# THE SAFARI

A Novel

## JACLYN GOLDIS

**EMILY BESTLER BOOKS**

**ATRIA**

New York   Amsterdam/Antwerp   London   Toronto   Sydney/Melbourne   New Delhi

EMILY
BESTLER
BOOKS

ATRIA

An Imprint of Simon & Schuster, LLC
1230 Avenue of the Americas
New York, NY 10020

First Emily Bestler Books/Atria Books hardcover edition May 2025

**EMILY BESTLER BOOKS/ATRIA** BOOKS and colophon
are trademarks of Simon & Schuster, LLC

For information about special discounts for bulk purchases, please contact Simon & Schuster Special Sales at 1-866-506-1949 or business@simonandschuster.com.

The Simon & Schuster Speakers Bureau can bring authors to your live event. For more information or to book an event, contact the Simon & Schuster Speakers Bureau at 1-866-248-3049 or visit our website at www.simonspeakers.com.

Interior design by Davina Mock-Maniscalco

Manufactured in the United States of America

1  3  5  7  9  10  8  6  4  2

Library of Congress Cataloging-in-Publication Data has been applied for.

ISBN 978-1-6680-6695-9
ISBN 978-1-6680-6697-3 (ebook)

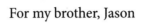
For my brother, Jason

# CHAPTER ONE

# JOSHUA

I hurry along the wooden path, nascent morning sunrays whispering across the gray sky, when it suddenly goes black overhead. I halt and gaze up at a tangle of vulture wings.

More vultures swoop down to join the party that's apparently being called. I duck, throw my arms up to protect my head. Once the flock passes by, I straighten, feeling foolish. Then the shrubs nearby shiver with movement, and fresh fear constricts my chest. I bob my flashlight around the dim bush.

Finally, reasonably certain that nothing menacing lurks close, I continue along the riverbank. The air is warm, perfumed by firewood, and tart blooming baobab flowers, and the whiff of eggs and sausage sizzling over the Skottel. Or maybe I'm imagining the last part, conjuring pure childhood mornings that were few and far between.

I check my phone again. No text. But Bailey will be at the firepit, waiting for me. She has to be.

Even though we were supposed to meet by the lodge. And Bailey—my reliable, quiet sister, who always does what she says she will—wasn't there. Not in her room, either, one of the property's five luxury suites she's sharing with our brother, Sam.

A fish eagle shrills, and a hippo follows with a series of grunts, sounding eerily close. More vultures whip by, and I run reassurances through my head about the unlikeliness of being injured on safari. An electric fence encircles the lodging grounds at Leopard Sands. And in the decades my family has been vacationing here, I am aware that monkeys, baboons, and sometimes even an antelope scrape by the enclosure, but rarely any predatory animals, like one of the Big Five. Besides, once the vultures swoop toward the trees, it means that the danger has passed.

Death has already come.

I wonder what died. An impala? A bushbuck? A wildebeest? And who executed the kill? A lion from the dominant Naru pride we saw on our drive yesterday? The circle of life, sure, but I always look away when an animal is about to pounce on its meal. Teeth gnashing, the vicious chase. The gore. Disney doesn't show you a lion emerging from a buffalo's cavity, fur matted in blood.

I prefer peaceful drives—watching hyena pups in their den, or a cheetah on the run, or lions lazing beneath a silver-flowered buffalo thorn—whereas my brother gets off on the kill. Sam is six years my junior, and my opposite in most every way. And yesterday he practically salivated when we got rare front-row seats to a hunt. Two lions chased an old leopard, then ripped him apart limb by limb. My brother didn't look away when the lions' incisors clamped down on leopard flesh.

I, on the other hand, looked away.

Sam was high on it; the rest of them too. I felt ashamed that I didn't share in the thrill. Sam taunted me— Would I ever man up? God gave me eyeballs for a reason, and I was a fucking sissy. Not the type of person who should be CFO of a huge, successful company—or next in line to command it. He said that pointedly to Mom. Fact is, Sam's hated me ever since he was seventeen, and I told Mom he was doing lines of coke off our dining room table. Still, the barb rubs up against my insecurities. I worried Mom may start to believe it. Or worse, that she was already thinking it herself.

I didn't defend myself, though. I just stared at my hands and thought, *I am a sissy*. But not for the reasons Sam said.

*Kill or be killed*, Mom said as she watched the lion feasting, trying to diffuse our tension, levying the edict in her calm, exacting tone that commands both the boardroom and our family. *Let the dead stay dead*.

And then sitting there in our open-air Jeep, we all added the obligatory statement, a ripple wave of irony that trilled out in unison. *The circle of life,* we intoned, almost like automatons, the axiom both apropos to the conversation, and also, the inspiration behind the name of our family company—Circ—that's worth at least a billion.

Mom's billion. Lest any of us forgets it.

I switch off my flashlight as light suffuses the horizon, dawn yielding to morning. Then I quicken my pace, passing the spot just on the inside of the electric fence, where I once watched a crocodile dismember a hippo on the shores of the river beyond. Aba kept my head steady on the sight, didn't permit me to look away. I can still feel his hand on my skull, the heat from his meaty fingers, the pressure on my neck.

Anxiety that began as an itch has now reached a peak in my chest. Everything is wrong. Starting with them getting *engaged.* Mom and Asher.

Or as Sam calls our soon-to-be stepfather: *Mom's new and improved right-hand Josh.* It's a one-two punch of a dig, as I despise being called Josh—it's such a fratty nickname. Sam is cruel, no doubt, but also right. I was once Mom's go-to, her favorite, her everything.

It's pathetic, isn't it? That I like—*love*—being those things to my mother. That every time she bestows her approval upon something I've said or done, I experience a dopamine surge. Which is why it's so out of character that I confronted her last night, that I didn't mince words. She accused me of threatening her—and still I didn't back down.

Not the golden-boy son any longer.

I round the bend amid a rustle in the trees. I stop. A few birds scatter in startled flight. The air is so heavy and humid now a pinprick could burst it. An owl hoots, and again I hear the hippos honking and grunting from the river. Hippos are the loudest animals on earth, which I quite respect, even envy. I wasn't loud enough with Aba, am usually not with Mom, and am not even with my wife. Though I am trying, on this trip, in fact, to cut this toxic trait of mine and express myself.

The sun, now almost violently red, bloats above the thicket of baobabs. Piercing vulture squawks zing down my bones. The birds are scavenging in the distance, I now see, beyond the memorial headstone for Aba, in scrubby brush that is tangled and overgrown, making it harder to identify the kill. I pass the firepit, with charcoal embers from the prior night's festivities.

I tried to go to bed early. After Mom and Sam fought, and then made up again, and then my brother massaged her shoulders, sucking up to Mom in a way that she invariably succumbs to. I'd had quite enough. Davina, many drinks deep, opted to stay out without me. I kissed Bailey's cheek good night, grazed my hand across Davina's back, then mumbled pleasantries to the rest of them. I returned to my suite to relieve Gwen, who was babysitting, after which I stared at Ruby in her crib for eons—my sleeping daughter's perfect frame, the reassuring rise and fall of her chest, the almost unfathomable way babies are able to sleep with nothing worrying them at all.

But when Davina finally slunk back to the room in a sorry state, I stormed out to talk to Mom. Heat creeps up my neck as last night lashes back. Mom's surprise, face flushed, as she lazed on the couch, still in her rehearsal dinner dress. How her surprise at seeing me morphed to indignation. Then anger. As I finally said the things that've built to a crescendo. . . .

Now my eyes skitter beyond the bonfire pit, toward the river. Elephants burrow their trunks in the murky depths, the stench of their dung pungent in my nostrils. And on the riverbanks, antelope graze amid spindly marula trunks, ears flicking.

*Where is Bailey?*

My footsteps slow as I pass the gravestone, tall, gray, and imposing, just like Aba in life, carved with a Jewish star insignia. *Aryeh Babel*, it reads.

Aryeh means "lion" in Hebrew. Fierce, to the ends. But Lion Sands was already a thriving safari lodge, so Aba called ours Leopard Sands. Because of all predatory animals, you don't want to be attacked by a leopard. A leopard will go straight for your jugular, suffocate and then eat you. You can be attacked by a lion and survive. But pretty much no one survives a leopard attack.

Thus, everyone who worked for Aba called him the Leopard. I think he secretly delighted in that moniker.

My eyes travel down the headstone. *Beloved Husband and Father* it reads at the bottom.

The sentiment always provokes a nervous twinge from my depths.

All of a sudden I freeze, breathless, as a few observations converge. First, that whatever is dead died within the bounds of the electric fence. When we built the bonfire encampment, with the memorial to Aba, the lodge extended the electric fence to enclose our family's beloved hangout. The place we always head after dinner to drink and chat and fight, when we reunite here in our South African home away from home.

The second thing that hits me is that there is something strange, something eerily human and hideously familiar, about the dead shape on which the vultures are feeding. Slowly, very slowly, my eyes absorb the details, then my brain. I stop suddenly.

A buzz mounts in my ears as I step closer to what is unmistakably a human hand. Though the vultures have ravished other parts of the body, the hand is intact, spotlighting prominent veins and long, thin fingers with age spots not completely eradicated by frequent laser treatments, to the previous chagrin of the hand's owner. I kneel down, my heart thrashing in my chest, taking in the glossy fingernails painted white, shaped in that trendy, witchy point that Davina has also adopted.

But the hand doesn't belong to my wife. Nor to my sister, whose nails are always bare and short. It belongs to . . . oh god . . . I can barely think it, even to myself.

Another person besides my wife who enjoys—enjoyed—keeping up with the latest trends.

Mom.

Nausea builds in my throat. As I teeter, my orientation unsteady, my foot crunches down on something hard, distinguished from the packed dirt. I bend down to pick it up, but even before it's in my hand, I know what it is. Mom's necklace. A large gold locket she wears on her neck, that since my earliest memory she has never taken off.

I glance around before I slip the necklace inside my chinos' pocket. Then I begin to scream.

# CHAPTER TWO

# VIOLETT

*Two Days Before*

If Tolstoy is right and every unhappy family is unhappy in its own way, then I am confident in saying that the Babels of Palm Beach, Florida, are unhappy in the darkest and deepest possible way.

Pardon. I should refer to them as the Babel-*Bachs*, considering Odelia Babel's recent engagement to Asher Bach, twenty-five years her junior. Asher is the head designer for the luxe basics line of Odelia's sustainable fashion empire.

Sustainable. Heh. Rich people are so deluded, or perhaps that's giving them too much credit—they waltz around courting the veneer of delusion, opting not to probe too hard into their own choices. From their smart homes and private jets, they champion climate change and sustainability with aggressive verve, *sustainable* being the new buzzword that makes a person or company touted on levels akin to Jesus Christ.

I must sound bitter, eh? Well, I am.

But back to the immortal words of Tolstoy, whom I've read extensively, which would likely surprise many people—both those in the decrepit town where my family lives, on the outskirts of Kruger National Park, and those who are my guests, whose any thought about me is a fleeting idea that I live to serve them. I'd like to challenge the author on the first part of his statement, about happy families—about whether they even exist in the first place. Because in all my years as manager for the most exclusive and expensive safari in southern Africa, I have not witnessed a single truly happy family. Where I come from, they think money brings about happiness. But for decades I've watched our guests parade through with their diamonds and their demons, and I know that assumption is a lie.

Maybe the happy ones sit in the wedge between fantastic poverty and fantastic wealth. Those with just enough.

I don't know anyone like that.

"Violett, how are you? A query for you." Jabulani walks briskly into the suite, sitting upon a zebra-skinned ottoman that flanks a pair of cognac-leather club chairs. I peer up from my squat in front of the minifridge, where I've just arranged the keto electrolyte drinks itemized on Odelia's rider. (The sixth-amended rider shared this morning by her assistant.)

"The baby . . ." Jabulani's small weathered face, perched almost precariously atop his massive body, muscled from years of outdoor labor, screws in confusion. "For Mrs. Odelia's granddaughter, they want . . ." He consults a printout. "A DockATot. Do you know what is such a thing?"

"*Ja*, Mandla is bringing it in from Jozi today, on the charter flight." I don't mention the part where we had the DockATot sent from Cape Town first, at great hassle and expense.

"*Sjoe*, but why is Mandla in Jozi?"

"To collect the kosher meat. And the DockATot."

"Ah." Jabulani shuffles the sheet to the bottom of his stack, revealing one of the color printouts of the Bora Bora engagement photos the Babel-Bachs provided to apprise the staff of our forthcoming VIPs. Asher Theodore Bach is typed on the top, and below it is a man who looks like he's stepped straight out of a desert island advertisement in his Panama hat and midthigh bathing trunks, impressive abs on display, his shoulder-length sandy hair as thick and luxurious as one of our lions. Whenever I imagined Odelia remarrying, I pictured a silver-haired titan of industry—not this.

"*Ja*, did you make certain Arno has the oat milk?" I ask, shifting back to the many tasks at hand.

"*Yebo*. Arno's got the oat milk without . . ." Jabulani shuffles his papers again and his dark eyes narrow at another printout. "Oat milk without . . . carrageenan. I'll get it now now. The fresh macadamia milk too. He's still working on that . . ."

I smile, and Jabulani smiles back. We both know that Arno making fresh macadamia milk will involve a trail of expletives.

"Every time the Babel family comes to Leopard Sands, there is a new milk to learn," Jabulani says.

I smile again, but this time it's an effort. Suddenly my walkie-talkie bleats. "Violett?" It's Amahle, one of the housekeepers. "*Yebo*, the main suite linens were laundered in . . . Laundress detergent. Scent is . . . *ag*, Santal 33."

"*Danke*," I reply. Then I turn to Jabulani. "When the milks are ready, bring them to me."

"When Arno finishes, I will add them to Mrs. Odelia's fridge."

"Let me, why don't you. Mrs. Babel is worried. So I'll do it, okay?"

"Worried?" Jabulani frowns.

"*Ja*." I stretch my arms behind my back, feel a crack and release in my shoulders. I avert my eyes from Jabulani's, make my voice light. "About her safety, I understand. She's asked that I handle all food and beverages in her room. Perhaps you missed it. It was in the *fifth* revised rider."

"Oh, sorry sorry."

I nod, think to tell him to pay better attention next time. That it's important we read every rider, no matter how mind-numbingly repetitive and ridiculous. But then I can't bring myself to, not on behalf of them. The flipping Babel-Bachs.

"Why is Mrs. Odelia worried about her safety?" Jabulani asks.

I consider what Gwen confided, whether to share it with Jabulani or keep it to myself. Gwen, who occupies a multitude of roles I don't really understand. She is a meek whippet of a woman who gives you the feeling that she's never in her sixtysome years expressed an original thought. Practically her every sentence begins with "Odelia would like" or "Odelia thinks," all said with utmost reverence, like Gwen is speaking on behalf of the Dalai Lama. Really, Gwen just occupies a multitude of made-up positions that sound fancy but boil down to the paid role of being Odelia's best friend. And in the past few days, gwentulchinsky@circ.com has been cluttering up my inbox with all measures of requests and revised requests. On Gwen's email salutation she's chief administrative officer (glorified assistant), head of glam (on-demand makeup artist), and spiritual adviser to the CEO (tarot card reader—I've seen her dole out those dumb cards to a delighted Odelia, excitedly predicting more money and success for her. I mean, if that's the criterion, well, hell, I can be a spiritual adviser, too!).

Rich people, I tell you—what they all have in common is scads of time spent searching for new, inane ways to use up their money.

As far as I can tell, from all the years Gwen has shown up with the family, trailing rapturously after Odelia, meeting her every need, almost like an adoring fan, Gwen's entire life is wrapped up in the Babels. Actually, the soon-to-be Babel-*Bachs*. Wonder how marriage number two is going to affect her. Gwen's always given off the vibe that, if she could, she'd lock Odelia in a cage and slip her inside her pocket to admire at will.

"Odelia is concerned about . . . well, poisoning, apparently," I finally say. I can trust Jabulani.

"*Jislaaik!*" Jabulani gasps.

"Ridiculous. But you know the VIPs. She's without her security and concerned. Just let me handle the milks. I suppose it's because she's known me a long time here. She trusts me." I pause, thinking to myself that she really shouldn't.

"But Arno is making the milk. And I will bring it to you. So . . . if we wanted to poison Mrs. Odelia . . . I suppose we still could." Jabulani clears his throat, flicks his eyes away from me. "But of course, we won't."

"Of course we won't," I echo. "Let's not inform her of the chain of handlers, how about it?"

"*Yebo,*" Jabulani agrees. By the slight downturn his lips have adopted, I suspect he's recalling Odelia's last visit, when she quietly berated poor Arno over a pasta that inadvertently contained gluten. But that was before Asher Bach. Before Odelia was all sexed up, which I've gathered is a foregone conclusion from the pictures we've been sent of their engagement in Bora Bora, folded all over each other, limbs contorted in ways I didn't even know limbs could contort.

Funny—Odelia's always seemed quite buttoned-up. Should be interesting, this second marriage. Quite a different husband from her first. Anyway, it's all good for my purposes. Let her be in a raring fine mood.

I give the fridge one last glance and adjust the line of house-made Snickers that Odelia requested, composed of Medjool dates imported from

Morocco, slit open and filled with natural almond butter, then dipped in sugar-free chocolate. I make a mental note to avoid Arno for the duration of the Babel-Bachs' trip.

I rise and survey the space, experiencing a rush of anticipation and anxiety. Glistening green leaves from the towering jackalberry rustle against the windowpanes, and beyond the teak sundeck and plunge pool, a zebra mum and foals are drinking from the river. Indoors, the color scheme of the suite echoes that of the bush—emerald marble-topped vanities juxtaposed with rock walls in the bathroom, and in the bedroom, a bespoke wooden bedframe handcrafted by local artisans, with lion-printed beige linen curtains. In the living area, artisan woven baskets line the natural stone walls, and midcentury modern side tables sit atop geometric-patterned carpets. The terrazzo floors are freshly polished, boasting stones from the Selati Railway that once connected Johannesburg with the port city of Maputo. A landscape by legendary South African painter Jacobus Hendrik Pierneef hangs above the bed; normally we hang a cheaper replica, but it's been swapped out for the original, which only emerges from its special climate-controlled storage on the occasion of Odelia's visits. I run a finger along the taupe linen cushions of a massive tufted couch, newly steamed. Then I fluff up a few crocheted throw pillows with gold yarn glittering in the reappeared sun.

It's February—summer, which is rainy season, and it's been a rainy doozy these last few weeks. Normally it just storms a couple hours in the afternoon, but it's been more prolonged and torrential of late. The air is perfumed by a morning downpour, and sun now streams into the suite from the open windows etched in black frames—the new style, courtesy of a recent renovation. It seems industrial to me, like an old factory, but what do I know of trends? I come from a small town baked into the mountains, called Graskop. It's not a wealthy town by any means, but certainly nicer than the shanty towns and townships and villages where people live without running water. Graskop hosts a small community of Afrikaners like me; we originate from seventeenth-century Dutch settlers. But my family has always been the poorest of the lot. Or we were—now that I make decent money, my grandmother's been able to replace the windows, shore up the roof, even erect a small wall around the house for needed security. But she's sick now, so my entire salary has gone to her treatments of late, with house maintenance and protection the least of our concerns. The small percentage of our guests who inquire about my heritage are always surprised to find out I come from nothing. I'm white, so I'm presumed to be privileged, well-off. Truth is, my family used to be guaranteed civil service jobs, or state-owned industry ones, until we lost everything after apartheid. Now, with the implementation of affirmative action and other employment equity programs, we must compete for jobs with Black South Africans. Well, sometimes when wrongs are redressed, there are casualties. That's the way the cookie crumbles, eh?

My chest tightens. I touch the waistband of my pants, feeling for my pistol in its holster. The pistol is pink, with a matching pink lock. Almost sweet, which is ironic, because there will be nothing sweet about me if I use it. Odelia certainly doesn't know I own a gun, that I carry it on the premises. It's legal, registered—a woman needs a gun in this country to defend herself. I'll leave it in my room when the Babel-Bachs arrive, but knowing it's nearby is a comfort.

Jabulani taps one of the daggerlike crystals on the chandelier with his fingers. "*Hawu!* If this fell, it could kill someone. Perhaps Mrs. Odelia should worry about this. Not poison."

"It's tight on." Even though as I gaze up at the dangling crystals, I can quite see his point.

"Sure. You're the boss." He smiles sheepishly, steps toward the door. Then he turns back. "Hey, I haven't asked lately, how's your *gogo*?"

I feel my breath suck in. "Oh, my grandmother is . . . Ouma's fine."

"You take her to a *sangoma* yet? Better than doctors many times, they are."

"No *sangoma*! A quack healer is not going to do anything for my grandmother." I'm breathless, angry at myself for spilling that, not remaining my usual even-keeled self. I summon calm and smooth my trousers; I used to wear the standard khaki staff uniform and try to shrink into the backdrop, for Odelia's sake. But now I am dressed beautifully, like the executive I am—shrinking into the backdrop no longer.

"There are experimental treatments, though, that Ouma could qualify for. What we really need is . . ." I rub my thumb against my fingers in the universal sign for money.

I realize too late that I shouldn't have done that, not to Jabulani. We've worked together for nearly three decades now. I spend more time with him than with anyone else; we are usually at Leopard Sands for three and a half weeks each month, with only a short break back to our families. We're friendly, but not exactly friends, as it's rare in our country for a white person and a Black person to be friends. The worlds we come from are still startlingly different. The end of apartheid catalyzed some progress, but our society remains exceedingly divided. It's ironic, because Aryeh Babel is the one who tried to imbue progress into Leopard Sands. No matter my disdain for that man, I can acknowledge that he was a progressive. That he saw, for instance, that the quarters for male employees, who are almost all Black, at other lodges were beyond subpar compared to the quarters for the white employees, who are more often in managerial and ranger roles. Aryeh tried to remedy that here, building quarters that are integrated and cleaner and nicer than quarters at other lodges, with the same conditions for all the under-staff, though rangers and managers, like me, have our own separate cabins. Aryeh wanted Leopard Sands to represent the best of South Africa. Still, Jabulani and I are not confidants; I should never have disclosed I'm hard up for money.

"I am very sorry, Violett." Jabulani's face craters in on itself. "I should not have taken your money. I wish I could give it back."

"Nonsense." I feel myself redden and hope he will stop.

"It means so much to my family, what you did. She needed—"

"Of course. Of course she did. And I gave happily and willingly. With pleasure. I would do it again." Jabulani's referring to his daughter, Iminathi, age six. I chipped in for her surgery for her cleft palate, back when I scrounged a little extra money to do so. Before Ouma became sick, and the bills began to pile up.

"*Eish*, you are an angel. May God bless you. I will pray for your *gogo*. For you, too, Violett." Jabulani's dark eyes are shining.

"*Danke*." I slap my thighs and hope he takes the sign that I'd like this conversation to end. I flip open the dustbin, to verify I've changed it out and put in a fresh bag, even though I quite know I have. Jabulani leaves, and before I follow him out, I spritz the entry with the Diptyque Baies room spray Odelia favors. One last spritz, amounting to five total. (Not six. A correction in one of the foking revised riders.)

Thing is, despite my layered feelings toward her, Odelia isn't unlikable. That is perhaps the biggest conundrum about her. In fact, she bubbles good energy and cheer. In the few weeks leading to this rushed wedding week, we have closed the resort, canceled bookings, all compensated by her, of course, as owner, and planned a caliber of festivities that would otherwise take months to pull off—for which, I acknowledge, Odelia has showered us with gratitude. And in a couple hours, she'll breeze in here with her smile and her heels and accept Jabulani's hot towel outstretched. She'll rub his forearm and declare, "You're a star, Jabulani!" And he'll feel faint with joy. He'll be ready to lie right down on the ground for her to walk all over him this week—flattered she even remembered his name.

She does the same thing to me. "Oh, Violett! You're a gem. A certi- fied gem. Everything is positively *lekker*." Odelia loves that word—loves sprinkling conversation with her glittering South Africa-isms, gleaned from the two years she spent in Jozi decades ago. She pulls from our eleven official languages proudly and confidently, as though unveiling a rabbit from a hat, unaware that she is speaking Zulu to a Tsongan, or Afrikaans to a Swati.

"What would I do without you, Violett?" she always exclaims, touching my arm in what would seem like genuine appreciation if I didn't know bet- ter, when I replenish her superfood powder, when I alert her each time her favorite animal, the giraffe, is at the watering hole. "*Danke*," she purrs, when my legs chug as fast as they might to run around catering to her every whim.

A familiar metallic taste floods my mouth.

When Odelia travels anywhere else outside of our safari resort, she sends a team ahead to prepare for her arrival. But she has known me a very long time. She trusts me to adequately prepare, to anticipate her needs, to satisfy every last one.

Ouma has always told me to work hard and God will provide. But that God only opens doors—it's my job to walk through them. It's how I worked my way up at Leopard Sands; typically a manager would only be selected from among students who graduated from hospitality school in the big cities, Durban or Johannesburg or Cape Town. My family didn't have funds to send me away to those schools. But when I was fifteen, I assumed my mother's role as waitress here after she died. In that way, God opened a door, I suppose. Ouma believes in God, but I can't say that—given how life's unfolded for me—I've ever been any great believer. But now, with Odelia and her family on a spontaneous trip to Leopard Sands, I find myself softening toward God. Because at a fortuitous time he's opened a door—and I intend to run right smack through it.

My jaw clenches as I step over the threshold of Odelia's suite. I recall the infamous line said by Julia Roberts when she was shopping on that ritzy street using Richard Gere's credit card.

Trusting me? Big mistake, Odelia. *Huge.*

# CHAPTER THREE

# ODELIA

I t's raining!" I stare out the window onto the tarmac, transfixed with excitement. "You know, my—"

"Favorite time at Leopard Sands is rainy season. Yes. You've mentioned it once or twice." My fiancé—my *fiancé*, insanity that—laughs and bends down, brushes his lips against my cheek. A peal of joy bursts out of me. I just can't contain it. In a life of many blessings, and also many obstacles, who could have predicted that at sixty-four I'd feel like I was just getting started?

"We haven't even deplaned, and already I'm gonna vomit," comes wafting down the aisle.

"Lovely," I say. That's Sam, ladies and gentlemen. Twenty-six years and two hundred twenty pounds of trouble and angst. My second, complicated son.

Reality settles, reminds me that I'm decidedly no longer in my love bubble.

"Enough," I add, my tone harsher this time. Sam stares me down with his fiery blue eyes, defiance inside them. But I can dish it all right back twentyfold. "I get that you have your own feelings to unpack," I say in a low, calm voice, "but I'm engaged, Sam. Getting married. This is done. We talked about it—I said that if you decided to come, there can't be any of this passive-aggressive stuff. So please, smile and be happy and just enjoy safari, okay?"

Sam doesn't bequeath me a smile, but instead runs a hand through his buzzed, ashy brown hair. My natural color—though I've been highlighting it bright blond for half a century now. Sam breaks our eye contact and stares at his phone, starts up a gloomy scroll. Fine, go right ahead, baby boy. He can steep in his misery. As for me, nothing is going to whittle away at my joy this week. Nothing.

The stewardess hitches open the door, and a dry gust hits my face, carrying the distinct scent of safari that lights into my soul. It smells like grass and brush and fire and freedom and romance. And danger. Can't escape that. The danger heightens everything, suspends you inside the glorious present moment. That's long been my theory on why safari is so intoxicating. The rest of life conspires to steal our attention. Watching animals in their natural habitat—that's the only meditation that's ever really worked for me.

"Be careful," Asher says as we file forward. "Those boots aren't made for—"

"They're Prada!" I laugh. "You styled them this season, with the low-rise cargo skirt and—"

"They're fine for models in a studio shoot," Asher concedes. "But not exactly practical for getting off a private plane in the rain."

I throw an unconcerned hand back. "I'm fine. Been walking in platforms since . . . I got this."

We meet rueful eyes. We both know I almost said something like—*since you were in diapers.*

"For richer and for closet full of shoes," I tease, leaning into my fiancé.

"So that's what I was agreeing to when I signed all those papers?"

"Yep. I had the lawyers bury it in the boilerplate."

He smiles, and I do too. I brush my hand languidly along the toffee-hued panel on the wall, the same kind of gleaming wood—rich-people wood, I've heard it called—that appeared everywhere on the three-hundred-foot yacht I chartered to the Mediterranean this past summer. Our last family trip of the Before Asher era. Once again, I feel the relief bubble in my chest that all the, let's call them *administrative* tasks, after our whirlwind courtship and Asher's proposal, went so smoothly. I was anxious about the prenup. Anxious about broaching it with him, at least. But Asher was a champ about it—as it happened, he wanted a prenup too. Because in his relatively brief career, he's made his own substantial money. It's one of the best parts of our union: not having to doubt that he's after me for money. And being able to assuage all the concerns my inner circle hasn't shied away from expressing.

"Did I also agree to give you three-quarters of the primary closet in that document?" Asher winks at me.

"Nine-tenths." I wink back. "Didn't you read the fine print?"

"Nine-tenths, eh? Well, it's all yours, babe. When you wore those pink Aquazzura stilettos for our first casual date at home, I started to understand your footwear fetish."

I laugh, remembering how I agonized over what to wear. Easy to dress for drinks or dinner, but at home, I suddenly felt unmoored. Strange for the woman who makes a living off fashion, who genuinely adores it. But I was mired in analyses. I figured the chill girl in her twenties that Asher was used to dating would wear Ugg slippers or some chunky white monstrosity of a sneaker that was the height of cool on TikTok. But I'm five foot three, and I'm not Hailey Bieber. Sneakers would have ruined my outfit, only annunciated me being a quarter-century older than Asher. And I felt the most me in those pink spangly Aquazzuras when I opened the door, after I'd decided to really let him into my world.

I shouldn't have worried. Asher loves me dressed up, or in my silk pink pajamas—even though his aesthetic leans more classic and neutral. He loves shopping with me, going painstakingly through the stuff my personal stylist wants to order, making edits, and then styling me himself when it all comes in. His skin care regime has more steps than mine. We have far more in common than I ever did with my late husband. Sometimes we're like two little kids, gleefully poring through the racks at Saks, or debating new designs. Asher knows my deepest failures, my biggest fears. Most of them, at least. We can lie in bed at night both in the same clay face mask and watch classic, feel-good TV, or even a romantic comedy, and cuddle and laugh. God, we laugh. With Aryeh, the house lacked laughter. But with Asher, work is fun is life is love. It all blends, one and the same. We're both intense that way, slaves to our passions, and now the joy of it is just doubled, doing it all together.

"He's the Kanye to her Kim circa the mid-twenty-tens," Sam mutters to Joshua. I bite back a retort. Asher is categorically *not* the Kanye to my

Kim, circa any year. But this week is going to be long. I need to just ignore Sam, not play into his hand.

"Huh?" Joshua says, distracted wrangling baby Ruby into her carrier. He probably doesn't even get the Kim and Kanye reference.

God bless Joshua. Bailey too. I have two compliant children, but that doesn't exactly ameliorate the noncompliant one. The *tsores* Sam's given me—all the drugs and rehab and money squandered. You're only as happy as your most unhappy child, isn't that the saying?

In the past, I've dovetailed with Sam—when he's sunk into a low, I've jumped down right there beside him in the trenches. I've spent my kids' entire lives trying to cushion things for them, but no longer. Finally, I'm happy as can be, and I deserve it. I deserve it all. Sam is going to ruin it over my dead body.

"Here ya go, honey." Asher's hand is outstretched, with a fistful of wasabi peas that he's separated from the snack mix.

"Honey! Gosh, you're the best." He transfers them to my palm, and I flush with pleasure. He's done this before, but it thrills me every time anew—how he observes the little things about me, how attentive he is to my needs. Let's just say, Aryeh never in his whole life would have picked through a snack mix for the wasabi peas for me. I don't even think Aryeh *knew* I love wasabi peas.

I consider eating them now one by one, savoring them, like I normally would, because they're fattening. But then I just stuff them all in my mouth and gulp down the joy.

Asher reaches up to the overhead bin for his fedora and plops it atop his newly shorn rich auburn hair. It used to be long, nearing his chest, a thick, impressive mane, but now it's shaggy and hipster-vibed, setting off his strong, gorgeous neck. Both hairstyles work on him; Asher's handsome as all get-out, but it's his quiet confidence that draws people in most. When he walks down the street, he draws every look: the women who want to be with him and the men who want to be with him too. Asher's bisexual—I've known that since we first got together. He told me it from the start, that he's monogamous and loyal but he wanted to be up-front. And at first, I wasn't sure how I'd feel about it, but soon I realized something surprising: I don't mind it. Maybe I even like it. I suppose in a weird way that makes logical sense; Aryeh was the opposite of liberal. My first husband believed in black and white, in men owning the world and women being subservient to them. And how Aryeh reacted to Sam coming out—that's a whole other story that fills me with anger. Anger at my husband's prejudices, and anger at myself for withstanding them.

But Asher is the complete opposite of my first husband. He's open-minded and wants everyone to just be who they want to be in the world. He doesn't need people put in boxes, or banished, to make himself comfortable in the world. And I've found myself powerfully attracted to that kind of self-assurance. Funny enough, the only time I've ever seen Asher nervous is with me.

A frisson in my chest—the power of that, the bliss of that. The persisting glorious surprise of such a late-life miracle.

As we descend the jet's stairs, the panorama of the bush adds a rush of contentment through my cells, the familiar verdant trees and endless brown rolling hills, the air warm and misty. Off the landing strip, on the tarmac, some of the entertainment staff are singing their indigenous songs and doing a great rollicking dance, and the greeting and waitstaff are in a row, saying smiley welcomes and *sanibonani*s and holding trays of warm towels and copper tumblers with straws. The tumblers contain Amarula on ice, I know, like Irish cream, a quintessential safari drink for everyone except me. I never partake, of course, too much sugar. One of the staff thrusts an umbrella over my head. Another who is vaguely familiar, with a high, bouncy brown ponytail, long lashes, refined gold hoops, and glossy red nails, hands me a tumbler.

"Welcome back to Leopard Sands, Mrs. Babel. This one has your keto electrolyte drink."

Asher guffaws, an almost childlike sound. He laughs with his whole face, his pale blue eyes dancing and the faint crinkle lines around his eyes deepening. It's the first thing I noticed about him: how for being an acclaimed designer, and a hot man in his prime, he doesn't do the stick-up-your-ass laugh, where only the lips crease faintly up. "Keto electrolytes. That's my fiancée!"

Sam laughs dryly. "Let's see if you're still laughing a year in."

"I will be," is all Asher says, lightly.

We all applaud for the dancers at the end of their show, and I squeeze Asher's hand, but I'm on edge. I can't pretend I'm not. Everyone together—was I insane, doing it this way? Sticking all the important people in my life in this blender and adding wild animals, to boot? Given all that has happened in this place . . . all the memories . . . the people who will still remember. But that's nothing new—what's new is the note that arrived in the mail recently, the image on a constant loop in my brain. The picture, a face circled in red marker. Mine. Scrawled above, in unfamiliar script: *You're next.*

There've been other notes, too, of late, notes that I've shoved from my mind and rationalized as a random stalker. Given how wealthy and public-facing I am, that happens sometimes. Notes that have said: *I know what you did. The countdown is on until you die.* But this last note hit me more sharply and made me question the identity of the person who sent the ones preceding it. The latest note—*You're next*—constitutes the first time I've seen that particular picture in many years. An entire lifetime, really. And I haven't stopped ruminating on how some random stalker was able to get ahold of it.

Asher pats Sam on his shoulder, a friendly buddy tap. I suck in my breath, hoping Sam doesn't punch him—he's far bigger than my fiancé, and if the past is any indicator, Sam doesn't shy away from physical altercations. But Sam just shoots Asher a tight scowl and grabs a drink, starts slurping it up loudly as he walks back over to join Bailey—his twin sister, and forever safety blanket. Those two huddled up in my womb, startling the ultrasound technician because at first glance they appeared Siamese. They couldn't be more different but have always been inseparable. In some ways, I envy my daughter. Sam has an easy, loving way with Bailey that he doesn't seem capable of maintaining with anyone else.

"I'll have a keto electrolyte drink too!" my daughter-in-law Davina says, smoothing her pale pink bob. It's a high maintenance do—her hair gets bleached blond, then the hairstylist highlights the top layer in the palest pink. It looks, I have to admit, impossibly chic. Especially with her tailored, body-conscious-with-French-sensibility ensembles that Davina pulls from vintage shops and intersperses with the coolest Circ items.

"Oh . . . well, I apologize, but we only have one keto electrolyte drink," says the pretty woman with the ponytail. "There are more, in Mrs. Babel's refrigerator."

"Okay," Davina says. "Just water then, please."

Davina's lost a bunch of weight lately, which, I mean, wonderful for her. She's one of those rare people who gives birth and then watches the weight fall off, without any effort, so she's far smaller than she was to start out. Even though she says she's happy at every weight, I can tell that, deep down, she's found getting smaller addicting. It isn't my business as her mother-in-law, but it *is* my business because she's been Circ's plus-size model for years—and she's no longer so plus-size. But even putting the business factors aside, in my opinion, Davina's weight loss runs against her personal brand. She has a popular Substack in which she eschews beauty and diet culture and calls out all the consumerism compelling women to shell out their money to antiaging products. I bite back my inclination to broach the topic of Davina's weight loss with her yet again. She knows what I think. We've gotten into it a few times—with Davina lecturing me that my having any opinion on the size of her body is not being body positive, or body neutral, or whatever they call it. Yes, got it, there are more interesting things to talk about than bodies, but this is business. Plus-size is profitable. The financials make it clear, and Davina is fabulous, the longtime face of our brand, having cultivated a rising star power and brand ambassadorship in her own right before she came to Circ and in short order met Joshua. Still, I'll have to raise the weight loss with her again later, or maybe I'll have Joshua take up the cause.

I stare up at the sky, where faint sunlight is beginning to poke through the clouds. The woman proffering my umbrella folds it up. "Rain's over," she says. "No more today."

"It's rained a lot lately?" Bailey asks.

"A lot! Twenty centimeters last Thursday! My cousin's car floated away and bridges split apart. Some roads are still closed."

"We always get perfect weather when we come here," Bailey says. "We're lucky."

"And we flew right in," I add. "So we don't have to deal with roads. We are blessed." I used to say *hashtagblessed*, but my kids have told me to stop that—that it sounds like I'm gloating. I don't intend to gloat; it's just that I truly do feel inordinately blessed. Especially of late. When I survey my family, my fiancé, my bank accounts. When I meet with the religious women with whom I volunteer, helping them start new secular lives as they desire, I count my blessings. All the ways my life has expanded and flourished since Aryeh passed a decade ago.

My gaze flitters around at my family, congregated in this place that means so much to us to celebrate my remarriage. For not the first time, I feel a twinge of regret. It's been just me and Asher, during our courtship and then in Bora Bora, when we got engaged. I was able to keep my two worlds apart. Then we jetted back to Palm Beach and moved his stuff into my place and told my children our news. We decided we didn't want a long engagement, or a grand affair—that a simple wedding in short order in Leopard Sands with my family would be perfect. So this trip, this plane ride, is our first time truly welcoming my progeny into our union. But on the plane, everyone slept. People—Sam especially—are far easier to contend with when they're unconscious. More worry tightens my chest. I knew this wasn't going to be easy. And then there's the notes . . . and who has been sending them. . . . Fear jolts through me anew. Maybe I should have waited a little longer to combine my worlds.

As if reading my mind, Asher mouths, *All good.* He presses me to his chest, bends down to kiss me again, his day-two scruff grazing my forehead. I sigh. His strong arms feel warm and protective, and his scent is intoxicating, evoking the outdoors, like a cowboy, hand on hip, proud at having just roped a calf. Lavender, cedar, pines. Funny—Asher couldn't be further from the cowboy type. He's an indoors person, epitomizes Brooklyn, where he grew up and where we spent much of our courtship when I was temporarily working out of Circ's New York office. Where he introduced me to the concept of having dinner at the bar. God, it's so much more fun—far less stuffy than a table. And you can touch each other's legs and flirt in this sensual, intimate way. Aryeh had preferred a table, an arm's-length distance between us. Always, unless he was angry. Then—no distance.

I shiver. Ten years later, and sometimes my body forgets that my late husband is dead.

I shake my head, shake it off, all the memories and comparisons and the fear that creeps in, of disappointing my children, or disappointing my soon-to-be husband, making him regret having jumped in the deep end with me. No. I banish that thought. Asher loves me. Even the hardest cynic in our circles has been forced to concede it. And I love him. Deeply. I'm not a romantic; maybe I was as a girl, but that stage has long passed. People may call me cold and calculated, planning five steps ahead, and they're not wrong, even here, even with this new love. I've approached it from all angles, thought everything through. No matter how it looks, Asher and I make sense. And at sixty-four, having found him, the last love of my life, I am more determined than ever to live life foremost for myself.

I clink my glass against Asher's. "Welcome to Leopard Sands."

"Thanks, sweetheart."

"Shall we get you settled in?" It's the woman in the ponytail again. She's tall, with a nice olive tan. Wait, is that . . . ?

"Yes, thank you . . ."

"That's Violett," Gwen steps delicately forward and whispers in my ear. "Violett DeVilliers."

"Violett! Of course." I smile warmly at her.

Shit. Violett. I can't believe I didn't immediately place her. She once faded into the backdrop—or perhaps I've tried to avoid her. But now she's unavoidable and shockingly glamorous, like the After on a makeover show.

Has she always been this beautiful? I suppose she has, naturally, even cloaked in the ordinary Circ uniforms that she's apparently decided to forgo. Given what took place between us in the past, I've always tried not to fix my attention on her. But she's luminous, her skin lit from within, wrinkle-free and tight, like she's had a good facial, or plastic surgeon, though, of course, that's not possible. You need money to do things like that, and I know what we pay her. Her hair's in a full, high ponytail that on most people would appear overly youthful, but on Violett somehow gives off a refined, sultry air. Safari managers typically wear the standard safari suits—khakis and smiles. But our manager is a glamazon, in flared white pants and a slouchy white blazer, with a pale green silk camisole beneath, showing a peek of a lace bra against pert cleavage. How old is Violett now? Davina's age, round-abouts, or a few years older—midforties, must be. We met when she was, what? Sixteen?

Shit, do I need this? Another potential complication in an already quite complicated week? I wonder, not for the first time, why I've continued to employ her all this time. The whole business is uncomfortable, to say the least. We hired her after her mother, a longtime employee, died. We felt obligated. But now . . . Perhaps she'd take a severance package and a recommendation to another upscale lodge. I'll speak to Gwen after this trip, see if we can work something out. Although there's always the threat that Violett could— Well, it will have to be handled delicately is all. And she's only ever been trustworthy. It's why I've asked Gwen to instruct her to preside over my safety this week. Of anyone, Violett can be trusted. Right?

"Everything is ready for you, Mrs. Babel. Just as you've asked."

I adopt a bright smile. "*Lekker.*"

I hear Sam groan, then say, "Can you speak English? You're *American*."

I fight to keep my smile wide. Honestly, I did live in Johannesburg for two years with Aryeh, before Joshua was born.

"Sorry for all the revisions on the riders, Violett! You are a gem—an absolute gem—for making things perfect for me and my family. This week—my wedding week—it's so important to me. And you're really wonderful to do it all on rather short notice." I stop, wondering if I've gone overboard with the compliments. Maybe I build people up too much, but in all my time as CEO of a huge global business I've learned that genuine appreciation always greases the wheels and helps smooth over little feelings of injustice that can accrue when people work for you a long time. And I *am* appreciative—it's a huge team that makes my life chug along nicely.

"With pleasure." Violett bows her head slightly. Not deferentially, though, which impresses me, because she quickly resumes eye contact. Then she points toward the lodge. "Shall we? You know the way."

Joshua smiles at me with excited anticipation, and I smile back. Despite his misgivings about my marriage that he's certainly conveyed, my older son cannot hide his eagerness about returning to this place that runs in his blood. Joshua, like Bailey, feels at home in Leopard Sands, perhaps more even than in Palm Beach. I watch Joshua adjust a sleeping Ruby cuddled against his chest in the carrier. So different from his father, I think, with a swell of pride. Aryeh never changed a diaper, that's to be certain. But this new generation of fathers want things to be equal. Asher too. When we got engaged, I said I wanted to take his last name. To become Odelia Babel-Bach. He shocked me by responding that he intended to become Asher Babel-Bach. That he wanted us to be a real family. That it was important to him to share our last names, not to present a united front against our inevitable opposition, but to feel the hug of my Babel around his Bach. That's what he said—cheesy as all get-out, sure, but it lodged inside of me, meant something enormous that I still can't quite tease out. He has this uncanny way of seeing exactly what I want before I even know it myself.

My eyes flit over to my daughter-in-law. Lucky Davina, who snagged

Joshua—a catch beyond catch, just like Asher. But Davina is not currently paying attention to her husband or daughter; instead, she's bowled over giggling at something Asher is showing her on his phone. A meme probably; Asher loves a good meme.

A smile freezes on my face. Nice, of course, that my daughter-in-law is welcoming my fiancé into the fold. But I watch them together, unable to shove back the startled feelings, the unkind thoughts—that the two of them look straight out of a magazine cover. No one would mistake them for mother and son, a jab Asher and I will eternally dodge.

"Got the same pride of lions as last time we were here? The Naru pride, I think they were called?" Joshua asks one of the staff as we head toward the lodge. Asher and Davina abandon their meme, and Asher returns to my side, slips his hand inside mine.

"Oh, yes. The Naru still control the territory over here. Markus will know more. He's here, as you know. Ready for the morning drive."

"Markus?" Asher asks.

"The ranger," I tell him. "You remember, I told you about him? We've known Markus since—"

"Since before we were born, right?" Bailey asks.

"Yes. That's right."

We arrive at the mouth of the main lodge. It's all lit up in paraffin lanterns in the dwindling sun, with the shop boasting those cool, fearsome African masks, and then beyond it, edging the river, is a long rectangular pool that I've never seen anyone swim in as long as I've been coming here. But it looks spectacular—the placid water against the untamed nature, adding an exotic, expensive feel. My idea, in fact, to have it, even though each suite has its own private plunge pool. And I quite think I was right. Well, I am about most things. Killer instinct. Exceptional judgment. It's not being conceited, just honest. Aryeh might have started Circ, but it was called Sports Plus when I met him, focused exclusively on athletic wear. The supply chain was in place, but I'm the one who turned it into a high-fashion, global enterprise. I'm the one who noted that sustainability and size inclusivity were starting to make mainstream waves, who foresaw the market pivot toward those frontiers. I changed the company name to Circ, to play on the catchy concept of the circle of life. I knew that our marketing team would be easily able to spin our mission and values into an impact on the bottom line. So yes, Aryeh might have provided seed capital, but no one can dispute I'm the one who took our family business to the stratosphere.

The staff begin to disperse us—Joshua, Davina, and Ruby to their suite, then Bailey and Sam to the one they are sharing. As my kids wander off and we all agree to meet at the lodge at seven for dinner, Gwen sidles up to me.

"I'll drop off my stuff, then come to you. Sound good, Dede?" She's the only one who calls me that. The only one left in the world who knew me when I was a child.

"Perfect. Bring a few shades of foundation, why don't you? I'm tanner than usual from Bora Bora."

"Sure." Gwen runs a hand through her auburn shoulder-length hair, and I avert my eyes, knowing what she's going to do. Pull at her hairs, yank them from her scalp—trichotillomania. An anxious habit she's had for decades.

When she's done and the hairs flitter to the earth, I notice Gwen's eyes travel to Asher's hand, which has gone for a leisurely walk down my back and is now resting on my butt, to my enjoyment. Gwen purses her lips; even though they're glossy and lined to perfection with Gwen's signature expert makeup touch, they've sprouted that old, deflated, crinkly look. I make a mental note to send her to my injector, as a little gift. Gwen's eyes are still on Asher's hand, like a laser willing it to move. She opens her mouth, then closes it again. Exhales heavily. But swallows down whatever is clearly on her mind to say. Which suits me, to tell the truth. We are best friends, yes, but Gwen knows that I live life as I desire, and that I don't take well to outside commentary. Prenups, age differences; we don't talk about dark, dirty things. A modus operandi that has served us well for a very long time.

Or has it? I think back to the threatening notes. I haven't told Gwen about them. Haven't wanted to ruminate on why . . . on the little shards of suspicion that have lodged themselves in my brain and refused to depart. Because, the only person in the world who knows my past . . . is Gwen. . . .

Asher clasps my hand, and my mind fizzes and swirls as we fork off from Gwen, following Violett to the best, most-isolated suite at the edge of the property. Violett enters, and I glimpse the familiar lion skin rug in the entry, which always makes me feel so rich when I pad atop it in the morning with my superfood latte. It's ethical, of course—a diseased lion skinned before scavengers could pounce. Everything's sustainable here, and the highest quality, utilizing South African designers and materials—steel-topped tables by Gregor Jenkin and a suspended cocoon swing on the deck by Porky Hefer.

Asher ducks under the entry, already oohing and ahhing. But I linger on the step for a moment and twirl my locket over my sweater, its weight soothing against my fingers, my eyes locking on to the words carved in gold: The Triple Threats—the words connected by an unbroken line through the tops of the capital *T*'s. Then I pop open the locket quickly, just to make sure. At the touch of cold, familiar metal, my heart swishes and settles back in my chest.

Suddenly Asher turns around. I snap my locket shut and scan his face. But he's all alight, oblivious. "Wait, don't come in yet!"

"Why not?"

He's turned back toward me, arms gathering me up. "Because we're getting married. I'm supposed to carry my wife over the threshold!"

I smile. "I think the tradition is after the wedding, not before. Anyway, you already did it in Bora Bora. And again in Palm Beach."

"Well, your fault then, that we have so many homes." My soon-to-be husband sweeps me up, and my eyes flutter closed as I soak in this feeling of being in his arms, in my favorite place on earth. At some point, I blink my eyes open and catch a sliver view of Violett, staring at us with a strange look on her face. I can't tell if it's envy or anger. Envy, I decide. Must be.

It's an exceedingly natural emotion, envy. What results when unhappy people spot happy ones, when the have-nots witness the haves. But I worked hard for all this. I've earned every last bit. And I sacrificed a hell of a lot.

I bury my head in my fiancé's neck and squeal.

# CHAPTER FOUR

# BAILEY

Sam bolts toward the sundeck, and I follow after him, anticipation flooding through me at the thought of seeing all my animals again. I wonder if Millie is still around—that obstinate elephant and I shared some sort of bond. I feel bonds with all of them, really. Often stronger than I feel with most humans.

I ease into the cane papasan chair next to my brother and dump my favorite backpack onto the stone ground. It's military canvas and I've had it for a decade, since I was sixteen and Aunt Gwen took me shopping for my birthday. She said we could go anywhere, get anything, and so she picked me up in her car driven by her chauffeur. Gwen isn't fancy at all, not like Mom, but she's a Nervous Nelly type and doesn't drive. When we were younger, this meant Gwen took a lot of taxis or walked places, but since Mom took over the helm of Circ, Mom's always paid for Gwen to have a chauffeur. Anyway, I asked the chauffeur to take us to this homey camping and skiing store where they had nice basic things. And Gwen didn't balk when I chose plaid shirts and baggy pants, stuff I felt comfortable and covered up in. Mom would never have indulged me like that—it would be Neiman's, with her insistent on getting me a nice homecoming dress, when I wasn't even being asked to homecoming, and had negative desire to go to it, besides.

That's always how things are with Mom—she's highly attentive, as long as you are fitting her mold of things she wants to attend to. But Aunt

Gwen sees me, maybe because we're both kind of oddballs. I feel grateful to have her.

Sam nudges over my backpack to make space for his Louis Vuitton one. "Love how you fly private, Bails, but your luggage situation screams poor backpacker."

"I only fly private because we're with Mom."

My brother smiles fondly at me, and I feel myself warm in his beam of love, something primal stirring in me. We're twins, after all. The love we have for each other is foundational. Other people misunderstand Sam, or don't experience his goodness, but I am lucky that I do. He is such a loving, kind person, to me at least. I wish he could open that side of himself up to other people, then others could cut him some slack too. Our family, most of all. But somehow they provoke the worst in him, and he in them.

My brother stands and sheds his black tee, revealing bronzed ripply muscles. Where I am soft and pale, what most people would call an average build, Pillsbury Doughboy in both form and skin tone, Sam is tanning-salon dark and jacked. He only has to look at a barbell and his biceps bulge up like Popeye. Sam kicks off his shoes, then peels off his socks, revealing his big feet with round toes. Just like my own. Most people's toes are ovals, but ours are fatter, Flintstone-like. We have other physical similarities, too—hair the color of dishwater, blazing blue eyes, dimples in our right cheeks. And we're both tall; I'm five eleven, not quite Sam's six four, but certainly taller than petite Mom, and even Joshua's five eight.

Jabulani arrives with a platter that could double as art: biltong and chips with pomegranate halves and glistening cheese, olives, sundried tomatoes, and sprigs of rosemary. He sets it on the teak table, and I sigh with delight, reaching for a chunk of cheese and staring out at the gray-slate infinity pool and the bush spreading out behind.

"Don't forget, Arno has a wonderful dinner in store." Jabulani's face creases with concern, which I quite understand. Hulking Arno with his stern grimace is intimidating to me too. "Everything okay?"

"Everything is wonderful, Jabulani. We'll just relax until dinner. Thank you." I rummage in my pocket and slip him some rand. Jabulani bows his head and disappears into our suite.

I watch through the glass as Jabulani crosses the sitting area and heads toward the front door, past the two queen beds spaced generously apart. Since we were kids Sam and I have always stayed in this very suite, talking and giggling into the wee hours of the night. We had our own rooms as kids in our parents' estate; coming here felt special—sleepovers every night. I turn back and stare out at the slew of crocodiles sunning together on the sandy riverbanks and beyond, the giraffes feeding at a cluster of acacia trees.

"It's fun to get to bunk together again," I tell my brother. "I love how we still do that here."

I look at Sam, to share this moment with him, but he's typing on his phone, lips quirking in a smile.

"Who's got you smiling like that?"

"What? No one." Sam stabs off a last text, then flips his phone over on his chest, but not before I saw it. A red heart from someone named O with a red heart next to the initial.

"O? Does broski have a new paramour?" I tease.

"Eh, lots of them," he says lightly, but something about the sparkle in his eyes, the heart next to the initial, and good old twinly intuition tells me this O is a cut above the rest.

"Well, is O the flavor of the week? C'mon, tell me. What's his name? Oliver? Otis?"

"No." Sam laughs. "Not Otis. Look, I'll tell you his name if it becomes serious."

"So it's not serious?" Usually, Sam's boyfriends have names in his phone like Jaques Bartender at Twist or Lotan Tan Man. I've never seen him put a heart after any of them.

"I'll just tell you that he makes me happy," Sam finally says.

I take in the words, but also his emotive tone. "That's amazing, Sammy. You haven't mentioned anyone since Alex." Even Alex didn't have a heart after his name; throughout their relationship he remained in Sam's phone as Alex Uber Driver.

Sam frowns. "There hasn't been anyone worth mentioning."

"Not even this new guy?"

Sam chews on a biltong. "Leave it, Bails. I'll tell you about him when I'm ready to. If there turns out to be something to tell."

"Oh. Okay." So it's like that, is it? He doesn't trust me with his love life? I wish I didn't feel hurt, but I do. Sometimes I wish my emotions weren't so tethered to my brother, but that's always how it's been. The feeling sometimes that we are really one person instead of two.

"Fine. Maybe this new guy *is* the flavor of the week. I met him on Raya a couple months ago," my brother concedes, allowing me a tiny smile.

Two months? In Sam Land, that's basically marriage. Alex only lasted a few weeks.

"Wow, that's great, Sammy."

Sam nods, then pops up abruptly and goes to stand at the edge of the deck, overlooking the panorama that is my favorite in the whole world. His hand is jittery at his side, and as I take that in, my heart grinds to a halt. The familiar signs: Sam's jitters, his irritability. Not that those are strange symptoms when he displays them to others, but to me, he's always been a teddy bear. Though it's hard to fathom when I witness him interact with anyone else.

"Are you— You're not using again, right?" I ask quietly.

"What?" Sam spins around, his blue eyes blazing, his jaw tense. "You're . . . that's not . . . no. I'm not using. You know what it took for me to get clean this time. I would never go back. I wouldn't. And besides, you'd *know* if I were using again."

I survey him and relax. He's right—I'd know. He's testy but not at an extreme, no constant runny nose and jarring mood swings. "Okay . . . you just seem—"

"On edge? Well, I am! Mom's marrying a child, and I'm basically at poverty level these days. I've taken out loans on the condo—I might even have to sell it!"

"Really? It's that bad?" A pit forms in my stomach. I didn't know it had gotten to this point. Aba left us all money to buy a place; I haven't used mine yet. But Sam bought a condo in Miami Beach with a massive mortgage. I thought he'd overextended himself—we all tried to convince him to wait, or to buy something less expensive, but he wouldn't budge.

"It's that bad," Sam confirms. "I even had to give up my Equinox membership, Bails. And soon I'll have to forfeit the G Wagon lease—"

"So Mom didn't give you the money after all?" I ask, even though I know she wouldn't.

I reach for a biltong, nervously chew. Sam is a photographer and has grand plans for this app he wants to launch called Say Cheese, a platform for people to liaise with photographers and book photo shoots with ease. Influencers, models, weddings, bar mitzvahs. Even teenage girls who just want to farm out their photo shoots on the beach and rack up stellar shots for Instagram. It's a good idea—I was impressed when Sam told me about it, because it's unique, and smart, but Mom's philosophy is Sam can do it on his own. Build it brick by brick, instead of the grand splash he'd prefer. Mom's offered him work at Circ, but Sam doesn't want to join the family business—he likes doing his offbeat artsy photography for smaller indie brands. Plus, now that he's clean he's bubbling ambition. He has his own dreams, and he wants the reins to them. Which I respect, even envy. But Mom says that if Sam doesn't want to work for Circ, she has nothing monetary to offer. And though I wouldn't say it, Sam had no business leasing a G Wagon in the first place. But as I stare at my brother, I wonder if his money problems are even worse than I suspect.

"No," Sam says, scowling. "Mom won't give me any more money. She's such a greedy bitch."

"She's trying her best, Sam," I say quietly. "Ever since Aba died . . . it hasn't been easy for her . . ."

"Oh, please." He spits out the words, the degree of his venom surprising me. "Like Aba's death didn't work to her benefit completely? Mom is living the life. Now, with her new boy toy. And she relishes how much we all need her. Need her money. Aba's money, don't forget. And *I* need that money, Bails. You know what I went through to get clean. I'm finally doing it, but I need money to really distinguish myself from every other Joe Schmo photographer and make the app a success. I *need* it."

I don't reply. *Need* is relative, after all, isn't it? My brother lives in South Beach, in an insane penthouse that isn't exactly commensurate with his income level. He doesn't just want to start his app, he also longs for a Porsche, assorted Gucci items—status symbols he's always cared about. Mom funded him for a while, after he got out of his last stint at rehab a year ago and really seemed to be making a fresh start. But now Mom's done doling out the money. She said Sam needs to stand on his two feet. To tell the truth, I respect that. But I wouldn't say so to my brother. I understand the hold our mother has over us. For me, Mom's strings aren't financial, but something more amorphous, like an umbilical connection I've never managed to sever. She's convinced me that I will make a way bigger impact on animals as chief conservation officer of Circ than I would ever make as a veterinarian, which is what I wanted to be as a kid. And she's probably right. But still, even though I love working with Joshua (and sometimes Mom), every day I spend in our offices on Worth Avenue, my soul feels more and more . . . plastic.

Is that right? Plastic? My mind circles the realization with slow dread. Sometimes, I do permit myself to wonder if I've chosen this path, or if it's been chosen for me. But mostly I manage to keep those uncomfortable thoughts at bay.

"I can give you money," I finally say. At least my Circ job is good for one thing, building my own savings account.

"No," Sam immediately says. "I mean, thanks, Bails. I'm not taking money from you. But I appreciate the offer."

For a while Sam spars with a few vervet monkeys who've come down to pilfer from our platter and cause their general ruckus; monkeys might be cute, but on safari they are ubiquitous and annoying. Sam grabs one of the heavy pottery vases and threatens to smack the monkeys with it and so eventually they retreat across the deck. I expect them to leap over the translucent guardrail but instead one of them jumps into the pool, then another does.

I laugh, but Sam darts up and goes to the edge of the pool. I try to keep from laughing as my brother growls at them, hands in the air like some insane person, but the monkeys merely look amused as they swim around and splash Sam.

Eventually, my brother returns to me, his face fired up.

"Fuckers," he says.

"They're just trying to play . . ."

"They're beasts!" He doesn't crack a smile. "The resort should find a way to get them out. An electric fence that zaps them harder . . . causes damage . . ."

"I don't think that's how conservation works," I say lightly.

He scowls again, and this time I scan my brother. Something is off, and I can't exactly tell what. If it's not drugs, then maybe it's this guy he was texting with . . . maybe my brother is even in love.

The only person I've ever been sure Sam loves is me. For a moment I wonder if I even want to share him, and I'm pleased when I realize that I do. I want my brother to be happy. I want that more than anything, perhaps even more than I've ever wanted it for myself.

Sam drops and rips off ten push-ups. "Wanna join me?" he grunts. "I need to move after the plane."

"Nah."

"Yeah, figured."

I laugh as I watch him—and think for the zillionth time how we couldn't be more different. I'm sluglike; it's hard to make me move, unless it's to go volunteer at the pet shelter, which is my weekly bright spot. Sam can't stop moving—especially since getting clean. Exercise is his drug of choice now, which his toned body makes clear.

After his quick workout, Sam disappears inside, then returns with his tallit bag. He pulls out his tefillin, wraps the black leather straps in the ordained way around his forearms, then heads to the edge of the terrace with his siddur, to pray the afternoon minhah. I watch him, his strong back still sweaty from his workout, the kippah on his buzzed head, and listen to the familiar murmurs of his prayers. Funny, I always think, how of all of us in the Babel family, he's the only one who kept Aba's traditions—who decided to remain religious. The rest of us shed it with relief, like skintight jeans that you unbutton the second you get home.

I eat a few lemony olives and munch on a cracker, and eventually Sam returns to hug me. He always hugs me after his prayers, if I'm around, a long sort of hug that makes me feel like he just got an extra ration of God and needs to spread some of it around. Then he sprawls out on the lounger. He places his tallit bag on the table between us. "I don't get it," I tell my brother, for not the first time. "Why you still do all this stuff . . . with Aba gone?"

"What stuff?"

"Praying. Keeping kosher. Studying with the rabbis. It's like you keep getting more and more observant, and it doesn't make sense to me. Orthodox Judaism means following so many rules. And you hate rules."

"I do hate rules," Sam says. "Generally. I like freedom."

"You do! That's why I don't get—"

"But freedom within a framework is so much better, Bails." My brother's eyes burn with excitement. "Religion is so beautiful. Ours has so much wisdom and kindness. Our rituals, prayers, all of it has meaning and intention behind it. Everyone else is just latched on to social norms, believing every tweet; they're all so *flimsy*."

"I'm not flimsy," I say, but my chest constricts, says that maybe I am. "And anyway, doesn't it bother you that some rabbis think being gay is a sin? It bothers *me*."

"You're lumping all the rabbis together when they're really all different," Sam says, his face puffing with passion. "And Rabbi Grossman isn't archaic or sexist or a homophobe! I wouldn't have finally gotten clean without him, I know that for sure. Judaism doesn't actually judge us or limit us, contrary to what you think. It calls us to be better. And it even calls us to question things! To engage with the texts, to debate. You used to appreciate it, too, Bails."

I'm quiet, because he's right. After Aba died and Mom said I could leave my religious school, I cut contact with that world. We're still Jewish, and proud of it; we celebrate the holidays with gusto, but we don't follow all the rules anymore, like being kosher and keeping Shabbat. And when I left Orthodox Judaism, I even cut contact with my favorite teacher, Mrs. Thatch, who was so kind and caring, who would call on me and ask what I thought about a point of halacha, praising my interesting take, even when the other kids in the class were so much louder and more outspoken. Mrs. Thatch survived the Holocaust, survived so much, and she was there for me. Really there for me, especially when things weren't easy at home. She used to find me lingering in the hall after class, not wanting to go home, and she'd invite me inside for one of her delicious homemade rugelach, and we'd talk. She told me about her sisters, Rivka and Tova, both of whom were murdered at Auschwitz, and she told me about how she tried to find non-Jewish neighbors to take care of her beloved pet rabbit when the Nazis forced her and her family into the Warsaw Ghetto.

And I told her things too. About how disappointing I was to my father because I wasn't a boy. How he barely even looked at me when he passed me in the house. Mrs. Thatch didn't try to tell me to see Aba's good side, like saying he provided a roof over my head, or that I shouldn't be so sensitive. She just listened. That was a lot—it was *everything*, really, to be honest. After Aba died, and I left Jewish school, I never saw Mrs. Thatch again. It was too painful to stay close to that world. I needed a clean break from all the trauma. And so I never answered Mrs. Thatch's calls. All her lovely emails.

"You used to love being religious," Sam goes on. "All the holidays. You used to love singing the songs on Pesach."

I bite my lip, thinking about that, remembering "Chad Gadya" and "Echad Mi Yodea," the latter of which each of us kids would belt out, taking on a different numbered stanza. Sam's right—I loved it; the traditions made something hum in my soul. But still, when I think back, I see Aba at the head of the table, leading the seder, turning to Joshua and Sam to read the parts of the wise son and the simple son—and not turning to me at all. Now we still have a seder, of course, put on by Mom's catering team, and it's beautiful. But we rush through the songs instead of how we used to do it, going painstakingly through the Haggadah, singing into the night.

"Anyway," Sam continues, "I just feel like being Orthodox gives me more than it takes from me. And the community is so generous, they lift me up."

I shrug. "Even if they don't agree with who you fundamentally are?"

"Even if *some* of them don't. There *are* open Orthodox communities— mine is. Rabbi Grossman says that on the issue of LGBTQ+ acceptance, halacha is in the wrong. That Jewish law should be consistent with our values."

"His opinion isn't exactly commonplace," I say.

"True. But sometimes you have to take the good with the bad. Just because you don't agree with something fully doesn't mean you throw it all out. And . . . life is hard sometimes. Painful. It hasn't been easy for us, you know, Bails?"

I nod and bite my lip.

"I need this community. It means something to me. And I guess it makes me feel closer to Aba too."

I'm quiet, don't feel like starting down our typical Aba conversation route, as to how Sam could possibly *want* to feel close to our dead father.

"You should try it, Bails. You could come to some events, Shabbos dinners. I would love it. I bet it would give you a new sense of meaning."

"I *have* meaning in my life," I say, feeling something stir in my chest. And then I realize it's the sensation that he's right. That I don't have meaning. Not nearly enough of it. But I don't feel like admitting that right now, or really facing it myself.

Sam squeezes my hand. We watch the monkeys, who are still splashing around in our pool. "I could call Jabulani to get rid of them," Sam says.

"What's he gonna do? Do your fierce monkey dance too?"

Sam gives me a tiny smile. He sighs. "How do you do it, Bails?"

"What?"

"How are you so . . . unfazed by things?"

"Them?" I gesture at the pool where the monkeys are making a rollicking mess, water sloshing over the sides. "I mean, it's not the end of the—"

"Not them. Everything. Mom and . . . *him.*"

"Oh." I shrug, manage a small laugh. "I dunno. She seems happy, doesn't she? He . . . I don't know, he's sweet, I guess."

"Sweet." Sam lets out a bitter laugh. "Sucking up to us is more like it. But I don't just mean Asher. I guess I mean—living the life Mom's designed for you."

My chest tightens. "I'm making a difference. I know I am," I say, so quickly I wonder if I'm trying to convince myself or my brother. "If we start to shift our leather making to vegetable tanning, like Mom's promised, and solvent-free finishing, then the environmental impact is gonna be huge."

"I didn't mean you're not making a difference. I just meant, you're not making a difference in the way you truly want to."

I'm quiet, because he's right on this count too. And I feel it in the pressure on my chest, and the same fears circling my brain, that I'm wasting my life. That I'm falling back on my old patterns, trying to please Mom. Forever caring about everyone else's opinions—to my own detriment.

"And sustainable leather is an oxymoron." Sam says it sharply, the final twist of the knife. "You know it."

"I know." I sigh. "Honestly, the most sustainable thing is to use what you already have. The industry isn't perfect. It can't ever be perfect." But I wonder if I'm just parroting Mom—not speaking to my own beliefs.

"It can't be perfect," Sam agrees, "because Mom will always want to grow and make more profit, and that in its essence is never going to cause the kind of environmental impact you want. Circ is all high on its morality, but recycled polyester? You mean, made from fossil fuels? Carbon neutral? Please. It's all BS greenwashing, regardless of what the tags say. In the end, your goal is the same as Zara and Shein. To entice people to buy crap they don't actually need."

"I didn't know you were so passionate about this topic," I shoot back, with more bite than I intend. I'm surprised, is all, by this diatribe of his. Sam acts like he's indifferent to Circ, so uninterested in everything Mom and Joshua love, obstinately I often think. But I didn't know he'd been harboring such skewering insights. Sam is smart, though. Smarter than anyone else I know, which most people would never suspect. He didn't care at all about school, barely expended effort, but still somehow casually emerged with mostly A's. Yet the many times he's gone to rehab has affected people's perceptions of him, even our own family's. But Sam is brilliant. He has a way of distilling things down to their truth in a no-nonsense way. And he's right, isn't he? Because though Circ uses organic cotton and linen and silks—presumably fibers healthy for people and for the earth—our ultimate goal is profit. Mom is constantly trying to decrease costs. She's pushing recycled polyester forward, even though the whole concept is a sham. It's toxic and will never decompose in landfills. It's the source of quite a lot of tension between her and me, and especially her and Joshua, too, of late. Because the whole point of our sustainable footprint is to keep our production integrity. And besides, if we start to close in on fast-fashion prices, we are not only going to lose the ethics of our mission, but we are going to begin to sell fast-fashion quantities. More toxic materials to pollute the earth, for people to discard after one or two wears. We can't deny that clothing production has tripled in the past fifty years. We are overproducing, and overconsuming, filling up landfills—and Circ is undeniably contributing to that.

Is that why anger boils in my throat? I'm not angry at my brother, am I? I'm really just angry at myself, for being a cog in the whole enterprise.

"You always give Mom the benefit of the doubt. You don't know what she's capable of. You have absolutely no idea." Sam stares off at the river.

"What do you mean, I don't know what Mom's capable of? What are you talking about?"

"Oh, forget it, Bails. Let's not get into it." Sam heaves a breath and leaps up, does a couple side stretches.

"No, really. What?"

"You're amazing. That's what I meant from all this. I honestly think what you're doing is amazing."

"I don't know if it is," I say quietly.

"Who says you need to be a vet? You have Sunny," he says, referring to my rescue mutt, whom I've left back in Palm Beach with my friend Junie. "Who says that just because you love animals, you need to be working with them? Maybe you've just figured it out better than me. How to deal with Mom, deal with life. You don't need much." He gestures to my humble backpack. "You should probably be telling me the secret to life, and not the other way around."

He flashes me a sheepish smile, and I smile back, though so many things are stirring uneasily inside me.

"You know, I think this trip is going to change things for us," Sam says, surprising me with his sudden optimism. He tips his face up to the sun.

"Really? Why do you think so?"

He shrugs. "Just have a good feeling. That things are on the up for the Babel twins."

"I'll drink to that." I clink my copper tumbler against his.

"To us." He meets my eyes, then downs his glass. He grabs his camera and aims it at me. I blush, but look off at the river, and let him click away. "Beautiful," he says.

"Ehhh." I shift in my chair, feel my body start to squirm. I'm so not photogenic. Not a model in the least.

"You *are* beautiful. You're related to me, after all."

I laugh.

"'Kay, I'm gonna go in and change." Sam springs up as if he's shot from a trampoline. It's such a simple moment but it causes me to smile, because it's also so my brother—he does everything with verve. Drugs, exercise, photography—the way he moves around the world too. He's not light-footed, tentative, unsure of himself and of his place in the world. Nope. Save that for the other Babel twin.

"I'm gonna stay out here until dinner and see if anyone comes down to drink from the river." I sift in my bag for my binoculars, already feeling that excited anticipation for tomorrow's drive.

"By anyone, you mean your animal friends." Sam nudges my arm, his tone teasing.

"The best kind," I say with a smile. "You always know where you stand with them."

"Ain't that the truth." Sam chuckles. "You're wearing that to dinner?"

"What?" I glance down at my olive sweater and my favorite khaki technical pants. "Dav told me that wide leg is in again."

Sam laughs. "I don't think she was talking about wide leg pants you get at camping stores."

"They're comfy," I protest. I smooth down my mass of dirty blond hair that has ballooned in the heat. It immediately snaps back out. Oh, well. My hair is fairly untamable, unless I resort to the straightening iron like Mom often tries to cajole me to do. But straightening my hair now will just show the awful job I've been doing cutting it myself. If Mom knew I was cutting my hair myself, she'd have a heart attack. When I was a kid, she always took me to her glamorous hair salons, but I only felt uncomfortable there, making endless chitchat—and a haircut took hours. A year ago, I decided to watch a YouTube video and even that was too much work—sectioning off, snipping so carefully. I've started just eyeballing my hair in the mirror and cleaning up the ends with a scissors I grabbed from the kitchen. It works, unless your mom keeps trying to insist you iron it into submission, which will only highlight the butcher job you did to your ends.

"Fine," I finally say. "I'm not pretending to be into couture."

"You've cornered the market on khaki couture," Sam teases.

I smile.

"Are we sure we're really related?" Sam laughs. My brother cares about things like cologne, and pants with whatever the trendy ankle width is, and the latest greatest Nikes. Like Mom. I, on the other hand, am missing that gene.

"We *are* related," I tell him, trying not to sound—or be—offended.

"I'm just teasing," Sam tells me, and his face takes a serious set. "No one in the world I want to be related to more than you. When I grow up, I wanna be like Bailey Babel. You're perfect." He squeezes my shoulders from behind and kisses the top of my head.

Yes, Sam and I might not have much in common ostensibly, but love is the biggest bridge there is. And my love for my twin is beyond that which I feel for anyone else in the world.

Sam goes inside, and I stare out at the river, thinking about the last thing he said. Thinking how it is, that with all my brother's problems, all the trouble he's caused, all his surliness and sometimes hatred of the world, he is the only one of us Babel kids who isn't working for Circ. Who is actually blazing his own path.

Am I the sellout? That's what he was implying, after all. Joshua is a natural-born financial whiz, at home in the role of CFO, so maybe Circ is his true calling. But me? Sam only called me perfect because of how I can contort myself into any box. And especially into the box Mom has wanted me to fit inside all my life.

I fumble in my backpack for gum and punch out four pieces. If Sam were still here, he'd puff out his cheeks imitating me. Want to know how different we are? Just look at how we both coped with Aba's death: Sam turned to drugs, I turned to gum. I return the gum to my backpack, my heart thumping. As I do the zipper, I spot my malaria medicine and realize I've forgotten to take it. I snap open the canister and slip a pill in my mouth, draining it with water. Then I put the gum in my mouth, savoring the chomp. But as my jaw is engaged in its familiar chew, the usual release doesn't come. I'm still on edge.

Everyone thinks I'm quiet, meek. Harmless. Fall-into-line Bailey. The opposite of daring.

But I'm not. And maybe it's about time that I show it.

# CHAPTER FIVE

# GWEN

I step back and study my best friend's radiant skin. So bronze and glowing, she's angelic—haloed. "Nah. Don't think you need any more powder."

"Let's do it anyway."

So I oblige and dust Dede's chin with Charlotte Tilbury powder, then study my masterpiece again.

"Gorgeous," I say, and it's not pandering. The simple truth. Anyone with functioning eyes would agree. We are a decade older than JLo and Jennifer Aniston, but Dede is just as beautiful and ageless.

Dede swivels her face in the towering oak mirror. "A little more contour on my cheekbones, don't you think?"

Asher pokes his head into the dressing area and deposits another one of those radioactive yellow powder drinks into Dede's hands.

"She doesn't need more contour, Gwen. Her cheekbones are already sharp enough they could cut steak."

Dede guffaws, a response that in my opinion is out of proportion to the hardly funny joke. I nod in a way I hope is polite but curt and reach for the contour anyway, because Odelia knows what she likes—and is never deterred.

But then Dede says, "Forget the contour, Gwennie. I'm good. Just setting spray, please."

I place the contour back into my kit and reach for the spray, feeling my hands tremble. I throw my other hand through my hair and pull out a few strands. I let the strands drop to the floor, marring Dede's otherwise perfectly spotless parquet. This feels satisfying, but in an empty way.

Dede throws her forearm up to cover her hairline and I spritz. Asher leaves, and I say quietly, "So this is how it is now, huh? Asher's opinion is the only one that matters?"

"You're being silly," Dede says. "He's right. I'm tan enough as it is."

I open my mouth, starting to say that contour is altogether different than tan, and what does Asher know? But then I close it. I know it—I am drowning in my humanness. I try so hard to be spiritual, evolved, to marinate in the marrow of my soul, and then that acute pain and separation of being human bubbles up.

I put down the setting spray, and Dede sucks through a straw on her radioactive yellow drink. A quiet balloons between us. But usually where I feel alight, comfortable, even joyful with her, my mind is now spiraling into dark thoughts. She didn't even tell me about Asher until after they got engaged. That's how little she trusts me. After everything.

Stupid me. I pull at more hairs—experience a dopamine hit each time they spring from their roots and fall to the ground. I actually believed her when she said Bora Bora was for work. Even if it was strange that she didn't ask me to join. Since Aryeh died we've been inseparable. No longer.

"This marble is gorgeous," Dede says, gliding a hand over the emerald counter. "I wonder if I should do emerald marble in the primary bathroom."

"I thought we're going with that gorgeous white Carrara marble."

"Well, I'm not set on it. Asher said he really loves this green one. And he has the eye, you know? Can you find out where it's from?"

Oh, *Asher* has the eye, does he?

"Sure," I say quietly, making a note in my phone. "I'll find out and we can discuss it with Ingrid." Ingrid is the head of the interior design firm Dede has engaged. "We have a meeting with her next week once we're back to go over the remodel plans."

"Great."

Dede frowns, staring at her long white nails, part bridal, part witch's talons. Her face is cloudy, impenetrable, and it bothers me I can't make out what thoughts are swirling beneath it. Where we'd normally be jabbering away, talking about the kids, and the cute grunt Ruby made, trying to de-cipher what her little personality is, or bemoaning some new awful thing Sam's done, instead we're stilted, like strangers.

"Gwennie, I need to ask—"

"Want me to pull cards for you?" I chirp at the same time. "Sorry." I stop, replaying her tone in my head—edgy, even desolate. "You need to ask what?"

A shadow flits across her face, and now I'm turbulent inside, my whole body thrumming.

But then Dede shakes her head and smiles, suddenly bright. "Sure. Pull me good cards!"

"What were you going to say?" I'm still holding my breath. "Ask me something?"

"Nothing." Now she's decisive, boardroom mode.

*Just spit it out*, I urge silently inside. We're both holding back so much. The tension is going to swallow me alive. And this isn't normal. We're not ourselves, the single organism that we used to be. If we were normal, there'd be no break between a thought originating in Dede's brain and my hearing it.

"Nothing," she says again. "C'mon, Gwennie, pull me some cards."

———

I PULL A THREE-CARD spread, then flip over the first one. The Moon. I suck in my breath. The moment I first learned the meaning of this card flings back at me. When I was in prison, at Camp Bryan in Texas, and another inmate taught it to me.

"Good or bad?" Dede asks, but I don't respond.

She's so binary, my best friend. Has a hard time contending with the betweens.

"Interesting," I say slowly, turning the second card over. The Three of Swords.

"Bad?" She tries to frown, but the Botox doesn't allow her to. "Oh, I hate getting bad cards."

"Not bad necessarily," I hedge. It's the same with my private tarot clients, too—everyone comes ostensibly for wisdom and guidance, but deep down, all we humans want is to be told the future is bright. I summon courage and flip the third card of Dede's reading. I swallow a gasp.

Death.

We both gape at the spread laid out on the green marble.

"Bad," Dede says again, shaking her head furiously. "No bad cards. I told you to eliminate the bad ones from the deck." She makes it sound like my fault.

"No such thing as bad cards," I say weakly. I start to grab them, shuffle them back into the deck, but she puts a hand on my forearm.

"No, tell me."

So I stop, stare at the spread, a warning signal flashing in my brain.

"C'mon, Gwennie. We're gonna be late for dinner if you don't tell me already. I can take it—I have to know what I'm up against this weekend. What's the Moon mean?"

"It means that there are things yet to be revealed, and everything is not as it seems," I say quietly. "It means you're being lied to."

"Lied to?" Dede laughs, sounding unconcerned. "Everyone lies to me. Production's on time, air quality won't suffer, the wage isn't minimum. Sam says he's clean again. All lies. Par for the course."

I don't respond, just stare at the card. "Not just lies," I say slowly. "It's more than that. It's like you're being manipulated."

"Oh, please." Her voice is cutting. "I'm not capable of being manipulated. I wouldn't have gotten this far if I were." But she can't conceal it, what flits across her face—something raw, uncertain.

"What?"

"No. Nothing. Do the next card."

She stares at it, and I do too. A heart pierced by three swords. As tarot cards go, fairly graphic and self-explanatory.

"Three of Swords means . . ." I sift for words that might soften the blow, but this isn't really a soften-able card. "Heartbreak," I finally say.

"Why?" Odelia picks up the card and stares at it aggressively, like it's set out purposely to offend her. "My heart's the happiest it's ever been."

I shrug. "It usually means an unexpected event. Something that comes out of the blue."

"I don't like this."

Dede touches her locket, plays with it. I remember mine, too, the weight of it when I used to wear it, though I haven't in decades now. The thing about remembering is that, if you do it too much, you're liable to go insane.

Dede tucks her necklace back beneath her top and then, in a flash of fury, flicks the Three of Swords across the counter. But she doesn't stand up, walk away, abandon this reading. I know her—she wants the whole reading. She isn't a quitter, folding her hand before she really gives it a full chance. In this way, we are markedly different. The past has proven that I'm willing to fold my hand—for her.

"When the heartbreak comes to light, and it will, it will be painful," I say slowly. "It will cause death." My heart lodges in my throat as I point to the last card. The pinnacle of the reading.

"*My* death?" Dede laughs, a shrill, awful sound. Normally her laughs are deep; she controls them. This one is different—the laugh controlling her.

"Too literal, Dede. It probably means the death of your former self." But as I say it, I'm not so sure. Because it *could* mean her actual death. I experience a rush of pain—but something else, too, something shameful. For the first time, I consider how my best friend's actual death would affect me. How it would massage things—some for the worst, some perhaps for the better.

"Well, my former self *has* died. I've been single for so long. I have a partner now. A true love." She's soft now, onward toward mush. But I can't melt with her, giggle girlie sleepover excitement. I feel steely. Suddenly afraid. Of her, of this week.

Of myself too. What the cards are trying to tell me. What truth they are beckoning me toward.

I rake my hand through my hair, tugging at the strands. I'm too frenetic, though; now the dopamine surge as the roots pry away is barely perceptible.

"Death can be like a rebirth," I say, trying to summon optimism, trying to calm, but I can't. Everything is on the edge of a cliff, an easy shove down.

So much is swelling in me. I remember a lifetime ago, when I spent those years in jail. You would think it was the worst time of my life, but it wasn't, not entirely. Unburdened of the outside world, all I had was time to spend with God. In that time of void, of quiet and stillness, God told me all his wisdom. Told me how separation is an illusion, and everything that is real is love. All we have to do is dismantle the blocks to love that reside within us. So simple.

I try to remind myself of it. Everything real is love. But no use—what swishes inside me is an overwhelming amount of hate.

"So that's it," Dede says decisively. "This weekend I am reborn. And if Sam tries something, well, he can't break my heart. It's unbreakable. Asher's responsible for that."

"What's that?" Her groom steps back into the room now, dressed for dinner, his usual edgy polished that I privately dislike. I like men rough and rugged, not so perfectly put together. Though I guess it fits Asher's brand, his olive cargo pants and brown leather boots, a boxy beige tee that shows the outline of hard muscles. All topped off by his earnest, boyish face. With its moony, swoony love, his hands, with long musical fingers that now caress Dede's shoulders, flitter down to her curves. I can almost imagine them making love—like a fucking symphony.

I'm ashamed when a surge of desire sweeps over me, the first time in a long time that's happened.

But Dede isn't paying me attention. Her eyes are riveted to his.

"I've just been telling Gwen that no matter what the kids say, what they do, how much they try to sabotage us, my heart is bulletproof. I feel so loved I could explode." She says it tenderly, staring up at him with this gushy look that is so foreign to see on her face.

"Don't explode, please." Asher leans down to kiss her. Tongue. God. I have the urge to say get a room, but that would make me the bitter, jealous old lady.

Plus, I'm *in* their room.

Still, something white-hot flares in me—my body betraying me. Disloyal. When you're in your sixties, when you haven't felt desire in decades, when no one's touched you since the Reagan administration, it shouldn't rise up. It should know to stay buried. But it doesn't.

I watch them, desire burning inside, like a festering wound I didn't even know I had. They're kissing, oblivious to me, as if I am some statue, or a servant.

Well, I suppose I am. Both.

They break apart. "Okay, dinnertime!" Dede says. "Ready, Gwennie?" She gives me a smile all alight, her eyes avoiding the cards.

I gather them up, place them back into my tattered box. "I need to go change, and I'll meet you there."

Her eyebrow flicks up. "You look fine."

It wasn't meant as an insult. And normally it wouldn't faze me. But suddenly, strangely, I don't want to look fine. I want to look beautiful.

I glance down at my olive-green linen set, the one the saleswoman at Nordstrom said was perfect for safari. I feel dumpy. Old. Like I don't belong here. Well, maybe I don't.

"C'mon," Dede says impatiently. "What you're wearing is perfect. This isn't a glamorous trip. It's what I love about being here. No pretense."

She stands, and I nearly laugh. No pretense, my ass. Dede's wearing skintight black trouser pants with slits at the ankle, black crocodile Khaite boots, a fur vest over a white silk Circ blouse, topped off with a full face of makeup. She hooks her arm through her Toteme T-lock bag, the one her stylist told her all the Gen Z girls covet. Dede looks like a million—no, make that a billion—bucks.

But I'm the sidekick. It's what I signed up for long ago. When we were kids—the world at our feet. Or at hers. And she's taken care of me—yes, she has. Still, fear bubbles in my chest, where before it's been calm. And the fear scares me.

I know what fear does. Hardens quickly to hate.

"Okay." As always, I follow after my best friend.

# CHAPTER SIX

# ASHER

Odelia and I walk toward the lodge as the sun is setting, about to collapse into the tree line. Thankfully I convinced Odelia to send Gwen ahead, ostensibly to check on the rehearsal dinner preparations, while we hung back and had a bit of alone time before more family togetherness. Gwen is ever-present; sometimes I just want to be one-on-one with my fiancée.

I watch the sun on its last descent, amazed at how red it is, how low it gets before slinking out of sight. In the States, there's pollution at the horizon, obfuscating the view. "It's all so . . . horizontal."

"Oh?" Odelia leans her head against my arm. "What do you mean?"

"New York is so different," I try to explain. "Everything goes up. Draws your eye up. Miami too. Even Palm Beach. But here there's no up, just out." She's quiet. I add, "The clouds are so close, it's like I could reach out and touch them."

"It's peaceful," she says.

"Extraordinarily."

"I'm glad you feel the same way as I do about this place."

"I do. It's special." My hand, woven inside hers, has hit its clammy threshold, beyond which it must be extracted from its hold, before it slides out and makes everything awkward.

"Sorry, sweetheart." I untangle my hand, swipe it on my pants. We're still at that shiny new relationship place, where a clammy hand embarrasses me.

"You're nervous?" she asks.

"A little."

Odelia shoots me a look that's sympathetic, but also sensual. Bedroom eyes, not obviated by my sweaty hands. Well, we did just have quick, excellent sex when Gwen left.

"Nervous about my kids?" She sounds surprised.

"Of course."

We pass a squat man clad in the ubiquitous khaki safari suit that is the staff uniform. He moves aside, giving us excessive birth to pass.

"Don't be." Odelia swats my arm. "I love you, and the kids will too. Anyway, Joshua and Bailey have been working with you for over a year now. They've only said wonderful things."

"That was before they knew we got together, though. Thinking of me as a work colleague is one thing, but as a stepfather is something totally other. I still think we should have told them about our relationship earlier . . . given them more time. But I understood you wanted to do it at your own pace. Still . . . you gotta admit—the vibe on the plane was weird. It didn't feel like your kids loved me, if I'm being honest."

"Davina does." Her tone is light, but I can sense sharpness behind it. "I noticed you guys getting pretty chummy on the flight."

"C'mon, that's ridiculous." But when Delia doesn't respond I add, "You're not insecure about your daughter-in-law, are you?" I stop, fix her eyes with mine. "We've been working together, too, for over a year. And I couldn't be less interested."

Odelia stares back, her big green eyes that remind me of Bambi, that are surprisingly youthful and vivacious for her age. It was her eyes that first transfixed me—when I looked inside them, I knew. I can tell she's insecure about the Davina thing, though, which surprises me. Insecure is not a quality I've really seen in Delia. She holds my eyes, and I return her gaze. For a few moments it's like we're back on that beach in Bora Bora, lost in each other, shutting out the world, everything but us. I liked that time, tumbling into the vortex of us, forgetting there are other things besides our love.

Finally, she blinks. "Okay."

"Okay," I agree and throw an arm around her shoulders. "Anyway, I get it if your kids haven't exactly welcomed me with open arms. I'm not much older than Joshua."

"You're nearly a decade older than Joshua. That's significant. And Joshua likes you. *He's* the one who hired you."

"He might have liked me before I got together with his mother, but I guarantee you he doesn't anymore."

"He does." She says it with zero qualms. Like a woman who is used to levying verdicts and having them adopted, no question. Delia has no doubts about the validity of her opinions, or imposing them on others. I admire that quality.

"I don't want him to like me because you tell him to. I want him to sincerely like me. For me."

She smiles indulgently at me. "That's sweet."

"He won't?"

"Bailey might. But Joshua and Sam? Probably not. Not so soon, at least. Sorry, honey. You're a threat. Mothers and sons." She shrugs. "It's a primal relationship."

Something skitters in a tree, and I start. I think about what I learned when googling this place. If you come across a poisonous snake, step back slowly. Don't run. That seems to be the theme with all these ferocious animals, though it defies human instincts. My breath returns as I watch something rodent-size scamper toward the ground.

"Just a mouse." I'm glad it's dark, that Delia couldn't tell the fear coursing in me.

"Not a mouse." She's still watching it, a smile quirking on her lips. "It's an elephant shrew. Look at his nose. How long it is."

I focus and indeed she's right—I note the long beak.

I sigh, taking in the quiet expanse, the lanterns studding iron posts, the suites all in a row, done in natural materials that achieve a seamless blend with this savage bush.

"How did you know that?" I'm amazed, really, that my decidedly not-outdoorsy fiancée has an apparent encyclopedic knowledge of the animals here.

"I've come here quite a bit, city boy."

I sigh. The air is crisp and impossibly fresh, as if pollution is a thing of hypothetical apocalypses, not anything that exists in our time. "I love being here with you."

"You ain't seen nothing yet."

"I'm happy," I tell her. "I'm really excited for this week." It feels inordinately true. The truest thing I could say. This will be a life-changing week.

"Me too. More than I ever thought I could be in my life." Her eyes are shining. "C'mon, you're gonna love the chef. He has a Michelin star. Oh! And you'll see where we're doing dinner tomorrow night. If you don't like it . . . if you don't like anything . . . I can just tell the staff, and have Gwen—"

"I'm going to like it." I return my hand into hers, glad it's no longer clammy.

"But if you don't, if you have tweaks . . . it's *our* wedding. I want you to have input."

"Our engagement was practically a wedding. Bora Bora was . . . incredible. Perfect."

"No cap on celebrations," she says firmly. "And it's important . . . I refuse to pander to the kids' . . . *feelings* about us. I love them, but this is my life. They need to respect my choices." She squares her shoulders as we walk into the lodge, past moss-green and bone linen settees, bookshelves with old leather-covered spines, and antique maps and zoological prints in slate frames. The windows are all timber-framed, sporting breathtaking views, and a fire is crackling in the lobby's stone fireplace. "This wedding has a message, you know?"

"Oh yeah, we're having a theme wedding, huh?" I tease. "Okay. What is it?"

"That you're not going anywhere." But Delia doesn't smile, only grips my hand tighter as we walk. Like the harder she grips, the more prescient she'll be.

"I'm not going anywhere," I agree, feeling the resolve behind my promise. The emotion bursting through my pores. "I promise you that."

———

AS WAITRESSES BUSTLE AROUND pouring biodynamic wine (Odelia), delivering Lion Lagers (Joshua and me), a beer shandy (Bailey), and brandy (Davina), I gaze around at my new family. If everyone weren't so serious, weren't treating this meal like a funeral, or a board meeting to be endured, it would be a comical scene with a diverse cast of characters. We are all dressed so wildly different that we look like strangers assembled at a country house for an Agatha Christie murder. I can practically picture Poirot here. An amusing thought.

"Doesn't this feel like a Christie setup," I ask Odelia.

She chuckles. "I hope not."

"Me too. It just reminded me." I pull at a memory and tug. "I used to watch Poirots with my mother on TV—before she went to prison." I immediately regret saying the word *mother* aloud, even though I've told Delia about my family background.

A shadow crosses Delia's face. She frowns. Eventually her face settles back to its usual placid state. "Who did it, you're saying, the murder on safari? Colonel Mustard in the library?"

"With the candlestick." I catch my grinning reflection in the copper mirror across.

Delia smiles and appraises her menu. "You know they're going to make you vegan stuff. Gwen made sure. It's not just game."

"Yes. Thanks, hon." I've already checked the menu, which is all kudu and springbok and venison, stuff that makes my insides curl. It doesn't make sense to me—how everyone can be so obsessed with conservation and respecting the animals in their habitat here, and then go ahead and eat them. But suffice it to say, not much in this world makes sense.

Everyone flips through the menus, and I look around, again finding the irony of all of us convened here, so different, but with one person in common: Delia, elegant in a fur vest and tight black pants that show off her amazing, round ass.

As Sam muttered on our way over, I admit that yes, I may skew Indiana Jones meets Bergdorf's in my designer safari gear. But Sam, on the other hand, hasn't veered from his leather jacket and tight jeans Danny Zuko uniform, complete with angst dripping from his pores and veins in his neck that pop from his hours a day in the gym. Bailey—the only one of the Babels around whom I can easily breathe—hasn't changed from the plane, still in her technical REI khakis and garishly turquoise top, her dishwater blond hair frizzy. Gwen looks her usual refined if not boring, having changed into a loose, long, lavender silk dress, her eyes darting around like a hunted animal. Davina's in a light blue cashmere beanie and olive cocoon bomber, appearing as unbothered as ever, and Joshua is in his standard khaki chinos, boring prep school look.

Since I was a child I've observed how people are often judged, even pigeonholed, by their attire. That's why clothes are so powerful, why I am obsessed with them, because they tell a story about who we are. Right or wrong, our fashion choices are one of the most potent ways at our disposal to express ourselves. Like, Sam: angry. Bailey: unassuming. Gwen: unoriginal. Davina: breezy. Joshua: perfectionist. Odelia: powerful. And if I could add another word for Delia, it would be uncaring. I don't mean it as an insult, though. I mean, uncaring about what other people think, or doing anything other than what she wants. It's one of the reasons that the relationship between Delia and Davina simmers with tension. They both do what they want, damn what anyone thinks.

And what word would I choose for myself? What do my rigid Prada cargos and Circ oat-colored boxy tee communicate? Stylish. Creative. Exacting. Sure. Can mix high and low; don't take myself too seriously. Uh-huh. But those things don't encompass all of me. Isn't that the problem with reducing ourselves to one defining characteristic? We miss the substance behind the facade. The everything behind the one thing.

Maybe my outfit doesn't convey that I am deeply spiritual, for instance. When I moved into Odelia's mansion, I felt dark energy. Houses hold their pasts, like people do. I had my healer come to cleanse the place. Odelia reluctantly agreed. My healer is ninety-two years old and blind in one eye; he nearly torched the place, truth be told, when he smothered our space in incense, sparks flying. He accidentally singed Odelia's new ecru couch. "Sorry, sorry," he said, turning to Delia with an exuberant smile. "The spirits were restless. But they are all gone now!"

"Wonderful," Delia said, then later told me she'd paid sixty thousand dollars for the couch. Now we do laugh about it.

My new family busies themselves with the menus, and I gaze off, thinking about what lies beneath all of us.

———

"SO ARE YOU TWO planning on having children?" Davina asks, nursing Ruby, barely bothering to shield her nipples. They've already slipped a couple times, and they'd probably be even more ubiquitous but for Ruby's thicket of dark hair—funny on a baby somehow. Still, it's unmistakable: Davina's breasts are swollen and on display. She's lost some weight—Delia has issues with it—but that hasn't diminished her breasts. I can feel Delia's anger radiating at my side. I clasp her hand under the table, but my eyes find it difficult to avoid looking at Davina.

"You know I'm not having more children, Davina," Odelia says tightly, her eyes fixed on Davina's breasts.

"I didn't mean *having* them," Davina says with a dismissive wave. "I meant, adopting. Or using a surrogate. There are so many ways these days. Especially if you have means."

I clear my throat. "Actually, I don't want kids. So it's not Delia's choice not to have them. It's mine."

"It's my choice too," Odelia says. "I don't wish to revisit the diaper stage." Her eyes swivel at Sam. "Or the rehab one."

Sam doesn't flinch. His eyes flicker at me. "You mean, you don't want kids, other than *us*, dear stepfather."

"Of course," I say lightly. "Ready-made kids who aren't in diapers. A dream come true."

"A total dream," Odelia says, sawing her venison with her sharp, jagged knife. "That satisfy you, Davina? Does that satisfy all of you?"

"I was just wondering," Davina says. "I wasn't trying to create conflict." Suddenly Ruby breaks away from her mother's breast and begins to wail, as if sensing her moment.

"Our daughter has exceptional timing," Joshua says, giving me a slight smile as he reaches for his daughter, thumps her back.

Davina takes her time pulling her shirt back over her breasts. I can't help but take in the magnificent view.

"Davina, really," Odelia says, fiddling with her locket. "In my day, we used tents and shields."

"It's stifling to the baby. Ruby likes to be out with the family, in fresh air. Why don't you want to have children, Asher?"

"I—"

"His mother is in prison," Odelia cuts in. "And his father was mostly absent. An alcoholic."

I swallow my bite of mushroom burger. My lips try to smile, but as always happens with the reveal of this story, they fail. There is a sharp collective intake of breath.

"Prison?" Bailey finally ventures. "For what?"

I pause. "Murder," I finally say quietly. "It's a long story. She was an addict. She was driving drunk . . . she killed a couple. Both in their eighties. Great-grandparents." I bite my lip, look away.

Gwen stifles a gasp. When I glance back, I see her face gone sheet white. I know she was in prison herself a long time ago, for a boating accident that ended in a death. So Gwen's startled reaction makes sense, her being triggered back to it. All the Babels are affected by Gwen's crime, I suspect—it's why Odelia's supported Gwen for all these years. Why she's allowed her into the family. Convicts don't have many prospects. I've never seen anything like Odelia and Gwen's friendship—a grown woman so entranced by another one, so indebted, but also maintaining some sort of power hold over the more powerful one. None of it makes much sense on the outside, but Odelia and I have talked about the deep things since the beginning. We haven't skirted over the hard or unpleasant stuff. It's why our bond is so tight, though we haven't been a couple long.

"Not everyone has a privileged upbringing with endless handouts," Odelia says into the vacuum of silence. The implication clear: *Like my children.*

"Handouts, *please*," Sam mutters.

"Oh, really?" Odelia says, her voice dripping with sarcasm. "So you've been given nothing, Sam? So your father didn't leave you money for your condo? And I haven't bailed you out many, many times? Given you the best of everything, your whole entire life? So I didn't take you all to Courchevel a couple months ago, what of it? You wanna know your problem—you have zero appreciation. No idea what other people have to do to persevere and prevail." She nods her head pointedly at me. "And Asher not wanting children—well, maybe that's because he realizes that sometimes kids are more trouble than they're worth."

"That's not what this—what my childhood is—" I protest, not wanting her to make a mockery of it, to use my lack of desire for children as a means to skewer hers. Anyway, not everything has a neat, fair rationale. I don't want kids because I like my life. I like silence, traveling when I want, popping over to Europe for fashion week, not having to deal with poop and vomit and little fingers and toes constantly in your space. Maybe it's as simple as me not wanting kids because I'm selfish.

"What?" Odelia tosses aside her menu. "They should all know. Of everyone here, you pulled yourself up by your bootstraps. Worked hard, put yourself through school, worked multiple jobs paying your way through your master's. In material futures, just like McQueen. You worked your way up. We were so lucky to poach you from Balmain." She nods at Joshua. "One of my son's finest moments."

Joshua flushes and rakes an anxious hand through his thick, dark hair, and I can tell he's not complimented by what she's said, but something opposite—hurt that his finest moment is linked to me. I like Joshua, genuinely. I find him sharp, quietly taking things in; talking when it means something, not just to hear himself sound smart. Though in my time at Circ, and now joining this family, I have gleaned Joshua's weakness: he has a bit of an Oedipus complex.

"You are an asset to Circ, sweetheart," Odelia says, running a finger along my cheek. "You and your— What did Yohji Yamamoto say? Oh yes— You and your *masterful monochromatic androgyny* are going to help catapult Circ forward. And your research using mycelium for textiles as a nonleather alternative is the future of fashion."

"Delia," I say quietly, grasping her hand, trying to impart that none of this is endearing me to her kids.

"What? Don't be modest, honey. I'm merely stating facts. I don't want anyone in my family to say you jumped on this gravy train and are just along for the ride. The opposite, in fact. Circ is so lucky to have you. You are just what our company needed. Just what *I* needed. And you earned every single thing you've achieved. You weren't handed a thing. Not *a thing.*"

Her eyes move around the table, holding each person's gaze, one by one. No one speaks, but the tension is palpable. Combustible.

Having made her point, Odelia signals for a waiter. "I'm craving one of Arno's delectable keto ice creams. Everyone ready for dessert?"

# CHAPTER SEVEN

# JOSHUA

We've finished dessert without incident, other than Sam's barbs about Mom's stinginess and her lack of taste in men. All of which Mom brushes off thanks to her seemingly impenetrable love bubble. I place my fork down, my stomach heavy with my two desserts. I overdid it, but couldn't choose between *malva*, sticky toffee pudding with apricot jam, and *koeksisters*, a twisted doughnut with syrupy goodness on top. I used to gorge on both as a child here, dishes laden with memories—Aba admonishing me, saying I needed to learn discipline. My phone buzzes in my pocket. I pull it out and steal a glimpse at the text. Lester from Circ. Sweat beads collect on my forehead. I read the text, then slide my phone back, my thoughts in a whirl.

"Joshua." Mom says my name in her disapproving way—enunciating the first syllable. She frowns.

"Ye— What?" She has this almost uncanny ability to see through me, to pry apart my thoughts before I can winnow them away. Conceal, conceal. But she can't have gleaned this one—she wouldn't be reacting like this. She'd be standing over me, raging, her voice hot in my ear as she reminds me who is boss. And I can't broach this text's topic, not until I think how to approach Mom the best way. How to finagle this, how will I ever—

"You know how I feel about you keeping your phone in your pocket. All that radiation, right by your testicles." Heat creeps up my neck. "You know it's bad for fertility. A million studies have said so, but it's common sense. I don't know how you allow him to keep his phone essentially right on his *balls*, Davina."

"He—" Davina starts to say, before I interject, "Sorry." I put my phone on the table, face down. Davina places a hand on my thigh, but I am shaking, too upset to feel my wife's support, or to want it.

"You can wear a man satchel," Mom says almost triumphantly. "Ask Asher. They're fire."

"Please don't say fire," Sam says. "You're not twelve. How do you even know that word?"

Mom ignores him and focuses on me. "They're cool now, man satchels. Asher has a couple himself. Circ makes a nice one. Or there's Gucci."

She tents her hands together on the table, like she has successfully identified a problem and solved it.

Asher says, "Delia, come on, let him live," but he doesn't appear to be put off by her brazenness. He's smiling, almost. Taking pleasure in my being talked down to. Maybe that's not fair, but it's how it feels. And Lester, on top of it. Everything on my shoulders, piling on.

"Look at our little pilot," Davina says, trying to distract me, I know. She's pinned the wings we got from the pilot on our jet to Ruby's jacket. "I always wanted to be a pilot when I was a kid. I was obsessed with airplanes. Can you imagine it, Pilot Ruby? Is there a feminine of pilot? Pilotess?"

I tickle Ruby's chin. "My little pilotess Amelia Earhart."

But I'm still vibrating with indignation at my mother when Violett approaches the table.

"Mrs. Babel and Mr. Bach—or should I say, the soon-to-be Mr. and Mrs. Babel-Bach?" Violett says, and I think I detect a note of teasing in her voice when she tumbles over that mouthful of a moniker. Davina would have insisted on a hyphen, too, except that her maiden name is Slutsky, and her feminist proclivities fell by the wayside on the maiden name retention point.

I launch out of my seat. "Violett! I barely got to speak to you on the tarmac. How are you? It's so good to see you!"

I've known Violett for . . . God, how long? Twenty-five years? Can that be right? Since I was a little boy and she was a teenager? Whenever I'm at Leopard Sands, we always chat and catch up. There is something about her that puts me at ease, that feels comforting and kind. We don't hug, though—that's not Violett's way. She's warm, but not touchy—very professional. Whereas I'm a hugger, but I get it, it's a strange thing, straddling the line between employee and friend.

"How is your grandmother doing?" I add.

Something dark flickers across Violett's eyes. "Oh . . . my grandmother is . . . thanks for asking. She's fine." I feel instantly I've said the wrong thing, especially when I notice my wife's body language, how she's sitting more rigidly, her jaw tense. I forget that Davina's never met Violett—never been on safari with us. She was pregnant the last time I came, and we both agreed that safari with a danger of malaria wasn't the place to endure one's first trimester.

"This is Violett, the manager of Leopard Sands," I say to Davina, taking my seat again, feeling a bit awkward. "And this is my wife, Davina."

"Pleasure to meet the famous Davina." Violett's face shifts back into friendly, professional mode. "You have a wonderful husband."

"Thank you," Davina says, but with a pinched, closed look, not saying anything more. My wife is normally open and friendly, and it takes me a moment to pinpoint this reaction of hers. Jealousy, is that it? Violett is gorgeous, and around Dav's age, I guess. Not that Dav has anything to worry about.

"I wanted to come and offer my services. Babysitting, for your little one." Violett indicates Ruby, now in her post-breastfeeding bliss face, which, from experience, can last a fleeting few minutes before she erupts back into her perplexing cries.

Violett bends toward Ruby and smiles. "Shame. Oh, *shame*." Dav pulls Ruby tighter at Violett's commentary, but I know that Violett says *shame* with a positive connotation, like when I was little and would color a nice picture. I'm about to clarify it for my wife, but then Violett adds, "Your Ruby is beautiful. I would be happy to babysit her while you're here."

"Oh!" Davina says, still clutching Ruby tight to her chest. "No, that's quite all right. We have Gwen."

"Yes," Gwen says brightly. "I enjoy babysitting. Auntie Gwen at your service. Ruby is like my honorary granddaughter, and besides, I don't even like animals much." She shrugs. It's true—it's why Mom didn't get the small yappy dog she wanted to get, after Aba died. Gwen, like Aba, is terrified of dogs both big and small. Bailey has a mutt, which has been a source of tension for Gwen; now Gwen works out of the guesthouse instead of the main one when she's helping Mom at home.

"Anyway, I like to have Ruby with me most of the time," Davina says.

"Can't on the drives, though," Violett says firmly, straightening up. "Frankly, babies are not supposed to come on safari at all. We have a policy at Leopard Sands. No children. Animals like to snatch them. And not too long ago, in Kruger, there was a little girl whose ear was bitten off by a hyena. Hyenas like little ones. So you must be vigilant. You must watch Ruby closely. Of course, for the Babel-*Bachs*, we've made an exception in our policy, allowing you to bring her. But still, no babies on game drives."

Davina shoots Violett a withering stare and places a protective hand on Ruby's belly as she wiggles around in her bassinet. "Please, let's not talk about animals snatching my baby or biting her ear off—"

"I wasn't saying biting *her* ear, just—"

"*Of course*, I won't have Ruby on the game drive," Davina says. "I never dreamt of taking her. I'll stay back tomorrow morning, or Gwen will. We'll see."

"I've already said—I'm happy to," Gwen says.

"It's really no trouble for me," Violett says.

"We're fine," Davina says, the implication clear: *Back off.*

"Maybe we should take Violett up on her offer." I eye my wife. "Gwen might like some downtime herself. Or to go on the drive. And Violett's been with the family a long time." I wince, realize I've inadvertently made her sound like the help. "I just mean . . . she's good with children. She didn't mind if we hung out in her office or her cabin when our parents were out on drives. She'd give us markers to color with, and biscuits and oat crunchies."

I don't say—don't think it would go over well with my wife to admit—that it wasn't just surface-level kiddie coloring with Violett. In later years, I had serious conversations with her. She's shared about her family, about how close she is to her grandmother, especially after her mother's death. We've spoken about Circ—she grew up not far from some of the artisan villages, where Aba used to employ local craftswomen, who used eco-friendly materials, before Mom did away with that for profit reasons after Aba's death. But Violett and I got deeper too. About apartheid, how its undoing affected Violett's family, too, as they struggle now as white people to find work. About how even with the advancements postapartheid, the effects of ingrained racism persist. At Leopard Sands, certainly—with the housekeepers and waitstaff mostly Black, and the management mostly white. And the owners of these parks, or stewards as we like to call ourselves, are generally white as well. Violett pointed out that, in fact, the land Aba purchased in the bush only came into our hands because other white people had claimed it earlier, though the indigenous people living on the land were the ancestral owners. I spoke about it with Aba sometimes, too—he felt deep guilt on this issue, surprisingly to me, because Aba wasn't emotionally sensitive about nearly anything else. He told me that he wanted to contribute to the solution and not to the problem, but often felt himself failing to do so because he was a white owner at the end of the day.

I used to talk about all this with Violett—I suppose now, looking back, that she helped me process my own thoughts, that she gave me an outlet to share without judgment. Violett's opened my eyes to other things, too—how huge the wealth disparity in South Africa is, the stark contrast between these over-the-top luxurious lodges and the villages bordering Kruger in dire conditions, often without running water.

Strange, I guess, that Violett has played such an instrumental part in my life, that she's taught me so much. And yet I've never told my wife about her.

"It's okay," Gwen says, "really, I'm happy to stay back. When you've seen one lion, you've seen them all." She smiles encouragingly.

"Yes, but there's the party tomorrow evening—Gwen really should be there," I say. "I guess we didn't think this through. Mom didn't want to bring a whole team with us, and you didn't want to leave Ruby with your dad."

Davina and I share a glance, engage in a silent disagreement. "It's okay," I finally say brightly. "Thanks, Violett, but we have it handled."

"Well," Violett says, "if you change your mind, I am here." Her eyes bore into my mine with such surprising force that I look away. When I return my eyes, I see Violett staring not at me, but intently at my daughter.

"*Danke*, Violett," Mom says briskly. "I'd like another glass of Sancerre."

Violett nods. She doesn't glance at Mom, just looks at me again with her penetrating brown eyes.

"Grace will take care of you." Violett motions to Grace, the rotund woman in a traditional navy dress and matching headscarf with a dazzling smile, whose patience is vast dealing with our crew.

Grace rushes over, and Violett swivels and leaves, her bouncy ponytail swishing behind her.

———————

I BURST OUT INTO the night, chirping crickets and hooting owls ablaze around us. Our cabins are blinking lights in the dark, and I cross the walk in a torrent of my own fears. I check my phone again—this cannot stand. I need to speak to Mom. Make her see sense. Or else . . .

I stumble, then right myself and gaze around, but no one's noticed. Mom and Sam are walking together ahead, Sam's hand movements sharp and big, indicating he's making some grand case, surely about needing more money. *Mo-mo*, as Davina and I would say to each other in the Ruby speak that's infiltrated our lives, mutually backing out of these sorts of conversations when they erupt. But Davina's not beside me. I look back. Bailey and Gwen are walking together, animated, probably talking about animals or some tarot card reading Gwen did. Gwen is Bailey's godmother, and those two are close, as close as one can be to Gwen, who is frankly slightly batty. Ah, and there is my wife, chatting easily with Asher, Ruby bobbing happily against Davina, roped into the baby carrier. They look like a picture-perfect family, I think uncharitably.

I'm the odd man out. Shame churns in my chest.

I felt like this a lot as a child, even before Aba died. He had his negative qualities, of course. He was often angry about something—an injustice, a perceived slight—and he bonded with anyone willing to be angry right alongside him. I preferred not to be angry, I found it uncomfortable. I could get over things quickly, whereas Aba stewed. Aba loved Sam—who could easily flex his anger. Sam was Aba's indisputable favorite. I'm convinced Sam never would have come out, would have stayed in the closet his whole life just to placate Aba. But he was forced out; Mom was switching out Sam's bed pillows once when she found his journal hidden in his pillowcase and decided to take a look. She read all his entries about his feelings for his friend Danny. When Aba heard, he forced our brother to go to conversion therapy with an Orthodox rabbi, to *pray the gay away*. He told Sam they'd solve this—that they'd get him back on track. That Sam had so much potential, it was all going to be fine.

It still fills me with helpless rage, how my brother tried to mold himself to suit what our father saw as the correct path.

All we boys ever wanted was to please Aba. Whether I was afraid of him or found my validation in him, I'm still not sure. Maybe both. Aba and I got along, relatively so—we both had minds for money, for the stock market, for economics. He taught me so much, about philosophy and Jewish mysticism, interests we shared at one point in time. But I was bullied a bit as a child, harmless stuff, maybe. I was a nerd, horrible at sports, picked last, things Aba cared about. He wanted me to be strong, to defend myself, and anytime I came home with a bruise, or had my glasses broken by the boys on the schoolyard, I could tell he was disappointed. Ashamed, maybe, that I would get weepy. I'm an emotional guy. I've always been that way, cried at the drop of a hat, but Aba thought that wasn't manly. That it was a sign of weakness. He never understood me. No matter how I tried to make him proud, it was never enough. I remember once I got the schoolwide math award, as a seventh grader. I even beat out the top eighth graders! I was so excited, and I almost sprinted home, thrilled Aba was going to finally sing my praises, and instead he looked at my certificate and ribbon and shrugged. Then he pointed to Sam, who was wrapping up his hands for boxing lessons. *Math is pedestrian, Joshua. A calculator can do it. What you need is street smarts. Strength.* Aba flexed his own bicep, bulging even in his suit. *It would behoove you to take up boxing, like your brother.*

Being strong—that was Aba's thing. He was the Leopard, after all. Sam is the one who inherited the Leopard's qualities, the indisputable one of us three Babel kids with superhuman physical strength and mental toughness. But that's not the only reason Aba put Sam on a pedestal. Sam also genuinely enjoyed the religious traditions Aba mandated we follow. I could never be to Aba what Sam could.

After Aba died, I stopped wearing a kippah every day, dropped out of yeshiva, and enrolled in a real university—all of it felt futile with Aba gone, his praise no longer a dangled carrot that I could never even reach anyway. I'd tried to fit in with Aba and Sam, but once Aba was gone, I admitted defeat. I shifted toward Mom's route—going all in on Circ, hoping that our bond would give me the feeling of belonging I'd searched for all my life. But

Mom's always dominated our relationship—given me my box in which to sit, and sit I've done, even when that box has felt stiflingly small.

When I met Davina, this strong, sure-of-herself goddess, I was instantly smitten. When she wanted me, too, when she loved my glasses and how I stick my tongue out while I do Sudoku puzzles and how I make us color-coded itineraries for our vacations, I thought I'd found it at last—my other half, the one with whom I didn't have to mold myself to fit. But lately I'm not so sure. Lately, I wonder if being with Davina—cool, gorgeous, star-quality Davina—gives me some semblance of confidence I should be able to find in myself. I've always liked strong women, perhaps because my own mother is that way.

Since having Ruby, Davina feels slippery to me, like a new entity in our shape-shifting marriage. She's so deep in her postpartum phase, her energy fiercer, her body changing and devoted entirely to Ruby, with little to no time or patience for me. Understandable, of course, that having a baby would alter things, but lately Davina's been dropping nuggets that make me feel like she's questioning us. Like the casual line she said a few weeks back, that she craves a bigger life. She said it after she came back from a yoga class, where she met a woman who is a humanitarian aid worker, and whose husband is a diplomat, and they move country to country every few years. Dav was radiating envy when she told me about this woman, and her incredibly flexible husband who was doing yoga there side by side his wife.

I, on the other hand, have two left feet. I never do yoga. And I don't ask—haven't had the courage to ask—if that bigger life Davina imagines is with or without me.

I can hear a lion's rumbling roar now, then the eerie laughter of hyenas in the distance. I remember the Hebrew name for hyena: *tzavua*. Before the twins were old enough to go on game drives, Mom would stay with them, and it would be just Aba and me out there at dawn. Aba used to love teaching me Hebrew words for all the animals: *peel* for elephant, *taneen* for crocodile. He once turned to me, a wide, genuine smile on his face, and told me that spending time with me on safari gave him *osher*. Happiness. It's the only time Aba ever said that—connected his own happiness to me.

The hyenas cackle again, louder, and then another lion roars. I shiver. I know rationally that none of them can get past the electric fence, that a lion can be heard from miles away, and that nighttime is when they are most active, communicating with their pride, staking out territory. Still, it's unnerving. Like at any moment something's going to pounce. I'm drunk, I realize, paranoid, maybe—I don't know how it happened. Normally I'm careful, not prone to overindulging, but . . . that text from Lester. My family. My new stepfather. Circ. Me—not knowing who I even am, if I'm not who everyone wants me to be.

I stare down at my phone, burning in my palm.

"Sam, I've had it!" Mom suddenly erupts, stopping along the path. "The answer is *no*. Stop asking me for more money. I regret giving it to you this long. You're twenty-six, and I'm done with the handouts."

"It's Aba's money!"

"It's *my* money! And don't you forget it. Aba already left money for your condo—that's plenty generous. And I've been thinking lately that I don't want you kids to have everything on my death. When I get back to Florida, I'm planning to change my will. You need to learn the meaning of work."

I stop in my tracks, feeling quite cold inside.

"Oh, so you're going Warren Buffett on us, is that it?" Sam leers.

"Yep. That's the new plan." Mom crosses her arms over her chest. "And this should be no surprise. I've told you it before, all of you kids, that it's something I've considered. Trust-fund kids aren't happy, not in the long run. I owe it to you as your mother to make you all self-sufficient."

"And so you're gonna . . . what?" Sam says. "Give all your money to Asher."

"Not all my money," Mom says, surprising me, "but some of it. Yes, even though I don't need to under our prenup, I've decided I want to provide something for Asher. Something substantial."

"Delia," Asher says, "we discussed this. I said I don't need it."

"I know you're successful. But maybe I want to give you some. Maybe that's *my* wish. And I'll give more to charity than I currently have done. It's important to me, to still support my Jewish causes, and conservation in South Africa, and ensure the continued success of Leopard Sands. Joshua and Bailey will have their positions at the company, their stock." Mom swivels to Sam with a satisfied set to her face, knowing that she controls the pocketbook and thus everything. "You'll thank me one day,

Sam. When you learn how to stand on your own two feet and create your own happiness."

My heart lodges in my throat as Sam positively erupts, practically foaming at the mouth. "You're so stingy! Aba was never stingy with us. No matter anything else. He believed in helping family! In having us together and supporting one another. You're a fucking bitch. You're such a fucking . . ."

We've all frozen. Sam's stopped under a lamppost, and the particle beam on his face has illuminated the menace upon it. He looks livid with red-faced fury, like he could reach forward and . . . I don't know . . . *strangle* Mom.

A figure appears, thrust through the moonlight, and my eyes focus and I realize we've reached the front porch of the lodge. "Mrs. Babel, may I have a quick word?"

Mom's eyes dart at the figure—Violett, looking . . . off, is the only way I can think to describe it. I think back to the Violett of our conversations in years past—congenial, warm. I was drawn to her as a kid, even hung around while she'd clean my room, while she'd tell me about growing up on the fringes of Kruger. Mom had told me I shouldn't disturb her, that the guests and help weren't supposed to mingle. That I was taking away from her work hours, but still, I'd get back from a game drive and find myself seeking Violett out. There was something calm about Violett, kind, a refuge from my family, I suppose.

Now, though, she seems almost feral. Like the animals who lurk out in the night.

"A word, Violett? A word about what?"

"About . . . the wedding."

"Ah." Mom nods. "Ash, shall we?" She starts toward Violett, moving to the lodge, but Violett puts up a hand.

"I'd like a word alone."

"Alone?" Mom's voice is knife-edged.

But instead of backing down in the face of Mom's bluster, Violett says, "Yes, alone."

And then to my surprise, Mom doesn't refuse, doesn't talk down to Violett, just says, "Okay." She pats Asher's forearm, ignoring Sam's stormy gaze. "I'll meet you in the room soon, honey." And then Mom trails off after Violett.

# CHAPTER EIGHT

# ODELIA

It's five thirty sharp, and we've all gathered for breakfast in the lodge. Bailey's foot is tap-tap-tapping the floor. I know my daughter—she wants to be out in the bush at sunrise. But I'm firm on this point. We need a good breakfast first. Or I do, at least. It's healthy for the metabolism. I put my hand on Bailey's knee because she knows the bouncing drives me nuts, and her knee stills. Violett walks past, speaking briskly to one of the servers.

"What did Violett want, by the way?" Asher asks from my other side, sipping his Five Roses tea with soy milk. As ever, I'm mind-boggled by a person who doesn't need multiple espresso shots to feel human in the morning.

"Huh?" I touch my locket, click it open, brush my finger inside, then upon feeling cool metal, snap it shut. I tuck the locket back beneath my collar.

He eyes me oddly. "When we were walking back last night and she came over, saying she wanted to talk to you alone. I forgot to ask you about it when you came to bed."

"Yes." I smile slyly at him, and he smiles back. "We got distracted by other things."

He nods, but still looks expectant. I consider what to tell him. I tell him pretty much everything; I don't censor much.

Finally, I say, "She wanted to know if I'd like to have my veil steamed."

The sun begins to break, a dim glow illuminating the giraffes feeding at the river. God, how I love giraffes. They're so regal—mother and baby, trotting together. I always wonder what it would be like to be an animal—how uncomplicated that love could be.

"That's what she asked?" He cocks his head at me. "Your veil?"

My chest crimps. "Yes. Why?"

"Oh. I just . . . no, that's—your veil—okay." He smiles.

As if she has some tuning signal, Violett arrives with my omelet. I requested—or asked Gwen to request—that Violett handle my food this trip. Because I trusted her. And now I realize that was quite stupid.

She avoids looking at me, just deposits the plate. "Mr. Babel," she says, and for a moment there is a pause, as all three men look up.

"Mr. Samuel," she says, smiling at Sam. "I wanted to assure you we've taken the highest precautions on kashrut." For a moment I'm not sure what she's said, and then I glean her intention. She pronounced the word "cash-rut," instead of the correct "kahsh-root." "Everything is very, very following kashrut," Violett says.

"Oh, thank you," Sam says, flashing her a wide, white smile.

For not the first time I marvel at it—my son's complexity. Despite how his father deployed a rabbi to attempt to try to convert him when we discovered Sam was gay, my younger son has nonetheless clung to the archaic religious rules my late husband imposed. Whereas the rest of us have freed ourselves from that bondage.

"I appreciate it," Sam adds. "Must not be a small task, to change the kitchen over. Please send my extra thanks to Arno." He takes a sip of his juice. "And tell Arno this pineapple juice is out of this world."

"It's been squeezed fresh this morning," Violett says.

"We never got to have pineapple juice here when Aba was alive," Joshua says, and the table falls quiet.

It's quite true—my late husband was allergic to pineapple. I shake my head, try to shake off the memories. It feels like Aryeh's ghost is lurking around every corner here at Leopard Sands.

"And my thanks, also, for making me vegan meals," Asher says, breaking the weird quiet. "They're outstanding."

I nod in appreciation, too, but I can't bring myself to look into Violett's penetrating eyes. Instead I stare down at the glistening omelet, with a sprig of rosemary atop. I reach for my double espresso and sip, thinking about my conversation with Violett.

About what I didn't share with my fiancé.

That Violett asked for—demanded—money. And that I refused.

Was I right to refuse her? Is she the one writing the notes? But how could she have found out?

Maybe I should just pay her what she wants. I admit, I didn't consider she had it in her. I picture the latest note, sitting at the top of my toiletry case when I flipped open the lid, which I snatched away before Asher could see, my heart rate berserk. Who put it there? That's the million-dollar question. Maybe before I could pretend my stalker was outside my inner circle, but now. . . . Anyone here had opportunity, including the staff, all of whom have access to my room. But what motive would any of the staff have to threaten me? Except for Violett. She could have done it, surely; until I lay in bed last night, ruminating about her demand for money, it hadn't occurred to me. This time the threat was an image of a clock on plain white paper, with the typewritten words, *Your time is running out.*

I shiver, then try to hide it behind a cough. I should never have left my security team behind. But I wanted privacy with my fiancé and my family, and I was starting to suspect even those I hired to defend me; now I think that foolish. Thing is, there is only one person who could send that picture of the three young girls and allude to what happened.

Only one person in the whole entire world.

Gwen.

But she would *never* use it to threaten me. I know that for . . . *near* certainty. But then this marriage hasn't been easy on her . . . but no. I can't believe that . . . it just doesn't fit.

Asher quirks an eyebrow, and I reach for my water, sip, and swallow hard. "I'm fine." I flash a smile to reassure him, then stare at my omelet, unable to bring myself to lift my fork and dig in.

Poison. It's ridiculous, the very idea, isn't it?

"I still don't understand why we can't do breakfast in the bush." Sam's smile is gone, replaced with a scowl, directed as always at me. "We always get out early. Before sunrise. By the time we get out there, we'll miss stuff."

"Because eating first is better for my hormones," I say, trying to be light about it. "And besides, Asher wanted to sleep in a little."

Sam mutters something under his breath and rolls his eyes.

I'm debating between giving him a warning look and ignoring him, when suddenly a shadow looms over me.

"Hello, Babel family!" That deep voice with his South African twang. I haven't yet looked up, but even before he spoke, I already recognized his shadow's shape.

"Markus!" Bailey rises first to hug him. Then Sam—a hug that I note bitterly is still far more enthusiastic than my son ever deigns to give me.

"Markus?" Asher asks over his porridge.

"The game ranger," I say. "Remember, I told you about him? He's worked for us for decades. He guides the guests on drives, and he's also a conservationist here. He culls the herds when the need arises. He'll guide us today."

"Ah."

Then I stand to hug Markus too. "You haven't aged a day." I don't mean it fully—he has aged. We all have. Lines have deepened around his eyes, cratered his forehead. But he looks vibrant in the way one only does at our age when you are doing the things you enjoy—his face tanned, blue eyes alight, thick tufts of blond-gray hair popping out from under his Leopard Sands cap.

"You're the one who hasn't aged."

"Ah." I accept the compliment, even if I know it's just the thing one says. "I'm glad you made it."

He laughs, his dry booming laugh. "You knew I'd be here. You summoned me. I was in Botswana." He pulls back, executes a little bow. "But no one refuses Odelia Babel."

"Soon to be Babel-*Bach*," I say, extending my hand so he can see the stunning six-carat oval diamond Asher picked out all on his own. He knows exactly what I like.

"Congratulations, yes. Or should I say mazel tov?" Markus reaches out to shake Asher's hand.

"Thank you. Nice to meet you." Asher rises, shakes back. "Excited to get out there. See some Big Five."

Markus smiles. "Yes, we'll get you some Big Five. That's what I'm here for."

Then Bailey launches up and says, "Is it time? Can we go now?"

"A few minutes." Markus chuckles. "Eager to get out?"

"Of course." Bailey grabs an empty chair from a nearby table and slides it beside hers. "I want to hear everything, Markus. All the new animal things. Everything that's happened since we were here last!"

"Well, I don't know that we have time to cover *everything*." He pats Bailey's shoulder and spins the chair around. Then he sits on it backward, resting his forearms on the back. I know he doesn't do this with his regular guests—with them he epitomizes professionalism. With us, he does, too, but loosens up some. He's been guiding our safaris for a long time, since early in my marriage to Aryeh, when Aryeh took me to this majestic place that now belonged to me.

As Bailey and Markus chatter on about a potential cheetah sighting, I gaze around. I notice Violett off in the corner of the room, by a life-size carved wooden totem, clipboard in hand, but staring at us. At me. She meets my eyes, jaw set and firm. I shiver, break our eye contact, and focus back on my family.

Gwen—on the other side of Bailey, a familiar balustrade—reaches over and puts a reassuring hand atop mine. Sam and his typical Big Infuriated Energy, sitting as far from me as possible, adjusts a camera lens. Joshua is bouncing Ruby on his knee. When he sees me watching, he smiles all the way up to his chocolate brown eyes. "Do you want to hold her?"

"Yes," I say, already anticipating her soft, wiggly bulk. "I would love to hold my granddaughter." I glance down, remember I'm wearing silk, but no matter—any smudges or stains are well worth a Ruby embrace.

Joshua rises, deposits baby Ruby in my arms. She's happy and gurgling and so very alive. It's primal, isn't it, things related to one's progeny? The ferocity of my love for her, even if I don't do the typical grandma things, like change diapers and devote afternoons a week to watching her, giving her parents a reprieve. It's complicated, these times with my granddaughter, because she often fills me with regret. That perhaps I didn't soak in these precious moments with my own children. I was so nervous as a mother—worried about every pitfall and scrape, fearing that I would lose them after I'd tried so hard to have them. Maybe I tried to control them too much, but I felt such little control in my young life, in my marriage, so I clung to the control I could assert, with my children. Still, maybe I could have been softer. I don't know. None of it was easy—I had all the time and money in the world, and still, sometimes in the dead of night I wake abruptly, sure that I've failed. That I should loosen the reins, trust my children to know what's best for themselves. But in the light of day I'm never able to relinquish the feeling that I know best. Because I generally do.

"You know your Lovie, don't you, sweet Ruby?" Ruby reaches her tiny fingers toward my face. I feel my smile widen, threaten to split off my face.

I kiss her cheek, then let it graze against my own, mink soft. "Your Lovie loves you. Your Lovie will always be here for you. No matter what."

Ruby coos and twines her chubby fingers into my silk Hermès scarf. "You like that? You have fine taste. When you're old enough, Lovie will buy one for you."

Davina smiles. "Our little fashionista."

"If she's into fashion this young," Asher says, "maybe she'll be a designer! Like her step . . . grandpa?"

Muted laughs at that.

Davina smiles again. "Or maybe she'll be CFO of Circ one day, like her daddy."

"Or running the place, like her Lovie," I say, appraising my strong, brilliant, beautiful granddaughter. It's like a drug, wondering the heights to which she'll soar.

"Maybe she'll be the head of the United Nations." Bailey laughs. "For her ability to bring this family together."

I laugh too. "True. We can all agree on the perfection of this little girl."

Then all of a sudden, Ruby's face shifts. Stormy, discontented—the clouds before the storm. I recognize the look from baby Joshua. Genetics—what a crazy thing.

Ruby erupts in a fit of wails, straining toward her mother. Davina comes, takes my writhing granddaughter from my arms. Immediately Ruby calms, dips her face toward Davina's chest. Davina sits, unleashes one ginormous breast. Ruby buries her face in flesh. Wails no longer.

I watch Davina breastfeed. She's lost weight, yes, but she's still supple, her face round and bright, youthful and beautiful at forty-three. When you are my age, weight loss in your butt mirrors the same in your face. Not yet in your forties, though. Davina has lines because she refuses to get Botox, calls it succumbing to the patriarchy. *Get to fifty or sixty* is all I privately think. *Then let's see whether you stand behind your beauty culture mumbo jumbo.*

It's ironic: you don't think you are young at forty-three; you think you are old as shit. But you are wrong, one of those wrongs you only know later. You can suddenly see clearly, but it doesn't matter anymore. I guess it's what people in their eighties think about me, at sixty-four.

You would think a plus-size model and antibeauty culture crusader (not *my* label, check her Instagram bio) might worry about projecting too much thinness, or at least try to assuage my concerns. But nope. Davina's brushed off every conversation I've instigated. She's told me, angrily, unusual as she's typically unconcerned about anyone's opinion but her own, that her value to Circ is in her essence—not her weight. Imagine that—Davina telling me, the CEO, what her value to me is. She stormed out of my office then, before I'd even dismissed her.

I felt ashamed, watching her go. Because I knew that deep down, her losing weight felt threatening to me personally, not to Circ. She is, of course, younger, but I'm thinner. Only now she's upsetting the rules I thought we'd quietly agreed to.

I love my children, but sure, I love them most when they act how I desire them to act. Isn't every parent like that? Davina, like Sam, prefers to color outside the lines—though less destructively. Davina wanted to wait a couple years after marrying Joshua before having children, so they could enjoy their newlywed life together. No matter that she was thirty-nine at their wedding. Indeed, she had no doubt that whenever she began to try for a baby, she'd get pregnant instantly. I privately thought that was insane. I struggled with infertility, after all, at an age far younger than she. But what do you know—Davina got pregnant on their first try. She didn't boast about it, but Joshua told me. And even though she was making me a grandmother, which I was pleased about, I felt a shameful surge of anger. How infuriating that she believed in her power like that, and not only that she believed in it, that she was right! When it took me so long to get pregnant . . . when it was all so goddamn hard. . . .

Maybe Davina triggers me even more so because I wish I had been like her in my youth. Doing what I want—damn the ripple effect. Ordering God around, even believing I could. I suppose it's my modus operandi now because I've lost so much of my past, have so much to make up for.

Davina's still feeding Ruby, her breasts on full display.

"Mom," Joshua whispers quietly beside me. "You're staring."

I whip my face away, embarrassed.

"I still think she should use one of those shields. It's what I did," I say hotly. Joshua nods but doesn't respond. Of course, Aryeh never would have let me flounce around like that, breastfeeding so immodestly. I remember how hot I was in that shield, how hot the babies were too. I busy myself with my omelet, feeling something surging in my chest. Anger—at myself. For letting myself watch my daughter-in-law with my emotions so transparent.

It's just, Davina has a quiet star quality that is surprisingly powerful. I feel excellent for my age, but I didn't at hers. I was a typical religious Modern Orthodox wife. I wore a wig over my real hair, I wore clothing to keep my *tznius*, my modesty. Doesn't matter how beautiful the wig, or how fine the fabric, I felt frumpy. In skirts long enough and shirts loose enough to meet Aryeh's—and his rabbis'—increasingly exacting standards.

Aryeh and I moved from Florida to his native Johannesburg for a couple years during our early marriage, before Joshua. Aryeh's business was expanding, and he was developing the property he owned in Kruger, at the infancy of transforming it into Leopard Sands. He was also moving some of his clothing production to local African artisans. And what was I to do in this foreign land? Mingle with the other religious wives. I didn't have to cook or clean; we had staff for that. Though I was responsible for the holidays, grand affairs for Rosh Hashanah and Pesach that required months with fifteen-plus courses to preplan, making both hard and soft *kneidlach* and ensuring the *kreplach* weren't mushy, and you couldn't offload all the tasks—Aryeh liked things just so. Still, I had ample time to shop—to go to all the fancy malls and buy pricey bags and shoes and admire the clothing I couldn't wear.

At those malls, I discovered kugels. That's the term for fancy South African Jewish Real Housewives–type women. They had the biggest rings, the most gorgeous, sexy clothes. They hung out at Hyde Park, at Melrose Arch, at Sandton. I became friends with a few kugels, browsing the racks together, all *howzit, babe?* and *how are you, darling?*, and then exclamations about how simply *divine* this was, and how *divine* that was, in their posh, nasally voices. And then going for coffee together at a kosher café. But they weren't real friendships. Not like Gwen and Rachel. Maybe I also didn't let the kugels get close—I felt ashamed of what I wore, how my inside wasn't reflected on my outside. This was just before Joshua, when I'd been trying for so long to get pregnant, when Aryeh blamed me for my dysfunctional uterus and threatened to leave me. When I privately wondered if this wasn't God giving me a sign—to leave my husband when I still could, before we had children. To try to start over.

But I'd grown up with so little—my parents were kind, but constantly fretting over money. I was beautiful, so my mother always told me I'd marry rich. And then her words came to fruition, when Rachel's husband, David, had a South African friend they knew I'd hit it off with: Aryeh.

By the time Joshua came, and my parents had died, and Aryeh had the money—all the money—I felt I was stuck. Aryeh was funny at first, he had a wicked sense of humor, could skewer a person instantly, which I enjoyed and partook in, until years later he began to direct that cutting humor at me. Funny, imposing, handsome, powerful, if not a bit rough around the edges—I wanted Aryeh at first, until the facade wore off and I learned he was distant, sometimes callous. When we first met, I was drawn in by his power—how confidently he walked through the world, unlike my own father, who was a bit meek, always deferring to my mother. Aryeh knew who he was, what he wanted, and I found that magnetic. I thought that together, we would be unstoppable. He was Modern Orthodox, like me, but slowly becoming more religious; at the same time, I found myself questioning religion, wondering why all these archaic rules should govern my life.

I should have left, I know that now, but then we had children, and a certain reputational currency surrounding our marriage, and, I admit it, I certainly enjoyed the money. I'd signed a prenup—if we divorced, I'd get next to nothing. And Aryeh told me several times—if I left him, I'd be out on the streets, more or less. What I'd get under the prenup for a year wouldn't even fund a month of my life. And he threatened to take the children, not to let me corrupt them with my secular-leaning ways.

As the years went by, I hated myself more and more, for staying. And now that I look back, I realize I didn't want to become a kugel. I wanted to *look* like a kugel, but actually *be* a bagel—the term for the powerful husbands of the kugels. I wanted beauty and power—both—and when Aryeh died, I claimed them.

After he passed, I removed the masks and the layers. I'm still exceptionally proud of being Jewish. I've felt the pinnacle of holy connection when I've prayed at the *Kotel* in Jerusalem, and every time I celebrate our holidays, I feel deep reverence and connection to the thousands of years of Jewish history, to all the people who sat down for a seder or lit candles on Shabbat. But I'm doing it my way now, without all the black-and-white rules, all the ways I could be deemed out of line. I was tired of being told my clothing was too tight, too colorful, to stop attracting attention. I still believe. I just no longer subscribe to a God who tries to make me more and more invisible.

The first time I showed an elbow in nearly thirty years, I felt brazen, like a sexpot. It's how Circ exploded in popularity, too—as I became far more fashionable, I shifted course on our lucrative and sustainable but not with-the-times athletic clothing and hired designers from the big design schools. Circ—rebranded—surged. I did, too, in tandem.

Still, no matter how great and glowing I am for my midsixties, I lost my whole youth, and every day I do mourn that. Before I had the twins in my late thirties, I remember wondering if Aryeh was considering trading me in for a new, younger wife. His being deeply religious was my comfort, knowing how he'd be shunned in his circles for forsaking his starter wife. My comfort, but also my fear. I didn't want to be traded in, and yet I wanted to be rid of him. Still, it sounded desperately scary to strike out on my own, to be a single mom, to relinquish my security without any career path to speak of. Plus, we had so many shared secrets, so many things to hold over each other's heads if it got dirty. The spiderweb that forms when you marry, and how, as a woman of my generation, it's impossible to extricate yourself without collateral damage.

Unless your husband dies. Yes, I consider the trajectory my life has taken since Aryeh died ten years ago—how I went from the unnoticed wife, the woman behind the man, to The Woman, with no one before her. The one in charge, the holder of the only opinion that matters. The captain of the whole ship.

As if intuiting my thoughts, Markus says, "Well, crew, shall we head out?" But he directs the question at me.

"Yes," I say. "We shall."

We all rise, and as we gather our things, I think how, indeed, Aryeh's death served me well. Neat and clean, most everything passing to me, with unfettered control. He'd been getting more and more religious with each passing year, relying on the marital and financial advice of those old rabbis with whom he studied, levying new verdicts on my clothing and friends and household attentiveness—and he'd also mentioned his intention to change his will. Put others in control of the financial aspects if he were to die.

But, instead, Aryeh passed away before he could implement those changes. His will was simple, made when we first married. Money to the kids for down payments on first houses, and the rest outright to me. Granting me unfettered control.

Spielberg couldn't have scripted a better ending of my old life and beginning of my new one.

# CHAPTER NINE

# BAILEY

Ready, Grumpelstiltskin?" Sam hops onto the Jeep and slides next to me. Then he clinks his flask of *moer koffie* against mine—coffee with condensed milk, a tradition of game drives.

"Can you not call me that? I didn't sleep well," I snap, a twinge in my chest. I spit out the wad of gum I've been chewing into a napkin and then take a sip from my flask, savoring the creamy deliciousness. I hate Sam's passive-aggressive nicknames. And I hate how ordinarily I snap a smile onto my face, because I'm supposed to be sunny Bailey, especially on safari.

But I'm decidedly not sunny Bailey today. I've woken up on the wrong side of the bed. *Woken* is a generous use of the word, really. I tossed and turned all night, anxious about everything. Mom and Asher, work, the cards-on-the-table conversation I need to have with Mom. I guess it's all churning in my mind. And it didn't help that Sam was texting even before our alarm rung, and the blue light expunged whatever fumes of melatonin I had left.

"Sorry. Why? You usually sleep well here." Sam adjusts the lip of his black Miami Heat baseball cap, then slips on his aviators, his tone softer now. The sun's barely broken the sky—I know he's only wearing sunglasses because he needs a shield from Mom and Asher.

"Can you just not text in the morning? Or go do it in the bathroom? You know I wake at the slightest thing." I dangle my hand outside the Jeep. We're in the front row of the vehicle, just behind where Markus will sit.

"Bailey Babel's No Good Very Bad Day." Sam flashes a smile.

I'm quiet. For some reason I can't muster my usual smile in return, can't put all the swirling voices inside myself to bed.

"Okay, okay." Sam raises his hands in surrender. "It's actually Bailey Babel's Fabulous Very Good Seeing a Million Lions Day."

"Elephants. But that's better." I grant my brother a genuine smile. "Who were you texting that early? Your guy?"

Sam doesn't reply, instead stares at his phone, thumbing down the screen. I peek over, but turns out Sam's not texting the guy, rather scrolling through his Chase app. I catch a glimpse of a number that at first I think is his account balance, but then I realize is how much he owes on his credit card. $46,845.

Shit. I immediately scoot over and look off, pretending I didn't see. That's bad. That's really bad, right? I didn't even know a credit card balance could be that high. Sam's money problems are far worse than I thought.

I try to push everything from my mind as I lean forward to introduce myself to our tracker sitting in his custom bonnet at the left side of the hood.

"We haven't met. I'm Bailey." I stick out my hand.

"Titus." He smiles a brilliant white smile and then shakes my hand with one hand and with his other, presses lightly beneath my forearm. It's a kind, respectful gesture, almost a formal version of a hug. Titus bows his head slightly, then returns facing out into the bush, eyes swiveling side to side, already taking in things with his senses.

"*Avuxeni*," I say. It means *the sun is rising*, a traditional good-morning greeting at the start of a game drive. It's Shangaan, the language most of the staff speak, the predominant tribe in this area of Kruger. They're known for being soft, kind, quiet people, and that's always been my experience with them, like Jabulani too. "*Kunjhani*?" *How are you?*

Titus turns again and this time he looks into my eyes. He's young, maybe my age even. Not more than thirty. "*Avuxeni*," he says. "*Ndzi kona.*" *Good morning, fine, thanks.* He nods again at me before returning to face forward, his *sjambok* knife at his side to cut through tall grass or bushes that get in his way—or deal with an animal in a worst-case scenario.

The sun is now peaking in the sky, the scents of dry grass and diesel in the air, and my anxiousness recedes. I'm filled with a familiar joy, an urgency to get out there. "Come on, guys!"

Sam's now adjusting his camera lenses, surely avoiding the bombs of Mom and Asher in the row behind us, hands snaking across each other's thighs. I wait for the rest of them to join, but Joshua, Davina, and Gwen are in a half circle, chattering tensely beneath the lodge's entry awning. I make out discussions over who is staying behind with Ruby—Davina saying she will, but Gwen insisting Davina needs to go on a game drive because she's never been, and Gwen already has, and then Davina's inquiring about Gwen's reflexes. She asks, in total seriousness, if a hyena were to get past the electric fence, if Gwen would be able to react fast enough. And so Gwen, in a totally ridiculous manner, is now leaping in the air to demonstrate her capacity to save Ruby. Which is kind of funny to watch, as I've never seen Gwen in a gait faster than a leisurely stroll. Gwen stops and smiles, so I can tell she's joking, that she thinks Davina is being a bit ridiculous, and Davina manages to laugh at herself, but still doesn't hand over Ruby. Then Violett pops in from the lodge, saying she's quite glad to babysit, but Davina brushes it off and says it's under control. Even though it clearly isn't. At last, Markus rounds the bend from the staff cabins behind the lodge. Markus's rifle is hanging at his side, and I feel myself leaping from my skin, wanting to shout for him to hurry up, to get everyone moving and whisk us away into the bush already.

Markus pauses to rally the troops, and I hear Violett offer to babysit again. Davina's still wavering—wanting to get out for her first game drive, but not wanting to leave Ruby behind. Mom and Asher are chattering close to each other, missing the whole frustrating thing. Finally, Joshua whispers something in Davina's ear, and Davina nods tightly. She bends toward Ruby's bassinet and peeks in on the sleeping beauty. I can see my niece from here—her matted hair stuck with a purple bow; her sweet face placid in sleep. Finally, Davina steers the bassinet toward Gwen.

"You'll stay in our room, right? Don't go anywhere, okay? And keep her covered the whole time, just in case."

"I will. Where would I go?" But Gwen is playful, undisturbed by my sister-in-law's slight condescension. Well, maybe I'd be as cautious as Davina if I had children. Though I can't fathom I ever will.

Violett retreats back to the lodge, and Joshua and Gwen climb into the last row of the Jeep. I expect Markus to come join us, too, but instead he follows Violett back toward the lodge. He taps her shoulder, and she swivels, face somber. I can't see his face, just hers, her mouth in a rigid scowl. They're too far for me to eavesdrop anymore—all I can make out is indistinct chatter. Their soft English with South African accents that I always find pleasing and almost musical, rounding the vowels, easing off the consonants, low in the throat, sometimes even guttural. But in contrast to the easy, lower register of their accents, their faces are tight, their lips moving fast and furious, their volume ratcheting up.

Finally, Violett turns on her heel and walks back into the lodge. Markus looks subdued, not exactly angry, but by the time he hops into his seat, he's entirely professional. He turns, sunglasses propped atop his khaki cap with the safari logo, a leopard on the leap, like Aunt Gwen. I chuckle to myself, suddenly filled with happy, excited energy.

"Everyone's got their *mozzie* spray on? Coffee flasks? Ready to head out?"

A chorus of yeses ring out, and it's the first time since arriving that all us Babel-Bachs are in unison. I feel a fizz of electricity among our group, something uniting us, bridging our gaps. That's what animals do, bring people together, and so does nature, especially this land that courses through our blood. It's why the only happy memories I have with my whole family are from here.

Titus says, "*Inyathi bamba,*" in a low voice to Markus. "*Ngala* feeding." And because Markus has taught me over the years the code that he uses to communicate with the trackers in Shangaan, I'm thrilled to know what that means before Markus tells us.

"Well," Markus says, "apparently one of our male buffalo was killed overnight, down by the Crocodile River, and the Naru lion pride are feeding. It caused a lot of ruckus with hyenas last night."

"I heard the hyenas!" Joshua says. "I woke up in the middle of the night to their cackles. I swear I thought they'd gotten through the fence."

Sam groans. "Don't worry, you've got Dav to protect you."

I glare at Sam, and he shrugs but mercifully doesn't continue, like we both know he well could.

"Well, shall we go check it all out?" Markus asks.

Everyone says an excited yes, and the engine rumbles as we head out. The wind in my face blots out all the chatter in my mind, and I'm only here. Only now.

"Quite brave of the lions," Markus shouts through the wind. "By having killed something so large, it's attracting the attention of the hyenas, and it risks bringing in other lions. Whether it be the Northern Avoca or the Ndhzenga males."

We speed down the dirt trail, then off-road through tall, brittle grass, the sun's orange glow now fanning the sky. As we drive, Markus points out the trees that elephants have pushed over, which is a problem, because elephant overpopulation can disrupt the ecosystem, knocking down trees that take hundreds of years to grow. We spot, at Markus's pointing, gray crowned cranes with their fluffy red throat patches and a pair of saddle-billed storks with their long, vivid beaks. Then Markus slows, pulling up about ten feet from a buffalo carcass overturned, its bloody belly splayed toward the sky. One huge lion looks like he's resting a few feet from the kill, and another lion circles the buffalo, then starts gnawing a hind leg.

"Impressive, eh?" Markus turns. "What a feat to kill a buffalo of that size."

I watch mesmerized. It's gruesome, but beautiful.

"Whoa, that's incredible!"

I turn back and see Davina with a wide smile that torches her brown eyes, the creases around her eyes like spokes on a wheel, as she cranes her neck out the side. I smile too—she's been bitten by the safari bug. I thought she'd like it here—she's adventurous, good at placing herself in the present moment. Whereas Joshua's face is frozen in a wince, eyes fixed on the marula tree beyond. I know what Sam would say if he turned and saw him—*You're such a wimp. You can't even look.* But I understand Joshua—my brother is sensitive and hates anyone or anything being in pain. When the lion breaks off a chunk of buffalo flesh, Joshua feels the buffalo's pain as it died as if it's Joshua's own.

I return to watching the spectacle. Mom and Asher are riveted, too, and Sam, of course. None of us averts our eyes. I love animals, more than humans probably, so perhaps my ability to watch lions devour their kill is on its face incompatible. But I was raised on this wilderness theater. Some animals have to die for others to live. I accept that. Not senseless deaths—of course not. I feel my chest constrict at that thought, then push it aside. This buffalo's death has meaning. No part will remain by the time the entire ecosystem claims its share.

"Wow. This is unreal." Asher snaps away with his phone, zooming in, his face exuding a sweet childlike glee.

"Isn't it?" I say, and Sam glares at me. I shrug, and he gives off one of those grunts that are his trademark in the gym, then grabs his camera and starts clicking away. It's just rare I'm with anyone on their first time out. I find that I'm genuinely happy my sister-in-law and soon-to-be new stepfather—weird, God still so weird—are down with safari. It's like watching a baby's first steps—encountering this new land to which they weren't before privy. It feels like an initiation, Mom bringing Asher here, even though I wish she'd have a longer engagement.

We keep watching, and I find that I fall into an almost meditation. Periodically the hulking lion emerges from the cavity, blood staining his ochre mane, looking sated and pleased. The sun glows behind him, adding an extra fiery tint to his fur.

Suddenly Titus turns and says, "Ingwe," which I know means leopard, and Markus nods, peeps a smile. "Plot twist, folks." He waits a few moments as the tension in the vehicle palpably escalates. "Check out the Flat Rock male leopard five meters away, hiding in the bushes. He's obviously been drawn by the smell and the commotion."

"Don't lions kill leopards, though?" asks Asher.

"Yes. They can. And this is one of our older males. Thirteen. That he's lasted this long shows how brave he is. And you see the bravery, that he's hanging out here by lions. But perhaps he's going to risk it. He's hungry, you can tell he's thinner than he should be."

The world freezes, the only sound that of chirping birds, a soundtrack that in its incongruence adds to the tension. The hairs on my arm prickle as I watch the leopard stalk the scene, the lions growling and feeding, unaware of what's lurking on stage left. It always astounds me how animals lack all pretense—we see them in their best and worst moments, and they can only be one thing, have only one mode: authentic. I envy it, I guess.

One of the lions grabs the buffalo's skin with his teeth. A cracking sound, when the leg breaks off. He feeds longer and then finally steps back, circles the buffalo, tail flicking, and gives off a deep growl. Then he settles a few feet to the side to take a rest and digest.

The leopard saunters toward the Jeep, and I hold my breath, expecting it to divert toward the buffalo. But instead it appears distracted by us and begins to approach our vehicle, heading right toward Davina sitting in the back.

"Oh god," I hear her breathe.

"No one move," Markus says.

The leopard is now inches away—my heart is thumping wildly, knowing that however unusual it would be, the leopard could easily leap up toward us. Markus starts up the vehicle, and I watch the leopard freeze. Davina makes a squeaking noise, and I can see her holding on tight to Joshua, her face wrenched. The leopard stops, then turns nonchalantly toward the lions feasting on the buffalo. We all collectively exhale.

"That was something," Markus says quietly, switching off the engine as the leopard now makes his move toward the buffalo. "They don't often come so close."

I can hear Davina exclaiming in a low voice about the encounter, but my eyes stay riveted on the leopard. He's swishing over to the buffalo, serving fierce face that was up close and personal to us only moments before. He dives into the buffalo carcass and begins to wrench at the joint the lion already pried loose.

"Brazen, isn't he?" Markus whispers.

"Brave," Sam agrees.

I grin at my brother, and he grins back.

Then one of the lions—the one most recently feeding—spasms, alert. A breeze sweeps through his mane, and the air vibrates with an anticipatory charge. The leopard stops feeding, and there is a moment of silence, a moment pregnant with so much—life and death both in the balance. The lion lunges, and the leopard gives one more jerk before the leg gives way. Then the leopard takes off toward the tree, with both lions ripping after in close chase.

Markus takes off and Sam and I exchange rapturous glances. I hang on to my hat as the wind whips through us. This is the stuff. The lions are in close pursuit along a stretch of sand. The one closest leaps, slashes a paw in the air, and I gasp as the leopard evades the strike by centimeters and dashes up a tree, dragging the buffalo leg in his mouth until settling on a branch.

"Lions can't go up trees?" Davina asks.

"Nope," Markus says. "That was the leopard's hope, that he'd make it up the tree with enough time."

The lion gives a few ferocious roars at the base of the tree, but eventually his face softens and he slinks back to the buffalo, digging into the cavity and soon emerging content again with his meal. No matter that it's minus one leg.

"What would it be to be an animal," Asher says, "and find it impossible to hold on to your anger."

"Dangerous." Mom laughs. "That lion may not be angry anymore, but there are still threats all around."

"Yeah, but at least he's happy now. It's a good way to be." I turn back. Asher sounds so serious, staring off in mid-distance, but maybe he's just like that—pensive, a bit melancholy. Not like I know him well enough to know the timbre of his moods.

"Isn't this amazing?" Mom flips up the brim of Asher's hat.

He nods, runs a hand down her cheek. It's unspeakably tender. I turn forward, unsettled, but unable to put a name to why.

"I can't, I really can't," Sam mutters, riffling in his camera case to swap out a lens. It's new, I note—that distinct woven, sumptuous leather that even I with my limited knowledge of designers know to be Bottega Veneta. Mom has a bunch of their clutches; she's mentioned offhand that they cost upwards of five thousand dollars each. Which is a figure that makes me nauseous, to be honest. What business does Sam have with a five-thousand-dollar camera case when he's tens of thousands of dollars in debt? All of which could be wiped out by a couple months of pulling a salary from Circ, if he'd come work on the graphic design team even temporarily. Stubborn Sam. My mouth opens to say something, but then I can't bring myself to do it. Instead, I give my brother a tiny shrug and try to smile, the anxious pitter-patter feeling back in my chest. I'm such a chicken. I pull a few pieces of gum out of my bag, unwrap quickly, and begin to chew.

"C'mon." Markus takes off again.

"Where are we going?" I ask.

"Somewhere truly special."

I close my eyes and savor the first burst of peppermint before it fades in my mouth. And we fly through the bush. Dust particles storm every inch of my skin that is open to the elements as we whiz through the vegetation made extra lush by rainy season. It's dense and grassy, and the watering holes and dams are overflowing, crocodiles lazing in their groups on the sandbanks. We rumble past, and I spot yellow flowers on the knobthorn tree and purple ones on the thorny tree. The wind whips my hair and my eardrums, making it impossible to tell Markus that I only know those things because of him. Because listening to him narrate the live drama of this place has taught me more about life and this world than perhaps anything or anyone else.

Eventually we make it back onto the main road, then dip off again. Suddenly Titus puts out his hand, and Markus slows. Titus says, "*Mdlovu*," with the clicking sound at the top, characteristic of some African languages.

I know that means elephant! I lean forward. If I had to pick one favorite animal in the bush, it would definitely be an elephant.

"Is Millie still around?" I ask Markus.

"She is," he says, "but we're on the trail of someone else. You know the Shangaan word for elephant?"

"You taught me."

He smiles. "I didn't know how much you retained."

"Everything," I say. And I think of all our lovely conversations, all the things Markus has taught me about the animals and about the world and about myself. Bushwalks just the two of us, occasionally with Joshua and Sam, or chatting in his room in the lodge, my feet kicking off the side of the bed, when I've disrupted his free time and barged in, suddenly burning with the need to ask him why leopard males don't help rear their cubs and how elephants have such incredible memories. Mom and Aba always admonished me, saying not to disturb Markus, he was there to work and I was disrupting his free time, but Markus said he didn't mind. He seemed to appreciate that I cared as much about the animals as he did.

"See that." Markus points to a cluster of marula trees, and a hush falls over the Jeep.

"What?" Sam asks.

"That." I follow the line of his finger point, and all of a sudden I hear a loud trumpet sound and then heavy footsteps that judder the ground. A waddly old elephant sidles up to a stout tree, continuing those trumpet sounds. Then the elephant begins to dig in the tree for the fermented marula fruit that elephants eat and sometimes get drunk on.

"Wow." I stare at the majestic creature whose left ear is extrafloppy, my heart cratering with love.

The elephant finishes eating, then dips her trunk down and lifts a stick from the earth.

"This one's famous around here. Her name's Masasana," Markus says. "That's a Tsonga word. It means *one can always make a plan*."

"I like that," Mom says. "A motto to live by. It's what I always tell you kids, you have to think ten steps ahead."

Sam rolls his eyes, and I stifle a grimace. Mom *would* like that. I wish she would have more integrity with her plans. As soon as I think the thought, I want to yank it back out of my mind.

"See that," Markus gestures again. "What she's doing."

I watch the elephant add her stick to the short tree, only now that I focus on it, I realize it isn't a tree, it's a pile of sticks all leaning against one another, in some shape that looks familiar but that I can't exactly puzzle out.

"It's a baby elephant." Markus turns around.

"Where?" Mom asks. I'm also scanning the bush, but I only see Masasana, making her trumpeting sounds.

"No." Markus shakes his head. "Masasana lost her baby a month ago. She's made this kind of totem elephant to resemble her baby, to remember him. It's why Masasana's here alone. Elephants usually stay in herds, but Masasana is standing guard in the place her baby died. Making this totem."

I gape at the thing I thought was a little tree, as the elephant shape of it leaps forth.

"She *made* this? The elephant?" Joshua asks. "That's . . ."

I turn back and see Davina chewing on her lip, face tight, and Mom looking off, too, brushing something from her eyes that can't possibly be a tear.

Mom never, ever cries. Not even when Aba died.

"Exquisite. Elephants are exquisite creatures indeed. They have such love and feeling. You can't deny it after you see this."

Indeed, we can't. I watch the elephant place a stick on her totem to her child and swallow a lump of emotion. The elephant trumpets again at us, tusks curled outward, and Mom brushes another tear away. This time the wet has traveled a line down her cheek, through her bronzer.

Sam glances back, and I can tell he's as surprised as me. By the elephant's touching way of mourning her baby, but also by Mom's emotive response that causes Sam to drop the angst that generally hovers over him like a rain cloud when he's around most of our family.

"I lost a child too," Mom finally says.

"What?" I ask, at the same time as Sam says the same thing, and Joshua says, "You did?"

My mind spinning, I say, "You never told us."

"Not a live person, Bailey," Mom says tightly, like I've said something cardinally wrong. Like it's my fault she lost a child I never knew about. "I lost a baby. An embryo, I guess. I was pregnant and lost it. It's not the same as this elephant." She gestures. "Who lost a real live baby. This made me think about it is all. Can we keep on? Yes, let's keep on."

But I have so much percolating inside. I know it took her years to get pregnant with us after Joshua. "When?" I finally say.

"Now. Let's go."

"No," Joshua says, his pitch rising, and I am thankful that this mythical sibling causes him to falter too. "She means when did you lose it?"

Mom presses her lips together. "Doesn't matter."

I notice that Asher places a hand on her thigh, doesn't look surprised. It hits me: He knows this. A thing none of us kids did. They aren't going to break up in a month, like Sam's predicted. Asher knows her secrets.

Markus starts up the car and my eyes meet the mother elephant's. For a moment I can feel her giant, shattered motherly love. And then we take off and the elephant gives off another large trumpet, breaking our eye contact, and I feel anxious again.

———

TITUS DIRECTS MARKUS TO tall grass where we wait a long time—waiting being the bedrock of safari, something I am good at and Mom and Sam are very bad at. They both lack patience, not that either would appreciate hearing the ways they are similar. Markus distributes *rusks*, large, hard biscuits, staples of game drives, and we dunk them into our coffees and eat. I try to enjoy the stillness and tune out Sam's fingers thumping the side of the Jeep. I ask Markus if the park has managed to make inroads on the awful rates of poaching. Markus says no, that in fact it's gotten worse, and poachers have gotten good at covering their footprints because they know they will be tracked the next day. Markus tells me that sometimes, the poachers have gotten so cunning and cruel they will cut off a baby elephant's feet and strap them to their own, so that when poachers lug out twelve kilograms of ivory, they conceal their paths with the elephant's own feet.

"No way," I breathe, the horror of that image stampeding through my cells.

"Unfortunately, way." Markus nods somberly, but then I can't ask more because about twenty wild dogs emerge and we follow as they dash across the savanna. The pack of them are a stunning sight with their rounded ears and white patches on black fur, emitting their thin almost birdlike calls and romping together. When the dogs eventually return to their den, Titus finds us a dazzle of zebras feeding at the river. *Dazzle*—that's the word for a herd of zebras, Markus tells us. Aba taught me the term, actually—he loved zebras, how they were always on the move, not staying still for a frontal picture so you'd catch only their behinds, fleeing, their majestic black-and-white stripes against the blue sky.

"Dazzle! That's the coolest word," Davina says, as we drive a bit farther to flat, open land, then climb out of the Jeep for a bit of a break. Davina thumbs through her photos. "The social media caption writes itself." But her face is expressive, almost childlike—fun to see her so awed, not her typical collected self.

We all sip from our flasks of coffees and eat our *rusks*. Davina creeps closer toward the river to photograph the zebras still drinking on the other side, and Sam slips an arm around me as we watch the earth do its normal things without the bombardment of human intervention we are used to. The sun now higher bakes down and birds chirp, such a rainbow varietal compared to the pigeons who like to poop in the garden at Mom's house. I watch insects zap around a pile of dung to my left.

As Joshua approaches, I say, "Watch your step."

He looks down and flinches. "What's that?" he calls to Markus.

Markus comes over. "White rhino droppings."

Joshua frowns and swats a horsefly away. "Is it safe to be standing here?"

Sam digs his toe harder into the dirt. "Dude," he mutters. "Markus has his rifle. You're fine."

"Sam." I nudge him with my hip.

Joshua flushes. "Excuse me if I want to stay alive for my daughter." He turns and walks back to the Jeep.

"That wasn't nice," I say as we sip our coffees. "Why can't you be nicer to him?"

Sam shakes his head. "I don't know. I try to, but then it just comes out."

"Well, try harder so it doesn't. He cares about your opinion, you know?"

Sam removes his aviators, rubs his eyes. "Joshua? No, he doesn't. He cares about one person's opinion: Mom. And maybe Davina's. But mostly Mom's."

"He cares about yours way more than you think," I tell him.

"No way."

"He does," I insist. "He respects you."

"Please. Joshua, the golden child? No chance." Sam's eyes shift to watch Mom and Asher, who are holding hands, Mom's head on Asher's shoulder, watching their own private movie while we are the spectators to theirs. Sam lifts his hand off my shoulders, and all at once I feel cold and exposed. He grabs his camera, snaps a few shots of me, and I feel my usual awkward, not sure how to stand or where to look.

"Gorgeous." He shows me the picture, and I make a face. I never like photos of myself.

"Stop," I say.

"You are." He zooms in on my eyes. Mom calls them blue on fire. Blue with hints of a flame. Just like Sam's. "These eyes are stunners. Even in khaki couture, they pop."

I groan. "You're just saying that because they're identical to yours. It's like you're complimenting yourself."

"You *are* gorgeous, Bails. I won't take it back no matter how much you want me to. Anyway—I'm gonna take a *bos kak*." He grins at me. That means a bush shit. Markus taught us the phrase when we were kids, claiming that it's the best way, out in open nature.

I laugh. "Enjoy yourself, broski."

---

WHEN WE'RE ALL BACK in the Jeep, Mom exclaims, "Those bastards! Another horsefly bit me through my shirt."

"They're vicious," Markus agrees. "But what do you say, Babels, have one more adventure in you before we head back?"

"Babel-Bachs," Mom corrects, still grumbly, rubbing her bicep.

"What?" Markus says.

"We're the Babel-Bachs now," Mom says again, indicating Asher.

"Oh. Right."

Sam snickers beside me.

"And yes, okay, one more adventure. Just get these damn flies away! And make it a good one."

"Your wish is my command," Markus says, his tone flat. "Back to where we started, how about? The buffalo kill. Apparently things are going down."

The vehicle begins to bump across the terrain, making it impossible to hold conversation. Normally I would enjoy time with my thoughts to absorb this beautiful place, and the majestic kingfisher bird with its blue-and-orange coat soaring above, but instead I find my thoughts in such a peculiarly dark place. The tension simmering between my brothers, with Mom and Asher, this bizarre new person in our family—but maybe most of all this sudden, all-pervading sense that I am playacting the role of Bailey Babel: loving daughter, chief of conservation at Circ. Knowing all too well that soon I am going to go back to Florida and spend yet another night sleeping in my childhood bedroom because Mom has said it's dumb to pay rent when I have a beautiful room to live in, no matter that such room has reams of pink satin and a chest of expensive porcelain dolls with creepy, uncannily real faces that Mom used to get me for gifts.

For some reason that mother elephant pops back into my consciousness with a force that nearly makes me weep. Piling sticks in her child's honor, forming it in her likeness. It hits me that to create a replica of her baby the mother had to really see him and know him.

As we whiz through the tall grass, watch a snake slink up a trunk and a warthog by a termite pile, my thoughts bake and broil and I think I might explode.

Back at the site of the dead bull carcass, our leopard friend is back to creep for more food as the lions laze, digesting.

"He's so daring," Asher says.

"Daring, or stupid," Markus says. "We'll see."

We stop the vehicle about ten feet away and watch as the leopard slinks back for more food. The lions sprawl out at rest, ostensibly oblivious as the leopard burrows into the bull carcass. But all of a sudden one of the lions stirs, cranes his head back, then snaps to attention.

"Oh, no," I hear Joshua say.

"Oh, yes," Sam whispers, a smile in his voice.

Suddenly the lion is not so much lunging but flying. The leopard is startled, jerks back. The air crackles alive, and I freeze. The lion growls as the leopard flees, but this time the tree is too far, and the lion is too fast.

My breath suspends, time stretches to infinity, and then teeth crunch into flesh. The leopard is writhing, but quickly the other lion is abreast him, and where moments ago life and death hung in the balance, now death has prevailed. I peek back and see Joshua looking away, biting his lip, but Davina is riveted, and Asher too. Mom is watching, as well, but something's off—she's stroking her locket, her eyes glazed, like she's somewhere entirely else. When I fix back on the leopard, one of his hind legs is pried apart from his body and is lodged triumphantly in the assisting lion's mouth. The leopard is still jerking though—and then nothing. The feast begins in earnest, a carnage of buffalo and leopard in a sea of pink meat. And two proud, feasting, growling lions.

"Well, Babel-Bachs, you got exceedingly lucky today," Markus says. "What a game drive, eh?"

"Good juju for the wedding tomorrow," Asher says.

"What, seeing a leopard murdered is your good juju?" Sam sneers.

"No, I just meant—all the excitement," Asher says quietly.

"Spare us," Sam says.

"For the last time, if you don't want to celebrate, then *you* spare us all and don't come," Mom snaps. "I won't say it again, Samuel."

Sam mumbles something incoherent, but doesn't say he's not coming. We watch the lions feed, and Sam suddenly swivels back. "Josh, you see it?"

"See what?" But Joshua sounds resigned. Also, he's not a Josh, he's Joshua. Always has been—no nicknames. Even Dav calls him Joshua, although she pronounces it Josh-wa, fast and a little Kardashian-y. So when Sam calls him Josh, we all know it's bait.

"The kill. Didja watch?" Sam asks, his tone aggressive.

Joshua opens his mouth, but before he can respond, Davina says, "So what if he didn't?"

"You need to look at things in life. Face them. And my brother's a hypocrite—fine using animal skins in clothing but can't look them in the eye while they're killed. Eh, PJ?"

Joshua reddens at that—of course. PJ means Perfect Joshua, the thing Sam can reliably say to scrape right up underneath Joshua's skin.

"The animal skins we use are carefully vetted, only from humane sources," Joshua says. "Not the polystyrene crap they virtue-signal by calling it vegan leather. That's what's actually polluting the earth."

A lion burrows his face into the leopard carcass and growls.

"Leave Joshua alone, Sam," Davina says wearily, placing a hand on Joshua's forearm.

"You're still ignoring all the greenwashing, Josh. But sure, if you want to ignore the hard stuff, that's your business." Sam shrugs.

"I don't ignore the hard stuff," Joshua says, shaking his arm free of Davina's hand. She looks surprised, maybe a little hurt. "And I can speak for myself, thank you," he says tightly. "I don't apologize for being sensitive. In fact, you could use a sensitivity chip, Sam."

"Sensitive?" Sam muses. "More like weak. News flash, family. A person who is weak shouldn't be next in line to helm Circ."

"Thank you very much for your expert opinion," Joshua says with a tone so spiteful it incinerates the atmosphere. My breath stills. I hate this—the two of them at odds. It reminds me of childhood, Mom and Aba fighting, Aba and Joshua fighting, Aba and Sam fighting, Sam and Joshua fighting. How I'd hide in that crawl space under the stairs with my fingers plugging my ears, counting to ten over and over and over again until the yelling abated.

"Boys." Mom puts her fingers to her temples. She turns to Asher, gives him a shrug, like, *Sorry my kids are such a mess.*

He smiles faintly, like, *They are, but it's okay.*

"Man, it's hot," Asher says and ruffles his hair from his neck. He has the type of hair and personality that would be suited by a man bun, even though I've never seen him in one.

I watch the lions consume the leopard, my heart drumming my chest.

"Well, kill or be killed," Mom says, but almost half-heartedly, twirling her locket. "Let the dead stay dead."

"*The circle of life*," I find my lips moving to say, and in unison, everyone else in the Babel family chimes in too. Like a cult incantation.

"Indeed," Asher says, but no one responds. Unsurprising, because even though the phrase flew out of us Babels like we are automatons, I know it makes us all want to throw up.

# CHAPTER TEN

# VIOLETT

The Babel-Bachs have returned, sweaty but subdued, without the usual postsafari glow but nonetheless exclaiming over all the animals they saw. Well, maybe they just saw impalas, and if so, I'll hear about it later from Markus. His job is to show safari guests the majesty of the bush, sometimes an impossible task when the animals decide to burrow in reeds or brush inaccessible to the *bakkie*, especially in the lush rainy season when the greenery camouflages things. And though the Babels are seasoned guests and in fact own the place, this perhaps makes them even tougher customers to please. First, they are used to getting what they want. Rich people, and such. And second, the measure of experiences becomes whether they outdo previous ones. So now it's not enough to see a lion, but they'd like him standing on his head.

Odelia is itching her arm where I'm assuming something bit her. They saw a kill, and zebras, and wild dogs, Davina tells me and confirmed that Gwen will be wheeling Ruby up here in short order. I smile wide at all this information. *How wonderful!* I'm used to it—my smile being forced up to the heavens, animals wielded like a checklist.

"There's my baby!" As Gwen wheels up with Ruby, Davina gathers up her beautiful daughter. Immediately, the baby begins to cry and paws her pudgy fingers at Davina's chest. Davina eases right down onto the pavement and feeds. I fight an itch in my throat and turn to Joshua.

"How was the drive? You had a nice time?"

He offers me a smile, but I notice it doesn't travel to his eyes. "How could I not have a nice time here?"

Yes, quite true. How?

"Ruby is beautiful," I tell him. "I'm so pleased for you. A family, Joshua. It's wonderful."

"Oh, thank you." He blushes. "I'm blessed. I never— Honestly, I never thought I'd find someone as amazing as Davina."

"Well, you are amazing yourself, so it's no surprise."

Joshua smiles. "Eh, I have my negative qualities, trust me."

"*Ag*, nonsense. I've known you a long time, and I've never seen a one." I wonder if this is something his wife has made him believe. I feel an urge that he know: He is perfect. He is handsome, and kind, and loving, and he wears his emotions and authenticity on his sleeve. Maybe he isn't the tallest or strongest or most outgoing, but he has a heart of gold.

My heart twangs with envy of Davina, an urge to go to her and shake her so she knows what she has. How lucky she is. I feel a sudden ache, and I know it's deep and always there, but I usually avoid feeling it. I've always told myself that it was enough to just have Ouma—the only one who knows everything about me, everything I've done, and loves me still. But Ouma's sick; she doesn't have much time. That's why I am determined to make the most of the Babels' surprise visit.

Joshua wanders off, checking his phone, and I walk toward Markus, who is chatting to Junior, one of the newer maintenance guys, telling him about a problem in the tire tread. I hear Junior say, "Yes, yes, will do it just now."

"You'll do it *right* now," I interject. *Just now*, as Junior said, in South Africa could mean in hours. I know he wants a smoke. This one—he's not a worker bee.

"Now, now." Junior's only looking at Markus for confirmation.

I wave my hand in front of his face to flag his attention. "*Right* now. Hear that? *Right* now." Junior meets my eyes.

"You heard the lady," Markus says cheerfully. "And give it a good hose down too."

Junior grumbles, then stuffs his cigarettes back into his pocket and makes his way to the driver's seat.

"Thanks, Markus! It was an awesome drive!" Davina waves from her breastfeeding perch.

"Even with the leopard nearly leaping up on you?" Markus asks, winking.

Davina laughs, though I can discern fear behind it. "Everyone needs a good safari story to tell when they go home. I'll totally milk that one."

"A leopard came close?" I ask. "See, that's why we don't allow children on safari."

"I never would have brought my daughter on a game drive." Davina glares at me.

"See anything good out there, miss?" Junior asks Davina, pausing.

I motion him along, but he doesn't go toward the car like I'm prodding, to drive off, fill up the diesel, do actual work. This one. He's not going to last. We need workers, not socialites, at Leopard Sands.

Davina's irritated energy toward me diffuses, and her face alights. "An elephant. My god. It was so moving. She lost her baby and made this statue in his likeness out of sticks. Really incredible. She won't leave the area—like she's standing watch."

"Oh my word," I say, though I'm surprised at the conversation burst. Despite her incontrovertible motherly inclination, in my short time around her, I've found Davina a bit aloof, snobbish. Maybe it's because she's very beautiful. But she's so emotive now, so heartfelt. Perhaps it's the motherly bond that brings it out in her.

"Ah, yeah. Heard about this thing." Junior pulls up his khakis around his hips and smiles congenially. "Where's it?"

"Where's it out there in the bush? No idea. Oh!" Davina's face sparks with recollection. "Close to—"

"Dav, no," Bailey says, emerging from the shop, unwrapping a pack of gum.

"What?" Davina is momentarily diverted, but then she says, "You know the juncture of Sabie River with Crocodile River, right before . . . oh, I know, by that spot Markus breaks at for coffees and—rusks!" She looks pleased she remembered the name for them. "You can't miss it—the sticks look like an elephant. Breaks your heart. You'll have to go and see."

"I will surely do that." Junior heads to the vehicle.

"Dav, I said stop!" Bailey's to us now, frantic.

Davina blows up her bangs. "What? What did I do?"

Bailey eyes me uncertainly. "Nothing. Never mind."

I know exactly what's in her head. Bailey didn't want Davina to share the location of the elephant with any of us staff. Fact is, poaching is big business down here, and often poachers find the location of the animals because clueless safari guests excitedly tell the staff about their game drives, who then tell their friends. Rhinos are typically more at risk in southern Kruger, but a lone elephant is a prime target, without the backup of its herd. But Bailey is too polite to cite her fears in front of me, lest I think she's accusing me.

"Violett." Odelia fluffs up her hair, waving me over, so I reluctantly leave Davina and Bailey. "Everything in progress for tonight?" she asks.

"It will be lovely." At her request, we are setting up a braai and bonfire at the special part of the property that Aryeh Babel designed, that we staff refer to among ourselves as "Babel Land."

"I'd like to see it, can we go over there?"

"Now?" Oh my word, I have about a million other things to do than listen to Odelia's minor corrections. I can already foresee the scene that sucks at least two hours from my afternoon. *Move the balloons a centimeter to the right. I want them on a tree with white flowers, so the motif stays neutral. Remember, I said neutral.*

I take a deep breath. Typically I am pure sunshine—those are the general reviews I draw from our guests. I am South African, to start. We are known as being sunny and warm and kind. And, even given how my life has unfolded, I am naturally good-natured. I have a good heart, no matter how the trauma of my past torments sometimes twists it. But Odelia tests my limits. My lips don't naturally curl up in her presence, especially after our conversation last night.

"Yes, I'd like to see the tent now," Odelia says, eyes flashing with irritation. Then she shifts her face into a smile, knowing, as she does, that smiles bring better service. "*Danke* for everything, Violett. *Danke* for making this just perfect for me."

I find that I can't muster a smile. That my lips refuse to budge. I simply can't fake things anymore. But clearly she thinks I will toe the line.

Even though she knows what she's done. I've given her an option, to do things the easy way. To make amends. To at least try. Give me money. But she refused point-blank.

Fine. What I want is bigger than money anyhow. So we will have to do things the hard way.

I slip my phone out of my pocket and check it quickly. Oh my word, a text from my tannie. I brace myself on the railing as I read. *Ouma is sleeping a lot but the pain medicine has helped. She is asking for you.* I text back quickly, even though it's unprofessional to do it while any guest—but especially Odelia—is waiting for me. *I am trying to get the money we need.* I send that off, then glance at Ouma on my lock screen for a moment—it's my favorite photo of my grandmother. I took it when she was in the kitchen making her famous plum jam, her dimple in her right cheek flashing in a smile meant just for me, wearing her favorite long blue cotton dress. Blue is Ouma's favorite color, because as she's always told me, blue is the color of the sky, and the sky is the most beautiful thing to look at besides looking at me, her beloved granddaughter. And then she says: *God has blessed me beyond wealth, because looking at both of you costs me nothing.*

And then she always pulls me into a hug, and I think now how, on the contrary, looking at me has cost Ouma quite a lot.

"Ready?" Odelia taps my arm and I shove my phone back in my pocket. Her face is pleasant, but with a clear irritation that I haven't leapt to her service as fast as she issued the request.

"Sure." This time, I manage to flash her a false smile. "Let's make this evening *perfect* for you."

Odelia kisses Asher. There are murmurs of a sensual manner that I hum a tune to myself to avoid overhearing. It doesn't work. I shiver. They irk me, the two of them. Odelia, of course, but Asher too. There's something slimy about him that I can't put my finger on, that I see through his Mr. Congeniality exterior. Strange that this young man is so taken by someone so much older, but of course that could just be the power of Odelia, and the favors she's somehow accrued from God.

No longer, I vow.

"Ready?" Odelia links her arm through mine. This woman is some actress.

"*Ja,*" I chirp.

As Odelia pulls me toward Babel Land, my eyes catch on Joshua, strapping a fed, gurgling Ruby into the carrier on his chest. I can't help but watch them, can't help but greedily mop up their sweet, ordinary movements. Then Odelia tugs me harder, and I tense.

I want this woman to feel pain. I want her to feel as powerless as I have. And I want money. She's finally going to pay up. Nothing will ever make me whole, but a good chunk of rand will help.

For now, though, I stay quiet and follow after Odelia like her obedient little chick.

# CHAPTER ELEVEN

# GWEN

"Aunt Gwen . . . would you . . . ?" Bailey bites into an oat cookie they call a *crunchie* here. She chews slowly.

I put down my teacup and feel myself leaning forward, hoping she's going to want a bit of girl talk about her mother and Asher. Normally I would be Team Dede, lips and ears sealed to any gossip about my best friend; of course, I still am, but in this situation, I need to confide a bit in someone. I haven't wanted to broach my own turbulent thoughts with Bailey, haven't wanted to influence her own feelings on her new stepfather situation, but if she initiates things, it's different. Then I can agree that yes, it's incredibly bizarre, and I, too, question Asher's motives, and her mother didn't even ask me to accompany her and Violett to check on things for tonight's *braai*—and before this marriage she would have assuredly done so. Dede and I have never strayed far from each other's side, unless forced to, but now this young, shiny man has come into our lives and sent all the Jenga pieces sprawling. . . .

"Would you pull some cards for me?" Bailey finally asks, brushing a crumb from her lips.

"A tarot reading?" I freeze.

"I'm just . . . yeah. I'd love a reading, if you don't mind."

"I don't mind at all. Of course." I reach into my canvas tote for my cards, a lump of disappointment in my throat. Well, maybe the tarot will help us broach things. I do want to confide in someone, but maybe it's selfish to expect that person to be Bailey. Bailey might be in her midtwenties but she's still a child in so many ways. Still so innocent, never had a boyfriend, doesn't even seem interested in boys. Always trying to please.

Living to please. Her mother, especially.

I shuffle the cards, and not for the first time do I think regretfully that my goddaughter is just like me. I stare out beyond the deck, where the day spreads bright and eager before us. The gray vervet monkeys are playing on the rail, and I know they are probably plotting how to pilfer our fruit plate, or crunchies, or peppermint crisp pudding. Monkeys are smart—social too. I've seen how they agitate the guests here, disproportionately to their little nuisances. Wealthy guests, including the Babels, like to be in nature, sure, but only insofar as the nature doesn't encroach on them. Monkeys encroach. And as they scamper toward us, making their grunting noises, I only respect them. Wish I could stand so tall and encroach upon others' space. Make my mark. But I've always been more comfortable in the shadows.

"What are you thinking about, Bails? What do you want the cards to answer?"

"Gosh." Her chin quivers. "So many things."

"Yes?" My goddaughter doesn't often unload, but I'm trying not to sound too eager, not to scare her off.

"Mom and Asher, of course . . ."

"Yes, it's quite a change for us all. Your mom didn't even ask me to come with her to check out the plans for tonight."

"Really?" Bailey says, but it sounds offhand, not affronted on my behalf like I hoped.

"Yes. She always wants my opinion, she knows I'm good at parties. I think of the details the manager misses. And I've helped with all the plans. She doesn't even have the checklist!"

"Mmmm . . ." Bailey shrugs. "I mean, that's Mom for you, isn't it? We're not going to change her. She takes charge. She thinks she knows best. Like, before the trip, I didn't go to the family doctor to get vaccines and malaria pills—I went to a different doctor. And she was all disapproving. As if she obviously knows best. As if her doctor is the only one worth seeing. And I couldn't possibly make a qualified decision on my own. It's classic Mom, you know?"

"Yes, well." I try to calm myself. Clearly Bailey doesn't understand our dynamic, how and why and to what extent Odelia relies on me. She couldn't.

"I guess that's what I have questions about, for the tarot," Bailey says.

"Questions about what?" I ask, not understanding.

"Mom." Bailey wrings her hands in her lap. "How she tries to . . . I dunno, run my life . . ."

"Run your life?" I look up, surprised. Bailey's always been such a dutiful daughter, doing all that's asked of her with pleasant agreement. The opposite of her twin brother. For the first time, I wonder if it's because of Sam that she's had to be this way.

Bailey flushes pink. "You won't tell her, will you? I need to have a frank conversation with her."

"A frank conversation," I repeat, thinking how unlike Bailey this sounds. "I won't tell your mother, no. You know you can always come to me and I'll keep anything you tell me private. This is about the doctor?" I ask, trying to follow.

"No, it's much bigger than a doctor. It's . . ." But she doesn't elaborate.

"Okay. Are you not happy, working at Circ? You've seemed so happy, rising in the ranks. Your mom is very proud."

"I know she is." Bailey stares off, doesn't respond. "No, look, I take it back. I don't need cards about Mom. I know what I need to do."

"You know what you need to do. Okay." I pause, waiting for her to fill it in, tell me, but she doesn't.

"What I really want to know about is the elephant."

"The elephant?" I ask uncertainly.

"Yeah, the mother elephant we saw on the drive. She lost her baby, and she's created this, like, replica out of sticks, and she's not leaving the area."

"Okay . . ." I don't see how this has anything to do with anything.

"And Davina came back and basically broadcasted the elephant's location to the staff. She didn't realize that poachers are often fed information by the staff here, to get a cut of the money from the ivory. I just want you to check if the elephant's okay." She's talking so fast, the words flying out, jumbled, in a way that is very un-Bailey. But Bailey does love animals.

An elephant she wants to chat about. Right. Disappointment floods my chest. Still, I close my eyes, feel into the cards, and pull three quickly. Then, spontaneously, I pull one final card. I lay them all face down.

"Do you know the elephant's name?" I ask.

"Yes. Masasana."

"Okay. Well, let's see what the cards have to say about Masasana." Before I flip them over, one of the monkeys makes off with my mango. Bailey laughs, and I do too.

Then I flip over the cards, one by one. The minute my brain collates the cards, I want to turn them back over and end the reading.

"What?" Bailey asks, leaning forward, her eyes fixed on the first card: the Tower. Otherwise known as one of the most conventionally feared cards in a tarot deck. "It's not good, is it?"

"Well, the cards are never good or bad," I say, which is always what I say when a skews-bad card comes up. "We always have free will."

"Masasana doesn't—not if the poachers come for her."

I can't argue there.

"What does it mean?"

I sigh. "Well, we have the Tower, the Eight of Wands, the Chariot, and the World. The order in which they've shown themselves is interesting."

"Interesting *bad*?"

"Not necessarily bad. That's too black and white a way to look at things. But yes, look, the Tower means *run for your life*."

"Me, or the elephant?"

"You. Yes, this is about you. But I do feel Mother Nature being harmed around you." A vision visits me, which happens often, but this is a rare one that makes me shiver. I consider hiding my reaction, steering Bailey around my own increasing sense of foreboding, but I vowed long ago not to mess with the cards. They only come up in a reading because they are meant to be shared. "I see fire. Gunshots."

"Gunshots?" Bailey gasps.

"Yes. You must move, and move with all your might. And the Eight of Wands is an individualistic card. Don't take others' advice, or trust others— you must do this on your own."

"This?"

"Whatever it is," I say, even though I see the elephant, see her fully now, her warm, tormented eyes. I wasn't on their drive, but I *know* this elephant. I've been reading tarot long enough to know I only get visions this clear when I'm accessing truth. But I can't bring myself to tell Bailey, to drive her into danger.

"You must do this on your own, but it's okay, because you know the way. The Chariot means you won't give up, and you won't lose any energy. Fate and Mother Earth are on your side, and are guiding you."

"Is this still about the elephant?" Bailey looks startled, and I am too.

"It's about life. And the positive thing is, you prevail!" I think I'm re-assuring Bailey as much as myself. "That's the whole message of the cards. The cards are saying, *Don't wait!* Now is the time to act on your beliefs. If you do not act, you will live under the illusion of safety and you may be hurt badly; however, if you go, you will also put yourself at risk but will come out with fewer scratches than if you stayed."

"That's positive, I guess?"

"Life isn't about being safe," I say, but as it comes out, I feel like a total fraud. My whole life hasn't been about being safe—not the early part, at least. But in the past decades, I've lived entirely in a veil of safety. The safe canopy of Odelia, more like it. And now I feel like the net's dropped out beneath me, and nothing is certain or ensured.

Bailey meets my eyes, and suddenly I feel very ashamed.

"You're a good person, Aunt Gwen," Bailey says, taking me entirely by surprise. I start to well up and swipe my knuckle at the corners of my eyes, before they betray me. "You're a kind, wonderful person, and Mom is lucky to have you. We are all lucky to have you."

"You're wrong," I say, because it's true. "I'm lucky to have your mom. So incredibly lucky." My heart twangs as my childhood smacks back at me. Flashes of him, my horrible father—footsteps closing in, fists raised. And then warmer memories: the haven and emotional support that Odelia and her family provided. Not just her shed, which became my safe place to retreat, but her arms, which always opened to hold me and reassure me. I would cry on her shoulder as she promised me with her typical Odelia confidence that she would always protect me. And so I promised to protect her back.

"And I'm so lucky to have all of you too," I finally say, biting my lip. "Without you guys, I have no one . . . no one in this world . . ."

"We're the lucky ones." Bailey stands, gives the cards one last lingering glance. "I think I'll go rest before dinner."

"Okay . . . rest. Yes . . ." Bailey bends down to kiss my cheek. Emotion chokes my throat. "But, Bails?" I get out, before she goes.

"Yeah?"

"Be safe, okay? Be very safe. I couldn't handle it—and your mother certainly couldn't—if something were to happen to you."

Bailey sighs, enunciating her frown lines, which are beginning to form—strange on someone so young. She gives me a small smile. "When have I ever not done the safe thing, Aunt Gwen?"

As I watch her go, I scrape my hand through my hair, yanking out a good chunk.

# CHAPTER TWELVE

# ODELIA

The setup for our rehearsal dinner is spectacular, though right now that feels beside the point. Violett weaves me around the tented expanse, pointing out all the admittedly perfect details. There are placards on the table with hand-drawn leopards, sporting the names of my family members. Crystal goblets and white flower petals strewn on organic deep leaf tablecloths made by local artisans, exposed bulb pendant lights strung from the ceiling, wooden cane-backed chairs, and black tribal totems and candelabras smattered throughout. A buffet's set up on the side for the *braai*. I've asked for unpretentious safari fare, the standard barbecue dishes. Arno's making all the South African essentials: *boerowors* and steak, lamb chops and chicken, and *pap and gravy*—Joshua's favorite, mashed potatoes with tomato and onion sauce. And garlic French rolls and a Greek salad, of course. South Africans love a Greek salad. The menu is the perfect juxtaposition in my eyes, glamour and extravagance—but make it bush.

My eyes swing to the entry, over which our initials are strung in white flowers—mine first, then Asher's to the right, an ampersand between them. I always notice when a couple is introduced who goes first, the woman or the man. When I was with Aryeh, it was always him first. Now, though Asher certainly holds his own, it is I who goes incontrovertibly first. I wonder with a start if that will be okay with him, if a power struggle could emerge that I don't anticipate. I deeply hope not. Aryeh and I were locked in a thirty-year power struggle—a struggle that he was winning up until his death.

"Does this meet with your approval?" Violett asks as staff members bustle about in the backdrop, steaming chair cushions and arranging china. "I know you wanted to see the stars, but rain is forecast for the evening. Better safe, no?"

"Safe." I manage a dry laugh. "Funny, in the end, you taking care of my safety."

Violett flicks her ponytail off her shoulder. Even though she is beautiful, she has a world-weary, heavy quality to her that my children do not. Because I have shielded them from it.

"Why is that funny?"

"Because you threatened me yesterday." I step over toward the entrance, so we're standing in private, beneath the huge initial wreaths wafting their heady, sweet aroma.

"I didn't threaten you." Violett keeps a level gaze with her serious brown eyes. "If I'd threatened you, you'd know it."

"Well, you asked me for money, and when I refused, you said I'd be sorry. If that's not a threat, then I must be out of the game."

Violett is quiet. A shadow flickers over her pretty, delicate features.

"I don't understand this," I say. "You know I could fire you in an instant. You've always been kind to me and my family. And we've always provided for you, given you a competitive salary, promoted you when we could have taken someone with far more training. I don't know why you'd decide to take this path."

"Because you forced my hand," she says softly, looking out at the bush blanketed in sun.

"I didn't do anything! I'm here to celebrate my wedding."

"It's always about you, isn't it? You and your husband—both of them. You take what you want no matter the consequences. And yet you think you have all the power, eh?" She lets out a sharp, scary chuckle. "Okay, I'll threaten you for real. Has it come to that? We both know I could ruin you."

Violett looks at me straight on, her expression fierce, nearly flattening me with her palpable hatred, with the bald threat. How did I never notice it before as she lurked in the background of our every family interaction? How did I underestimate this woman? I'm usually on my game—aware of everything swirling around me so I can manage it. Control it.

"You work for me," I finally say. "You're paid handsomely. I could fire you right now. It feels like you are forgetting that." But my voice lacks punch. I think we both know now that she's got the upper hand.

"I'm paid handsomely." She practically spits the words. "*Please.* Nothing could compensate me for what you've done."

"What I've do—" My chest is churning, my anger surging, and yet, I know I need to tread carefully. I take a deep breath and finally I say, "Look, communication is the most difficult business. That's what I always say. I think you're misunderstanding me. I don't want to fight now. I'll pay you what you've asked for, okay? But just that. Nothing more. Not ever. You'll let this go and leave me and my family alone. Do we have an agreement?"

She doesn't smile like I hope, just stares me down. Finally, she whips her ponytail off her shoulder and says, "I'll text you my bank account details."

Violett turns, but I reach for her shoulder, grip her harder than I intend. "Stop sending me those notes. And stay away from my family. You're playing a dangerous game here. You don't know what you're up against."

She shoves off my arm, meets me with defiant eyes—familiar eyes, so familiar that I feel like weeping.

"You don't scare me. Maybe you did once. But not anymore."

And then she whips off, leaving me in the magnificent tent, alone.

---

WE EMBARK ON A second game drive, this one less eventful than the first. We see a white rhino and a female leopard named Xidulu, whose eyes are the color of rainbows, and her two leopard cubs. We watch giraffes bucking around near Crocodile Bridge, and a sweet hyena cub who looks like a stuffed animal and isn't as annoyingly chirpy as I usually find her parents to be.

We have sundowners on a rocky hill Markus calls a *kopje. Kop-yay, kop-yay, kop-yay,* I murmur to myself as we head back to the lodge. I notice my family, other than Davina, is generally frosty to Asher. Whereas my fiancé and Davina have a banter going that irks me, especially when Asher holds a cooing Ruby and looks the very picture of an adoring father. It's sweet—how much he's taken to my granddaughter. He spots me and hands Ruby back to Davina, then comes over. He snuggles into me, and I feel him harden a bit, as he kisses my neck, breathing up to my ear, how he knows I like. But I can't settle in it, not now. I can't help but wonder if Davina has turned him on. And if I'm going to worry like this for the rest of my life.

Back at the lodge, the rest of my family heads to the tent for our rehearsal dinner, while I slip back to my suite to change. Gwen offers to freshen up my makeup, and I gratefully accept, even though it's not on the itinerary we've already agreed to. After she sprays a new round of setting spray, I swap my safari attire for a Cult Gaia halter-necked confection that features white crochet rosebuds from the neck to midcalf. It's midi length, but see-through past the thigh, with cutouts at the smallest part of my waist. Perhaps it's too revealing for a sixty-four-year-old celebrating with her family but when I tried it on, I felt so alluring, like the Odelia Babel-Bach I'm close to becoming. Yes. If I were alone, I'd do a power pose to feel strong and embodied, but I stop myself from it in front of Gwen now. We *are* sisters, aren't we? Suddenly I feel so vulnerable and unsure. Not emotions I'm used to indulging.

"Do you want to take off your watch?"

"Oh." I glance down at my Apple watch. "No. But I will tomorrow, for the wedding."

Gwen nods. I twist my watch around.

"Are you okay, Dede?" Gwen asks.

"Oh." I stifle a little gasp. I consider asking Gwen point-blank what's tip-top on my mind. But god, I don't want to do this right now. I want—need—to enjoy this night. And suspecting Gwen—I have to be wrong.

"Yeah, why do you ask?" I nod at myself in the mirror, adjust my locket so it's tucked beneath the fabric and doesn't mar the neckline.

"You really want to wear that tonight? It sort of clashes with your dress," Gwen says softly, and my heart grinds to a halt.

"The locket? Of course." I almost say something about how she doesn't wear hers, but then I decide to switch tactics. I wasn't going to broach the topic, but Gwen bringing up the locket feels fortuitous. "Gwen, if something were ever to happen to me, I want you to look in my locket."

"Happen to you?" Gwen's head jerks. "Why would anything happen to you?"

"The Death card earlier," I say, attempting to keep my voice steady. "Just—"

"Oh." Gwen smiles. "The Death card doesn't mean you dying. You're taking it too literally."

"Just the same, I wanted to say it."

"Your locket?" Now she eyes it. "I don't understand, what's in—"

"I had to say it. Don't worry, Gwennie. Shouldn't come to that. Everything will be fine." Yes, I reassure myself. It's all going to be fine because I have the will and resources to make it so. Odelia Babel is no longer. Long live this new chapter. I am on top and I will make sure I stay that way.

"I'm sorry you'll have to leave early tonight," I tell her. "Davina is sensitive about who watches Ruby. Joshua's told me that he's convinced Davina to let someone from the staff stay with Ruby during the wedding tomorrow so you can be there too."

"Yes. I'd like to be at your wedding," Gwen says. "I know how important this fresh start is for you."

"Yes. Of anyone, you especially do." I clasp her hand, feel her familiar tight grip. I know it's a concession, how hard this must be for my best friend, but I can't help her process my marriage and what it might mean for our relationship. Not with everything else going on.

"So Violett will stay with Ruby tomorrow?" Gwen asks.

"Absolutely not. No, Violett won't be getting anywhere near my granddaughter. You can be certain of that. I need to have a word with Joshua."

"Not Violett?" Gwen asks uncertainly. "But she's very kind."

"Not Violett. *No.*" It's all coming at me like an avalanche, crushing on all sides.

"Okay," Gwen agrees deferentially, like normal. "Gosh, Dede, you're stunning." We both appraise my reflection in the mirror. "More beautiful now than when we were kids. Truly."

Her voice is a bit pandering in a way I usually enjoy, but today it grates on me. Sometimes honesty is preferable to unabashed cheerleading. Especially when I feel a bit insecure, uncertain whether she actually means her compliments or is just saying them because she is—and always has been—blinded by her devotion to me.

"Thank you, Gwennie. I love you so much. You're the best friend I could ever imagine. Truly." I choke with real emotion.

"And you are too," she whispers. Then we hug the tightest tight.

When we break apart, I stare at myself in the mirror, faking a smile. But once I've faked the smile, joy actually descends, and I find something unfurling in my chest that has been clenched.

That's what people don't understand about faking it. Faking it isn't something negative. The more you fake the person you want to be, the more you actually become her.

"Let's find my fiancé and start the party!"

---

NO ONE BUT ME has changed into more festive attire, and I'm slightly put out by that. I know tomorrow is the wedding, and everyone will get dolled up, and safari is a casual affair, but still, the lack of effort annoys me, makes me feel like this occasion isn't receiving the reverence it deserves. Even Asher hasn't changed. I'm about to bemoan that to Gwen, but she's staring at the huge floral wreath arrangements boasting my and Asher's initials with a strange look on her face. Great. Just great. I can't deal with her jealousy now.

"You look like a snack," Asher tells me, his gaze wolfish as he slips his hand into mine. Then he makes a little growling sound, informing me that looking like a snack must be a good thing.

"It means you're hot," Davina whispers as she slides a glass of champagne into my hand.

"I know that," I say, testiness creeping into my tone. But come on— I know I'm not a millennial like her. No need to hammer that fact home.

"You look beautiful, Odelia," Davina says.

"Thank you." I should say, *As do you*, but I can't bring myself to. The truth is, my daughter-in-law looks more beautiful than ever. She's positively glowing in a way I hope is attributed to Ruby or Joshua and not to my fiancé. "You look gorgeous, too, but no one would mistake you for our plus-size model anymore," I finally settle on saying.

I expect her to balk, but she just shrugs. "No, I suppose I'm midsize now. That's in, too, FYI."

"Maybe, but we have other models who cover that market. And besides, it's not your brand."

"You mean *your* brand."

She wields it like an insult, but I say, "I don't control the market research, Davina."

"So you've said." She sips on her own champagne, so seemingly unbothered. Anger burns in my throat.

"Look, I understand your position on my weight, Odelia. You've made it perfectly clear. And I'll say this: No one will tell me how to look or what my brand is. Not my CEO, and certainly not my mother-in-law. *I* am my brand. And if I'm not your brand, I'll survive. Actually, I'll thrive." Davina tips her champagne glass to me. "Cheers to you and Asher and your *every* happiness."

And then she turns and struts off, brushing her hand against my fiancé's arm as she goes. He says something I can't make out, and Davina peals a laugh that I suspect is extraloud and exuberant just for me.

# CHAPTER THIRTEEN

# JOSHUA

've been looking for the . . . perfect words to toast my mother and new *daddy . . .*"

Sam glints a broad smile, and anxiety chinks through my chest. I watch my brother puff his shoulders back and then my eyes flit over to our soon-to-be new stepfather, who smooths his sandy hair and shifts uncomfortably.

New daddy, though—ha.

On its face it's ridiculous, and there is something satisfying about the barb, especially as it was said by my brother, and I didn't have to be the one to voice it. I mean, though Asher appears genuinely besotted with Mom, I am wary of this marriage. I knew Asher as our designer before Mom announced they were together. Hell, I hired him. And I found him a creative genius and amiable to work with—and the customers have certainly responded positively to his designs. He has a revered reputation among Gen Z and millennials, the likes of which haven't been seen since Jenna Lyons with J.Crew. No one can dispute that our luxe basics line with its androgynous flair has been responsible for the lion's share of our profits this past year, an even more important feat given our overall revenue decline.

But to find out after the fact that Asher and Mom got engaged has been . . . difficult.

"Samuel," Mom hisses, a rictus smile on her face.

My cheeks go hot, like I've been admonished too. I can't eradicate the constant sense that I am responsible for my brother, that if I'd done something different or better I could have prevented his misdeeds. Maybe I feel this burden because Aba heaped it on me. *You are the older brother, Joshua. You have to protect him, even from himself.*

As Sam got older and came out of the closet, I became the object of Papa's anger, perhaps even more than Sam. *Set your brother straight. If you see him talking to boys at school in a certain way, I want you to tell me.* Shaking my shoulders, like it was I who'd offended Aba's sensibilities, like it was I who was the ever-disappointment.

"Don't worry, Mother, this is a toast, not a roast." Sam's words pull me back to the present, though the familiar shame is still there. I rub my neck, which now feels like it's flaming. I creep my collar up, though I already know my ubiquitous hives have begun to sprout.

"What I want to say is that, when Aba died, everything changed." Sam bites his lip and I rub my neck as my hives intensify. "We lost our father, yes, but suddenly we had a new mother too. Conventional thinking is that couples grow to resemble each other. I wouldn't know from personal experience . . ."

That's for sure. Sam goes through men like water; no one ever holds his interest long.

"But I'm told when you're together long enough," Sam says, "you acquire the same habits and quirks. And that's what we saw as kids. Mom was religious. She made Shabbat dinner, cholent on Saturday afternoon. She was pious and she loved God. Everything Aba stood for too. But after he died, she transformed into a different mom."

My eyes flit over to Mom—her face stony.

*Don't go there,* I want to shout at my brother. *Stop this. Abort.*

"She lay in bed and watched romantic comedies for a straight month."

I remember that. We were in mourning. All the mirrors were covered with sheets, and we had to wear black and pray and talk to all the mourners while Mom stayed in her bedroom and people asked about her, and we had to make up excuses, like she was sick. Periodically, during the prayers, when everyone was somber, you'd hear voices from her room—Reese Witherspoon, Kate Hudson. Followed by laughter—Mom's.

"And when she came out of her bedroom, she was a different mom. Gone were her wig and those skirts down to her ankles."

"This isn't a roast?" Mom says tightly. "This quite feels like a roast, Sam. And I'm not having it. If you don't want to celebrate my marriage, then you can go."

"This isn't a roast," Sam says evenly. "I'm trying to say, we watched you become your own person. You were Mrs. Babel before Aba died and then you became Odelia, queen of the world. And even if we disagree at times . . ."

"At times," Mom repeats dryly. "Sure."

"Even if we disagree most of the time," Sam says, "I still respect that you became your own person. We should all be our own people, not answering to anyone, or following anyone else's path."

There's a distant howl of some animal as I ponder that.

"So, a toast to Mom." Sam tips his champagne flute her way, and for a moment I think this is going to be okay. That Sam's actually trying to be decent. But then I see it—how Sam's eyes darken when they latch on to Asher, who is rubbing Mom's shoulders, bending down to kiss her cheek. "To Mom and *her boy toy*." Sam fixes his gaze on Asher, and Asher stares defiantly back.

"To Asher: Mom says you're two peas in a pod. Her version of a compliment, I guess, but I'll leave that to my dear family to decide."

A shiver spikes down my arms. The air crackles with Sam's anger, the heat. It's like we're all frozen, watching the implosion, but powerless to stop it.

"We *are* two peas in a pod, Sam," Mom says, with a warning tone. "And I would watch yourself. You're skating on thin ice."

"Am I?" Sam draws up to his full height, his voice thick with fury. "Oh, well, now I'm scared. I'm so fucking scared. And peas in a pod, eh? You and Asher? Maybe. Maybe I can see it. You both have good hair, good style, although . . ." He laughs mirthlessly. "There's a bit of an age difference. Still, cheers to you, Asher. Anyway, Mom says you are generous and kind, which she is surely not. I hope that's true, because when Mom inevitably turns into you, when she molds herself around your likes and dislikes, like she did with Aba, maybe she'll stop being such a stingy bitch!"

I gasp, and so does Davina beside me. On my other side, Bailey breathes, "Sammy," her voice brittle.

Jabulani's eyebrows are pinched together as he replenishes my water glass, avoiding looking me in the eye. If he did, I know what would be written there: *I'm sorry this is your family.*

Sometimes I'm sorry too. Sometimes I wonder how I even got here. If it weren't for Bailey, I'd feel like an alien inside this family.

Rage bubbles in Mom's eyes, but she waits to unleash it. I watch her mold it, prepare it for maximal impact, but then she surprises me and drops her tone to a whisper, sounding desolately sad. "Your father wasn't a saint, you know? You think he was, because he's gone, so you've placed him on a pedestal. He's the one who couldn't accept you as you are. I'm the one who didn't blink an eye, who wants you to love whomever you love. I'm giving you the chance to fly free, baby boy. Trust-fund kids aren't happy. Believe me. Making you make it on your own—I'm giving you the keys to your own happiness."

"Oh, that's rich," Sam erupts. "That's rich, coming from you, who got handed the keys to the golden kingdom by Aba conveniently dying. And don't pretend that you aren't the one who read my private journal entries. You're the one who went straight to Aba. You're the one who forced me out of the closet. You've never protected me. So don't pretend now that you are."

Mom stands, and with an almost robotic calm she lifts Sam's champagne glass from his hands.

"You won't be needing this anymore," she hisses. "Get out. I want you to leave."

He reaches for it back, his face one big sneer, but fear pools in his eyes. I know that fear—it comes out like defiance, but he cares. He cares what Mom thinks. He needs her. Needs her approval, and her money even more. "I'm not drunk, Mother." He snatches the glass, drains it in one fell swoop. "Just having fun on this *happy* occasion."

"I don't care if you drink, Sam," Mom says tightly. "I don't care what you decide to do. I meant you won't be needing this drink, because I'm kicking you out."

"Kicking me out of . . . South Africa?" Sam laughs. "As if you're the president or something." But I can tell the sudden uncertainty laced behind it. "Like you have the power to tell me where I can be. You're so full of yourself."

Mom's fury is controlled, but unmistakable. "You can go wherever you please. But out of this resort. Which I own. I told you in no uncertain terms: this is my new chapter. All I wanted tonight—this whole week—was to unite my family, for us all to have a *jol*."

"A *jol.*" Sam rolls his eyes. "God. Just say have a good time. You aren't South African. Dad was! And that's your problem, you know you can never take his place, no matter how hard you try."

"I'm not trying to take Aryeh's place. Your father is long gone. And I'll speak however I like." Mom grips Asher's hand and stares defiantly at Sam. "And if you can't celebrate my soon-to-be husband and me, then you're no longer part of this."

"This?"

Mom gestures around. "This celebration. This *family.*" Her eyes are blazing, but I can tell she's sad too. "I'm so goddamn tired of this, Sam," she says quietly. "Just get the hell out."

———

IT'S FRONT ROW SEATS to a theater production for which none of us wanted tickets. An explosive three-act arc. Because of course Sam doesn't leave, and of course Mom doesn't actually want him to go. And both of them feed off each other—almost revel in the fight. He's a lion, she's a leopard, and they're circling each other, both ready to pounce.

There's Sam pacing the length of the bonfire pit where we've now relocated since the forecasted storm was a mere drizzle and has already come and gone. The fire crackles, a worthy blaze, reminding me of childhood times, when we'd all gather around here and Markus would tell us fables about lions that could fly and hippos that were hungry. Grand stories that riveted us kids, that even our parents abided by, joining in the fun, pressing pause on their argument-du-jour. But now Sam injects my eardrums with his all-too familiar tune, an indignant diatribe on money, always money with my little brother. Always the injustice, how he's been eternally denied. Stalking past Aba's grave, invoking the old man—actually young when he died, relatively, only sixty.

"Hey!" Asher says, stepping up. "Stop. Just stop. This is your mom you're talking to, Sam. Sit down. Show her some respect."

"Respect!" Sam whips his head around. "That's *rich.* You don't know what you're talking about, Asher. You've been around for what—five minutes? You think you know all her secrets? You sit down, Asher. *You* sit down."

Asher stays standing, which I respect, but it's clear he's not quite sure what to do. My nervous system feels jangly now, hijacked by Sam's rants, his cutting remarks about how Aba wouldn't want my brother to struggle any further, would want to support his photography venture so he can be a strong, ambitious man. Mom shooting back that Aba would want him to stand on his own two feet, as Jabulani adds more logs to the pit and the fire roars anew. Then Sam gets in Mom's face in a way that makes me want to shrink back. He spits, "Have you ever stood on your own two feet? Let's not forget the only one among us who benefited from Aba's death."

Something passes over Mom's face—something odd, which I am aware I will think about later. "What are you implying, Samuel?" Mom asks.

"I'm not implying anything." Sam shrugs. "I'm saying I know about the autopsy. How you covered it all up. How Aba didn't just drop dead—he was *murdered*."

That accusation blasts through us as sparks fly up from the firepit and white smoke billows over to where Davina and I sit, her long, manicured fingers resting on my thigh. She scrapes her fingernails over my chinos, up toward my waist, thumbing the skin beneath my belt, making it burn.

"Is that true?" Davina whispers in my ear.

I strain my neck, crack it side to side to ease the tension and so she can't see my face. "He says crazy stuff like this all the time. You know Sam. You can't pay attention to him."

"I *do* know Sam. But I've never heard him accuse your mom of murdering your dad."

No. I hadn't, either. My eyes flit over to catch Mom's infuriated face. Asher prods the fire, causing it to surge and send up more sparks.

"And there's more too. None of you knows anything about anything!" Sam's veins protrude in his neck, his cheeks nearly puce. "What Mom has done . . . why Aunt Gwen was *really* in prison . . . Aba told me . . . he told me *everything* . . ."

"What?" I shake my head, not putting two and two together at all. "That's literally ridiculous. What possibly . . . ?"

Bailey has leapt up toward Sam, and I can hear her talking soothingly but firmly, hopefully dropping him back down to earth. Asher's now whispering with Mom, their faces coming in and out of the shadows as the fire crackles.

Why Gwen was *really* in prison? What does that even mean?

Jabulani tiptoes up and delicately sets out the marshmallows in stakes on the firepit ledge. He hovers, looking nervous, like he's arrived at intermission and wants to make sure to jet out before the next act, which is sure to be even bloodier.

I manage a smile. "Thank you, Jabulani." I reach for a stake and extend it marshmallow-tip first into the fire. White ribbons of smoke billow back. I know that later my clothes will smell of this smoke, that when I am home days from now, I'll bury my nose in them before throwing them in the laundry—a shred of nostalgia for this place, even though the night's been hijacked by my brother.

"Do you need anything else?" Jabulani asks.

"No, I think we're fine," I say, as Davina says, "A refill would be amazing, Jabulani. Thank you beyond." She flashes him a winning smile and pats his shoulder. He blushes, looking flattered. God, Dav—she could flirt with a wall.

"Sure, I'll get that for you now now."

"How many is that, hon?" I ask lightly, when Jabulani's gone.

"I can handle my alcohol, thank you." But there's something slack, loose about her eyes, which I don't often see.

"I know, just . . . maybe you'll sleep better if you cut it off here."

She ignores me and punches at her phone, a smile creeping on her face. "Who's that?"

"Nothing." She slips her phone back in her pocket and smiles encouragingly at me.

But then I notice Asher angled in his canvas chair away from Mom, typing into his phone too.

Understanding lashes my bones. "Are you texting with *him*?"

"What?" Davina asks, staring into the fire and not at me in a way that feels deliberate. I feel my hives instantly reignite.

Asher's now taking periodic swigs of his beer shandy, his phone in his pocket.

"You are, aren't you?" Tears poke at my eyes that, god, I need to keep at bay. "When did you even exchange phone numbers?"

"We're family now. And we work at the same company. It's no big deal at all. I just texted him to see if he's okay. This whole night is pretty full-on for someone new to the family."

"*You* texted *him*!?" It comes out squeakier than I intended.

Jabulani returns. He nudges over the kerosene lantern on the stump between us and sets Davina's brandy beside it. I nod at him in thanks, then lower my voice. "You know it's a big deal, Dav. And . . ."

I can't bear to hash it all out again. It makes me feel so insecure and stupid and weak. Of course Dav and Asher are going to work together—we're all at the same company. She's the model; he's the designer. Of course he's going to have to be up close to her, pinning stuff and making alterations, but lately, I've been taking more trips from my office across the floor to the studio where they're often working and laughing. Sometimes with other people, sometimes alone. I've never seen them doing anything compromising, but when I pop by, Dav gets weary. Whatever laughter infused the space, existed between them, fizzes, and I wonder—I can't help but wonder—if something's brewing with them. Even though Dav has always vehemently denied it. Now, with Asher—surprise, surprise—marrying Mom, I should be less insecure, more certain of my wife's fidelity. But I'm not. And now they're texting, and I'm scared. I'm scared that this life I have and love, that lately has felt like I need to navigate a tightrope to keep, is one step from total erasure.

Davina sips from her brandy and then looks me in the eyes with zero apology in hers. I used to get lost in her almond-brown eyes, which had so much depth and complexity within them, used to feel so safe and secure with her, and now she feels like a stranger. Like I don't even know the woman who sleeps beside me.

"Asher doesn't need you," I say, still stunned. "And the time you're spending texting him—you could spend with us." I know I sound needy but I can't help it. "I need you, Dav, and Ruby needs you—"

"I'm with you and Ruby all the time," Davina says fiercely. "And I strongly object to the implication that I'm not."

"I don't mean that. It's just, I haven't even . . . I haven't . . ." I stop, because I don't know how to tell her, but all of a sudden it's all bubbled up. Everything I've been feeling that I've been stowing away.

But instead of eliciting compassion from my wife, she amps up the indignation. "Maybe I need *him*. Have you thought of that, Joshua? Have you thought that maybe I'm struggling postpartum, and that sometimes being on the outside of all these Babels, but always dealing with your family's craziness, makes me want to confide in someone who doesn't have the last name Babel? Especially after my mother died, and Dad's in a total depression. And now Asher's also marrying into the family, and so he gets it. He gets that I've been having a hard time. But do you? Do *you* get it, Joshua?"

"I get it," I say, feeling socked in the stomach. "And . . ."

I can't bring myself to say it, not again, how beautiful she is, how inadequate I've felt. That I'm here for her, even though it doesn't seem like she wants me to be. Dav's always been beautiful, garnered looks from men, but lately, she's been losing weight, and to my surprise, flaunting her new shape in even more body-conscious attire than previously. It's rocked my feelings of security, I suppose, making me wonder where I stand—and now it's confirmed, what I guess I already suspected. Davina's talking to Asher, growing closer to him, confiding in him.

And what else beyond that? It would take a person with the confidence of George Clooney not to wonder or suspect, and George I am not.

"You and Ruby," I finally say, in lieu of voicing the rest. "That's all I care about. All I want to do is be here for you both."

Davina softens, but I wonder if it's just at the mention of our daughter. Where did the splinters come from? When did we crack? I stare at the soil, damp from the touch of rain. I watch an earthworm coil up.

"Joshua, I . . ." Dav returns her hand to my thigh. The heat of her hand feels like a burn, like it's singeing my skin.

But before Dav can continue, something else diverts our attention: Sam hovering over Mom, speaking words I can't hear. I hold my breath, waiting for the next explosion, but to my surprise my brother extends his hand and Mom puts her hand in his. He helps her up, and the two go off to the side, near the outlook onto Crocodile River. For a while, Sam's talking, gesticulating but not angrily so, and I keep waiting for the inevitable dovetail to the storm that will sweep us all back inside. But suddenly my brother bends down to hug Mom, and Mom reciprocates, pressing her small frame into my brother's hulking one. The hug lasts a while, and when they break apart, Sam steps briskly over to Asher too. Extends his hand to our forthcoming stepfather.

Asher stares, which makes me respect him more, like he's not just going to cave to Sam's childish behavior. But instead of sulking at the snub, Sam raises his hands in surrender. "Sorry. I really am, Asher. I promise no more disruptions to your wedding weekend."

Asher looks wary, but he eventually reciprocates the handshake.

I make eyes with Bailey. *What did you say to him?* I mouth. *You're a magician.*

She gives me a small smile, but it doesn't reach her eyes. Yes, my sister is an old-hat mediator, a role she never asked to occupy. She used to do it for Mom and Aba, too, trying to be cute, break the tension with a cartwheel, or a story about some new animal in our backyard, though Aba would eventually tune her out and walk away before any real resolution could be fixed.

"All right, let's have a real party now." Sam rubs his hands together. "What do we say? Sorry for all of that, family. I'm just . . . emotional. I didn't mean to cause a . . . well, I'm ready to celebrate now. Let's celebrate for real."

I shake my head, feeling whiplashed. How has this gone from zero to one-eighty and back again? This is them, though. I don't know why I ever think it will be any different. Mom and Sam suck up all the oxygen in the room. This is how it is. How it's always been. How it always will be.

Now Sam's gone back behind Mom, and is rubbing her shoulders, and Mom's leaning her head back cautiously, sneaking glances at my brother, like, *Is this real? Has he really come around?*

The bar is set so low for Sam that he makes one grand concession and comes out like Jesus in Mom's eyes. And what about me? I try so hard—all I do is try—and yet Mom never caves. It's her way or the highway. I try so hard and get bamboozled and just take it. Roll over. Joshua the puppy who just wants to be loved. Joshua—you can pull the wool over his eyes and he'll keep on being your loyal soldier.

Ever since I spoke to Lester about Circ this afternoon, I've felt a pounding in my ears, a migraine mounting. This was before I found out about Dav and Asher texting, back when I was sure she was on my side, and she was pushing me to stand up for myself. To stand up for us. It's our company, after all. We're the future. Mom and her archaic practices with no integrity have to be the past. Or else.

"Or else, what, though?" I had asked Dav, faltering then at her pep talk, not seeing another way.

"Or else, period-on-the-end-of-the-sentence energy," she'd said, decisively.

I channel that now. Period-on-the-end-of-the-sentence energy.

I stand and walk over to Bailey. The only one I can confide in. And I must, before I combust.

"Bails, can we talk?"

"Now?" she asks.

"No." I glance around. "Not now. Tomorrow morning. Early. Before breakfast, before sunrise. Five thirty, okay?"

"Uh . . ." Bailey's eyes are flitting around, everywhere but at me. She's scattered, eyes bloodshot—kinda strange, it occurs to me. It's the wedding, must be—Mom and Sam's fight and then slapdash makeup. This weird trip to celebrate a marriage all of us secretly, or not so secretly, dread.

"Tomorrow, we'll meet at the front of the lodge and then walk back here to the firepit, okay? To have privacy."

"Um . . . okay?"

"Just you. Don't bring Sam. Don't tell him, either."

"Okay. Is this—are you—"

"I want to say something!" Mom raises her drink, and all the chatter stops.

I nod encouragingly at Bailey and mouth, *We'll talk in the morning.* I make my way back to my seat. Davina's put her phone away and is looking at me with question marks in her eyes, but I don't have the energy to answer them, or to raise the issue of her secretly talking to Asher, which is still burning in my throat.

"I want to say to all of you that I am very happy you are all here. And Sam talking about Aba—"

"I'm sorry," Sam says with unusual contrition. "I'm really sorry again. I—"

"It's okay." Mom lets out a strained exhale. "I've forgiven you—just no more, okay, Sam? I can't take anything else—this is the very last time."

"I promise," my brother says earnestly. "I'm really going to try. Wait, this is a great shot. Hang on." He retrieves his camera from his side and aims it toward Mom, clicks.

Mom draws her shoulders back and pivots; she knows how to ensure her angles are right. When Sam puts his camera down, Mom's smile fades. "Do more than try, Sam. Be the kind person I know is inside you. Truth is, I know how hard it was—and still is—for you kids to lose your father. And we're so close to him now." Mom indicates the gravestone, a hulk in the dim night, its inscription lit by the firelight. "It's made me think, is all, about death. About *my* death."

My chest bubbles with an uncomfortable sensation.

"Sweetheart, can you please think of *life* when we're celebrating our impending marriage?" Asher says.

"I am!" Mom says, suddenly fervent, and I have this sense she's not putting on a show, that this is real. The realest she ever is or will ever get. "I'm thinking of life, too, at the same time as my death! I'm thinking about how lucky I am, for this second chance. I love you so much, honey. I am the luckiest to have found you, Ash." For a moment Mom looks so bathed in genuine contentment that it's like staring at the sun, like I'm about to be blinded. "In Hebrew, Asher means happiness, and that's exactly how you make me feel. Life with you is like one great sleepover with my best friend that I never want to end."

I look at my stepfather; his eyes are glistening, fixed on her.

"Maybe it's safari that makes me think of death too," Mom says, as Asher rises to stand beside her and take her hand, circling her palm with his thumb. "Seeing the lions kill the old leopard today. Maybe death isn't a bad thing is what I mean. No, hear me out—death is just love recycled into something else, isn't it? I want to tell you all, whenever I die, let me stay dead. I don't want any of you to spend your energy grieving. To wonder if you should have done something different. Said something more to me. God knows I've made mistakes. As a mother, as a best friend, as a person . . ." Mom's eyes roll back, and her face wrenches in a pain that makes me feel breathless. "Just . . . right now, I am very happy."

"And rather drunk," Sam says, but with a smile.

"True!" Mom laughs. "And if this is my last hurrah, well, it's a pretty spectacular one."

Mom's tipsy, maybe, but her words are clear, an arrow to my heart.

"Delia," Asher says, looking as uncertain as the rest of us. "Please stop. I don't want—let's get one thing clear. I plan on having you around for a very long time."

As he folds her into a hug, Mom says, "You never know when it's your time, is all. I just wanted to get this off my chest."

I watch them, my heart pummeling my rib cage. Mom had to get a lecture about *death* off her chest? What about what *I* need to get off my chest.

And I've been waiting . . . waiting for her to get back from galivanting in Bora Bora with Asher, waiting for this farce of a wedding to pass, and now I feel it churn in me, everything I've repressed.

I'm telling Mom tonight that it's over. If she doesn't make things right, then I will.

## CHAPTER FOURTEEN

# ODELIA

I sink onto the couch as the room tilts and spins.

I didn't think I drank so much, but I suppose I did. I suppose the staff kept refilling my glass. And I didn't eat much . . . didn't have much of an appetite. Extreme happiness—heart-explosive love and unbelievable sex—is, on one hand, a nice little appetite erasure. But then there was Sam's speech, and all the business with Violett and the notes. Appetite killers.

"Want one of your Snickers dates?" Asher asks, kneeling in front of the fridge.

"Nah. But thank you."

He shuts the fridge door, then patters back over. I tilt my head back as he looms over me, the date-Snickers between his lips. "Sorry, I'm eating more of these than you are."

"What's mine is yours, honey."

"Do you think Arno will mind if we ask him for more? My abs have never looked better since I started your keto ways."

I laugh. "The date-Snickers aren't actually keto. They're my sinful treat. I only have one a day."

Asher freezes, his face aghast. "You're telling me after I've had, like, ten!"

I giggle. "Well, it doesn't seem to be affecting your hot bod—" My voice cuts out at a sudden rap at the door. Asher gets up and starts toward it.

"God, if that's Sam with a complaint about some new egregious thing I've done, please tell him I've hit my limit tonight."

"Don't worry. I'll be your bouncer."

I turn to watch the door swing open and, to my surprise, Joshua is standing in the frame.

I wave. "Hi, sweetheart. I thought you went to bed a while ago."

Joshua stuffs his hands in his pockets, his face strangely grim. "I was waiting for Dav to come back and take over with Ruby."

"Oh—okay?"

"Can we—" Joshua eyes Asher.

"It's fine, babe." I nod at Asher. "Can you give us a moment?"

"Okay." Asher disappears out onto the deck, closing the screen door behind him.

"Everything okay, Joshua? Is it Ruby?"

"No, Ruby's fine. She's sleeping. It's just— I spoke to the office today. To Lester."

"Oh." I feel everything in my body tighten. God, this? Now? Lester's my COO. He's supposed to have my back.

"Yeah." Joshua stands stiffly in the foyer, and I motion him over toward the couch, sighing.

"And you felt the need to come talk business with me at"—I check the clock embedded in the wall—"eleven fourteen on the night before my wedding?"

"It's not business, Mom! It's everything that's going on with the—" He lowers his voice. "Sweatshop labor. Lester confirmed it."

"Well, he shouldn't have," I say, trying to steady myself. Lester's supposed to be my fucking vault. And we're fixing this. We're going to fix it all, but it takes time to sort this stuff out, that's what Joshua doesn't get in his little bubble of numbers, divorced from reality.

"What, he should have lied to me? I *knew* something was going on by—"

"You're the finance guy—this isn't your forte. Back down, Joshua. Our revenues are down, as you know, and I'm doing what needs to be done. Like I always do. Someone has to make hard decisions sometimes. We can't all live in fantasyland. And anyway, this isn't the time to talk about it."

"You promised we weren't using that factory anymore! They've been slapped with so many violations—"

"Nothing's been proven! And I got us out of Xinjiang. We're in compliance with the law. So I don't know why you're coming at me."

Joshua inches closer to me. "It's not enough to be in compliance—we're supposed to be doing better. To be doing the *best*—treating the people who work for us just as well as the planet we're trying to save. You promised me, Mom. This isn't the company we're trying to build. Or, it wasn't, when I joined. But it feels like our whole mission is running away from us. Everything we stand for is being compromised. And you're going behind my back on things. I'm having to find out from Lester! I'm supposed to be your right hand. Do you know how that makes me look? How I feel?"

"How *you* feel? How about how *I* feel? I've poured my whole soul into this company. You think I don't care about its success? Sustainable Zara is an oxymoron, Joshua. You know it and I know it. One of those ambitions has to come slightly above the other."

"I know, Mom. Don't I know it. But that's the thing. That's where we fundamentally disagree. You want to build us closer to a fast-fashion behemoth, and I want us to contribute to a world that Ruby's generation will be proud of. Our mission statement isn't just words for me. It matters. It matters to Bailey, too! And it feels like you don't even ca—"

"You know what, Joshua?" Suddenly I'm at my limit. "When I'm gone and you're in charge, do what you please! Make the company you want to make. Evolution is a good thing, I know that. The circle of life. But right now—" I sit up taller. "I am very much alive, and Circ is mine. My baby. I make the rules. I say how it goes."

Joshua stares at me. His face, already pale, is now ghostly white.

"I can't do this right now. I can't. Not on my wedding night. This feels like a complete slap in the face, you coming here and— What? Threatening me? Is that what this is?"

"You're deceiving the board," Joshua says. "Cutting corners in costs, materials. Labor. And god knows what else. I don't feel like you're being up front with me. I feel like there's more you're hiding."

"Hiding?" I ask, my tone scathing. "Hiding like what?"

"I don't know, but now that I know we're still using that factory, and your marriage to Asher . . . you're saying you're gonna change the will, and you haven't told me how that might affect me. My role at the company."

"Ohhhhh. I get it now, so this is about money. Of course. I've told you a million times—the company is yours! You'll take it over, when my day is done. What, you think I'm lying? Playing you? I love you, Joshua. I trust you. You just don't trust me. And it really hurts me that, when it comes down to it, it's always about money with you kids."

"I'm not Sam, Mom!" Joshua bursts out, looking as angry but also as sure as I've ever seen him. "But you can't deflect from the stuff I'm saying anymore. And I can't stand silently by when our company values are being compromised—when we're deceiving—"

"Get out. I want you to get out." I stare numbly at my son.

But Joshua doesn't budge. "Mom, please. Please let's talk about this. I don't want to threaten you, that's really not what I came here to do."

"Isn't it though?"

The screen door screeches open, sending a gust of warm air inside. Asher steps in. "Joshua, I think your mom's tired. You can continue this another time. But not tomorrow. Not here. When we're back in Florida, back at work . . ."

"Yes. Okay." Joshua reddens. "I'm sorry—I didn't—I just had to say—"

"Another time, Joshua," Asher says, kind but firm. My partner, backing me up. I should be grateful, but I'm too upset.

I stare at my son, and he stares back, and I think about everything I've done to make him mine. Does he have any appreciation of all the sacrifices I've made to give him a good life? A good, privileged life where his biggest worries are what the world is going to look like in thirty years. God, my worries are so much more immediate. That's the problem with trust-fund kids, no matter how smart and hardworking they are, like Joshua; they will never have to claw their way up. They will never have to make the truly impossible choices that the generation prior had to make to facilitate their silver spoons.

Then Joshua turns and walks quickly out without even saying I love you. That's what we always say to each other, always, after every conversation, and today he broke our code. That's how I know he's serious about threatening me. Something occurs to me, and I stare. The notes—could Joshua be behind them?

No, I reassure myself. He couldn't. But what if somehow . . .

I shiver, feeling spent. It's all too much.

Asher's staring at me with concern in his eyes. "Wanna talk about it?"

I consider it. Do I? It's not like I've kept it from Asher, the chasm that's growing between me and my kids who work at Circ. We all want a sustainable company, what's good for the planet. But the problem is, what's good for the planet isn't always good for business. So sometimes I have to make difficult choices. When they take over, they can do what they want. But for now, I'm in charge. And Asher, like me, is a realist. But still, I don't want to talk about sweatshops and exploited workers right now.

"No." I shake my head. "No, I really don't wanna talk about it. Right now I want to forget all of it."

"Let's go to bed then." My fiancé extends his arm, and just the simple phrase—his deep, sensuous tone, his smoldering smile, the brush of his rough fingers—it all shoots in a straight line to my down-there. My pussy, as Asher calls it, his breath hot in my ear as I gasp. *Your pussy feels so good.* Aryeh never even referred to my vagina, by its technical name or otherwise, in our two-plus decades together. We never had sexual intimacy.

I take Asher's hand and let him lift me up. I follow him to the bedroom, my mind tumbling forward. Already playing out the way we will unite, how his thighs will lock against mine, how I'll squeeze his butt and he'll groan and then lick me in all the good ways. All the ways I never knew could exist, until him.

Asher kisses me, then goes to the bathroom. "I'll meet you in bed."

"Hurry up," I tell him, unzipping my dress. Then I peel back the covers and slip inside the Charlotte Thomas bespoke sheets that I picked out myself, with twenty-two carat gold woven into the fabric, letting the silky bliss pull my thoughts from me one by one.

I hear Asher washing his hands, then the light flickers off. My body prickles with anticipation as Asher slides beneath the sheets and groans, as our bodies meld together. He enters me and it's fast and rough—just how we like it. We don't finish together—now I understand that's the stuff of romance novels. Rather, Asher takes care of me first, and then I take care of him, and when we're done, we're slick with sweat, our mouths pressed together, not kissing anymore but sated.

I flop over and burrow into his chest, feeling our hearts beating together, syncing up. Despite tension with my family, with Gwen, despite these mythical threats, and the problem of Violett that I must handle, right here and now, I feel safe. Protected. Secure.

"I feel so alive," I tell him.

"Me, too, sweetheart. I love you." Asher rubs his hand over my hip, then closes his eyes, his face gone slack. In the moonlight that spills into our room, I can see how tired he looks, how spent, and I feel the power of having been the catalyst of his reaction.

For not the first time, I whisper a thank-you to God for Asher, this unexpected last love of my life. I still remember life with Aryeh, unable to fully shake it. Sometimes it rises from the abyss, almost threatening to reclaim me. How afraid I felt, dead inside. In Hebrew, the word for husband also means "owner." And that's how I felt—a kept woman. I recall how Aryeh's religious proclivities demanded that we abstain from sex, even from sleeping in the same bed, for my menstrual cycle and for seven "unclean" days after. So, like many Orthodox couples, our bed was composed of two separate ones, which we would move apart during my unclean days and move back together afterward. Aryeh would ask me, *Is it time yet to reunite?* And I would lie and say, *Not yet.* Dreading our coming back together. So angry. So hostile. So sick of fighting over every last thing. We were fire and fire. Two big personalities—no midpoint at which to meet. Those days sleeping apart during my first marriage were the only ones I slept peacefully. Back reunited with my husband, I would lie awake, deeply unhappy. Or sometimes our passionate fights led to passionate sex. Hate sex, really. Explosive, but not actually satisfying or enjoyable.

When I think back to those times, above all, I feel ashamed. Ashamed that I was weak, that I didn't rise up sooner and claim the life that was meant for me, no matter the consequences.

But for the last decade ever since Aryeh died, I've experienced power. Power in commanding a boardroom, commanding my family too. But this power I've experienced with Asher—with a true, soulmate love—is different, and dare I say more potent? Because I know, no matter what anyone thinks, that this man loves me.

And power derived from love—well, that is a whole other drug.

# CHAPTER FIFTEEN

# ASHER

Bashing cymbals in my eardrums—a dream? I roll over, flutter my eyelids, then flinch as light spikes in. As I blink my eyes fully open, the fuzzy shards of morning crystallize into a clearer picture, and I register that the other side of the bed is empty.

The wooden door that Odelia has informed me is reclaimed pine from old railway carriages reverberates with more thumping. I stare at the ceiling as my eyes acclimate, my brain off spinning stories, my body still thrumming with the weight of my fiancée.

"Coming." I scramble from the bed. My heart rate revs up.

I throw the door open, thoroughly surprised by the person who is standing there.

Joshua.

Till now we've only ever exchanged pleasantries. The initial Circ interviews, of course, and later meetings with the larger team. He's fairly vanilla, Joshua. Pale chinos hitched up by brown leather belts and an array of button-downs over undershirts, the vibe very 1950s grandfather. And always a somber face that at first glance makes you wonder if someone died, but the problem winds up being some financial or sustainable ethics quibble. So far I've gravitated to Joshua's wife far more—Davina's spicy, doesn't take anything lying down, has a wicked, witty sense of humor. Whereas Joshua shares his mother's propensity for an unreadable demeanor. You don't know how Odelia or Joshua really feel, unless you're in their inner circle. And I am not in Joshua's inner circle.

"Are you looking for your mother?" I rub my eyes, feeling self-conscious in my boxer briefs, the vent overhead rousing goose bumps on my bare chest. "She's not here . . . I don't know where she is. Maybe she went for a—"

"She's dead."

"Wha . . . ?" I freeze. "What . . . what did you say?"

"Dead. I said she's dead."

He stares at me, and my heart hitches in my chest. Stops its beat. "That can't be," I finally say. "That . . ."

I stand motionless as the words dribble off. I feel like I'm going to be sick. I look blankly at Joshua. For once, I can tell how he feels deep down. It's stamped on his face as he bites down on his lip, unable to hold back tears.

"I just found Mom lying by the bonfire pit, and the vultures—she's been . . ." He shakes his head so vigorously that it shoots me back to another life. To my childhood dog trotting out from the water and shaking himself off.

"Asher, you have to come now. Mom's been . . . killed."

———

ONE LOOK AT MY fiancée's body—what's left of it—and I dash to the side and vomit. I kneel down, scraping my hair off my face, and more comes out. More. I glance to my left and realize I'm vomiting by the grave of Odelia's ex-husband. Even now, the irony does occur to me.

I stop, panting, a glug of emotion in my throat. I'm vaguely aware of voices, sobs, screams. The sun vaulting up through the clouds, burning onto my neck. I don't know how long I kneel like this. But at some point, piercing cries jolt me to a stand. I wipe my mouth, then stumble over to the chairs that encircle the firepit. I gaze around, the evidence of the tent that housed us for last night's celebrations already swept up by the efficient staff when we moved to the firepit. The firepit flashes back at me, leaning over to roast marshmallows amid the crackle, the heat, as I sat beside Delia, our thighs pressed together, the familiar electricity between us. Her warmth and touch still caress my skin. . . .

"How . . . how . . ." Gwen. She's speaking, but nothing more coherent emits.

My vision blurs, then focuses, catching Gwen and Joshua in an awkward, almost motherly embrace. Gwen is bereft in a way I recognize . . . I know. A tightening in my chest accompanies a memory of my own mother. Joshua is rigid, his hands by his sides, allowing Gwen to squeeze him like a stress ball. I spot Sam by Delia's body, staring at his mother, his body motionless. And now I register footsteps clomping down the path. Soon Violett appears, with her luminous skin and high, lush ponytail, her lips perma-pursed, like she is prepared to volley a customer complaint.

"I've called the police, but they've said it might take time to get here," she says. "Some of the roads are still closed by Skukuza because of the recent flooding. Since they're clay soil roads, they mud up and become impossible to traverse. And it's supposed to storm again soon. So the cops'll have to come by chopper."

"H-How?" Gwen is sobbing now, crouched by Delia's hand, saying incomprehensible things, or else things I just don't feel like hearing because I have my own ticker tape of horrifying thoughts. I flit my eyes back at the body and then regret it. My throat constricts again, and I send the bile back. Odelia's hand is about all of her that remains recognizable.

"It's obvious how it happened," Joshua says quietly. He points, and I follow the line of his hand to a rifle on the ground by her body.

"Is that . . ." I start, my brain still whirling. "Is that . . . Markus's?"

"Yes," Violett says. "But I don't see why . . . I mean . . . why would Markus have killed Odelia? And left his gun right out in the open? You have to kill at a long range with that gun. It means . . . someone stood thirty meters off. Someone who knew how to shoot. And—"

"Where is he?" I ask. "Where's fucking Markus?"

"Not here," she says. "That's what I started to say. Odelia gave Markus the day off today. With the wedding . . . and you didn't have a drive planned this morning. Markus goes back home to Hazyview on his days off—it's an hour away. His car's gone, so that tracks. I checked just now . . . after I ran into Joshua . . . after . . ."

"So Markus could have killed her and then fled," I say. "But why would he have left his rifle behind?"

"Maybe—" Sam starts, but then stops. "He must have done it." Sam approaches me and stabs a meaty finger into my chest, knocking me off-kilter. "Mom's boy toy."

I step back and laugh bitterly, wiping at a tear that's brushed down my cheek. "Please. Get off me. What motive would I have to murder my fiancée?"

"What motive?" Sam grimaces. "One of the wealthiest women in America. What motive, he asks?" Sam laughs, a shrill noise.

"Money?" I pose, my voice rising. "If the motive is money, don't look at me. I get nothing. You heard her! She was going to add me to her will, but she didn't. Who inherits then? *You.*" I point at Sam, shaking now at his proximity, not wanting to touch him. "*YOU.*"

"I saw him," I hear, and it takes me a moment to associate the soft voice with Gwen. "I saw him coming out of Markus's room. I saw you, Sam."

"When?" Sam asks, after a beat of silence. "When do you think you saw me?"

"Yesterday evening." Gwen's lower lip trembles. "After I'd put Ruby to bed, I was looking out the window from Davina and Joshua's suite. They're closest to the lodge, not far from Markus's cabin. I'd seen Markus go out, duffel on his shoulder. And not much later I saw Sam at Markus's door. He must have come back during the dinner."

"Before or after he ripped his mother a new one during his wedding toast?" I ask.

Sam shoots me a penetrating glare.

"Did you see him go inside?" Joshua asks.

"No . . ."

"Or come out with the rifle?" Joshua eyes his brother warily.

"No," Gwen finally says. "Ruby started crying, and I went to her."

"And you didn't tell anyone," Sam taunts. "Convenient . . . that when you're a suspect, too, all of a sudden you start spinning a tale."

"I'm telling everyone now." Gwen puts a hand to her throat. "And I'm not spinning anyth—"

"I didn't steal Markus's gun! And I'm not trying to hide anything." Sam turns to all of us. "Gwen's right, I did go to Markus's room, but only to ask him to do a game drive this morning after all, just for me and Bailey. But he wasn't there. Anyway, I'm assuming he puts his gun in a case or a closet or something that requires a key, or a passcode. How would I possibly access something like that? Maybe Gwen—maybe you're trying to deflect. Maybe *you're* the one who took the rifle. You could have snuck out while we were all celebrating, left Ruby there on the monitor. Maybe you're the one who killed Mom! And you're trying to pin this on me."

Gwen gasps. "I would never leave Ruby alone, monitor or not. And how would I know his passcode anyway?" She stops, breathless. "I didn't kill your mother. I can't believe you'd even suggest it. She was my very best friend!"

"Yes, we know." Sam laughs mirthlessly. "But recently someone else stepped into your shoes. A man who was to be our *stepfather.*"

"How dare you." Gwen's lips are almost blue, pressed tightly together.

"Okay, stop this." I step between the two of them, before this escalates further. "This isn't helping anything."

Sam elbows me away. "And besides, I was talking to Bailey forever last night. For hours after we got back from the bonfire. There's no way I could have gone out and killed Mom. Bailey'll vouch for that."

"Speaking of . . . where *is* Bailey?" Joshua asks.

"Oh." Sam looks around uncertainly, and now the rest of us do too. "Maybe at the lodge?"

Violett shakes her head. "No. She wasn't."

"What time were you talking to Bailey until?" I ask Sam. My eyes flicker toward Odelia, and I snap them back.

She's dead. I shake my head. My fiancée is really, truly dead.

"Until at least ten after one," Sam says. "I saw the clock. Even commented on how late it was. Bailey'll tell you."

"Mom could have been murdered after that," Joshua says.

"Well, Bailey is the lightest sleeper in the world," Sam says. "So if I'd left, she'd have noticed."

"That's true," Joshua concedes.

"Well, there's an easy way to tell when Delia . . . when she died." I kneel to the ground, where Delia's phone rests beside her body, making no attempt to wipe loose tears from my cheeks.

"How?" Sam asks.

"Your mom's Apple Watch." I motion to her still intact wrist, with the watch. "It synced to the Health app on her phone. Monitored her heart rate and stuff. You know—she was big on counting her—"

"Steps," Joshua fills in. "Jeez." He mashes his palm to his forehead, his voice thick with emotion.

"Yeah. So we should be able to see when her heart stopped." I pick up the phone, punch in her passcode, feeling my own pulse ticking faster.

"You know her code?" Joshua asks, staring at me oddly.

"Of course," I say quietly. "We shared everything."

I punch it in—0301. Three children, one grandchild. I don't tell them the meaning of her code, but later I suppose I will. Their mom was sentimental, and she loved being a mother and a grandmother, even if she didn't always show it in the most stereotypical ways.

I thumb to Odelia's Health app, then scroll and stop. "See." I show them. "12:24. That's the last time the app clocked her heart rate."

Everyone crowds around me to get a view.

"See!" Sam says. "I couldn't have done it. We must have gotten back to the room around eleven, and Bailey and I stayed up talking till at least two. Ask Bails. She'll tell you! Wherever she is . . ." He looks around uncertainly.

Joshua glances about and asks again, "Where *is* Bailey?"

There is a moment that we all stare dumbly at one another. Then we launch into action—a search. We scavenge around the property, and the staff members help too. At first we're subdued, stunned by Delia's murder, unable to process, floating through the luxurious space like robots, sure Bailey will turn up any second. But then, when Bailey doesn't pop out from around a corner like we all expect, the search turns frantic. Sam bursts out of the suite he's sharing with his sister to reveal that her phone is plugged into her charger. She's gone out without her phone? Strange. Thus Gwen has the staff mobilize, splitting up to check all the rooms. Sam searches behind drapes so flimsy they are see-through, but what do I know? What can I say? I have zero clue where Bailey is, even if I don't think she's liable to be playing hide-and-seek.

We'll find her; we must. All my emotion is so heavy in my body, I feel like I'm lugging boulders. If I allow myself to dive inside it, I know I'm going to collapse.

At some point amid the tumult, Davina emerges into the lodge, Ruby strapped to her chest.

"Odelia . . . *and* Bailey . . . no. I don't believe . . . Bails, where's Bails? She has to be here."

"We'll find Bailey," I try to reassure her, my chest still a tornado of funneled grief.

Davina dashes frantically around, and again, we all look in the storage closets and offices, across the grounds and the lodge. We even push our way into the kitchen. As if Bailey's stumbled into the freezer. (We check there too.)

Every nook and cranny is probed until we are finally forced to acknowledge: Bailey is nowhere to be found.

# CHAPTER SIXTEEN

# VIOLETT

It's chaos until the police officers finally arrive from Skukuza. There was some hullabaloo about getting a chopper pilot. Unsurprising—besides weather issues, the police around here often have the reputation of being bumbling idiots, taking forever to do things. Also, sometimes chopper pilots are drunk. It's not unusual to have to wait for them to sober up. It's served me, though, having some time to think things through while the officers delay and then are finally en route.

I greet the chopper as it lands, and four officers spill out. I instantly recognize the ones in charge. Whenever we have poaching incidents nearby, they spearhead the hunt for the criminals. I shoot my shoulders back and try to make my face look innocent. Then I shake brisk hands with Officer Lerato Monala, a Black woman in her midfifties who is so tall that even I have to crane my neck up to meet her eyes. In previous interactions due to poaching issues, I've found her to be quietly astute, listening more than talking, but then sharply identifying the best way forward.

"How you?" Officer Monala says, at the same time as I say, "Howzit?"

"Ah, shame." I grimace. "Okay, fine. Show you the way?"

"*Ja.*"

Next I exchange greetings and extend my hand to Officer Johannes Botha, a paunchy, bald white man who has the tendency to clear his throat in a grand way and say, "*Sjoe,* I wonder if . . ." as if he's about to crack the case with some very wise insight and then finish, "I wonder if I could get some more coffee! Powers the brain." And then looks at me like he expects me to be impressed at the huge size of his brain. And like why am I not hustling off for his coffee?

Privately, I've suspected him in the past of having connections to the poachers and making an undercover cut, thereby intentionally letting them get off. Not a surprise—police are often corrupt; bribery here is the order of the day, how you get out of any speeding ticket or the like. I've considered reporting Officer Botha, even talked it over with Ouma, but I never did. Because Ouma and I both worried it could come back to bite me, and I couldn't risk losing this job.

It occurs to me that a potentially corrupt officer could be an asset now.

I show the officers to the *boma*, the firepit, and around the crime scene, where their lackeys begin cordoning off areas with tape. This conjures a memory, another time with officers and tape, and I shrug that from my mind, prickles in my heart. One of the officers is bagging up the rifle. Another is bent over the body—I don't look. It's raining now, lightly, but heavier rain is forecast, and so the officers are working quickly, inspecting footprints and the like, I presume. Not that they'll be able to tell anything from them. The entire family—and me—have been traipsing about the bonfire area, both last night and today, so I find it unlikely they'll be able to discern the murderer's footsteps from everyone else's.

"Where are they?" Officer Monala asks. "The family?" Her eyes flit skyward, where it's now more gray than blue. "Shame, we need to get a move on. The weather isn't going to wait. And we won't be able to take off in lightning."

I nod. I knew this; in fact, it pleased me as I watched the forecast shift in the last week, portending storms on Odelia's wedding day.

"*Ag*, the family is in the lodge. In hysterics." As it comes out, I wonder if I sound heartless, but Officer Monala just nods.

"Let's go," she says to Officer Botha, and from that I glean she is in charge.

I can't decide whether or not I'm thankful that someone competent is.

When I enter the dining room, where I asked Jabulani to watch over the family, to tend to their needs but also to make sure no one leaves, the first thing I notice is that the baby is crying. Funny how those small creatures can make the loudest noises. It's like we learned as adults to restrain ourselves, but perhaps that's not always a good thing. I look anywhere but at Ruby, my insides tight, squeezed in a wince. I'm angry. Red-hot. But I can't show it. Rain pummels the windows and the world looks bleak, mirroring the mood inside. As the officers begin their interrogations, I whip the staff into action, to serve hot teas and coffee. Maybe some pastries, too, soothing carbohydrates to console the family in their mounting worries about Bailey, in their fresh mourning over Odelia.

Even though that bitch doesn't deserve to be mourned.

———

SAM DRUMS HIS MEATY fingers on the table in a way that makes me want to reach over and rip his hand off his wrist. Then every few seconds, he pauses his drumming fingers, flips his phone over, and says, "Nothing. Joshua?"

And Joshua shakes his head and rubs his eyes. "Nothing."

Ruby, now her happy self again, smiles up at her father from her bassinet, and Joshua manages a sad smile back. He tickles Ruby's chin and she wiggles her whole body and gurgles with delight.

"Where *is* she?" Sam says. "Where's Bails?"

"That is the magic question," says Officer Monala. "And where is Markus Bloomfield? That's another."

"Who killed Odelia Babel is another magic question," Officer Botha says with verve. He wiggles his pants up over his protruding stomach and reaches for another *melktert*.

Officer Monala manages the herculean task of preventing her eyes from rolling. "Now, as I've said, we will be conducting an interview with each of you individually, but first we wished to gather you all together. To see, collectively, what you have to say."

"Who we think did it, you mean," Joshua says.

"That too. But also what you noticed, what sticks out—"

"Last night," Asher says quietly, then stops, like continuing is taxing him beyond that which he can bear.

I look at him, really take him in—Odelia's second husband. It's not that he fades into a corner. He is really quite handsome and magnetic, but quieter than her, more thoughtful. When I heard about their age gap, I thought what everyone thinks. Gold digger. But then I overheard the family talking about it—how Asher has his own money; apparently, he's very successful. And Odelia didn't even provide for him in her will. Not yet, although she was planning on it. Still, there is something about the guy—he's too . . . perfect. Always saying and doing the apparently right thing. I don't trust him. But I do grant that he looks very genuinely sad now.

"Last night," Asher says, his voice raw. "Last night, Odelia had words with several of her children."

"Had words?" Officer Monala asks.

"Fought with," Asher says, but reluctantly, not appearing to relish in it. "Sam—"

"I told you I was with Bailey!" Sam erupts. "I couldn't have done it. I'm literally the only one, other than Bailey, who has an ironclad—"

"Where is Bailey, though?" Joshua erupts, his hands springing out from his sides. "I want to know where Bailey is, Sam!"

"You think I know? You think I'd ever do anything to her?"

"You did say quite horrible things to your mother," Asher says in a low, calm voice. "And I know you need money. I'm sure we all know that . . . for how many times you've asked just this trip."

Sam darts his eyes around, the prominent vein in his neck bulging. "I didn't kill my mother! I don't care what you all say. I didn't kill her! I swear it on Bailey's life. I didn't!"

"I don't know what to think." Joshua shakes his head, his face pinched. "I just can't believe . . . Mom . . . and now Bailey. I can't understand . . . where did she go . . . where did Bailey possibly go? I was supposed to meet her this morning at the bonfire p—"

"Why?" Officer Monala interjects.

"Why . . . what?"

"Why were you going to meet your sister so early?" Officer Botha asks, cutting off his partner, leaning forward with piercing concentration. "And why not at the lodge?"

"We . . ." I can see Joshua's mind working. I've never known him to lie, but of course, I don't know him well. Just the casual chats we have when he's here. But from them I've gleaned that he is honest. Kind. That he operates with integrity. Something about his reaction gives me pause, though. Like he's hiding something.

What could Joshua be hiding?

"S'okay," Officer Monala says. "We will adjourn to talk to you all privately soon. You can tell me then. You *will* tell me then."

"*Ja*, you will tell us," Officer Botha adds importantly. "You will tell us everything."

This time I can't restrain my own eye roll. When my eyes return to their resting place, they fix on the breakfast buffet draped in ivory silks and satin. Odelia wanted the entire wedding day to be special and spectacular, start to finish. I think of all the cooking and baking over which Arno has presided, of the truckloads of flowers delivered yesterday and the couture dress and veil that Ahmale already painstakingly steamed. All for naught.

And I think of the wedding cake that Arno worked so hard on—the four-tier masterpiece in white fondant with a smattering of king proteas, the national South African flower. I thought it interesting that Odelia wanted that especially, given that her late husband was the one of South African origin, not she. The flower signifies strength. Courage. Resilience. It survives in extreme climates. But all I felt looking at the spectacular cake was bitterness. Because if anyone signifies the qualities of that flower, it is not her, but me.

Officer Monala turns to Asher. "Which other child did Odelia fight with?"

Asher fans his face. "I'm sorry?" he asks, his eyes bobbing around, landing on the spectacular breakfast spread. He stares at it numbly, and I realize for the first time: this was meant to be his wedding day too.

"You said Odelia fought with several of her children. Sam and—"

"Joshua," Asher says.

"When?" Officer Monala asks, just as Joshua whips his head around.

"We didn't fight! Just . . . talked."

Asher shrugs with a wary cast to him. "You came to our suite and summoned your mother. And then you shouted at each other. That's how I remember it, at least."

"We didn't shout." Joshua says it calmly, but his dark eyes are blazing.

"Did anyone hear this fight?" Officer Monala asks.

"I certainly didn't," Davina says.

"You were drunk, though," Asher says, a bit apologetically. "And it happened in our suite. It sure sounded like a fight to me."

In a flash I see—the fall. The crack. Her reaching for me, and then . . . gone.

I clap my hand over my mouth.

"Violett?"

I shake my head, willing myself back to the present moment. Officer Monala is looking at me oddly, as if she's managed to snoop inside my brain.

"Yes?"

"Did you hear this fight? Or did any of the staff?"

"Shame, I did not. I went to sleep after we cleared the bonfire. *Ag*, so hectic today. Or was supposed to be . . ."

I force myself to meet the officer's eyes, hoping she can't see through all my lies. "You must check with the rest of the staff. Perhaps someone else heard."

"*Ja*," Officer Monala says thoughtfully. "Shame you didn't hear. And Gwen? Did you hear this fight?"

For the first time this morning, I look at Gwen, really look at her. Her gray-green eyes are vacant, her cheeks ghostly pale. She looks despondent, like a cardboard cutout of herself. Officer Monala waves a hand in Gwen's face, causing her to snap to. "Oh. Sorry. I heard . . . yes, I . . ." She shakes her head. "I just can't understand. I can't understand anything."

Davina slips an arm around her shoulders and says, "Shhhh, it's okay."

"It's not," Gwen says. "It's *not* okay. This is all my fault."

"What do you mean by that?" Officer Monala asks sharply.

"I mean . . ." A hush falls over the room as we all wait for Gwen to continue. "The tarot cards," she says, inconsolable now. "I gave them readings. I gave them both readings."

"Oh." Officer Monala straightens, and I can tell she's disappointed. "You're some sort of . . . psychic?"

"You may make fun of me, Officer, but the tarot cards aren't wrong. They're dangerously accurate here. For Odelia, they predicted dark things. The Death card, but I thought—"

Gwen stops, her eyes rolling back, thinking. "Where is her necklace?"

"Her necklace?" Officer Botha says.

"Her locket," Asher explains. "She always wore it. Actually I didn't see it anywhere. I wondered . . ."

Officer Botha rises to consult with one of the officers who has come in from outdoors. When he returns, he says, "There was no necklace."

"Maybe one of the vultures flew off with it," Joshua says.

"Unlikely," Officer Monala says. "Necklace, you say—"

"A locket. A gold locket." Gwen describes it.

Officer Monala makes a notation in her notebook and then swirls a spoon in her teacup, looking out into the mid-distance.

"Are you going to send out a search party for Bailey?" Joshua asks. "Please, you have to find—"

"We already have," Officer Monala says. "Rest assured we are going to find your sister. But it is starting to rain now. The search will be more difficult. We will have to wait it out."

"They'll find her," Davina says. "Joshua, they're going to find her." I can tell Davina is a woman with strong convictions. A woman who is often right. Joshua looks at his wife, like he needs very much to believe her.

"You really think?"

But then Davina falters. "I . . . yes, I do." She nods staunchly, but in her moment of doubt, I can tell she's lost Joshua. Davina pulls him to her chest, and he weeps openly on her shoulder. I chew on my lip, feeling something break inside me, too, that I need to stay contained.

"The elephant," Gwen says, crying herself, pulling hairs from her scalp like she always does. "You have to go to the elephant!" Her eyes are enormous and urgent, like a child claiming there are monsters under the bed. "That's where you'll find Bailey. I'm sure of it."

"The elephant?" Joshua eases his face up from Davina's shoulder and wipes his eyes. "What are you talking about?"

"Yes, what elephant?" Asher asks.

"I don't know," Gwen says, "I wasn't on your game drive. But it was in the reading. The elephant is the key to everything. I know it!"

Officer Monala eyes Officer Botha, and this time I can tell the two of them are in aligned agreement: Gwen is a bit of a loon.

"Okay," Officer Monala says. "We'd like to speak to each of you individually and—"

"You'll follow up on the elephant, though, won't you?" Gwen asks frantically. "Talk to Markus about—"

"Don't worry, of course we want to speak with Markus. His rifle appears to be what killed Odelia, after all. We are locating him," Officer Monala says.

"You haven't found him yet?" Davina asks in surprise.

"Not yet. We will." Officer Monala presses her hands against the tabletop and eases to a stand.

"The elephant! The mother elephant." Gwen shoots up, too, yanking at her hair. "I swear, I know what I'm saying. Bailey must have gone after it. I'll do another reading. Let's see what the cards say!"

"Oh my word," I say under my breath. This woman is certifiable.

"That's— I'll keep the offer in mind," Officer Monala finally says. "Now we'd like to speak to each of you. Violett, you first. And the rest of you—stay close."

"Certainly," I say, my mind whirling. Me first. But why? Could they know about the blackmail? No, they won't have already probed Odelia's financial records. They certainly will, but not quite yet.

In which case I plan to tell the officers a version of the truth now— a version that omits some things. Because I'm not finished with my plans here. Not even close.

# CHAPTER SEVENTEEN

# GWEN

After my interview, I stumble out of the lodge into apocalyptic rain.
"Gwen! Gwen!"

Voices muddle in my ears, then crystallize. Joshua. Davina. I continue out into the day so dark it feels like night. Something about the rain makes everything that seems so horrifically unreal disappear for the moment.

A fleeting shoot of relief, then it's back, the dread that's drowning me. "Gwen! Come back!"

I don't turn around. I know if I do, I'm going to be asked about my interrogation. I'm going to say things I shouldn't, because right now, I forget what I'm supposed to conceal and what I'm allowed to disclose.

I continue along the walk, instantly drenched, fighting sudden gusts of wind. I have to find the locket. Before it gets into the wrong hands.

Back at the firepit, the world is wet and angry. Tape cordoning off the crime scene snaps in the downpour and detaches from the stake, flaps at my face like those elastic slap bracelets the kids once had. Odelia's body is gone, the footprints all erased, turned to mud.

"No," I scream, tipping my face to the slate sky. "How could you? How could you?"

God answers back casually, with more rain.

I dive to the ground, choking from my sobs. The first time I've cried this much since the accident all those years ago. The mucky ground sags beneath my knees as I scoop up the earth, digging for the locket.

As I kneel, I can't stop the memory assailing me: Odelia admiring herself in the mirror just last night, saying *I love you so much* to me. Gripping me tight, telling me that if anything happens to her I should look inside her locket.

What did she mean by that? Why didn't I probe?

I think about the locket, its cavernous interior. Most have just enough room to store a photo, but our trio of lockets were bigger. Not flat but protruding. Box-shaped. Where each of us once stored a copy of the same key.

A fleeting recollection that yanks me back—the three of us chortling in Odelia's parents' shed in Hollywood (the Hollywood in south Florida, teeming with Modern Orthodox Jews instead of outposts of Chanel). Rachel's just moved and it's been instant, how we've absorbed her into our fold. We can't stop asking Rachel to say British words. At our cajoling she must repeat, "Would you like a biscuit?," exaggerating the word *biscuit* a million times.

Odelia's parents are kind; her father is a well-respected rabbi, but for a religious authority he's surprisingly soft, unassuming, and yet witty and self-deprecating. Odelia's mother is a *balabusta*, the perfect homemaker and an amazing cook, and she's opinionated and spicy and loud. Like Odelia. They let us use their shed as our clubhouse; I think they know that Rachel and I don't have such warm, fuzzy family situations. Maybe that's why we both glom onto Odelia like magnets. Anytime I hear my father's plodding footsteps, or hear his rage-filled voice, I sneak out my window and beeline to Odelia's backyard, straining at the shed with the little key, terrified my father will follow after and spoil my hiding place. And Odelia's always there to take me into her arms, to tell me it will be okay, that we are sisters and sisters protect each other. Always.

I cry out again now, something shrieking and awful, a hurricane of pain in my chest. Pain for my best friend, who shielded me from my father's abuse when I needed her to. Pain for me, too, that I didn't protect her enough after that portentous tarot reading, when I should have known she needed me. Even worse, perhaps, I let her go to her death without celebrating her happy ending with Asher like she well deserved. Celebrating her with my whole soul.

I wipe my eyes, scanning the area, trying to discern beyond the sheets of rain a place where the locket could be. I know the police didn't find it—

I heard them whisper so. It must be caught somewhere. Hidden. Buried. Where?

I haven't worn my locket in decades, but Odelia never takes hers off. I understand why, but I don't understand why she told me to look inside it. Of course, when I answered the officers' questions, I avoided telling them that part.

———

I'M NOT SURE HOW much time passes as I dig frantically around— a minute, an hour, could be either. But all of a sudden, I hear my name again, and this time, when I turn, they're all there. My family, sort of— what's left of them.

Davina, Joshua, and Asher. Sam too.

"Have they found Bailey?" I ask.

Joshua shakes his head. "Not yet."

"They'll check the elephant, won't they? That's where . . . I know it, Bailey will—" I gasp. "The elephant. That's where."

"I . . . I'm sure they'll look for her there." Rain cascades down the planes of Joshua's face. "But Gwen—"

"And the cops? They're not looking?"

"They left," Joshua says. "You didn't hear the chopper?"

"No." My heart is in my throat. "I was— I was—" Crouched over the toilet bowl, throwing up last night's meal. Venison from the prewedding party, delivered by Jabulani to the suite since I only stayed for appetizers before Ruby was ready to go down.

"How could the cops just *go*?"

"It's mmmming," Asher says, drowned out by the rain.

"What?"

"It's storming!" he yells, as if I can't tell, just as lightning crackles and shakes the earth. Every time it hits, which is frequent now, a row of vertical spikes light up throughout the bush, making the trees glow, which is beautiful and also eerie. Asher gestures us under a nylon awning the police set up, and we all move over and huddle beneath. "The police had to get back before the storm, otherwise they'd be stuck here. Gwen, come inside with us."

"Why didn't they arrest Sam?" I point toward him. "I don't understand I saw you in Markus's room. You must have taken his rifle!"

"That's ludicrous," Sam says, his usual defiant. "Why would I do such a thing?"

"You hated her."

No response—he can't refute the truth.

But my heart races as I think about what I claimed to the police, as I wonder if my memories are even true or just more lies to heap upon the pile. "And you fought with Odelia. You hate your mother—hated—and now you'll inherit—"

"But Sam claims to have an alibi during the time of the murder," Davina says, flickering her eyes at her brother-in-law. "And anyway—anyway—"

"Sam wasn't the only one who fought with Mom late last night," Joshua says. "You can say it. *I* did." He hangs his head.

Davina doesn't look at Joshua, just says, "And Bailey and Markus are missing is what I was going to say. The cops don't think anyone's in danger." Though she sounds doubtful. "They said they'll be back to question us further when they have more information."

"More information . . ." My heart contracts. "Like what?"

Asher shrugs. "Finding Bailey, to see if she'll corroborate Sam's alibi or not. Finding Markus too. And reading the will," he adds. "I assume that will be of some relevance."

"The will." I feel my breath suck in. "We have to find Bailey. I can't believe the cops left like that! Left us here. Left her out there—without sending out official search parties."

"They did send out search parties, but with the rain they've had to pause. They said we're not to leave," Asher says.

"Where would we go?" I reach for my hair, tugging, pulling. I wait for the relief to flood in, but it doesn't. "And why aren't they looking for Bailey? They have to look for her! At the elephant, I told them—"

"Gwen, they can't look for Bailey now. Not in this weather," Joshua says, exchanging a glance with Asher, like they're having to reason with a nutcase. "They said they'll send search parties and choppers as soon as the storm passes. And anyway, they want to perform an autopsy, on the . . . remains. See if they can find any further evidence."

"Evidence, *pah*. You saw the same sight I did. You think there was any evidence left?"

"Come with us, Gwen. Please. Dry off." Davina extends a hand.

"No!" I shrink back and duck outside of the awning. "I need to find the locket."

"It's not here, Gwen." Joshua kneels down and reaches for my forearm, right as hail pelts down. It hurts my scalp, my face—but it also reminds me that I'm still alive. That I can avenge my best friend's death if I just think and find the locket.

"Come on," Joshua urges, reaching out to pull me back. "It's not safe out here."

"No!" I snap out of his grip. "Not until I find the locket. And if they won't look for Bailey, I will."

"How?" Asher asks. "It's hailing now. We have to wait this out. No matter how difficult it is. It will let up, and we can go out and search. But we can't do anything for Bailey now."

I press my hands over my ears, trying to drown them out. I reach for a clump of hair, sopping wet. But still I find the roots and yank. The pain is sharp, knifelike, but doesn't last nearly long enough.

I rub my scalp, then dig again in the ground. All of a sudden, I spot something shiny. My heart surges, and I yank it up. Damnit, just a glinting rock! Disappointment barrages me.

Asher kneels down too. "Gwen, really, it's not safe to be out in this storm." As if in punctuation of his concerns, lightning crackles in the distance.

"Today was your wedding day," I say numbly. "Rain is supposed to be good luck."

Asher nods grimly. "Delia would have hated this weather."

"*Hated* it. On that we can agree."

Asher stands and joins the others back beneath the awning. Of course, they're talking about me, how to get crazy Gwen inside. Maybe one or all of them have ulterior motives, want me not to find the locket. I stare up at them: Asher gathering his sopping hair off his neck. Sam checking his phone again, shielding it from the rain with his shirt. Davina with an arm looped around Joshua. Joshua shifting his weight from left to right, thrusting a hand into his pocket. . . .

"Oh!" I bolt up.

"What?" They all stare at me, perplexed.

My mind replays what I just saw. Puzzle pieces rejigger. I wonder . . . I wonder if—

"Oh god, I—" I stand frozen, finally convince my neck to move my head side to side. "Nothing. I-I thought I found the locket."

"But you didn't?" Joshua stares at me oddly.

"No. I didn't." I accept Davina's arm. "Okay, let's go back. I'm done here."

I'm speaking the truth, at least. I don't need the locket after all. I have what I need. I just have to piece things together now, before I confront him.

# CHAPTER EIGHTEEN

# JOSHUA

Ruby is hysterical, emitting a shrill screech/scream at a decibel you wouldn't think possible to come from such a tiny human. But it *is* possible, a fact of which I am aware every time I try to sift through my thoughts as yet another earsplitting Ruby wail causes them to scatter.

Davina keeps trying to mush Ruby's face into her breasts, to feed her into submission, as we sometimes joke. It usually works, but Ruby's having none of it, just keeps wriggling and roaring, her skin—normally pale like mine—now a splotchy tomato red.

"It's like she knows what's happening around her," I say.

"Of course she does." Dav wriggles her boob so Ruby gets a good latch. "Babies can read energy better than anyone. She probably knows who did it."

"Who did what?" I wonder if Davina's going to say, took Bailey. Or even worse. *Killed* my sister. I suck in my breath.

Bailey has to be okay. She has to. I can't let my mind go anywhere else.

"Who killed your mom. What did you think I meant?"

I press my fist against my trembling lips. "Bailey. Bailey's what I thought you meant—"

What if Gwen's right? What if my sister really went off on some quest to save an elephant? I shake my head—it sounds insane. Bailey is the most levelheaded, thoughtful one in our family. Even if she worried or wondered, she wouldn't go out at night into the bush by herself. She'd know that's akin to a suicide mission. Which means . . .

"What if whoever killed Mom also killed Bailey?" I whisper.

"No," Dav says firmly. "Don't go there, Joshua. Bailey's going to be okay. They're going to find her. Anyway, if the person who killed Odelia killed Bailey, don't you think her body'd have been there too?"

"I don't know. I don't know how this murderer's fucked-up mind works." I take a few deep breaths as a question rises to the top of my mind. "Dav . . . you didn't, like . . . I mean, you were sleeping the whole night, right?"

"I was right there next to you," she says sharply.

"I know. I slept like the dead." I stop, realize what I've said. "I know you didn't kill my mother. Of course I do. But I also know you argued last night—"

"About me being Circ's plus-size model! Trust me, Joshua, I'm not hurting for work. I'll find other stuff, and my Substack is blowing up. I wouldn't kill your mother over a work dispute."

It's not only a work dispute. It's her texting Asher, too, behind my back, basically. And my mother's back too. But I don't have the energy to get into that right now. "I know, I'm just saying—"

"You're saying you don't fully trust me is what you're saying."

"I do trust you," I protest, but I know it sounds weak. False.

"Look at me, Joshua." I force my eyes to meet hers, which are fierce and angry. I've seen her eyes that way, seen her when she gets riled up, but we've always been on the same side before. It's been her defending *me*, against my mother, against the world. And now . . .

"I didn't kill your mother. But apparently, you fought with her too. Not that you told me about that until it came out when were with the officers. You could have gotten up in the middle of the night too. We both slept like the dea— We both slept deeply, it sounds like, after I pumped and dumped and fed Ruby that bottle when I got in. Thank god she slept a few hours, after her jet lag bonanza that first night." Davina glances down at Ruby sucking happily. "Little night terrorist."

Davina and I stare at each other, but don't say anything more. It's like— How has it come to this? We aren't really suspecting each other—are we?

My phone bleeps, startling me. Bailey?

I grab it and see a text from Sam:

*Went out to look for Bailey with Titus but it's raining too hard. Bridges are flooded. We have to come back.*

My breath stalls. I stab back: *No sign of her?*

The ellipses of Sam typing, then: *Nothing, but we didn't make it far. Still, I don't understand where she could be in this weather.*

I sit on the bed and look numbly out the window, watching rain pelting the deck. Then I shake my head at Davina, stand, and go wordlessly toward the closet. I peel off my shirt, then my pants, balling them up and throwing them in the hamper with force. I stare at the hamper, wanting to take it and turn it over and throw it across the room and roar. But I don't. All that rage twists in my chest as I shrug back on a dry shirt and pants.

"Joshua, can you bring me a diaper?" My fists ball at my sides at the sound of Dav's voice. It's new, this surge of antagonism toward her. Maybe I'm just mourning—maybe it's the anger over finding Mom like I did, and Bailey missing. Maybe it's that my last moments with Mom were shouting at her. Or maybe it's that my wife was texting Asher last night behind my back. If she was hiding that, then what else do I not know?

"One sec!"

I switch off the lamp with its bronze base that illuminates the walk-in closet. I have a nagging feeling I'm forgetting something, and suddenly I remember—the locket. I dig it out of my pocket, my stomach twisting. I can't believe I almost forgot that I had it, that I lied to the police about finding it. After I discovered Mom's body, I had the fleeting thought that I should hide the necklace somewhere on the property, in case the police eventually searched me, but then I forgot to do so. And thankfully, though they did search our rooms, they didn't search my person. Maybe they didn't think the necklace was very important. Or maybe they bought my theory that a vulture flew off with it.

I bounce the locket in my hand. Then I snap it open and I'm only half-shocked when I pull out a mini USB flash drive—not even an inch in length.

I stare at it for a few beats, my brain whirling.

God, I know exactly what this is. And I don't want to face it.

Damn you, Mom. Damn you!

There's sudden banging on the door. I hasten out of the closet, stuffing the flash drive back into the locket and slipping it inside my pocket.

"Who is it?" Davina asks.

"Dunno, maybe Gwen. Or Bailey!"

I throw open the door, hope surging in my chest.

But it's not my sister, or Gwen. It's Violett. She's drenched, hair slick to her scalp, her umbrella at her side, misshapen, ravaged by the wind and rain.

"Have you . . . found Bailey?" I ask, but already my hope's fading, because I realize she would have said so right away.

"Unfortunately, no." She smiles sadly at me. "Joshua, I . . . I'm so sorry. I'm so very sorry. With everything . . . I feel like I haven't adequately expressed that."

"Oh. Thank you."

"Joshua," she whispers. She comes closer, but doesn't hug me. She smells like gardenias—I remember that somehow, from how we used to chat when I was a kid, when she was watching us or tidying up our suite. "Joshua, it's okay to fall apart."

"What— What do you mean?" I ask.

"I mean you're the one who holds your family together. I always thought that. Not your mother. Not your father. You. But sometimes the person who holds everything together needs to fall apart."

Her words do something to me, make something start to break inside me, and I feel tears at my eyes. But they stop midstream when a voice snags me back.

"Joshua?" Davina says, sounding weary. "Do you mind taking Ruby for a little? I just want to close my eyes for a few minutes." When I turn, I see Davina brandishing a gurgling Ruby, smiling as though she wasn't scorching earth with her cries only a couple minutes prior. Dav's eyes flit from me to Violett. I can't tell what she's thinking.

I avoid my wife's gaze and reach for Ruby. "Violett was here to express her condolences."

"Oh."

"That's not it," Violett says. "Not *just* it. I wanted to see if you would like help with the baby. Gwen is—well—"

I nod. We don't need to say it, the thing we all are thinking. Gwen's manic with grief.

"Hi, baby," I say, trying to imbue a lightness to my voice I don't feel. I take Ruby and thrust her above my head like she likes, and she gurgles with delight. But my arms stiffen, put out by the exertion.

"We're quite fine, thank you," Davina says tightly.

I feel myself shift uncomfortably, returning Ruby to chest level. Davina clearly didn't like seeing me in deep, familiar conversation with Violett. Violett is beautiful, granted, cheeks always pink, full lips.

"Dav, I—"

How to say it, that Dav needs support. That we both do. That we're both on the precipice of losing it, and we need help, and clearly Gwen won't be up to lending a hand. How to say that I want to collapse, and I need to take care of some things. I could tick off the to-dos to Davina, like email Mom's lawyer and relay the news, and request a copy of the will. Notify Circ's board. Ask the lawyers to draw up a press release for me to review. But I won't tell her the other stuff, like checking the USB, if I muster up the courage to face what's on it. And I certainly won't tell my wife that I need space from her. That I can barely look at her, that her flirting and texting with Asher are making me question things.

No, that has to be back burner now.

"Violett's very trustworthy," I finally say. "She used to watch us sometimes here. And Dav, you're overexhausted. I am too. Even though we had uninterrupted sleep last night, it was what—four hours? We need to rest. And I'd really like to . . . have a moment with my feelings and thoughts. I'm sure you would too." I rub my forehead. "And . . . I need to email the board and Mom's lawyer."

"About the will?"

I nod. "And when the rain lets up, I'm gonna go search for Bailey."

"Well . . ." Before Davina can continue, Violett reaches for Ruby.

"You—" I start to say that Ruby can be finicky around strangers, but my daughter makes her cute belly grunt, smiling at Violett.

"Yes, hello. Hello there, sweet Ruby!" Violett offers an open smile to Davina. "I can watch her here, while you rest. So she's close by, and you don't worry."

I look at my wife, and our eyes engage in a silent conversation.

"Yes, okay, thank you, Violett," Davina finally says, to my enormous relief. "I was up a while last night after the celebration feeding this one—" She eyes Ruby with fondness. "And then the stress of . . . Odelia and Bailey. I'm going to lie down."

"We'll be here, won't we, Ruby?" Violett smiles. "While Mama rests?"

"Mom," Davina says, and I watch her soften. "I'm just Mom."

"We'll be here while Mom closes her eyes."

"Thank you," Davina says gratefully, depositing a kiss on Ruby's head and then walking toward the bed.

"I'll go to the lodge, then," I say. "Take care of . . . things. And when it stops raining, I'm going to search for Bailey."

"Okay." Davina throws the covers back. "I'll come for lunch in a bit, okay? Hey, check on Gwen, too, J? You don't think she's doing anything crazy, like going out to search for Bailey in this weather by herself?"

"I'll check on her," I promise. I return to the closet, slip on a raincoat, and grab my things. Then I head over to the bed and crouch down to give my wife a hug.

"I can't believe this day," Davina says, her voice throaty with emotion.

My chest crimps, but I force myself to pull it together. "I know," I murmur against her hair.

I untangle from my wife, then walk back over to the entry, where Violett is holding Ruby. "Bye, Ruby-Rube." I kiss my daughter's soft cheek. Then, not thinking, I kiss Violett's cheek too.

"Oh!" she exclaims, but not in a bad way.

"Oh, I—" I catch Davina looking at me with narrowed eyes. "That . . . I didn't mean to—thanks, Violett. I'll see you all . . ."

I mumble something else that I'm not sure are words and duck out of the suite into the torrential but somehow welcoming rain.

# CHAPTER NINETEEN

# GWEN

I let them escort me to my suite, assure them that I'm fine, as fine as one can be on this horrific day. Then I sit on my bed, sopping wet, and stare at a painting composed of splashes and blobs of red and black paint that apparently represent artistic expression. Am I making too much of this suspicion of mine? No. It has to be . . . My brain whirls, and then I gasp at a memory. From the rehearsal dinner, before I departed with Ruby. Oy . . . so it's true. So he—

Tears are rolling down my cheeks as I reach for my tarot cards on the nightstand. I shuffle them, dripping water onto the cards. My tears, or the rain, I'm not even sure. This is my favorite deck, and I'm ruining them, making them soggy, but what does that matter?

*What do I do?* I ask the cards and pull.

Knight of Swords.

I stare at the knight in his armor, brandishing his sword, charging ahead on his powerful horse. Wind barrels toward the knight, but he continues forth on his mission. He doesn't let the wind stop him. He doesn't let anything stop him. The Knight of Swords doesn't hang back waiting for something to happen. He makes the first move.

The first move . . .

*Think, Gwen!*

I scan the room, my eyes landing on the heavy brass lamp base. I don't stop to second-guess—the Knight moves swiftly. I scoot over, grab the base, and yank off the lampshade. I unscrew the bulb, my hands shaking so hard it takes a bit of wiggling to get it off, and I bend down to yank the plug from the wall. Then I wrap the cord around the base and stuff the whole thing beneath my raincoat, which I haven't even removed.

I vault up from the bed, my mind cycling forward. I'll go to his suite— don't care who hears. I will call him out in front of anyone. This ends now. And if he retaliates, I have protection.

Down the wooden walk, to his suite, but he's not there.

Oh, I bet I know where he's gone.

I stalk down the walk again. I'm the only one seemingly outside in this entire place. Understandably, in these conditions. It's impossible to see an inch beyond my face as the rain rushes down like an angry God. And for good reason—betrayal of the highest order has been done. I can't believe I missed it. All the signs and clues. It was staring at me right in the face this whole time.

As I make my way slowly, sadness swells over me. The anger and fear are still there, but momentarily recede. I am desolate at the tragedies that curl forth like tsunamis. Desolate at the part I've played. My best friend taken from me . . . and before her, another . . . and now, maybe Bailey—but why?

If it's possible, the rain seems to accelerate its tempo. In a few minutes, I've made it back to the familiar high ground, the firepit, overlooking the river not fifty feet away.

My bones are cold, my hands chapped. I look around but see nothing. Maybe I was wrong. Maybe—

I spot a flicker of movement behind a tree. It's him, walking toward me. "Looking for me?"

————

I TIGHTEN MY GRIP on the lamp base beneath my coat.

"I know what you did! I know everything. I can't believe I didn't see— that I was so stupid—and oblivious. But you're—you're not going to get away with it. This ends now . . ." My teeth are chattering wildly, my tears mixing with the rain. "This has to end now! Please . . ."

Shame bubbles up. The Knight isn't supposed to beg. The Knight isn't supposed to cry.

I tremble as he reaches beneath his raincoat and pulls something out. I'm startled—it takes a moment to process. He's brandishing the exact lamp base I'm clutching beneath my own coat. Like we both had the same idea. A duel of lamps.

I unveil my own, and instead of looking at all intimidated, he laughs.

"Great minds, eh?"

I scramble back from him, toward Aryeh's headstone, but he pushes forward. "It was you—" I sob. And I point at him—manage to get my pointer finger right up into the thing that proved it to me.

Suddenly he's vicious, like a snake up to my face. "And you take no responsibility for your part?"

"I'm sorry! I'm so sorry. If I could go back—"

"Well, you can't. The damage has been long done."

"I'm so sorry," I say again, and I really do mean it.

He raises the bronze lamp base and I mirror him, but, my god, it's heavy, and slippery, and I don't even get it to eyebrow level. Odelia kept telling me I needed to work out with her trainer. Lectures about sarcopenia and losing muscle mass every decade.

"We're past the point of sorries, don't you think? Look, I didn't want to do this. It was her. She's the one truly responsible . . . but I knew you figured it out, and so—I guess I'm sorry too."

I freeze—everything's in slow motion as he aims his elbow at my bronze base, knocking it easily from my hands. I watch in horror as my only means of defense topples to the mud. When my eyes return to the scene directly before me, it's his base I see launching in the air, far above his head, before it starts the descent down toward me. I scream and throw my hands up toward my head, but it's too late.

Crash. Impact.

And in the moments before I lose consciousness, I think: *the irony*. I've lived only hours without my best friend, my first venture out of her shadow. And now I'll be condemned back into it.

In heaven or in hell, wherever I'm heading to join her.

# CHAPTER TWENTY

# ASHER

You have to eat when you're in mourning—that's what Jabulani insisted as he led me to the dining room, propping an umbrella up over my head as we pass through the breezeway. A friendly face where the rest of them are anything but, as I force a few bites of some vegan muesli thing into my mouth and survey the odd detritus of my would-be wedding. Flowers, the buffet draped in silk. I'm reminded of Delia's dress still hanging in our closet—her scent on the sheets. . . .

I stifle a sob. I truly loved Odelia. No matter what any of them thinks.

"I don't understand where Bailey is," Sam says. Grace gently slides our plates in front of us and then retreats. Sam grips his burger and bites, spraying meat juice straight across the table my way. He chews quickly, then reaches for three fat fries and chomps on them all at once. "Why she hasn't come back yet."

Silence. I'm sure I'm not the only one thinking there could be a horrible reason Bailey hasn't shown up, but I'm not about to say so.

"I hope . . . I really pray she's okay. Bailey's a survivor." Davina's feeding Ruby again—wild, that baby might as well be sewn to her breasts.

"She *is* a survivor," Sam says. "I know she's okay."

"How would you know that?" Joshua runs a hand through his dark hair, his face wan and pinched.

"Twinly intuition. I would know." Sam sounds so confident I almost believe him. But none of it makes sense.

"You better hope she's okay," Joshua says, "because she's your alibi."

"Fuck you," Sam says, flicking Joshua a middle finger that's covered in disgusting meat juices.

"He's right," I say quietly. "Sam, if you—"

"Killed our mother? Is that what you're seriously accusing me of, Joshua?" Sam puts down his burger and leans across the table, getting in his brother's face.

Joshua flinches, but to his credit, doesn't skulk back. "You said horrible things last night. You hated her and—" He flicks hesitant eyes over at me. "Asher. You hated them together. But you hated her the most. Ever since Aba died, you've hated Mom. C'mon, Sam. Admit it."

"I didn't! Once Bailey comes back, she'll tell you—she'll tell you all—"

"Right. Whatever." Joshua bites his lip and tears stream down his cheeks. "Mom's dead, Sam. *Murdered*. Her body—did you see it? Do you have any feelings? Are you even sad?"

"Of course I'm sad," Sam says venomously.

"Really? Could have fooled me. You seem entirely unfazed by it. Happy she's gone."

"You have no idea, Joshua! None!" Sam smacks the table with his huge palm, vibrating my teacup. "Maybe I've just been crying my eyes out over in my suite, which I was sharing with my missing twin. I'm allowed to have complex feelings. Yes, maybe death is just what Mom deserved. But that doesn't mean I did it. Anyway, she did horrible things . . . things you have no idea of . . ."

"Like what?" Joshua counters. "Just what did she do? Other than love us and provide for us and survive as a single mother and—"

"Survive as a single mother." Sam laughs a throaty laugh. "That's rich. Not hard to survive when you make off with a billion dollars. Anyway, you don't know how Mom actually got to the top."

I stand. "I won't listen to you talk about Delia like this!" I scream.

The entire place goes silent. I take a shaky seat, my throat scraped raw. I knead my knuckles into my cheeks, then out toward my ears. Odelia used to rub my ears—she knew just where to touch me to make me sigh with pleasure. I knew how to touch her too. Memories flash, but I keep them at bay.

Finally Joshua pierces the quiet. "Where's Gwen? Did anyone tell her we were going for lunch?"

"I stopped by her suite," Davina says. "She didn't answer."

"That's weird," Joshua says. "I stopped by earlier, too, and banged a couple times. She didn't answer then, either, but I figured she was resting. Sort of weird." He checks his watch. "It's been over an hour. And Gwen isn't a napper."

Davina smiles ruefully. "True. She's always said she has too much energy."

"She does," Joshua says. "Aunt Gwen's an Energizer Bunny. Even more than Mo—" He stops, then reaches slowly for his water glass. I can see his hand shaking as he lifts the glass to his mouth. "I hope Gwen didn't do anything crazy, like go in search of that elephant."

"She must be resting," Davina says firmly. "Or else she's just a wreck. Maybe she needs privacy. This has been a terrible day for her. You know how she loved your mother."

"Of course," Joshua says tightly.

"Hey, Joshua," Sam says, lacking his prior menace. "Have you heard from Mom's lawyer?"

Joshua frowns. "I emailed him, but it's not even morning yet on the East Coast."

"I emailed him too," Sam says, and I can tell that agitates his brother.

Joshua says, "You emailed him? Why?"

"I don't need to explain." Sam crosses his arms over his chest defiantly. "You did the same exact thing."

"Yes, because the police have asked for a copy of the will. And because it controls the business, we'll need it to figure out who's in charge now; have you thought about that?"

"I have thought about it. Yes. So you talked to the police some more?"

Joshua nods. He removes his glasses and rubs his eyes. "Officer Monala said as soon as the storm lets up, they'll come over in the chopper to interrogate us more. Frankly, Officer Monala seems like she's doing everything right, but the reputation of the police down here isn't so great."

"What does that mean?" Sam asks.

Joshua shrugs. "Like not following processes. Losing evidence. Everything's handwritten apparently—like the witness statements we signed. I guess nothing goes into a computer. I'm only saying it in case we need to bring in our own investigation team or something."

"That's a little first-world centric." Davina clucks her tongue. "Don't you think, Joshua?"

"It did take the cops a lot of time to get over here," Sam says. "And then they just left."

"Yeah, Dav," Joshua says. "Anyhow, Violett's the one who told me this stuff."

Davina visibly stiffens at the mention of Violett.

"It's not being first-world centric," Joshua rushes on, "but this country has been through colonialism and apartheid. There are still a lot of kinks to work out in the system, so we'll see. The cops have confirmed the time of death, though. The coroner estimates the same window as the last data records on Mom's Health app."

"See." Sam punctures the air with a triumphant fist. "See! What did I tell you? When I was with Bailey. They can interrogate me until the sun comes up, and I was still nowhere by the bonfire pit when Mom was killed. Can't they do anything more productive, these officers? Like check CCTV footage? Hey!" His face lights up. "That's an idea—can't they see where Bailey went based on whatever cameras are around?"

"No. We don't have cameras." Joshua frowns.

"None at all? That's wild, at a place this ritzy and remote," I say. "Almost negligent."

"Our father." Joshua shrugs. "He was big on secrecy. My mother too. Neither wanted anyone spying on them is how they saw it."

I manage a small smile. "I could see Delia feeling that way. What about the guard, though? There's a guard at the front twenty-four seven, isn't there? So if Bailey left the property, he should have seen her, right?"

"I've already talked to him," Sam says. "Obviously."

"Me too," Joshua says.

"And?" Davina asks.

"He didn't see her," Joshua says. "But . . ."

"But basically every time I've ever seen that guy he's sleeping in the shack," Sam says.

"Yeah." Joshua heaves a sigh. "Amogelang. I don't put too much stock in his guarding. Bailey could have left without him seeing. Especially at night. Not that I can possibly comprehend why she would do that."

"And Markus?" I ask. "Have the cops found him?"

"Not yet," Joshua says. "He left his phone at home, who knows why, and the police by Hazyview checked in on his house. He's not there."

"What the hell," Sam says. "And now Gwen's gone, too . . ."

"Gwen's resting," Joshua says.

"How do you know? You've seen her?" Sam says. "Maybe Aunt Gwen's disappeared, too, which, I mean, what the fuck . . ."

"God forbid," I say and shiver. "This whole thing is starting to feel like *And Then There Were None*."

"Huh?" Sam asks.

"Agatha Christie. You know, where everyone disappears? Never mind . . ."

"Right, you used to watch with your mom," Sam says. "Can you not impose your fake murder mystery on our actual family situation?"

"I'm worried about Gwen, Joshua," Davina says. "We should go check on her."

"Yes." Joshua stands with a weary look to him. "I'll go now."

"There's something I still don't understand too," Davina says, mindlessly stroking Ruby's thick hair as she feeds. "Why Odelia was found by the bonfire pit."

"Whether she was forced there or went by her own volition, you mean?" I ask.

Davina nods slowly.

"Officer Monala told me there's no sign of a struggle," Joshua says, "but—"

"The vultures decimated the evidence," I say. "But if she'd been lured out of our room, I'd have heard it. And I heard nothing."

"Tell us again," Sam says, even though I've already told them, and the cops.

"We were both so exhausted," I say. "We practically fell right asleep."

"And you heard nothing?"

I manage a small shrug. "I sleep like a rock. The next thing I heard after kissing Delia good night was banging at the door in the morning. Joshua."

"So maybe Mom went out to meet someone, or to find something . . ." Sam shoots a death stare at Joshua.

"Don't look at me," Joshua says. "I certainly didn't kill Mom."

"Well, I certainly didn't, either," Sam says. "And between us, I'm the one with an alibi."

"Davina can attest I didn't kill anyone in those hours!" Joshua says.

"But Davina's your wife. She'd say anything!"

"And Bailey is your twin! So would she!"

Both brothers lean forward, menacing. My money's on Sam, though—he towers over Joshua in both height and musculature and he oozes champion energy. If either of them had a gun, my money would be on Sam to pull the trigger first.

"Go fuck yourself, PJ," Sam says.

"Mm, I'll be sure and do that," Joshua says, his tone fairly venomous. *Nice boy's got some edge*, I think. Makes me respect him more, knocking his brother down a peg.

We all eat, or pick around our food, in silence for a while until Ruby starts crying. Again. God. The sound is becoming a bit like a tiny person who lives inside my head, knocking on the sides of my skull with a hammer. Violett comes over and offers to take her. I half listen—apparently she was watching Ruby before, and now she's brought some sort of carrier wrap and has offered to walk Ruby around the dining room. Davina's objecting, but Violett is taking her, wrapping her in this expert way, and Ruby quiets and almost fist-pumps the air in delight, and Davina has an eyebrow raised but isn't protesting, and Joshua isn't even looking—he's staring dazed out the window. So in the absence of further protests, Violett takes off with a gurgling Ruby to stare at the rain out the window, and Davina looks unmoored, like her body is used to having a function and doesn't know what to do with this stillness.

Joshua spurts with something that sounds like a sob, then stands and shoves his chair in. "Sorry, sorry. Dav, I'm gonna go . . . check on Gwen again." He gathers up his computer bag, and Grace brings over his raincoat, which has been drying on the side.

Joshua hurries off and then it's just me, Sam, and Davina. "*And Then There Were None*. You called it, Ash." Davina ekes out a smile.

"I can't believe the cops didn't stick around to protect us, with a murderer on the loose," Sam says.

"They're not bouncers or private security," I say. "They need to be back at their station to investigate."

"Yeah, but I agree with Sam." Davina's eyes travel over to Violett and Ruby, and she visibly relaxes. "It's like . . . they came and then quickly left without making a single arrest. And they're not even looking for Bailey!"

"They did and they will. But they can't in this rain." I'm speaking louder—we all are—because the rain is drumming the roof so hard that it's difficult to hear one another.

"Well, when's it supposed to stop?"

I check the weather app again. "Tonight."

"But they can't always fly after sunset," Sam says.

"Oh," I say. "Well, then we should be prepared for them to not be able to pick things back up until tomorrow morning."

"I'm not waiting," Sam says. "I'm going to look for Bailey again after lunch."

"There's no way Titus will go with you right now," I say quietly. "It's not safe out there."

"I don't care if I die out there looking. I don't care if I have to go on foot by myself." Sam's jaw is set, like he won't budge on this. And I get it— if someone was out there whom I loved that much, too, I wouldn't hesitate either. After all, if we are truly good sons and brothers and husbands, we will go to the ends of the earth for the people we love.

"I'll go with you," I say.

Sam eyes me in surprise. "I don't need you to. I didn't ask—"

"I'm offering."

He opens his mouth, like he wants to protest more, but then he shuts it and stares stonily away. He doesn't say okay, but he also doesn't say no.

Then Joshua is back, breathless, peeling off his raincoat and splattering drips all over the table.

"Joshua, what—" Davina bolts to a stand.

"Gwen's gone!" Joshua's eyes are darting frantically around. His voice is raised, attracting the attention of the staff. "I went to her suite, and she didn't answer, and so I had one of the staff let me in. But she wasn't there— I looked everywhere!"

We all stare at one another, dumbfounded.

"I—it—" Davina starts to say, but then she stops at a commotion coming from the entry of the lodge.

I swivel and that's when I see her.

Bailey!

A veritable wreck, but seemingly alive. And there's— Well, I'll be. I am shocked to see who's trailing behind her.

# CHAPTER TWENTY-ONE

# VIOLETT

It's a good thing I am here to calm the baby, because everyone else has erupted in hysterics. Bailey is back—happy news.

And Markus is at her heels.

Don't get me wrong; I'm thrilled Bailey is safe, and apparently in one piece, albeit caked in mud, with scratches on her face. Markus, too, though he has a larger wound apparently, which needs to be cleaned. But despite my attempts at soothing Ruby, she's glommed onto all the frantic energy and is wailing. I assure Davina that I've got her and take Ruby to the side, where I sink down into a plush velvet chair in the lounge area and give her a little gripe water from my bag. Ruby drinks and then immediately calms. I suspected it would come in handy. Gripe water is magic: a mix of sodium bicarbonate, dill seed oil, sugar, and the key ingredient, 4.4% alcohol.

I watch Davina usher Bailey away. Bailey is soaked, and her back quakes as she walks. Then Markus goes, too—they're both heading to clean up and be attended to with first aid. As they leave, exclamations rain down. Confusion. Calls made to the police—assurances the officers will arrive as soon as the rain has ceased.

They have more questions, apparently. Well, of course they would.

Ruby is warm in my lap. I stroke her cheek and watch her perfect tummy heave and fall with her breath.

Finally they return, Bailey in a sweatshirt and sweatpants, both with the Circ logo. She tightens the blanket around her shoulders, and Markus follows after her, in similarly warm nonsummer gear, albeit not Circ branded.

Then their big reveal ensues. And, boy, is it a doozy.

Apparently, from Bailey's frantic tale punctuated by Markus's somber interjections, Bailey decided to go off in the middle of the night to save an elephant she thought to be in danger. Gwen was right about that, inexplicably so.

"But how did you know the elephant was in danger?" Davina asks, as confused as I.

"Gwen gave me a tarot reading," Bailey says, confounding things further as everyone begins to speak at once. But Bailey fidgets her fingers in her shirtsleeve, doesn't answer any of them.

"Where is Gwen?" Her eyes dart back toward the entrance. "And where's Mom?"

Joshua avoids answering and deftly gets back on track. "Bails, are you telling us you went after an animal in the middle of the night by yourself? That's . . . insane." I can tell he intended to use an even stronger word but restrained himself. "How did you navigate at night? Even know where you were? You left your phone in the room . . ."

"I know." Bailey looks vacant, almost dazed. "I don't know how—that was stupid of me. I took the flashlight, and as for navigating . . . I just know this place. I've always paid attention to Markus, I guess, when he explained stuff."

"Stuff?" Sam asks.

She shrugs. "Like how termite mounds in the Southern Hemisphere grow leaning to the north. So when I passed them, I could tell I was still going east. Stuff like that."

"Termite mounds." Sam whistles, but not sounding impressed as much as disbelieving. "How did you even get past the electric fence?"

"I stepped over it. There are sections where it's only about a foot high." Bailey seems, mercifully at this point, to have dropped the inquiry about her mother. And Gwen. Right. Gwen's gone too? How—

But then my thoughts dissolve and I'm listening, rapt and disbelieving, to the story that ensues. Markus cuts in now, explaining how he'd left for his day off and was home for some time when he cycled back over his conversation with Bailey earlier. He says Bailey had cornered him after the evening game drive, seeming frantic about the elephant and potential poachers and how Davina—with this Markus flits apologetic eyes at Joshua's wife—apparently let slip the elephant's location in front of Junior.

Junior? Oh yes, I remember Bailey admonishing Davina over that. But really, Junior, in with the poachers? Not that I've ever thought that man amounted to much. He lazes around most of the day, munching on biltong, smoking cigarettes, littering his *stompies* all over the place. He needs a lot of galvanizing to do a spit of work. . . .

"I replayed our conversation in my mind, and something bothered me," Markus says. "And all of a sudden I felt an awful foreboding. If I had to pinpoint it, I guess it was the look in Bailey's eyes. She looked . . ."

I look at Bailey's eyes now. I guess we all do. And I see it—she's beady-eyed, almost unhinged.

Strange. Very strange. Out of all the Babels, Bailey's always seemed like the last person to take a death-defying mission into the bush at night.

Has she forgotten she's in rural South Africa, where life is dirt cheap?

But she's had a horrific ordeal. So perhaps her being out of sorts is her coming down from the shock.

"So you came back?" Asher asks.

Markus nods. He rubs his shoulder and winces. I see it's dressed in gauze, and I presume that one of the staff must have cleaned and bandaged a wound. Grace, probably—she's the most motherly, and proficient at first aid.

"I came back. Must have been two in the morning by then, and when I went to my room and saw my rifle was missing, I immediately assumed Bailey had taken it."

"How would Bailey have even gotten into your safe?" Davina asks.

Markus flushes. "Well . . . Bailey's been in my room before. She's seen me lock my safe. I speculated she'd seen me do the combination."

"You were sleeping with Bailey?" Joshua shrieks, looking apoplectic.

"No, no, no," Markus says. "Absolutely not."

"No!" Bailey says, aghast.

"Bailey and I talk sometimes, is all." Markus coughs and looks away like he's supremely embarrassed. As well he should. He's not supposed to be entertaining our most important VIP guests in his room. And certainly not a girl so much younger than he.

"About the animals," Bailey says softly. "That's all we talk about."

"Oh," Joshua says, but shifts uncomfortably, like something isn't sitting well.

"Anyway, I didn't take the gun," Bailey says.

My mind spins, trying to follow everything. Ruby peals sudden laughter, and I lower my face toward hers, smiling back.

"*Ja, bokkie,*" I whisper. "Everything's okay. Violett will take care of everything."

"So what happened then?" Davina asks.

"Well, thankfully I had my pistol on me. Never without it, unless I've got the rifle. Anyway, I got back in my car and followed Bailey's tracks. I saw that she'd gone past the guard shack—"

"How? Amogelang said he didn't see anyone," Asher said.

"Amogelang was out cold." Markus grunts, then presses his palms together and rests his cheek there, imitating a snooze. "And as I figured, I followed Bailey's tracks toward where we'd seen that elephant. I wanted to call the police then, but I realized that I left Hazyview in such a rush I'd left my phone behind at home. And when I arrived, when I saw Bailey—"

"When he arrived, he saved my life," Bailey whispers.

"It's a long story," Markus says, a solemn set to his jaw. "We could have died. Honestly, we almost did. Because she was encircled by poachers with rifles drawn, and we could have gotten into a shoot-out. They outnumbered me, anyway. If I hadn't known one of the poachers from my town, if he hadn't realized the risks—"

"So the poachers didn't kill us," Bailey interrupts manically. "Markus convinced them he'd already called the police, genius on his part."

"A complete bluff," Markus says soberly, "because I didn't even have my phone."

"Yeah, so they got on the phone with whoever was in charge," Bailey says. "I heard him on speaker, the Big Man, they kept calling him. And the Big Man said it had already spun out of control, so they had to abort. They tied us up in a snare, though, to give them time to escape, and they took the keys to Markus's car and drove off in it, so we couldn't use it to get away, and then they left quickly without hurting Masasana—"

"Bailey got there just in time to save her," Markus says. "It was truly a miracle."

Bailey half smiles.

"But I was injured." Markus indicates his shoulder. "So hyenas smelled our blood—"

"And we had to get out of the snare quickly," Bailey says, back with that wild, almost frenetic energy, but understandably so in light of this straining-credulity story. "The hyenas were licking their lips. It was . . . scary. And Markus couldn't kill them all with his pistol, not tied up like that, so he kept snarling at them, so I snarled too. And he said *Bugger off*, so I did, too, but then obviously we weren't gonna keep them at bay for much longer, and so we finally freed ourselves and climbed a thorn tree!"

"Wait, you actually . . . climbed a tree?" Sam stares at his sister with a mixture of horror and awe.

"Yeah. And we were up there for hours . . . through the start of the rain . . . until I realized it was going to be heavy and dangerous. The branches we were on could collapse," Markus says. "So we finally climbed down and made it back here—"

"And we saw a lion too!" Bailey interjects, almost like it was exciting, though, instead of terrifying.

"Yes, that was— It was quite a thing," Markus says quietly. "When we were trapped in the snare, I noticed two little sparks of light. Close to the ground. I thought it could be a buffalo at first, but they lift their head when they're threatened. And these eyes were closer together. Meaning a lion. Lions don't really attack humans unless the humans are threatening their cubs. So I kept my flashlight shining in her eyes, and thankfully she didn't wind up pouncing. Because truth be told, humans are the best meal passing in the dark. Honestly . . . Bailey and I are very, very lucky to be alive, with all our body parts intact. I thought—a couple times I thought—we were going to—"

"Die." Bailey is still shaking. "Me too. It was horrible, but also . . . I mean, we made it. And so did Masasana."

Markus reaches over and places his palm on top of Bailey's hand, and the two look at each other with some solemn, mutual understanding.

"Yes," Markus says. "But, Bailey, even with Masasana . . . elephants are vegetarians, but she could have easily crushed us. It's not a joke to be out there in the bush at night, without a rifle. Even with a rifle . . . the night is for predators."

"I know," Bailey says and looks like a lost child for a moment. "I'm so sorry. To Markus, to everyone, for causing so much stress and worry. I'm glad I did it, I guess, but I don't know what I was thinking really."

Markus pats Bailey's hand again. They haven't yet broken eye contact, and in their eyes, I discern something else. Some flicker of . . . I don't know. Something they've left out, haven't shared.

Huh. I wonder if—

Suddenly everyone starts shooting out additional questions in unison.

"Can we take a pause?" Markus says above the fray. "We'll answer all your questions later, but we— Bailey's just been through an unthinkable ordeal."

"Junior!" Bailey smacks her palm on the table and glances around. "Where is he? I know he called his poacher friends. I know that's how they got Masasana's location. They need to arrest him."

"Okay, Bails," Joshua says distractedly. "I'll call the police and tell them. I'm sure they'll want to question him. But—I'm sure they will."

Silence, as we cotton onto his drift. That Junior's responsibility, or lack thereof, of sending poachers to kill the elephant is important, albeit low on the list of collective problems right now.

"Now Bailey needs to relax. And rest." Davina slings an arm around Bailey's shoulders, quite motherly and kind. And on Bailey's other side, Sam kisses her forehead, expelling an audible breath.

I nod at Grace, communicating without words. They need hot water, tea, sustenance. Immediately. She scurries off.

Thank goodness I've trained my staff well, that I can trust Grace in the dining hall, Ahmale in housekeeping. As for Junior—well, the vehicles can go to shit at this point, doesn't matter. All that matters is that things are taken care of here, and that all my brain space is freed for what I still must do.

I feel my phone buzz in my pocket. My heart swishes over itself. I soak in another glimpse of Ruby to give me the courage, then I check my phone.

More bad news. Well, it usually is.

I feed Ruby a touch more gripe water, feeling slightly guilty that I didn't ask her parents if I could. If Davina knew about the alcohol content, she'd likely refuse it.

But sometimes people don't know what is best for them.

"Bails," Sam says, "can I ask one question? Not about what happened out there—but do you remember what time you left our suite? Because we talked for a long time . . ."

Bails puts a hand atop her brother's. "We did. It felt like a sleepover, chatting into the night with you. Like we were kids again."

"Well, you live far away now."

"Sam." Bailey smiles. "I'm in Palm Beach. You're in Miami. We're basically neighbors."

"Farther than we've ever been our whole lives. So, do you remember—"

"Yeah. You were Mr. Chatty. At one point I was tired, like around midnight, but then you kept talking, and by the time you fell asleep it was 1:22. I remember, because you started snoring, and I wasn't tired anymore, and I couldn't stop thinking about Masasana—"

"One twenty-two?" Sam looks around. "Everyone hear that? It couldn't have been me." He looks at Joshua. "See, Josh?" he taunts. "I'm the only one in this place with an alibi."

"An alibi for what?" Bailey asks, voice hitching. "And where's Mom, by the way? And Gwen? Getting ready for the wedding, I guess?" She glances around, her wild hair matching her wild blue eyes. "But aren't they worried I was gone? Or has no one told them yet?"

Her eyes continue to dart around in the thick silence. "What? What aren't you all telling me?"

Ruby begins to squirm, as if she can intuit how this conversation is about to dovetail.

Poor Bailey. I feel for her intimately. Both of us had the misfortune of being born to the wrong mothers.

"Shh, *baba*." I stand with Ruby and head out toward the lobby, so Ruby doesn't have to witness what comes next. As I walk, Ruby whimpers and wiggles her long legs, gazing up at me with her big, brown, beautiful eyes.

I ease my phone out of my pocket as we walk and see a text back from my tannie. *The trial is not an option anymore, Violett. Money won't help, we just need to make Ouma comfortable. She's not going to make it. You must accept that. And come see her soon. The doctor says there isn't much time.*

I feel my knees buckle. I manage to make it over to the sofa by the shop, tears misting my eyes. Ruby must sense I am upset, that something is wrong, because she squirms and begins to fuss. I find myself weeping silently. It's all spiraling so far out of my control. My plans, to naught. How have I found myself here? Now?

What a God, I feel like screaming with my fists at the heavens. What a God with horrific timing.

Or perfect timing, I realize.

"It's okay, *shongololo*." I bounce her on my knee, a new plan crystallizing. I wipe the tears from my cheeks with the back of my palm.

"I am here, Ruby. *Ja*, I am here, and I am not going anywhere."

# CHAPTER TWENTY-TWO

# JOSHUA

It's only two in the afternoon of the longest day of my life. Jabulani replenishes my coffee, and I reach for it over the scattered remains of a sandwich I've only picked at. I nod gratefully at Jabulani and lift the cup to my lips, hoping the coffee will quickly do its work. Give me energy, clear my brain. Bring me a badly needed dopamine spike. My fingers shake wildly as I set down the cup—and I suspect it's not the caffeine. Yes, I'm overwhelmed with relief that Bailey is back, but still, nothing is clear. Not least of which is why my little sister struck off alone in the middle of the night to rescue an elephant. But that's not the pressing thing now.

The pressing thing is helping Bailey process Mom's murder. Which is hard when the rest of us have hardly processed it yet ourselves.

Bailey breaks down at the news—of course she does. And so Sam and I huddle around her, arms gripping one another tight. Sam and I, locked in a temporary truce. I am surprised to feel love course through me, *gratitude*, for both my siblings, no matter how complicated my relationship is with one of them. I am thankful that we are all still here, what remains of my family intact. Rain continues to drum the windowpanes and thunder bursts, sounding close, giving the whole scene an air of the end of the world.

This circle of us reminds me of being kids too. Sometimes Mom and Aba would scream horrible things at each other, but more often, they'd be engaged in a ruthless silent-treatment competition. "Bailey, tell your mother to bring me another piece of chicken," or "Joshua, tell your father that we're having the Goldsteins over for dinner tonight." They could last weeks, months, entire vacations.

"Will they get divorced?" I remember Sam and Bailey once asking me, because they were young, like eight, and divorce was the worst thing they each could imagine.

But I was older—fourteen. I would reassure them. "No. They won't get divorced."

But I knew, in some deep place, that our family wasn't normal. And even more, that we were already broken.

And I was right.

———

SAM AND I TAKE Bailey to their suite. Bailey showers, but her sobs sound from the bathroom and burrow into my bones. Sam and I don't speak, just sit on their couch and stare grimly into the bush. As we wait for Bailey, I call Officer Monala and relay the news that Bailey has returned but Gwen is missing now. That we think she might have gone out to find Bailey. Officer Monala assures me, again, that as soon as the storm ends, they will take a chopper over.

When I hang up, I tell Sam, "Let's not tell Bailey about Gwen yet. She has enough to—"

"Yeah," Sam says. "I agree."

When Bailey's fresh from the shower, shaky in her threadbare old robe, we help her into bed. "Is this real?" she asks. "You really saw Mom—you saw her all—"

"We saw her." I tuck the sheets up to my sister's chin. "I'm so sorry, Bails. It's horrible."

"I'm so tired," Bailey chokes out. "I'm so—so—"

"I know. I'll sit with you while you fall asleep." I squeeze her hand, limp and cold in my own.

"I'm going to do a quick workout on the deck," Sam says. "I need to get this energy out. I'll be here when you wake up, Bails. I'm not letting you out of my sight ever, ever again." He kisses Bailey's forehead and she peeps a weak smile up at him.

My brother scrapes the sliding door open and then bursts onto the deck, sending a rush of hot, moist air into the room.

"I'll close it," I say, standing, but my sister reaches out her hand.

"No. Leave it. It's—"

"Okay." I sit. I get it. The air is a distraction, or a reminder of life outside this surreal place and time.

I watch my brother. Instead of stopping beneath the overhang, Sam walks right out into the rain, up against the translucent rail that borders the river. He stretches out his arms wide and even though all I can hear is rain, I know that he's screaming. I know because it's what I want to do too.

"I'm sorry I wasn't there this morning," Bailey says quietly. "I'm sorry you had to find Mom all by yourself."

"You have nothing to be sorry about, Bails."

"Was it horrible?"

I pause, trying to bat back the images that return. "It was horrible," I finally say.

Bailey bites her lip but doesn't cry again. "What did you want to talk about?"

"This morning? You mean, at the firepit?"

"Yeah."

"Oh." I think about it. My fight with Mom. Everything going on with the company that I'm afraid will be exposed. That I'm afraid will ruin us. And it all feels so irrelevant now. "Stuff with Circ," I finally say. "Let's put a pin in it, though. Talk about it when things calm down."

"Will they ever calm down, Joshua? Mom's gone. I just— I can't—"

"The sea always calms itself," I tell her, something Aba once told me at the beach, in a moment of shared wisdom that felt true and sacred.

It's the same thing I told my siblings after Aba died. But this time, I'm not sure I believe it.

"Sam's gonna be broken. Their fight . . . the last things he said to her—"

"I'm not sure our brother is the type to break. Not over Mom's death, at least."

"You're wrong." Bailey shakes her head vigorously. "Sam's sensitive. More than you know."

"Well, he does a good job hiding it then."

"He's all bluster. No bite."

"He's got a good bite, Bails. For everyone but you."

"You're wrong. But I'm going to be here for him. Someone needs to be. You have Dav. Sam's gonna need people to lean on. Well, I guess it's good that . . ."

"What?"

"I think . . . I think he has a new boyfriend."

"Really?" That's news to me, but I mean, our brother has a new guy in constant rotation. So this isn't exactly groundbreaking.

"I think it's . . . I don't know, more than his usual flings. Sam was kind of evasive, almost . . . protective about talking about him. You know, normally he's an open book. With me, at least." She frowns. "Sorry."

I shrug. "Can't dispute the fact that I'm the last person Sam would be open with about his love life."

"The guy—Sam's guy—he was in his contacts as O with a heart next to it."

"A heart. Serious, then."

"Yeah, he didn't want to elaborate, but—"

"You did your twin thing and got it out of him." I feel a flash of . . . I don't know what—hurt? I guess I always felt it was special, their twin-dom. Felt it would have been nice to have that kind of bond. Bailey and I were close enough, but six years was a big age difference when we were younger. I mostly existed like my own island, left out of their twin speak and closeness.

"No, the twin thing didn't really work on this." Bailey smiles, not realizing I said it facetiously. "But Sam told me this new guy makes him happy."

"Okay, well, I'm happy for Sam, if he's happy. It would be good for him to settle down."

"They've been texting a lot. Sam looks—I don't know, he's different when he talks about this one. So I hope—well, maybe this guy can be there for him now."

"You're a good sister, Bails." Emotion chokes my throat. "You've always been such a good sister to us both."

Bailey wipes her eyes on the sheet. Then she stares at the ceiling. "They need to arrest him—Junior. Did you tell the police? How he must have informed the poachers—"

"Yes, I've told the officer in charge. She's promised to look into it."

"She has to do more than look into it! It has to be him, Joshua—after Dav—" She stops, eyes widening. "I know Dav didn't mean to . . ."

We're both quiet, because Bailey already vocalized this in the dining room—her suspicion that Davina led the poachers to Masasana. When she realized what she might have done, albeit inadvertently, Dav felt so guilty. Which turned into Bailey hugging Dav and consoling her. Even after her whole ordeal. Even after finding out about Mom.

But that's my sister, kind to a fault. Always putting everyone else's needs ahead of her own.

Bailey rubs her eyes. "It's too much—it feels overwhelming. Like it's all going to crush me. Or already has."

"I know."

The way she says it, so distraught, reminds me of earlier. The looks that passed between her and Markus. The frenetic energy, which could have been a result of their death-defying ordeal, but also gave me pause.

"What really happened out there, Bails? I feel like . . . it feels like we're missing part of the story. You can tell me. Whatever it is."

Bailey responds by twisting away from me, curling up on her side. "Nothing happened. I told you it all. I'm so tired, Joshua."

And then she closes her eyes and I watch her for a very long time, wondering if my sister is sleeping or very good at faking it.

———

WHEN SAM RETURNS AND I've transferred Bailey duty to him, I leave their suite and pause on their porch, readying myself to rush back to my suite in the downpour that's still not let up. I wrangle on my raincoat and then check my phone.

Two messages have come through—first, an email from Mom's attorney. I scroll through the pleasantries and condolences, spotting two attachments. One being the "Last Will and Testament of Odelia Tisdale Babel." And the second titled, "Letter from Odelia to Gwen."

Letter to Gwen? I check for any other letters, like to me—wouldn't Mom want to send me a letter on her death? As CFO . . . as her son . . . But nope. I click on the letter, my curiosity mounting, but it's password protected. And then I see it, in the lawyer's email missive to me, the directive that I should send the letter to Gwen, and that Odelia has said Gwen will know the password.

Great. Just fucking great.

I check the other message on my phone, this one a text, and see that it's from Officer Monala. They've managed to track Gwen's phone, and she'd like me to give them a call.

I scramble in my head, try to make a new plan. Plans are my forte, what I rely upon when the world is going to shit. As to shit it has gone.

I'll call Officer Monala back. And then go deal with the will, and also force myself to finally check the USB. No matter how much more calamity it reveals. I can't bury it anymore, this horrible sense that the worst isn't over. That we're not even yet in the eye of the storm but rather in the middle of something with a looming, amorphous end. I need to face it all, figure out how to run this to its end.

Before anyone else I love disappears or dies.

# CHAPTER TWENTY-THREE

# BAILEY

I come to, disoriented, and my eyes flicker, testing out whether they want to rejoin the day or stay buried in the dark.

"Bails." Sam's voice snaps me to, and I struggle up in bed, staring at my twin in the same chair Joshua was sitting in before.

"Mom's dead? That wasn't a nightmare?"

"Not a nightmare. Sorry, Bails."

I nod, not trusting myself to speak. I lean back in bed. The effort of sitting up was almost too much. When my head hits the pillow again, I feel dizzy, like everything's not spinning as much as swirling—I see Mom, her checklist for my life, the security of being told what to do and when, even as I struggle to breathe. I see Masasana—that regal, proud, grieving elephant. Her glorious tusks, and the evil poachers who came to claim them.

It was insane, wasn't it, like they all say, to go after an elephant in the dead of night in the African bush? In some intellectual part of me I'm having trouble accessing, I know it was insane—but all I actually felt was the anxious drumbeat of my heart as Sam and I chatted into the small hours of night. I love talking to my brother, love sharing a room on vacation, even though we could have each easily taken our own suites because Mom closed the resort to tourists this week, and there are five in total. Leaving one spare—the suite on the other side of Mom and Asher. Sam and I never get sleepovers anymore, now that we're adults and he's moved to Miami, so both of us savor the opportunity to be roomies for a bit.

But my brother had so much to say, so much to discuss, about his app and Circ and how maybe he and I should backpack the world together, and all I could think about was Gwen's tarot reading and Masasana out there, so vulnerable, building her stick statue of her baby.

So I crept out.

But what I don't tell Sam—what I dare not tell anyone—is that somehow, I blacked out. That I barely remember the moments—the minutes or even the hours, who knows—between when I left our suite and when Markus arrived to save me.

———

"WHAT HAPPENED OUT THERE, Bails?" Sam asks, jolting me back. "Are you ready to talk about it?"

"Not really. I don't know." I press my lips together.

He runs a finger along my forearm beside where a vertical gash bisects it. Grace, who is gentle and good with a needle, stitched it up with inordinate care, but said I should get a doctor to look at it when the storm lets up.

"I can't believe you did that," Sam says quietly. "Please promise me you'll never put your life at risk like that again. I couldn't handle it, Bails, if something happened to—" He breaks off and squeezes my hand like a stress ball.

I open my mouth to promise, but I find that I can't. I'm too wound up. Almost possessed. Maybe it's just grief. An ocean that so far I've only waded into.

"It was horrible, Sam," I finally say, because describing it will maybe get me out of my awful, twisting mind. "They had knives and rifles and a tranquilizer dart. They'd already shot Masasana with it, and they were getting ready to saw at her tusks when Markus came. He didn't have his rifle—well, now we know someone took it." I study my brother as I say that, because Joshua told me that Gwen apparently saw Sam coming from Markus's room.

Where is Gwen?

But Sam doesn't hesitate. "I didn't take the rifle, Bails. I wanted to ask

Markus if we could still do a game drive this morning. Just me, you, and him. I know Mom wanted the day to be all about the wedding, but it's such a shame to be here and not do what we came here to do. Not be out there, you know? I thought I'd surprise you. But his door was open, and he wasn't inside, so I left."

"Oh. Okay, that was nice of you." It makes sense. And I don't want to second-guess my brother on this point.

"Anyway, you know I was with you when Mom was murdered. I didn't kill her, Bails. Tell me you believe me. Tell me you have zero doubts."

"I believe you," I finally say, and I can't decide if I mean it or if I need to mean it. Even though Sam hated Mom, I can't imagine him doing something so evil—something with ramifications for us all. Even though I imagine this is going to change everything financially for Sam—and for all of us—and I can't help but think it's a neat answer to his money problems that I've learned this trip are pretty extreme.

"Thanks, Bails. I needed to hear that." He heaves a sigh. "So what happened with the poachers? I still can't believe—"

"Yeah. I don't know, it's all hazy, sort of. There was a knife, and the main guy, his name is Andre. Markus has encountered him before." I shake my head, shivering as I remember him. I might have blacked out for most of it, but this part is clear, how he grabbed me, said I was crazy, asking to be killed, by him or a lion, he didn't much care.

"Markus convinced Andre—said we'd already called it in to the cops. That they were tracking us—that we wouldn't have been so stupid to come out into the bush without backup. And thank God—" I breathe out. "He bought Markus's bluff. He talked to the Big Man—someone on the phone—then tied us in the snare. They left, and that's when the hyenas came, and we had to—god—it was so close—"

I gasp, remember the hyenas approaching, their cackling calls, the moonlight blazing as Markus and I managed to free ourselves. As he dragged me up the tree, shouting for me to go faster. As a hyena nipped at my sneakers, and I used all my might to scramble up, my elbows scraping against the bark.

"That's insane, Bailey. I literally don't know what to say."

"Yeah, that's not the end of the insanity, though," I say quietly.

"I know. You saw a lion too."

"Yeah." I exhale deeply, my nerves absolutely shot. "But that's not what I mean."

Sam cocks his head at me, studies me with his blue eyes, mirrors of my own. We're fraternal, different in so many ways, but our eyes are the same. Like Mom always says—said, fuck—*blue on fire*. Blue with hints of a flame.

When we were finally safe from the hyenas, high up in the tree, I looked at Markus. So many things could have ticked by in my head at that moment, but the one at the forefront was the last thing Andre said to us when he left us in the snare.

*Your daughter, eh? Same eyes.*

I steadied myself on a branch and looked disbelievingly into Markus's eyes. I'd seen them a hundred times before, but this time I really looked. And in the moonlight, I could see.

Blue—on fire.

---

SAM LOOKS AT ME without saying anything as I tell him how Markus admitted he's our father. How he explained that he and Mom slept together a few times—how he said Mom was unhappy with Aba. At that Sam mutters, "Captain obvious."

I tell Sam what Markus told me, as we sat on a tree branch in the dark amid howls and crackles and a free, alive Masasana below, beginning to rustle, no longer inert from the dart. How Markus said the doctors called Mom's pregnancy with twins miraculous, because she'd been trying to get pregnant after Joshua to no avail. Markus said he agreed to give up claim to us because his life in the bush wasn't conducive to being a father. Not to Odelia Babel's children, at least. And he couldn't imagine living anywhere else. But he always enjoyed it when Odelia came to Leopard Sands, and he bonded with us.

Remembering him saying that, a lump forms in my throat. I've always felt a kinship to Markus. He's always made me feel like wanting the simple life—not having much ambition, preferring quiet and nature and the company of animals—isn't a bad thing. He doesn't call my love for animals crazy or frivolous. He doesn't try to mold me into a Circ puppet, or ignore me, like Aba did. Something jagged scrapes my chest, as I remember how I once asked Aba why he named me Bailey, when he chose biblical names for Joshua and Sam. And he told me because he liked Baileys in his coffee sometimes. And then he looked me in the eyes for maybe the first time ever and asked me to make him his afternoon coffee with Baileys. *A Bailey to bring me my Baileys.* He kind of chuckled to himself. And it became his thing—asking me to make that for him. And every time I made him his coffee with Baileys I seethed, thinking of how he'd chosen a sacred name for each of his sons, and a common liqueur for mine.

Now, with Mom gone, I feel grief but also anger that she kept us from our real father. And anger, too, that I am not ready to face, that Markus let himself be kept from us, or just didn't want us enough. But I'm sure Markus is our birth father—if the eyes didn't clinch it for me, and his explanation, another thing did: our feet. Sam and I both have the same kind of feet: huge, ugly, flat feet, with round Flintstone-like toes. Totally different from Mom's slender, petite feet, and Joshua's ordinary, regular ones. But up in the tree, when I was resisting full acceptance that Markus is my father, he took off his shoe and showed me his bare foot. And I gasped. Because his feet are exactly the same as ours.

"You're saying Aba's not our birth father," Sam says slowly.

"No. He's not. And I know you loved Aba, but c'mon, you can't pretend he wasn't horrible. That he cared about himself and Judaism and Circ way more than us. This isn't the worst news, is it?" But I'm holding my breath, because I suppose I know for Sam it will be.

"That some Hicksville safari guide is our dad? And that Aba's not . . ." Sam turns his head and blinks back tears, wringing out my heart. "It's— No. Just no. And I reject the things you said about Aba. Sometimes I feel like you and Joshua grew up in a different house."

"Sammy," I say gently, "I feel like you have a revisionist memory. Are you forgetting how Aba sent you to that rabbi to convert you? To smack out your gayness? I literally heard him say that word for word. Is this the person you're longing to still be your father?"

"He was raised that way!" Sam bursts out. "He couldn't help it! The whole Torah and Talmud and some of the Orthodox sect say that being gay is contrary to the tenets of the religion. He couldn't help but do what he'd been taught to do, but—" Sam bites his lip. "He always told me, *You are my brilliant, strong, wonderful son. The sky is the limit for you. We will fix this, Son."*

"Fix this? Sam, he meant fix *you.*"

"Aba couldn't help who he was any more than I can help who I am. He couldn't help the millennia of history and tradition that paint me and people like me in a certain way."

"I don't know that I agree with that, Sammy."

"You can think what you want, but he loved me. I'm damn sure that he loved me. And respected me. *Valued* me. Maybe more than anyone has."

"More than I value you? That's not fair, Sam."

"It's different, Bails," Sam whispers. "It's just, Aba . . ."

"You idolized him," I say slowly. We were so young. Things were bad at home. Maybe I never saw this, how Sam looked up to Aba to the exclusion of anyone else. Maybe I never wanted to see it.

"Maybe I did. Don't most boys idolize their fathers? And ours was a great one. He achieved so much, persevered despite having nothing. And Mom didn't make things easy on him. You and Joshua rewrite history, but you've always put a halo on her head she didn't deserve."

"I don't think that's true. You made her the devil, so anything less than that meant us being her yes-men."

"You are her yes-men!"

"*Were,*" I correct him quietly.

"Truth is, Bails, and I don't say this to offend you, but let's be straight with each other. Mom liked lackeys, and Aba liked independent go-getters. He liked that I talked back to him sometimes, that I had a point of view. That I stood up for myself, that I was courageous. I was his favorite, I think."

"I know," I say quietly. "You were."

Sam smiles slightly and I can tell that, even now, this means something to him. "Because even though he disapproved of me being gay, even though he refused to accept it, he saw things in me no one else has ever seen. And Aba created Circ. He built Leopard Sands! No matter what awful things you all say about him, he cared about the land, about doing good for the earth and the people here, about sustainability long before it was the cool thing to care about. He's the one who had local artisans weaving the fabrics. And he paid them a fair wage. Remember that? How Circ used to support those women weavers? How we went to the village to see how they worked that time? Mom's the one who did away with that arrangement after Aba died. All for the dollar signs!"

I grimace. It's true, that part. Aba, like all of us, had many layers, and some of them were good, I admit. But the good Sam just cited were the outer layers of Aba's onion. At home we got the core of him. And the core was rotten.

"And Aba came from nothing, Bails—from Lithuanian Holocaust survivors who had nothing. He wasn't like the wealthy fifth-generation South African kids, whose parents had come to mine gold."

"I know." Aba didn't talk about his childhood much, but I know it was traumatic. I remember how every time he said Yahrzeit for his parents, his face got blank in this scary way. I remember how he once told me that his parents had found it hard to show him affection because they were afraid he'd be taken from them, or them from him. *And so it marches onward through the generations*, I think bitterly. Though, fortunately, Joshua's broken the mold.

"Aba came from nothing," Sam says, "and he fought his way to the top. He built everything . . . Circ . . . for *us*. That's why I hate it . . . hated it . . . every time I asked Mom for money and she refused. Aba wouldn't have refused. He fought for us to have this life. He wasn't stingy. He wanted us to enjoy it!"

"Maybe I don't want this life, though," I hear myself say.

Sam scoffs. "Saying you don't want this life is something only someone privileged can say. I bet most people on this continent would gladly trade places with you."

"Maybe." I feel the world shift its tectonic plates, jolting the ground on which we're standing, carrying Sam and me to a new place. Somewhere that feels painful to be. It's a cards-on-the-table talk, putting words to our childhood that before, we've always talked around or buried deep.

Something's nagging at me now, though, in a new way. That Sam went to Markus's cabin the night of the party—before everything went down. The rifle. Someone had to steal Markus's rifle . . . had to know the code to his rifle closet. . . .

"The code," I whisper. "You knew the code."

"What?"

"I told you years ago . . . how weird it was . . ." My veins go ice cold. "I was in Markus's room, bugging him about the animals, to tell me stories, and I watched him open his safe to get the rifle. I saw him punch in the code. And I told you later—what a coincidence it was—that the code was 0402—"

"Our birthday," Sam says flatly. "I barely even remember you telling me that. That must be years ago now."

I digest that. "Are you telling me the truth, Sammy? Did you really not remember?"

"I really didn't, Bails. Jesus. How would I possibly remember something like that?" He shakes his head. "I didn't take the rifle. Any number of staff probably know the code. Or someone else. But it wasn't me. And, god, you're telling me Markus used our birthday as his code? That's so—fucked-up."

I don't respond. My mind is still spinning through all of it, but landing on nothing that feels substantial.

"And by the way, Bails, Markus isn't in the clear. He could have killed Mom with his own rifle! So before you leap to conclusions, before you suspect me, consider that."

"Yeah." I let out a big breath. "The thing is—about all this—Markus being our father—"

"*If* he's our father. It's still a big if. I don't buy it."

I'm quiet. Sam knows it's true. But I get that he doesn't want to face it yet. It all makes sense, the code being our birthday, our eyes. How we look nothing like Dad. I could tell Sam about the feet thing, too, how ours are the same as Markus's, but I don't, because I know inside that extra substantiating facts won't make a difference right now. I have to take this at Sam's pace.

"Fine," I finally say, "*if* Markus had something with Mom—if he's telling the truth, and he's actually our father, then—"

"Then he could have had a motive to kill her," Sam says flatly. "Yep."

"Yeah." I think through it again, but it's all so fresh, not exactly gelling. "I can't really imagine Markus having killed Mom, but I guess it's a possibility." My brain whirls through possibilities—money? Anger at not being promoted? "Regardless, it's a connection that no one knows about. We'll have to tell the police."

"What? And make it public—that Aba's not our biological father? No! No way, Bails. You can't ask me to do that. Not now."

"Sam!" I'm startled at his reaction. "We can't keep this from the police.

What if it helps the investigation? I mean, I don't really think it's Markus, but—"

"No. If you love me, Bails, you won't say anything to anyone about this. Not right now and not ever. I'm gonna go daven in the lodge and just—" Sam scowls in a way I've seen him do before, of course, but never at me.

And then Sam grabs his tallit bag and tefillin and stalks off without looking back.

# CHAPTER TWENTY-FOUR

# VIOLETT

'm in my office, talking to my tannie, when Markus bursts through the door.

"*Yoh!*" I give him a perfunctory wave, then motion to my phone. *Fok*, I should have locked the door.

"What's that?" my tannie asks.

"One moment."

I turn my back to Markus and face the window, which is open. From it, I can see the workshop guys, smoking and then throwing their *stompies* on the ground even though I always tell them not to. They're chatting loudly beneath the rain-battered overhang, shouting my *bru* this and my *boetie* that, always very loud, because in their culture they don't like to talk behind people's backs. They don't want to hide secrets. So they are friendly and very loud. Often, I tell them to be quieter. When I am trying to do paperwork, their booming voices are distracting. But now, I am thankful, and I hope they will drown out any vestiges of my conversation that filters toward Markus.

Still, I lower my voice. "*Ag*, Tannie, I have to go. I'll see you soon." I listen. "*Ja*. I understand. I don't know when—but as soon as I can. Tell Ouma I love her."

And then I click off. I make my face light.

"Markus, this is a surprise. What an ordeal you've been through— I thought you'd be resting. But here you are looking great."

He cocks his head at me, like he's trying to work something out. "Didn't make it this far in my life for a poacher to take me out."

"No, but a lion or leopard can do that, as well." I smile. "Sounds like God was watching out for you."

"If I believed in God, it would sound like it indeed."

Markus smiles back, but his smile doesn't reach his eyes. I have this sense that we are two actors, both playing astutely in quite different scripts. I assess Markus, wondering if I need to worry. He's wearing one of our army green fleeces, with the leopard insignia over the breast. A cut is bandaged over his eyebrow, and he rubs his shoulder, where he injured it, but otherwise he does look well, like I said. It's hard to believe, the story he and Bailey relayed. Something is off in the whole thing. Maybe that he went after her—without his rifle—

"It's quite a horrible thing you came back to, eh?" I ask.

His eyes darken. "Absolutely. Odelia was—absolutely. And now Gwen is missing. I don't understand how that could happen."

"I'm sure she'll turn up."

In fact, I'm not sure of that at all.

"Who do you think did all this?" Markus asks.

"The son, of course."

"Which?"

"Samuel. Not Joshua."

"No," he says thoughtfully. "No, you wouldn't think so, would you?"

"What's that supposed to mean?" My breath hitches.

"Were you involved, Violett? I hope you'll forgive me for asking you outright, but you and Odelia—well, I came to tell you—I'll need to tell the cops what I know."

I force myself to take a breath. I don't know what he's talking about; he can't possibly know. "And what of what *I* know?"

"What do you mean by that? I've already talked to the police on the phone, told them everything I told everyone else." He tries to play it off, but I can tell that my hunch is right. That there is something relevant he's not said.

I smile in a way that I hope is mysterious. "The cops will be here soon enough. It's supposed to stop raining by nightfall, so I expect they'll be here in the morning."

"Well, that's a comfort," Markus says, his voice dripping in sarcasm. "Because we know how competent they are."

"Officer Monala is competent," I say, drawing up and throwing my shoulders back, so we're nearly the same height. "Maybe she'll figure it out."

He looks thoughtful. "Maybe so." I expect him to interrogate me further, but instead of doing so, he stuffs his hands in his pocket and says, "Watch yourself, Violett."

"Is that a threat? Don't play with me, Markus," I say quietly, trying not to show I am suddenly afraid.

"I'm not . . . but I've seen you with Joshua. I *know*."

The way he says it makes me shiver. Because all at once I put it together—our conversation before the family went on their first game drive yesterday—when I was talking to Davina and Joshua—and Markus intervened. . . .

"You couldn't."

He shrugs. "I do. And I don't know how it fits with Odelia's murder, but you have to tell the police, Violett. If you don't, I will."

I gather all my wits. I'm seething inside, but I won't let him see that. I'm quite a good actress. I think I've proven that by now.

"I *will* tell the police, Markus. In fact, I plan on it. It doesn't have anything to do with Odelia's murder—you're barking up the wrong line of inquiry—but it doesn't matter. Clearly you don't care that you're going to hurt people. Because if you say what you *think* you know, you are going to hurt people!"

"I do care," he says softly. "But it's the right thing to do, Violett. Odelia . . . she was a good person. A good mother. She tried." His face twists, like someone pained by her death, though I can't possibly conceive of why. Unless . . .

"*Ja*, if you say so." I shove my phone in my pocket and slap my thighs, to signal this conversation is over. "When the police arrive tomorrow morning, I will tell them everything."

I don't tell him that by the time the police arrive, it will be too late, anyhow.

---

SHE TRIED. THAT'S WHAT I keep hearing in my head, Markus's voice. *She was a good person. A good mother.*

If Odelia Babel was a good mother, then call me Mother Teresa.

I close the door to my office, sit in my chair, and stare at the framed picture of Ouma holding a six-year-old me on her lap, both our smiles glittery, authentic. Beside the picture is another frame, containing an old drawing of a family of zebras that's yellowed at the edges.

I feel tears about to break the dam. How can this all be happening? *Now?*

*She was a good mother.*

Odelia wasn't a good mother!

*No, stay here, don't make me go back,* I whisper, but I'm powerless. Dragged there all the same. To the dark on the brink, screaming at each other, finally everything out in the open. I felt like a wild animal, frothing at the mouth—so angry and distraught that I really could kill her.

And then I did.

# CHAPTER TWENTY-FIVE

# ASHER

We've all gathered in the lodge again at the request of Joshua, our de facto leader. We're at our same corner table—the one I sat at with Odelia, just yesterday, our hands playing in each other's laps. How was that only yesterday? It's not even yet dusk. I exhale deeply, longing for my bed, to curl up in a ball and cry and process everything that's happened on this awful, never-ending day. Instead it's Groundhog's Day back in the dining room again, but not for a meal. Down to business. Stapled packets laid out in front of each chair.

"No sign of Gwen yet?" Sam asks.

"None," Joshua says. "But Officer Monala said they're tracking Gwen's phone and she'll be in touch as soon as they've identified its last location. It's not in her suite, so maybe it will point us to her . . ."

Bailey emits a strangled sound. I know she just found out about Gwen. Joshua and I walked over together—he emerged onto his porch as I passed, on the way to the lodge. Then he thrust his umbrella over my head to cover us both. As we walked, Joshua said he'd come from filling Bailey in on Gwen's absence. Apparently, Bailey broke down at the news, inferring that Gwen might have gone after her. After all, Gwen is the only one of any of us who correctly suspected that the elephant we saw on our game drive was the impetus for Bailey going missing. I for one gave that possibility zero credence when Gwen went on about her tarot reading. I've heard Gwen with

Odelia, of course, and I've always thought tarot a lot of fluff. Even though I do believe in healers, like the one I hired to clear Odelia's house of wayward spirits, cards have always seemed like quite a load of bullshit. Or maybe I'm prejudiced, as I felt Gwen was always using the cards to manipulate Odelia to do what Gwen secretly wanted. But now Gwen's missing, and I can understand why Bailey might feel guilty about that.

"So I had a call with the attorney." Joshua consults a yellow legal pad, where he's jotted notes in his neat, squat script. "It's kind of complicated, with all the tax language and provisions for the company, but I think I understand the gist. The lawyer said he could do this on Zoom with us, but I figured it's a bit much to add another person to our fold right now."

"Yes, I don't think we need a Zoom." Davina places a supportive hand on Joshua's forearm. With her other hand she rocks the stroller with bassinet where Ruby's currently making quiet fussy noises, on her way to snoozeville.

Sam's already leafing through his copy eagerly beside me, not waiting for Joshua to expound. I stare numbly at the words: Last Will and Testament of Odelia Tisdale Babel.

If she'd had time to amend it like she said she intended to, it would say: Last Will and Testament of Odelia Babel-Bach. I keep that observation to myself.

"So all right if I run through it?" Joshua asks.

Bailey's across the table, looking—to be frank—a wreck. Blond frizzy hair in a low ponytail, blue eyes wild, flinching at every little sound, like she's trying to escape her body. I wish I could say something to console Bailey, but I know that I can't. Trauma shapes people; I can't pull platitudes from my hat, pretending she'll be fine.

"Yes, please, Joshua," Sam says agreeably. "Take us through this mumbo jumbo."

"Fine. So first off—" Joshua looks at me apologetically. "Asher. I believe you are already aware of this, but Mom left nothing to you. As you know, in your prenup, you waived all your rights to any assets at her death. Perhaps you might think that's unfair—because Mom just talked about amending her will to leave something to you above and beyond her obligations under the prenup, but obviously . . . she didn't get to it in time." He removes his tortoiseshell glasses, rubs his eyes, then slides the glasses back down the bridge of his nose.

"It's fine, Joshua. I didn't expect anything. Like I said." I think of how to say this without bragging. "I wasn't marrying Odelia for her money. I have plenty of my own."

Silence, until Davina says, "Of course you do. I think it's respectable you signed a prenup."

"Respectable, hmm? I don't remember you signing one," Sam says.

"Shut up, Sam." Davina stares daggers at her brother-in-law. "Don't drag my marriage into this. What would you know about partnership—about trying to build a life with someone and sharing everything together?"

Sam opens his mouth, but then closes it. "Nothing," he mutters.

"Back to the will," Joshua says, his voice strained. "Please, can we just get through this without fighting? We're all running on empty here."

A chorus of reluctant mm-hmms.

"Okay." Joshua reaches for his water glass but it's empty. We've asked the staff to leave us in privacy, so who's going to refill it? Joshua, no matter how grounded and seemingly uncorrupted by the silver spoon with which he grew up, is used to water fairies filling his glass. Eventually, he places the empty glass down and sighs.

"Okay, so let's start with the first gift. It's to Gwen, and it's a big one. Before disposing of the company, which goes to us kids—"

"Well, that's a relief." Sam's shoulders slump. "I didn't know if Mom was going to do something crazy."

"Well, before taking care of us kids in the way that Mom did," Joshua says, not totally shutting down Sam's fear of something crazy, I notice, "Mom made a very generous gift to Gwen. Fifty million dollars, outright to her, along with a letter and her locket."

"*Fifty* million dollars," Davina repeats in a low, disbelieving voice, echoing, I'm sure, what the rest of us are thinking. "And the locket? We still don't know where the locket is, though, do we?"

"No," Joshua says. "Still missing."

"Wow, that's . . . a lot of money," I finally say.

"A lot," Joshua agrees.

"What does the letter say?" I ask.

"I don't know," Joshua says. "It's password protected. The lawyer told me he doesn't have the password. Mom was clear on not giving it to anyone. She said only Gwen would know it."

"Where *is* Gwen? I don't understand where she is? And why the rain means search parties can't go out." Bailey stares out the window. "Can we hurry this up? I want to go looking for her."

"Bails, no," Davina says. "You can't. That's really not a good idea, not after what you've gone through."

But Bailey has never looked more to me like her mother in the defiance that torches her eyes, her jaw in a menacing set.

"I'll make one thing crystal clear," Bailey says, her voice sharp, leveling a steady gaze at each of us in turn. "If I want to go look for Gwen, which I do, I'm gonna go, and no one's gonna stop me. My mother is dead, and that means that no one—*no one*—will ever get to tell me what to do again."

# CHAPTER TWENTY-SIX

# JOSHUA

It's shocking to hear Bailey so vehement and unhinged.

"Okay, Bails," I finally say, trying to sound soothing. "Let's just finish reading the will." I'm hoping that since she's not storming back into the bush, we can table her concerning statement that she's going to take off again.

"So, after the gift to Gwen, which is very generous—"

"Fucking nuts, you mean. That's so much money," Sam says. "And it's not like Gwen needs it. Mom pays her well, and she doesn't have kids. She's not into all the designer stuff Mom's into." He pauses. "Was into."

"Well, nuts or not, that's what Mom did. Anyway, before I get into the disposition of the rest of the estate, I want to tell you all that Mom's will contains provisions related to Circ. I understand from the lawyer they're fairly standard, but one provision was . . ." I think how to say it. "Important," I finally decide upon.

"So not standard," Sam says.

"Not *not* standard," I counter. "Just . . . okay, she named me CEO of Circ, which—is not a surprise, right?"

"Right," Sam says, after a pause.

I nod. "But she also assigned me all her voting shares."

"Wow." Sam whistles. "Big brother on the block."

I blush. "I was really shocked, to be honest."

"C'mon," Davina says. "Of course that's what Odelia did. The company is in the best hands with you."

"I don't know about that, but I'm going to try my best," I say quietly. "I love this company. Bails, are you—is that . . ."

She stares at me dumbly. I know she doesn't want the company—to own it or to run it—but she works there, same as me. Chief conservation officer—what we were supposed to chat about this morning, before I found Mom's body. In what feels like another life.

"This doesn't change anything about your role at Circ," I say to Bailey. "Mom was so proud of you. She would definitely want you to keep on—"

"Keeping on," Bailey interrupts.

"Uh . . . what?"

"Keep on keeping on." Her voice is eerie, almost singsong. "That's what Mom would want. Yep. Well, I won't be."

"Okay." I clear my throat. "What you want to do going forward is up to you, obviously. And no one has to make any rash decisions, not now."

"Right," Davina says encouragingly, and our eyes beam messages back and forth.

*Do you know what this means? My taking over Circ?* my eyes ask hers. *I do*, hers respond back.

"Anyway," I finally say, "the rest of Mom's estate, including her ownership of Circ, go to us kids equally, with a few caveats."

Sam props his elbows on the table and leans forward. "*What* caveats?"

"Well, first, our money doesn't come to us outright. It's put in trust."

"Okayyyyyy," Sam says. "Which means what?"

I tell him what the lawyer said, trying to make it sound technical and standard. "A trust is a vehicle to hold an inheritance that's managed by the trustees."

"And who are the trustees?" Sam asks.

"Well, the trustee," I say, correcting it to the singular, "is . . ." God, he's going to freak. Give me strength. "Fine, I'll say it. *I* am the trustee of your inheritance, Sam."

Sam turns beet red. "What? You're telling me I don't just get my money? That *you* control it?"

"What I understand from the lawyer," I try to say calmly, "is that this is pretty standard. For tax reasons, a trust makes sense as a vehicle. And there is a distribution standard giving the trustee—"

"You," Sam says, like he's accusing me of asking for this thankless job.

"Me," I agree. "Giving me discretion to make distributions to you for your health, any further education, and reasonable comfort. And . . ." God, I don't want to have to say this part.

"And what?"

"And Mom put in a specific proviso."

"For my trust?" Sam asks. "Or for yours and Bailey's too?"

"Just for yours," I say quietly. Man, this sucks. As much as I think what Mom did was warranted, I know this is going to enrage my brother. And I get that it's unfair. Kids should be equal in the eyes of their parents, shouldn't they? Only we've never been.

"What? What is it?" Sam asks.

"She specified that no distributions should be made to enhance your quality of life beyond that which you experience from your own professional acumen." Sam's boiling rage is clear, so I hurry on. Might as well pull the Band-Aid straight off. "And she said that no distributions should be made to fund a business in which you are engaged, unless that business is Circ."

"I see," Sam says, so calm I am almost afraid. "And what about the trusts for you and Bailey? Who is trustee of *your* trust, Josh?"

Fuck, it grates on me when he calls me that. But I can't let on, give him the satisfaction. "Well . . . I am, alone," I admit. "And Bailey is named as the sole trustee of hers."

"So it's just *me*," Sam says. "Just me who gets screwed. Of course. I should have expected nothing less of our mother. And what about if something happens to you, PJ? Who becomes my trustee then?"

Davina grabs my hand. "Nothing's going to happen to Joshua, Sam. Please don't go there."

"I'm only saying what if!" Sam's eyes flash with rage. "No one will live forever, Davina. Not even your precious PJ."

I keep my tone as steady as I can, even though I feel wobbly. "Well, if something were to happen to me, then you and Bailey are named as cotrustees of your trust."

"I see," Sam says, in a way that scares me. I've never been terrified of my brother, but maybe . . . maybe now I am. I note for not the first time how the left bow of Sam's top lip puffs up higher than the right when he's not smiling. The asymmetry only amplifies his menace. I suppose it's how I've always felt around my brother—like nothing is balanced and calm, like he's always unpredictable and liable to pop off.

"So Bailey and I would have to agree on distributions?" Sam muses, his face softening.

I know what he's thinking—our sister is a pushover when it comes to him. She'd kowtow to whatever he wanted.

I wave a hand in front of his face. "Hello, I'm still alive here, Sam. I plan to be for a very long time."

"I figured." Sam shakes his head violently. "I should have figured. Even if I inherit millions upon millions, I actually am getting nothing in my bank account." He stands up, walks over to the window, and lets out an earsplitting roar. "ARGHHHHHHHH." Then he pounds his fists on the windows with such vigor that his kippah flings off his head.

"Sam!" Bailey vaults up and goes to him. I stare at Davina, at a loss for what to do, and she just gives me a tiny shrug. There's no rulebook for this trip.

I wish Mom were here. She'd know what to do.

My phone vibrates at my side, and I'm grateful for the excuse to slip away.

"I'll be right back," I say, brandishing the screen as evidence, so no one thinks I'm taking the easy way out and bailing because of Sam. "It's Officer Monala."

When I'm out of earshot from my family, the officer and I exchange pleasantries. She expresses yet more reassurances that the police will return as soon as the weather makes it practicable, then asks if anything else has developed.

I say, "You mean anyone else dead? Not yet, but the day is young." I chuckle, though it doesn't feel at all funny.

"Joshua." The officer pauses, and it tells me she's about to deliver bad news.

"Yes?"

"We tracked Gwen's phone to her last location."

I steel myself. "Where is she?"

A pause, then Officer Monala says, "Joshua, it's showing that Gwen's phone is not far from the bonfire pit—"

"Jeez, really? She's still out there? I thought someone looked there. But the weather—maybe she's, I don't know, hurt or something . . ."

"No, Joshua." Long pause. "Unfortunately, the last broadcasting location of Gwen's cell phone isn't at the bonfire pit, but farther down the hill."

"I'm not following—down the hill is past the electric fence—I mean, that's close to the river—"

"Yes. Unfortunately, that's what I'm saying. Gwen's phone is tagged to the banks of Crocodile River . . ."

I feel numb—outside of my body—when I return to the group.

"What?" Davina asks, immediately spotting my face.

I call Sam and Bailey back from the window. Sam must notice that something's changed, because he obliges without protest. I tell them what Officer Monala just told me, trying to be as calm as possible so that everyone else stays calm too.

But calm is not what ensues.

Because Bailey launches up and starts screaming at a decibel so high and shrill she sounds like a person possessed. And then before anyone can react, she takes off sprinting toward the front door.

# CHAPTER TWENTY-SEVEN

# BAILEY

I don't remember running down the walk, shedding my clothes as I go. But Joshua tells me they found my sweatshirt at the juncture by the pool, and my sweatpants draped on Aba's grave.

I do remember leaping over the electric fence barrier, screaming "Gwen!" I do remember staring into the abyss of Crocodile River, rushing with water because of all the fresh rain, and standing on my tiptoes, prepared to dive in. Being absolutely convinced that Gwen went there for me, to find *me*, and that it was my responsibility to find her. And find her I would.

I do remember shouts—distant though—and a snort—maybe a hippo, or a crocodile. I remember the scratching of a porcupine, and how I watched a dung beetle pushing his ball. I remember the way mist chilled my bare skin, and how I wasn't afraid. Not at all afraid.

I remember screaming, "Gwen!" one more time, and that I heard her respond. Actually heard her—her sweet, low tone. Of course she responded—she's always there for me, always around the corner, more motherly to me than my own ever was.

"Yes, Bailey, I'm here. Come in and save me!"

Then I remember hands on my back. Gripping my arms. Pressure.

They're trying to cage me. But I need to get to Gwen!

I struggle and scream, but the cage is stronger than me.

Then I black out.

When I come to, I'm in my bed at Leopard Sands. My hair is damp, I feel it dripping down my back through my shirt.

They're all there, my family, but not Mom and Gwen.

"What happened?" I ask, blinking rapidly.

"Bails . . ." Sam passes me a glass of water. Concern riddles his features. "You . . . I guess you freaked out. You really worried us. Do you . . . do you remember—running and—"

"I'm fine," I say, and I try my hardest to look it. I feel like an animal at the zoo, performing for the people who've bought tickets. My heart is still thwacking my chest, but I don't dare admit it. I can tell how they all relax at my display of fineness. I can tell how much they don't want me to be crazy.

"I just freaked out. About Gwen." I bite my lip.

"I know, Bails." Davina squeezes my hand.

I wish I could explode again.

"I need air." I bolt to a sit. "I need you all to go."

"Sure." Davina nods and stands. "Sam, you'll—"

"Of course. I'll be here."

As my family shuffles around and touches me and hugs me and murmurs unhelpful assurances, about the police being here in the morning, as if that's going to fix anything, I find myself hovering above and watching everything. I know this day is horrific. That I haven't begun to process what's happened. And that there is still a murderer on the loose. And Gwen's missing. Maybe dead, in Crocodile River.

But I'm suddenly quite lucid and aware that it was crazy to try to run into the river in an attempt to save Gwen. So I wonder: Am I just in awful pain at Mom's death, or is something else happening to me?

The door opens, and hot air billows in, diluting the blasting air-conditioning, and I think about blacking out. About the things I still don't remember. And a question flashes in my brain:

Am I being drugged?

# CHAPTER TWENTY-EIGHT

# JOSHUA

My head is pounding with the start of a migraine when we leave Bailey with Sam in their suite. Davina and I don't speak, just walk toward the lodge to collect Ruby from Violett. Thankfully Violett was in the lodge when Bailey burst out, so we asked her to take Ruby and then raced after Bailey. We retrieve a happy, gurgling Ruby in her bassinet, then walk her back to our suite as she swipes at her squishy ball toy thing that dangles from the handle.

"Nice of Violett to stay with Ruby," Davina says, breaking our silence. "She's sweet with her."

"Yeah. I tried to tell you that."

"I know. I'm saying . . . you were right."

It doesn't feel like any sort of victory now. "I'm worried about Bailey, Dav. Worried something's wrong with her. Like beyond everything that's happening."

"I know. Me too."

That lands with a thud. Davina isn't one to get worked up unnecessarily with fears. If she's worried, then I'm right. Something is seriously wrong.

"What do you think it is?" I ask.

"I don't know. But it's not just your mom . . . and Gwen . . . even before, Bailey going after the elephant. It's so reckless. Like asking to—"

"Die," I finish. "I know."

The rain has stopped now, is only a fine mist. The sky is charcoal heading to black, night closing in on the last faint shards of day. My phone rings. Officer Monala.

We're at our suite now, but I motion to Davina. "I'm gonna take this outside." She nods and I hold the door open for them, and Dav pushes Ruby inside.

"Hello?"

"Joshua, hello. How are you?"

"I'm . . . I don't quite have a word to describe that right now."

"*Ja*. I understand. Well, I am calling to tell you that we will indeed be returning in the morning. No more rain is forecast, but the roads from Skukuza are still flooded, so we definitely will take the chopper. We will take off shortly after sunrise. We intend to question everyone again and—"

"And you'll send out search parties for Gwen?"

A pause, and then Officer Monala says, "We will, but Joshua—the phone on the riverbanks, outside the boundary of the electric fence—you can't delude yourself. That's not a positive sign."

"There could be many reasons it's there. Maybe it fell . . . and went downhill in the floods . . ."

"Perhaps," she says, sounding skeptical. "By the way, we've processed the rifle. There were no fingerprints on it."

I'm quiet, digesting it. "Which means what, the killer wiped them off? If Markus's prints weren't even on—"

"Joshua, I'd like to ask you a question. Who do *you* think killed your mother?"

"I honestly have no idea." I exhale slowly. "Maybe one of the staff. I don't think you've looked enough into all of them."

"Maybe." But she sounds doubtful. "What would the motive of a staff person be to kill your mother?"

"Who knows. Blackmail. Revenge. My mother's a powerful, wealthy person who had the tendency of pissing people off. I'm sure there was no shortage of people who wanted to kill her."

"We're looking into every angle, but . . . Joshua?"

"Yes?"

"I would advise you to lock your doors tonight. That goes for the rest of your family too." She pauses. "You don't know who is still out there. What they still have planned."

I take a deep breath, then say, "We will, Officer, thanks. See you in the morning."

Back in the suite, Davina's sprawled on her stomach on the bed, in front of her laptop. She looks up, gives me a tepid thumbs-up. Meaning Ruby's already sleeping in her DockATot. I peer over; I hope she won't surprise us with another jet lag bout, or a sleep regression. My own body burns for sleep. My eyelids feel like weights, pressing my eyeballs down into their sockets.

But first I need to shower. Snap back to life. To think. And to finally look at the USB burning in my pocket.

"Whatcha doing? Oh, your Substack." I ease onto the bed and rub Davina's shoulders.

"Yeah."

I peer over and see the heading: *The Menace of Beauty Merch.* And the subheading: *Your Bucket Hat Branded as Sun Protection Is Contributing to Global Warming.*

I frown. "Don't *you* have a bucket hat?"

Davina groans. "No. C'mon. I mean, I do. I have Circ's bucket hat, that's sustainable, and I only wear it because it's cute, not for its branding. But I own that one hat. Do you know how many other girls have?"

"I don't know . . . two?"

She rolls her eyes. "Try like five. And they wear each a grand total of once. Buying an extra one is just augmenting the levels of stratospheric ozone and is actually increasing the UV radiation reaching the planet."

"Those are fair points." We bonded over this stuff when we met— how both of us saw the holes in greenwashing companies claiming to be sustainable, and how badly we wanted to make the earth a truly more habitable, sustainable place. And Dav's Substack is amazing—she has tens of thousands of subscribers, and she talks about important things, about the toxic chemicals present even in the clean beauty products, about how bras constrain lymph nodes and can actually contribute to breast sagging, contrary to popular opinion. How kids as young as ten are being sold "antiaging" skincare regimes on TikTok. Stuff no one else is talking about much. Stuff that helps women navigate and take a stand against our often absurdist culture. Stuff she opened my eyes to and I am proud of her for discussing.

"Thanks." Dav smiles.

I sag back onto a pillow. "I can't believe you have the energy and brain space to work on your Substack right now."

"You called the office, too, Joshua." Davina's eyebrows pinch together. "This is work. And a distraction, honestly. Plus, I'm not releasing this tonight. Obviously, that would be tone-deaf. I've already sent out a blast with 'thanks for your patience during this difficult time.' But I'll have to release a newsletter in the next week. My subscribers don't just expect it, they pay for it. They help pay for our family."

I restrain the impetus to argue, because that's hardly true. Even though it's amazing, and I'm very proud of Dav, her Substack isn't pulling in meaningful money yet. Our Circ jobs are what pay for our family, but I am hardly about to make that point now.

"I'm just putting on finishing touches. And don't think I didn't hear you talking to Lester. Or that I don't know you went to confront Odelia last night about work. About Lester—apparently you really got into it."

"How . . . how do you know—"

"Asher told me." Dav shrugs. "We're both workaholics. Don't make me out to be the only one."

She's right. Fine. We *are* both workaholics; we hit it off early over that. How lucky we both felt, getting to make our passions our jobs. How work was fun! We didn't understand people who felt otherwise. But something she just said—not the workaholic thing—has knocked the wind out of me. "You talked to Asher about me?" I ask, hating that I can't let it go, that I feel so insecure.

Dav rolls over and props up to a sit, facing me. "Oh man, please tell me you're not going down that road again? I can't take it anymore. For the last time—nothing is going on between me and Asher."

I'm quiet. Not sure what to believe anymore.

"You need to manage your insecurities. I can't constantly be bolstering you up."

"*Bolstering* me?" I stand, now quaking with anger.

How have we become these people? I think about the *we* of years ago, working together at the company, getting to know each other slowly. Growing more comfortable to be my nerdy, shy self and happily surprised each time as Davina accepted the parts of me I once thought I needed to fix. She showed me acceptance and kindness—and sensuality. She taught me how to flirt, how to banter, how to find humor in intimacy. I'd always felt such anxiety to perform, felt like women were judging me, finding me lacking, but Davina made me feel comfortable, at ease with myself, like exactly how I was, with my fumbling moves, was okay. More than okay—wonderful. For the first time in my life, I felt special. That this majestic woman had chosen me over everyone else. And her spicy melded well with my mild. Or it did then, I guess.

"How dare you say you're bolstering me up? Acting like you-you—" My hands flop to my sides. "You know what? I can't do this right now. In case you didn't notice, my mother was murdered today," I whisper, feeling totally defeated. "And Gwen is missing, and my sister might be losing it." But then it surges in me again, my anger. "So fucking excuse me if I don't have the energy to chat about my insecurities right now."

I stare at my wife, breathless. God, we never speak to each other like this. *I* never speak to anyone like I have on this trip. But I've felt so irate, so pushed to the edge. Maybe she's right, though. Davina clearly wants me to step into a different version of myself, and so maybe it's time she met New Joshua. Maybe it's time everyone did.

"I'm gonna go back to Bailey's suite," I say. "Make sure she's all right."

"No." Davina's up now, practically vaulting toward the door.

"What do you mean, *no*?"

"I mean, no! I'll go. I'm her sister, too, and she needs a woman right now. Motherly energy, after . . . after Odelia. And honestly, Joshua. I need a break. I don't want to be in this stifling room right now. *You* stay with Ruby. I need fresh air."

But she doesn't wait for me to agree, just stalks out and closes the door behind her, quietly, of course, because she is a mother, and Ruby is sleeping.

———

FINE, I SEETHE, SHEDDING my clothes and going into the bathroom to run the shower. *Fine. She gets to escape to—* For a moment I wonder if she's actually going to Asher. Not to Bailey.

*No, stop it, Joshua,* I order myself, as I let the water gush around, cleanse me, or try to. *You're grieving, and afraid, and this is the craziest, most fucked-up day of your life, so you're spinning out.*

When I've showered and toweled off, I return to the room and realize it's nighttime. The sun hasn't set so much as disappeared, the gray sky transmuted seamlessly to purple blackness. I turn on a table lamp, put on pajamas, and then dig in the chinos I was wearing for the locket. I grab my laptop and prop it on a pillow on the bed, my back against the headboard.

Time to finally face the USB.

I stare at the locket—The Triple Threats in block, almost ominous script. I know, of course, that the triple refers to Mom, Gwen, and Rachel. Best childhood friends, until Rachel died in a boating accident while Gwen was driving the boat. That's why she spent two years in prison, for manslaughter. It was a slam dunk case—Rachel's nanny saw it all happen from their lawn. This was before I was born. Mom hardly ever spoke about Rachel, though I've seen the pictures, three girls impossibly young, holding one another tight. I know from the rare time Mom spoke about it that, when they were kids, each of the girls' lockets held a key. The keys were all identical, able to open the shed in the backyard of Mom's parents' house. It was the girls' safe place—I realize I never asked why they all needed one.

Mom kept that key in her locket always, as far as I knew. But last week I saw her fiddling with the locket, popping it open, and I noticed a flash of metal incompatible with a key. A USB? The key was gone, I realized. But why would Mom have substituted it with a flash drive?

Lester and I have been chatting in secret lately. Neither of us is happy about the direction the company is taking; Lester thinks further machinations are underfoot, that Mom is cutting costs to the detriment of our mission and possibly even human life. Bailey thinks so too. That's why I wanted to chat with my sister this morning. Get ahead of things and present a united front. Maybe Mom could fend off any of us on our own, but all of us together would be a far tougher fight.

I spin the flash drive in my fingers. What will I do if Mom's hiding something even more egregious than I'm aware of, something else Circ's perpetrated? I'm CEO now—it will all crash down on my shoulders.

I slide the flash drive into the port on my laptop, and when I open the first file, I gasp.

This isn't what I expected at all.

It's much, much worse.

# CHAPTER TWENTY-NINE

# BAILEY

There's a knock at the door, and Sam launches up, like he's happy to have something practical to do. Whereas my whole body clenches, anticipating more bad news.

When Sam opens the door, I hear him say, "Hey, Dav. What—you forget something?"

My body whooshes with relief, but that only gives me a second's reprieve before the stiff foreboding seizes hold again.

"No. Just thought Bailey might like . . . I don't know. Thought I'd check on her." Davina's talking softly, as if she doesn't want me to hear, but obviously I can. They're treating me like I'm five, like I need to be babysat.

"Yeah. It's been a helluva day." He cracks the door open.

Davina comes over to where I'm pacing by the windows. "Hey, Bails." She tucks her pale pink hair behind her ear, looking more nervous than I've ever seen her.

"Hey, Dav. You and Sam are twins."

I don't say it with humor, just an observation. They're both in all black. Dav's wearing a maxi dress with her boobs hitched up. It veers a bit sexy-funeral, odd for this rainy, grim day, but then, ever since giving birth, Dav's been dressing more body consciously. Sam, on the other hand, is in black athleisure, a bicep-straining crew neck and close-cropped athletic shorts that highlight his muscly thighs. And a black Miami Dolphins cap. That's his typical uniform, unless he's in its more formal iteration that involves ripped black denim. All black always—a good color for him, accents his perma-tan.

Sam shrugs. "Yeah. Guess we are. Hey, Dav. If you're gonna stay and—" He eyes me hurriedly, like I won't figure out they're arranging babysitting duty for me if they don't say so explicitly. "Maybe I'll go look for Gwen?"

"Yes, that's a good idea," I say, even though in my heart of hearts, I think it's futile. Before, I might have thought I could find her—save her—but now I'm back in reality, and the odds seem low of finding her alive. I may have survived the elements today, with Markus protecting me, but the fact that the two of us made it out there at night in the bush is like having been struck by lightning. Mom's gone, and Gwen is as strong as a pincushion. I can't imagine how she's made it to this point out there, unless lightning truly does strike twice.

"At night?" Davina asks. "Is that safe?"

"I'll just be an hour. And besides, is being in here safe when there's a murderer around?"

Davina doesn't have a response to that. "I'm sure Markus would go with you too," she finally says.

"No," Sam snaps, and I watch Davina's face color in confusion. "Titus can drive, and he's a better tracker anyway."

"Okay, good luck."

"Be safe, Sammy," I whisper.

He laces up his trainers and kisses my cheek.

"I need air," I say, and push open the screen door before Davina can answer. I walk out into the night and begin pacing the back deck.

"Hey, Bails." Dav follows after me.

I don't stop pacing. I know how I must look—a crazy mess. Normally I'm a lug. Not in a bad way, but I can chill. If ever we're all at Mom's, hanging out over lunch, Dav and Sam start to get antsy, ready to make moves, but not me. I can sit there forever and chat and eat. I'm not an Energizer Bunny type, but right now, I feel positively manic.

"Hey, Dav," I finally say. "Thanks for coming to babysit me."

"I'm not." She flushes. "I mean, I don't— I know what it's like to lose your mom, Bailey."

"Oh." Shame swells in my chest. How did I briefly forget that Dav lost her mom a couple years ago? It was horrible, Lou Gehrig's disease. They were really close. I remember at the shiva that Dav referred to joining the Dead Parents' Club. Aba died a decade ago, so I suppose I've been a member for a long time. Now, it suddenly hits me that I'm an orphan.

"I'm sorry, Dav," I say slowly. "That was—I'm—don't pay attention to me."

She waves a hand and unpeels a sad smile. "Bails, don't feel like you have to be a certain way for me right now. Just be how you are. I really understand. It's the worst day of your life."

"Yeah. It is." I remember, our first full day here on game drive, Sam saying something similar. I forget how he put it—Bailey's No Good Very Bad something or another Day. Which is ridiculous, even comparing that day to this one. That game drive seems like another lifetime ago, a lifetime when I wasn't freezing down to my bones even though I've taken like four hot showers by now.

"I'm so sorry, Bails," she says. "About your mom. About Gwen. This is all so . . ."

"Thanks." I stare up at the stars—the first time I've really looked since I got here. I could've the first night, of course, and last night certainly I was close enough—up in that tree. But even last night aside, when the name of the game was survival, I've felt anxious since coming here in a way I usually don't. Usually I feel more or less able to snag the present moment. Even when I have a ticker tape of anxieties. But here . . . I've been more distracted than usual. I tip my face up now and manage to focus a few seconds on the warm air, not its typical muggy, but cooled by the storm, the world drenched and ravaged but still chugging on. Buffalo in the distance at the river, and the endless starry night.

"Will you distract me, Dav? Tell me something?"

"Something . . . like what?"

"I don't know. I just want to talk about something normal. Something that's not Mom gone, and Gwen, and poachers, and—"

"Yeah. Okay. Ummm . . . Joshua thinks I'm flirting with Asher."

"What?" I goggle at my sister-in-law. "You can't be serious?"

"No. I mean, I'm serious." She shrugs and gives me a tiny, sad smile. "It's unreal. He's always been jealous—"

"Not jealous," I say quietly. "Maybe insecure."

"Yeah. Insecure. But, like, cheating on him with a guy who was going to be his new stepfather? Obviously, I'm not," she adds. "That goes without saying, right?"

"Right," I say slowly. I mean, I do believe her. She and Joshua are great together. Granted, Dav does flirt with Asher—but she flirts with everyone. I saw her flirting with Jabulani earlier too. She's open, she's curious about people, loves talking to them and finding out what makes them tick. Joshua's introverted, but that's why their dynamic works. Even though he keeps to himself, he opens up to the ones he loves, to me and to Dav.

"To be honest, Bails, I feel like he's the one hiding things from me. Joshua is kind of flirty with Violett, have you noticed that?"

I stare at her in disbelief. "Violett—the manager, you mean? You can't be serious."

"Yes. She's really sweet with Ruby, I'll give you that. But I swear, she and Joshua are like . . . friends. And he never told me that before we came here. And now I realize—they have this whole relationship he kept from me. And the way she looks at him . . . it's like— I don't know, Bails. Tender."

"Tender," I repeat doubtfully.

"Yeah. How's that for a distraction?" Dav forces a bright tone.

Now I smile. "Dav, I don't think you have anything to worry about there."

"I know he's your brother, Bails. I'm not trying to make you take sides. But honestly, Violett's all over him . . . constantly checking on him."

Gosh, she's really serious. How do I make her see she's being ridiculous, without calling her hormonal, or anything else condescending?

"Violett," I say again, and suddenly I gasp.

"What? Bails, what?" Dav asks.

"Nothing."

"No, Bails, tell me. What?"

"Really, nothing." But a lump's lodged itself in my throat. I rub my shoulders.

"Dav, can we go in? I'm getting cold."

"Oh . . . yeah." She extends her arm, and I shrug it off.

"I'm not a child, Dav." I walk fast inside ahead of her, go into the bathroom, and close the door.

I try to clear my mind, sift through things and group them together in a way that makes sense. But I can't. Am I crazy, or am I finally seeing things clearly? I keep ping-ponging between the two possibilities and can't be sure where I've landed.

I change into pajamas and wash my face and brush my teeth, my thoughts in a whirl. When I come out, Dav's on the couch, drinking from a glass with clear liquid inside, an empty minibottle of tequila on the coffee table.

When Dav spots me, she smiles with visible relief, like she worried I was going to escape out the bathroom window.

"Here, Bails." She hands me another glass, fuller than hers, with clear liquid too. "Yours is water."

I'm parched, but I hesitate before accepting it. Finally, I take the drink and am about to sip when Dav says, "And I was thinking . . . here." She sticks out her hand, curled into a fist, and when she unfurls her fingers, I see a pill. She drops it into my palm.

"What's that?" I ask, the hairs prickling on my arm.

"An Ambien. I just thought—Bails, you really should get some sleep."

"How do you have an Ambien? Is that even safe . . . while you're breast-feeding?"

"Sometimes I can't sleep," she says, but doesn't answer my second question. "I really think you should take it, Bails. You need a good night's sleep. Things will look different in the morning."

"They won't," I tell her and stare at the pill, vacillating. Oh, whatever— I slip it in my mouth and follow it with water.

Dav looks pleased, and as I place the cup back on the coffee table, I hear a key in the door. Sam bursts in.

"Did you . . . ?" I ask him. But I trail off, because I see it in his face— he didn't find Gwen.

Dav stands, her face weird and unreadable now. "Okay, Bails, I'm gonna get back to my crew." She hugs me goodbye. "Tomorrow the police will arrive. They're going to sort this all out. Sleep tight."

I can only muster a tiny nod in response.

Sam shows Dav out. When he returns to me, he opens his mouth, but suddenly I don't have any energy to talk. None. "I have to go to the bath-room," I say, then return there, close the door, lock it, and splash my face in the sink.

When I finish and wipe my face, I stare out the tiny window that over-looks the front porch, where I am surprised to see Davina standing, looking out. She must have been standing there for a minute by now, for no reason I can discern. I see her glance around, as if someone's lurking around the corner, but there's no one I can see anywhere. No one watching her, other than me.

She checks her phone, writes something, then slips it back into her pocket. Then she flicks her eyes left, in the direction of her suite with Joshua and Ruby. But instead of going left, she walks briskly to the right instead. She turns once, looking back over her shoulder, then continues on, faster paced this time.

There are only two suites to our right, I realize. The one immediately to the right is the empty suite, and the one to the right of that, at the end of the row, is Mom and Asher's. Now occupied by only one person. The man who was meant to become my stepfather.

————

I DON'T KNOW WHAT to do. If I tell Sam, he's liable to overreact. To do something . . . I don't know what . . . I need time to sort it out in my head first.

Why did Dav tell me her suspicions about Joshua and Violett? It was so odd—no way would Joshua ever fool around on her. Dav knows that. She must know that. In which case, did Dav tell me to deflect? To throw me off the trail of her and . . . Asher? And apparently, Joshua's jealous, insecure—which says something, doesn't it, for my not-prone-to-overreacting big brother?

I crawl into bed, hoping the Ambien will take effect soon. Erase all my thoughts.

"Sleep well, Bails." Sam comes over and kisses my forehead, then turns off the lights. "Things will look better in the morning."

"Yeah," I say, even though I know that he's lying. The pain's going to be there in the morning, waiting for me.

I listen to a distant howl of some animal and take another sip of water. I feel so horrible—so unlike myself—

Am I being drugged? I'd wondered earlier in the day, but now it feels increasingly possible. The sleeping pill? Why did I take it . . . especially now that I know Dav went skulking over to Asher's when she said she was going back to her family? Was it even an Ambien? Or something else . . . something else that would explain this strange way I'm feeling . . . and acting. . . .

That's my last thought before sleep pulls me under.

# CHAPTER THIRTY

# JOSHUA

I gape at my screen, scrolling through the contents of Mom's flash drive. Pictures. Mostly screenshots, as far as I can tell, of notes. All typed.

I know what you did.

You won't get away with it.

The countdown is on until you die.

I gasp. What the hell? What are these threats? Who sent them? To Mom?

My mind spins forward, assessing. This changes everything, doesn't it? Someone's been blackmailing Mom. Whoever sent these . . . murdered her. Right?

I can't believe Mom's been receiving these and didn't tell anyone. Didn't tell me. Or at least, the police. If she didn't tell anyone, does that mean she's done something horrible?

I click on the other file, and this time it's a picture. A *screenshot* of a picture, in fact, and I glean that it accompanied one of the notes.

It's a picture I've seen before: three young girls, arms wrapped around one another. Mom, Gwen, and their best friend, Rachel. The one who died in the boating accident, when Gwen accidentally ran her over. I remember the one time Mom relented and told me the details. How Rachel had married a rich *macher* who lived in a lakefront South Florida mansion. Mom was married, too, by then, to Aba, a friend of Rachel's husband, David, both of whom ran in wealthy circles. They were in their late twenties or early thirties, and Gwen was single, but the three of them were still the very best of friends. They decided to have a ladies' day, going out on David's boat. Rachel was waterskiing off the back, and Gwen was driving, but she didn't realize Rachel had fallen, and Gwen somehow wound up running right over Rachel in the water. Rachel was killed instantly by the boat's propeller. It's a horrific story—Gwen accidentally killing her best friend, then serving jail time for it.

But what's really horrific about this photo is what's scrawled above the smiling young girls, written in the same red marker as the circle around Mom's face. Two words: *You're next.*

———————

I PULL UP GOOGLE, and into the search box I type: boating accident Rachel Gwen Odelia Lake Worth.

I scan the previews, and a few entries down, I see an article from the *Palm Beach Post* with the headline: "Jury Convicts Hollywood Woman of Manslaughter in Boating Death of Best Friend."

I click on the article and scroll rapidly through.

The driver at the helm of a speedboat when it ran over a woman in Lake Worth, killing her instantly, was convicted today of two counts of manslaughter.

Gwen Tulchinsky, 30, was driving a boat along the lake's southern shore on July 15 when she struck 30-year-old Rachel Taubman Balsam, a citizen of the United Kingdom and resident of Palm Beach. Tulchinsky and Balsam were friends, spending the afternoon waterskiing and boating along with a third friend, Odelia Tisdale Babel, 31.

"It was devastating," Babel said. "It's very difficult for me to talk about. I never imagined that the three of us would go out for a fun afternoon and that one of us wouldn't come back alive."

Deputies say Tulchinsky was recklessly driving the 28-foot boat, going 65-70 mph. Balsam had been waterskiing off the back of the boat, and Tulchinsky testified that she didn't know Balsam had fallen when Tulchinsky circled back and drove the boat right over Balsam. Balsam was killed instantly by the boat's propeller.

The only eyewitnesses, besides Babel, were Balsam's son, Oshri, 6, and his nanny, Olesia Ratajczak, 48, who were playing on the swing set of Balsam's property when the accident occurred right in front of the house.

"It was horrible, absolutely horrible," Ratajczak said. "When they pulled the body in, it didn't even look like [Balsam] anymore. [Tulchinsky] was at the wheel, looking absolutely bereft. But I certainly don't think [Tulchinsky] intended to do it. And she wasn't a drunk, like the prosecution tried to say. She was driving recklessly, far too fast. Such a tragedy. Those three were the very best of friends."

Tulchinsky will be sentenced in late April.

———

I READ A COUPLE more articles, all similarly disturbing. I can't believe I never googled this, but it happened so long ago, and I guess I've been like most children, absorbed with my own problems and concerns instead of digging into my parents' pasts. It's hard to believe, though—the court case, the allegations, the terrible way Rachel died. It must have shaped Gwen's entire life, and Mom's, too, in ways I've never contemplated.

But I still don't understand how it all jibes. How the accident, and what Gwen did, intersects with these threats. . . .

Is it a coincidence that Mom was murdered, and now Gwen's disappeared? Can't be, can it, now that I know about this picture and the threats? I know I'm missing something big, but my mind can't wrap around what.

I pull up Mom's letter to Gwen that the lawyer sent over and attempt a few more passwords. I try Rachel, then TheTripleThreats, then all variations of GwenRachelOdelia.

Nothing. None of it gives me access. The police will be able to break the barrier, I'm sure. But not tonight—and I want to know now.

I stare out into the black night. Why did Mom corral all these threats onto a flash drive that she was keeping in her locket? Who has been sending the threats, and what does it all mean?

As I try to parse the facts, I zoom in on a picture in the newspaper article, of Rachel's little boy. Oshri. It's clearly a candid; he's walking away from the camera toward the water, a dog trotting at his feet, but someone—Rachel, likely—must have said, *Look at me*, and so the boy swiveled and did. He's wearing a light blue collared shirt and blue checked shorts, and he's sucking on a red Popsicle that I can see has dripped down onto his collar. He's gangly and has what looks like a blobby birthmark on the back of his neck, but the thing that strikes me the most is how happy he looks here. How happy he once was before he watched his mother die. Before he was simply playing in their yard with his dog, just waiting for Rachel to come home.

The shadows on the walls dart to and fro. I glance out the window to the suite in the distance that belongs to Bailey and Sam, wondering if I can see Davina, see my siblings—craving signs of life. But the drapes are drawn— I see nothing. I am alone. I've tried to glom onto them, I guess—Dav and Bailey. Aba and Mom, too, in some ways. But they're all slippery. It feels like all of them are gone.

I stand and go to Ruby. She's so still that for a moment, my breath clogs, until I spot the tiny protrusion and then contraction of her stomach. I remember doing skin to skin with her when she was a newborn. Davina was the one feeding her, and I was generally Davina's butler, a role that I was more than glad to adopt, so that my wife could focus on her herculean tasks of recovering from her C-section and nourishing our daughter. But I wanted that contact with Ruby, too, that connection. I remember lying on her floor in those first few weeks, the scratchy carpet against my back, and Ruby on my chest, as my heart burst with fireworks. I love Davina dearly, but I'd never felt that before, such pure, primitive love. I can't deny it—with Ruby's belly against my mine, I thought about my own parents then, about whether they held me that same way when I was weeks old, about whether love coursed in them with the same ferocity. Whether they looked at each other in delight, their eyes screaming, *He's ours!*

I think I know the answer now.

# CHAPTER THIRTY-ONE

# VIOLETT

Just before nine in the evening, I'm hurrying along the walk toward Joshua and Davina's suite, nearly to the door, when I spot Davina down the walk, in the distance. I stop, wait for her. She's coming from Odelia's suite, I can see. Odelia and Asher's. The farthest from the lodge. Next to it is the empty suite, and then Bailey and Sam, followed by Gwen, and then Joshua and Davina, located here, closest to the lodge and staff housing. I wonder what Davina was doing with Asher at this late hour.

"Oh, hello, Violett." Davina looks not at all ashamed that I've caught her in the act of . . . what, exactly? "Nice that the rain has finally stopped for us, eh?"

"Yes . . ." I open my mouth, about to ask her right out, but whether and why she was with Asher at night is none of my business. I try not to stare at her *tet*, straining from the tight bodice of her dress.

She must notice me looking, though, because she says, "When the milk comes in, they get gargantuan."

"Oh." I blush. "I was coming to tell you and Joshua—the police will be here in the morning. Now that the storm's done."

"Finally." She leans on the rail, then fishes out Chapstick from her pocket and applies it to her lips. "Thank you for letting us know. I'll sleep better, knowing that."

I take a deep breath. "And I wanted to see if you'd like me to watch Ruby in the morning? When the police come? They'll want to interview you . . . and I'm happy to watch her. She's such a sweet baby."

Davina's face morphs into a smile. "She is. She really is. Her little personality is starting to come through too."

"Oh?" I ask. I've gleaned it—Ruby's a go-getter. Demands what she wants. But I wonder about Davina's interpretation.

"Yes. She's fierce. Doesn't take no for an answer." Davina says it in the proud way of a mother.

"I've noticed the same thing," I tell her.

Her smile gets wider. "Yes, actually, that would be wonderful, Violett. If you could take Ruby in the morning, we would really appreciate it. We'll pay you extra, of course."

I wave a hand. "No bother. This is all part of the VIP service."

"You're wonderful with children," she says.

I manage a smile and nod. "Thank you. So I'll come around . . . six, shall we say? I assume she's an early bird, Miss. Ruby."

"Oh . . . you don't need to come so early. She'll probably wake around five . . . and then feed a while . . ."

"So six it is. It's no bother. I'm up with the sun. That way you can sleep a bit longer after feeding. After this day, I'm assuming you'll need it. And—the police—you'll need your strength."

"Oh." To my surprise, Davina lunges forward to hug me. "You can't imagine how I appreciate this. Joshua will, too, I know. Today was horrible— I'm just so exhausted—"

"Yes. You need your strength." I pat Davina's shoulder. She is a sweet person. Perhaps I misjudged her. Except, why was she coming from Asher's suite?

Davina nods. "Yes. Tomorrow is going to be another doozy of a day. With the police, and finding Gwen . . ."

"Yes," I agree, but now we avoid each other's eyes. *Finding* Gwen. Whatever that will mean. "Okay. Well, I will see you bright and early. Sleep well."

"Thank you again, Violett." She gives me a warm look, and I can tell she's wondering if perhaps she misjudged me. "Sleep well too."

"I will." I touch the gun in my holster, hidden beneath my jacket. I smile as I head back to my room behind the lodge, glad Davina said yes to the morning's plan.

Because I could also do this the hard way.

# CHAPTER THIRTY-TWO

# JOSHUA

Dav finds me standing over Ruby, still watching her. "Watching her breathe?" she whispers, draping her arm around me.

"My favorite hobby." Davina's arm feels heavy and cumbersome, but I allow it to lie there and suppress my desire to throw it off.

*You were gone a long time*, I think of telling her, but I know I'll sound bitter, even more insecure. Voicing my suspicions, my fears, that something is going on between her and Asher. That when she said she went to Bailey's, it was really a cover to go to him, in his empty suite, now that Mom's gone.

I finally slip out from under Davina's arm and go to the bed. I lie down on the coverlet embroidered in giraffes, a headache still simmering from my forehead up through my scalp.

"Exhausted? You must be," she says, slipping off her dress and changing into pj's.

I'm momentarily caught up in the sight of her—her silky skin, her delicious curves. My beautiful wife.

"Joshua?" She turns, her pink pajamas matching her pink hair. I am reminded that she is perfect. She is mine—for as long as that lasts. For the first time I realize that maybe I've been holding my breath ever since I met her, waiting for the other shoe to drop, for her to leave me for someone more . . . more, I don't know what. Just more than me, more than I can offer or be.

"Oh," I finally say. "Yeah. I'm matcha-level exhausted."

She laughs. That's an inside joke, a reference to Davina getting a speeding ticket when Ruby was a newborn. Davina got pulled over and pointed to Ruby in the back seat, telling the officer she was a new mother and completely exhausted. But the officer wasn't compassionate and started writing up the ticket, and Davina got agitated, saying this is what happens with the patriarchy, new mothers are demonized. And the officer said, "Ma'am, you were going fifty in a thirty-mile-an-hour zone and drinking coffee at the same time." To which Davina screamed, "This is matcha!"

Davina's smile fades now. "Matcha-level exhausted is justified, babe. I feel it too. This has been the worst day."

"The worst," I agree. I open my mouth, think about telling her what I found on the USB, but something stops me. "How's Bailey?" I ask.

"Oh." Davina props up the monitor on the nightstand. "Having a hard time."

She flicks the light, sinking us into darkness. My body prickles, waiting for my wife to curl into me, needing it, but she doesn't.

"Violett said she'll watch Ruby in the morning."

"Oh. That's great." I'm about to say that I'm glad Davina's grown to trust her, but I don't want to do anything to disturb that trust, to make Davina question it. "Violett's good with children."

"Ruby seems to love her," Davina agrees. "No stranger danger there."

"Ruby loves Gwen too," I say.

Silence, then Davina says, "She does."

I'm glad she doesn't say *did*. I know both of us need to believe Gwen's okay. That somehow, by some miracle, we're going to find Gwen alive.

---

I AWAKE IN THE middle of the night, knowing with certainty that Gwen's not all right. Knowing that whatever is going on is right in front of my nose—right on the flash drive—and I'm failing to figure it out.

I'm failing, and Gwen's time is running out.

I glance to my side. Davina stirs, but doesn't wake. I softly peel off the covers and slide out of bed. I press the side button on my phone and use the glow from the photo of Ruby on the screen to guide my movements. I grab my laptop from the nightstand and pad over to the closet. Inside, I close the door and switch on the light, then spontaneously change into a fresh pair of chinos and a blue-and-brown plaid short-sleeved button-down that Dav says makes me look like an even more dashing Don Draper. I need to be in work mode, need my brain to switch on. I'm tired to the bones, but adrenaline floods on top.

Mom was murdered. Most likely by the person who was blackmailing her. No matter Mom's faults, she didn't deserve her inglorious end. I remember on her sixtieth birthday, how she wore a long, slinky, neon-yellow, attention-grabbing dress and got up to give a speech. She clinked her glass with a knife for quiet, looking radiant, and said, "Happy birthday to me! I was once asked in an interview, who is your greatest hero, and I didn't know the answer. But now, I do know. My greatest hero is myself." Some of the audience tittered, and Mom said, "Bear with me, please. I'm not a total narcissist." More laughs. Mom laughed the hardest—she could often poke fun at herself. "What I mean is, in my six decades thus far, I've made many mistakes, and indeed, I have many regrets. But I hope my life would be characterized by how hard I've tried. How I've been knocked down— so many times—and I've gotten up, again and again. I've gotten up for my children and for myself. So yes, excuse me if I say that I am my greatest hero. I've earned that title. And I intend to continue to live up to it."

I am racked with sobs. I grab a spare pillow from the shelf and cry into it, so I don't wake my wife or daughter. Eventually, when the sobs have abated, I reach for my laptop and open it. I click on the letter from Mom to Gwen, and I rethink the password. I try Mom's birthday, then Gwen's. I wonder if I could find Rachel's. I search through Google a bit, but don't find anything. I read the article again, the first one I found earlier. Then I pull the locket from my pocket and study it once more.

The Triple Threats. Already tried that. I focus on the girls' names, all those *T*'s.

Gwen Tulchinsky. Rachel Taubman. Odelia Tisdale.

The Triple Threats, with three capital *T*'s. I try another password, TTT. Nope. I'm about to give up, when one more thought occurs to me: TheThreeTs.

I punch it in, and the pdf pops open.

———

Gwennie,

If you're reading this, then I've been murdered. I've been thinking how they will do it. Poison. A knife. A cord around my neck?

Someone's been threatening me for weeks. Sending me notes, telling me I'm next. Next for what? Well, whoever's threatening me sent a picture of me, you, and Rachel.

They know, Gwennie.

I should have told you, but I worried. A little part of me worried it was you. That you're the one who's been threatening me.

But you wouldn't. You're my best friend! We know all each other's secrets. But I know that my imminent marriage to Asher hasn't been easy on you. That you aren't exactly happy about it. You pretend you are, that what makes me happy makes you happy. But I don't think that's true. I think that we have been a crutch for each other in many ways, our whole lives. Aryeh wasn't an obstacle to you and me. But I know you fear that Asher is. Well, maybe you're right.

You would never murder me, Gwennie. Because I know that you love me. As much as you've ever loved anyone.

I'm not ready to die. Of course I'm not. And I don't actually think it will come to it. But of course, I can't go to the police. We are going to Leopard Sands tomorrow, and I'm not bringing my security team. Why, if I'm afraid for my life? Well, lately I've begun to suspect that perhaps one of the team is the person blackmailing me. What if we didn't vet them enough? It can't be my family who is targeting me. Or you. I hope we will arrive in Leopard Sands and that I can enjoy my marriage. Enjoy with you and my family. When we are home, I am determined to figure out who is targeting me. To solve this once and for all. I don't know how, but I will. If I've proved anything in this life, it's that I am a survivor.

But if I am wrong, Gwennie, if it's someone close to me who

wants to murder me, and if this person succeeds, then this note is for you. In addition to the copies of the threats. I'm not giving you this information to bury. I'm giving it to you to expose it. Expose what I've done. What you've done for me. I can't live with myself if I'm not certain that my death will set you free.

I'll never be able to repay you, Gwennie, no matter how long I'll live or how much I give to you. You are the best friend any girl could have. Truth is, I probably never deserved you.

Don't worry about my reputation. Once I'm gone, none of that matters. You've lived your whole life with this hovering over your head—something you never even did. I should have taken responsibility, but Aryeh swooped in so fast. Paying off the nanny. I don't even think I knew what had happened. By the time I came down from it all, it was done. You'd agreed to take the fall. The nanny had agreed to lie to the police. No one else saw.

No. I can't put it on Aryeh, not this. I did it. I was at the wheel. Me. After far too much vodka, me.

If they'd known it was me, the sentence would have been so much worse. I was drunk. Well, of course you know that. I drank so much back then—you know how it was. How horrible the infertility was. And my marriage with Aryeh was falling apart. I was waking up at six, taking a pregnancy test—negative, always negative—and then pouring myself a tumbler at seven. I know it's not an excuse. Of course it's not, but I started drinking that morning after I got up. Aryeh and I had a huge fight. He said it wasn't normal that I couldn't fall pregnant. He said I needed to stop drinking, that it was my fault the babies weren't sticking. That his parents hadn't survived the Holocaust for their lineage to die out—that be fruitful and multiply was a mandate from God. He called me barren. I couldn't figure out another way to endure other than to drink more.

It was all me, though, Gwennie. I don't want you to think I'm not taking responsibility. I shoved you aside—I grabbed the wheel. I wanted to feel powerful, feel the sea air in my face. I wanted to feel like I was at the helm of something—anything—in my life. You tried to push me away. You screamed at me to stop. I didn't see Rachel. I didn't see anything. I just wanted to drive that boat as fast as I could, fast enough to drop out of myself, out of my life. I felt like such a failure, as a woman, as a wife. Every woman is supposed to bear children, that's what it said in the Bible, Aryeh told me. And here Rachel was—with little Oshri, a son, like Aryeh wanted. And another baby on the way. I burned with envy

But I swear to you, Gwen, I didn't run Rachel over on purpose.

I suspect you've always wondered. Even though you loved me too much to ask.

I loved Rachel. To the ends. You know I did. She was a sister to me as much as you are. I was so out of my mind. Sure, maybe I envied her a bit. David was so kind and gentle; Aryeh was gruff, more acerbic, angry, even though I did love him then. But I didn't kill her intentionally. I swear to you, I didn't.

I didn't think you'd serve time. I thought they'd let you off the hook. I wanted you to get married, Gwennie. I wanted you to have a full, happy life, and I've wondered a bit, if I stole it from you. You were always timid around men. You never dated much. I wondered if it was because of your father—if men scared you. But you were young—you still had your whole life in front of you.

Remember, Rachel and I used to tell you, you were going to find your T.B.! Just like we had. After all, I became a Babel, and Rachel became a Balsam—so your guy, surely his last name starting with a B, had to be on his way! Remember how Rachel and I flipped through the phone book, poring over the B's? We all laughed and laughed. It was meant to be, we told you. Destiny, we said. The Three T's with their B's. And then you were sentenced to prison, and it was never the same after that.

I'll never forgive myself for those years I took from you. For the trial and the prison sentence, and everything that followed. For every time you've ever had to admit you are a felon. You insisted you wanted to take the fall. That it wasn't just Aryeh convincing you—that you agreed it was the only solution. You said you could handle the jail time. But maybe I've always known that even if you could handle it, I shouldn't have let you.

You are the reason I could go to South Africa with Aryeh after the trial. Try to put what I did behind me. You are the reason I have Joshua, and Sam and Bailey too. If I'd gone to jail . . . for decades probably . . . I never would have survived. I was the drunk one; you didn't even have a sip that day. You knew it all, and so you took my place.

I can never, ever repay you.

You will always be provided for. I've always told you that, and I've always meant it.

Clear your name now. Tell the truth. To my children, to Asher, to them all. Let the dead stay dead. That's what I've always said, isn't it? When it's my time to go, it's my time, and maybe when I'm gone, you can find it in you to really live. To figure out what makes you happy, when you're no longer so fixated on my happiness. You've always been a better friend than me. A better person. I've left you more money than you can possibly ever need. Have fun, Gwennie. Have a beautiful life.

I love you with all my heart,

Dede

---

I STARE AT THE wall, numb.

Mom killed her best friend Rachel. And she let Gwen take the fall.

Not even let—Aba set Gwen up. He paid the nanny to say Gwen had been driving. It's despicable. Unthinkable.

I sit for a long time, questions swimming in my mind, trying to deduce what this has to do with Mom's murder, and Gwen's disappearance.

Someone knows. Someone was blackmailing Mom. But who? Something's nagging at me, something off. . . . Something someone said, maybe. What?

Suddenly I gasp. And I think that I know.

# CHAPTER THIRTY-THREE

# JOSHUA

I burst up from the floor, teetering, feeling unsteady. It can't be— Am I grasping at straws? It still doesn't make sense.

Only I am suddenly certain I'm onto the whole thing. I snap my laptop shut, slip the flash drive back into my pocket, and shut the light in the closet. I check my watch—3:24 in the morning. Still two hours until sunrise. I watch my family in the moonlight streaming from the curtains I didn't fully draw. I pass by Ruby, still sleeping, and Davina, too, her mouth slack.

Will they be okay if I— Should I wake Davina up—

No.

Should I wait until morning? Until the police arrive? No, this can't wait. I need to confront this *now*.

I stare out the window, toward the bloated moon. *Help me, Aba*, I say quietly, the first time I've ever talked to my father since he left this earth.

*Be courageous, Joshua*, I imagine him saying. Or maybe he'd call me Yehoshua, my Hebrew name that he sometimes used. *Be strong, Yehoshua! You have Babel inside you—a whole lineage of survival and strength.*

Even though in all likelihood he wouldn't believe I'm strong enough, after all.

I swivel on my heels and head to the bar area. I rummage in the top drawer, then find what I'm looking for. I stick the sharp knife into my pocket and head for the door.

———

I LOCK THE SUITE behind me, wondering if it's very reckless to leave my family slumbering alone when there is a murderer on the loose. But then I reassure myself: I am going *toward* the murderer. I am going to handle this, so my family will be safe. I grip the handle of the knife.

I walk to my right amid howls and scratches. I try not to think of snakes and scorpions and hyenas and all the other things that are probably lurking close, just shine my flashlight and convince my feet to walk. It feels like I'm the only living thing on this planet, but then the bleats and hoots and cackles of the bush remind me I'm not.

All looks quiet at Sam and Bailey's suite, but I stop. I wonder.

I think through it again.

Rachel Taubman Balsam.

Odelia Tisdale Babel.

Gwen Tulchinsky.

The Triple Threats. The Three T's and their B's. I was so fixed on their names that I neglected what was important about it. In Mom's note to Gwen, she wrote that all she and Rachel wanted was for Gwen to find her T.B., too, just as her two besties had.

But there's another person in our mix with a T middle initial, B at the end. Asher Theodore Bach.

I've witnessed his signature on many contracts, so of course it's been staring at me in the face all this time. Even down to the floral wreaths of Mom's and Asher's initials, hovering above the rehearsal dinner entrance. I remember that I caught Gwen staring at them oddly at the rehearsal dinner, which I chalked up to envy. Could be a coincidence—but is it? Has he adopted Asher as an alias, and changed his middle and last names, but preserving their original initials?

Then I stop abruptly, shot back to that conversation with Aba when I was ten on safari. Aba sitting in the Jeep beside me, telling me the Hebrew words for all the animals we saw. Then how he sighed, and in a rare moment, said he was happy. That being on safari with his son in his favorite place in the world gave him *osher*. Happiness. Oshri must be a derivative of *osher*, I piece together, my mind scrambling, drawing on my rudimentary knowledge of the Hebrew language. Both words have the same root letters. And in tandem, I remember Mom's speech the night before she died—how she said that Asher's name means happiness, and that happy was what he made her.

A chill zaps down my spine. It can't be a coincidence, can it? That Asher and Oshri are both Hebrew words meaning "happiness"?

Is Asher Theodore Bach actually Oshri Taubman Balsam, the son of the woman Mom killed?

---

I ARRIVE AT THE last suite in the row and bang on Asher's door, everything swirling in my brain. I thought something was off with Asher. I *knew*. My alarm bells have been blaring. I've wondered if he's having an affair with Davina—I'm still questioning that.

I cup my ear to the door, listening, but all I hear are the sounds of the bush—something skittering in the tree off the porch. I grab hold of my knife in my pocket. Then I see a shape emerge—a porcupine. They're night creatures. Not dangerous to humans, but shit. What am I planning to do if it attacks—stab a porcupine to death?

Thankfully, the porcupine scurries off, probably more afraid of me than I am of it.

I bang the door again, and a dim light switches on. But still, no footsteps.

"Asher!" I shout, pounding my fist again. "It's Joshua. I need to speak to you."

My hand not doing the pounding is in my pocket, sweaty and slippery against the knife's plastic handle.

As I wait, my heart positively slamming my chest, I wonder if I've leapt to the wrong conclusion. If I'm inventing links that aren't actually there. What if I'm about to confront Asher about nothing? Maybe my jealousy is coloring things. Obviously, Davina's not in his suite; I've just left her sleeping in our bed. But what if . . . now something strikes me like a lightning bolt. What if Dav was in on murdering Mom with Asher . . . Lately, Davina's been encouraging me to stand up to Mom, to advocate harder for Circ's sustainable mission that Mom was ruining. And Davina's certainly not been pleased with how Mom was pushing back on whether Dav qualifies as plus-size, on her weight, on her mothering. Maybe Dav wanted Mom gone, wanted the money and control I'm coming into as a result, and got with her boy toy to make it happen.

I slept soundly the night Mom was murdered—god only knows if Davina was actually sleeping beside me too.

Now I hear rustling inside, and another light inside the suite. A shadow flits by the window, but then nothing. The knob doesn't turn.

Maybe I should go back. Leave this to the morning. Suddenly standing here, I feel foolish. A knife in my grip. What am I doing? Who do I think I am? I should talk to my wife first. That's what I should do.

I turn, but then something happens. My synapses are firing, making connections.

I remember a conversation, the day before Mom was murdered. All of us in the lodge at dinner, perusing our menus, when Asher told us his mother was in prison because she killed a couple while driving drunk. It occurred to me then, the similarity to Gwen going to prison for the same reason. But I didn't think anything nefarious of it. Now that I know more, now that I have my deep suspicions, I wonder if Asher invented that story to get under Mom's skin. And under Gwen's skin, too . . .

The door hitches open, and there is my almost-stepfather, rubbing his eyes, throwing a hand to his brow to deflect the moonlight.

"Joshua, what can I do for you?" His tone is tight, his jaw set. He's shirtless, in gray sweatpants that show off his more-than-six-pack. "You do realize it's the middle of the night."

"Yes. I'm sorry about that. Actually, no—to be honest, I'm not sorry."

Asher's compact but muscly frame is leaning against the door, and I slide sideways and elbow my way past him.

"Joshua, I don't know what this is about, but can we do this in the morning?" He throws out an arm, tries to block me in the entry.

"No. No, we can't." My eyes flick around the room, the crackled leather headboard and rumpled bed, the gauzy mosquito netting still perfectly drawn toward the four corners of the bed. Clothes in a clump beside the tree-stump footstool, and Mom's wedding dress still hanging on the closet doorframe.

"I know, Asher," I tell him. "I *know*."

"Okay?" He sounds like he's losing patience. "You know *what* exactly? And again, can we do this in the morning?"

"No, we can't. Because I think you killed my mother. Actually—I'm sure of it."

"Oh god." He laughs. "Are you serious? What reason would I possibly have to do that? You kids are the ones who are wealthy now. I gain nothing."

"You gain nothing. Maybe. Maybe that's right. But maybe you weren't trying to gain, you were trying to rid . . ."

"Rid?"

"Exact revenge. You—"

"Oh, sure. Revenge. Got it. I thought you were the together one of Odelia's kids, but now I see you're as crazy as the rest of them." He's still looking at me, acting amused, but I note something hard in his eyes. "What would I possibly be exacting revenge for?"

"Your mother," I say simply. "Rachel Taubman Balsam. The way she died. I *know*, Asher. Or should I say *Oshri*. I know everything."

"I don't know what the fuck you're talking about, Joshua." But his face is locked now, resolute, and he steps closer.

"Really? Because I think that you do. I think you know exactly what I'm talking about. Where is Gwen, Asher? What did you do with her? Did she figure it out—somehow she figured it out, didn't she, that you're Oshri? That you saw what my mother did to yours?"

My brain spins rabidly through all my questions, all the things that still don't make sense. There's some missing piece still—something I just know I'm neglecting to see—

And then I gasp. I stare at the bed again, how rumpled it is.

On both sides.

Asher's not been sleeping in there alone tonight, but with *someone*.

Not with my wife, but with—

"Oh my god!" My whole body feels weightless, like this can't be, this can't—

"You're O!" I hear myself say, staring dumbfounded at Asher, as I hear a creak behind me. "O-with-a-heart, who Bailey said Sam's been texting. The guy who makes Sam *happy*. . . . Holy shit— You're Sam's boyfr—"

A creak—and I swivel to see my brother emerge from the bathroom, shirtless, his face somber.

"Joshua," Sam says, arms raised as if in surrender, walking toward me.

But I don't hear the rest, because something hard smashes from behind me into my skull and turns everything black.

# CHAPTER THIRTY-FOUR

# ASHER

I take Sam's hand and squeeze it as Joshua comes to. "It's going to be okay."

"Is it, though?" he asks dully. "You could have given my brother a head injury when you bashed him with that lamp."

"Nah. I hardly touched him." I don't say that I know where—and how hard—to hit to cause a head injury. Or to cause worse. I eye the knife on the bar, the sharp one I used to cut fruit. Nothing is fair, I've learned in this life, and a long game is the most potent kind. Sam will come around to his brother needing to go. We've agreed we will do anything—anything—for our love. For our goals.

And I know one thing for sure: Joshua Babel is the last big roadblock in the way of our goals.

I watch Joshua squirm in the leather club chair, cry out, or try to, until he realizes there is a gag in his mouth. A makeshift gag—one of Odelia's silk scarves. Joshua's eyes dart wildly around, and his hands and feet yank futilely at the restraints. We did that—the restraints. Or, really, I did it, alone. Sam's useless right now, one giant freak-out, a fire hydrant spewing endless questions and concerns.

I've had to think fast as I assuage Sam's fears and simultaneously deal with his brother. Fact is, I didn't expect Joshua to come to my room now, in the middle of the night, or to have figured out so much.

"The police are going to be here this morning," Sam says urgently.

"Morning," I say. "Still a ways off. So." I pat Sam's arm and walk toward Joshua. "Joshua, my friend. Would you like me to take your gag off?"

Vigorous nodding of his head, tufts of black hair, not a receding hairline like his brother. Though I love Sam's shaved head just as it is. He's perfect, the whole package. Everything I want—everything I've dreamt of all my life.

"Well, if we're going to take your gag off, you can't scream. If you scream, I'll put it back on. And . . ." I walk toward the bar, grab hold of the knife. "I have this. And now you know what I'm capable of. So don't try anything stupid. Okay?"

More nodding, and I peel the scarf from Joshua's mouth. He looks at me like an animal, gnashing teeth, like he wants to bite me, or eat me, or skin me alive.

I quite understand that feeling.

He struggles against the restraints and opens his mouth like he's going to scream despite my warnings.

"The suite next to us is the empty one," I remind him. "No one on our other side. So if you scream, no one's going to hear you. And I'll put the gag right back on."

Joshua glares at me. "You killed my mother. I can't believe . . . and you." His head swivels to Sam. "You . . . and him, Sam . . . you . . ."

"Yes." I help Joshua along. "But before you paint us as monsters, let's go back to what you came in here saying. You figured it out—I can't understand how. But you know now that your mother killed mine. Framed her best friend. Covered it all up. You know the whole story, so you can quite understand why we've done what we've done."

"*Understand?*" Joshua spits. "I understand nothing. That—what? You infiltrated my mother's company, got her to love you, to marry you, seduced her son—the police would have read your texts eventually. How did you even plan to get away this?"

"Our texts were on Signal," I say tightly. "They disappeared. There is no evidence of Sam and me talking. None at all."

Joshua gapes at me. "So all this—all these careful plans because—all because our mother killed your mom in a boating accident when you were a child?"

"An *accident*? First off." I dart eyes at Sam. "I love your brother, so let's put that to bed right now. And let me tell you one more thing for sure, my mother's murder was no accident."

I let those facts sink in. "Your mother was drunk, and jealous of mine! I saw the whole thing. They were driving in front of my house, and Olesia said, *Look, there's your mother up on the skis.* Mom had been practicing, trying to get up, wanting to show my dad that she could water-ski, one of his favorite activities. Gwen was driving the boat. I remember them still, my mother's best friends—Gwen had this long cinnamon hair. She was the one who paid attention to me. And Odelia—the one who didn't look at me, even when I showed her my best artwork and magic tricks. Odelia was the one who always had a cup with a straw in her hand, whose breath smelled like rubbing alcohol. Your mother grabbed the wheel—I saw it all. Every sickening turn. How *my* mother fell, and was screaming, and your mother turned the boat around and ran her right over. Purposely. Because she was jealous of her!"

"It was an accident!" Joshua says. "She didn't do it on purpose!" But his face is pallid, like he isn't totally sure.

"My father told me everything," I hiss. "How envious your mother was of mine. He told me it all before he started drinking so much that I lost him too."

"I see," Joshua says evenly. "So your father is the one with an alcohol problem. The whole thing about your mother being in prison for a drunk driving accident—that was meant to toy with my mother more."

"Well, I needed a plausible reason my mother wasn't in my life to celebrate our wedding. And anyway, Odelia deserved it," I respond. "She deserved everything I did to her and more. I was *six*, Joshua. And both my parents fell like dominoes at the hands of fucking Odelia. Your mother was envious of mine, that's the goddamn truth. My mother was wonderful and beautiful and kind. Everyone loved her. She loved being a mother. She was pregnant again—with my baby sister—did you know that?"

I can see by the way Joshua flinches that somehow he does.

"And your mother couldn't get pregnant. Aryeh was horrible to her, and she resented my mother. Was jealous of her!"

"That doesn't mean she meant to kill her," Joshua says, but softly, barely audible.

"She was drinking and driving," I scream. "So does it fucking matter?

Aryeh covered it up—he paid off my nanny, got Gwen to lie, and when I told my father otherwise, when I said what I'd actually seen, he didn't believe me! He told me to stop—that I had to accept it, that I had seen things—but I had seen the truth! After the trial, Dad moved us to New York. He thought that if he got me away, I'd drop it. I'd forget. But how could anyone ever forget that? Did you read her statement, what Olesia said? She said Gwen was *bereft*. Can you believe anyone bought that bullshit? That a recent Polish immigrant who spoke broken English would legitimately know the word *bereft*. And yet everyone did buy it, hook, line and sinker!"

I ease down on the bed and take a few deep breaths. Reliving this story now is sucking everything out of me. It's so rare I've shared it. This is only the second time. The first was with Sam, after we met at Circ, early on in my employment. I'd originally planned to ingratiate myself in Odelia's company, to topple her business, to cause her life to implode from the inside. But then I met Sam at a holiday party, and it was lust at first sight. We started sleeping together, but it was a couple weeks before I even knew his last name.

When I found out Sam was a Babel, I feared I'd sunk my entire plan. That there was no way I could seduce his mother anymore. But as Sam and I grew closer, I realized things could be used to my advantage— in particular, how much he resented his mother. He confided in me how he despised his mother, because she'd killed his father, though he couldn't prove it. And then she'd stolen the money that was rightfully Sam's, with-holding it, conditioning it, whereas Aryeh had been free-handed with the funds, he had believed in Sam, would have wanted him to have what was his. After all that, I felt safe enough to share my own sordid tale. The Odelia Babel destruction tale. And then Sam agreed to help me take his mother down.

I try to slow my rapid breaths, try to regain calm and control. It's all devolved, spiraled so far beyond my careful plans. And the worst part—the part I haven't even yet admitted to Sam—is that I don't feel the whoosh of relief I expected.

No closure.

No beginning of a new chapter.

I thought I would—that Odelia alive was the only thing keeping me from letting it all go. But I don't think I realized it, how making her the focus of my entire life would affect me once she'd gone. Even though I am responsible—even though I pulled the trigger—tracking her down, hunting her, deceiving her, making her pay, all that gave me purpose. And now it's all gone. And where I thought I'd feel full, whole, ready for this new life, I feel hollow inside. Empty.

An Odelia-size hole.

"Now you know, Joshua." Sam eases down beside me, and I slide a comforting hand down his thigh. My hand pools sweat onto his skin, matted in fine blond hairs.

Sam says, "So can you understand—"

"Understand?" Joshua's suddenly so calm it unnerves me. "Understand why you got with this guy to . . . murder our mother? No, Sam, obviously I can't."

"She murdered Aba!" Sam erupts. "You know she deserved everything that came to her and more."

"She . . . what? What are you even talking about? Mom *didn't* murder Aba. He had a heart attack."

"No. You're wrong. No, that was the party line. I heard her on the phone, with someone she paid off— There was pineapple in Aba's system."

Joshua gapes at his brother. "What the hell are you talking about? *Pineapple?* No. He was allergic—he wouldn't—no—he had a heart attack."

"He had a heart attack catalyzed by anaphylactic shock," Sam says, triumphant now, but not taking glee in it—just finally able to trumpet facts Joshua's averted his eyes from. "It was in the original coroner's report. There was pineapple in his system. You know what that means, Joshua." Sam stares at his brother, and Joshua breaks eye contact, leading me to think he knows exactly what Sam's talking about. Sam's told me, how once on vacation his parents were fighting, a particularly vicious fight, and Odelia ordered a plate of pineapple, even though pineapple was verboten in the Babel household, because juice could have spurted over toward Aryeh. If he hadn't already left the table in a rage, that is.

"Yes, of course you remember it too," Sam says. "Obviously Mom slipped pineapple to Aba in some way, but she got it struck from the report. She killed our father, Joshua! God knows how many people she's paid off in her life to get her way."

"Sounds like Aba paid off Oshri's nanny over here. So Mom's not the only one." But Joshua's face is sheet white—clearly he's stunned by the accusation, but more so, by knowing it all fits.

"Well, there's no excuse for Aba's behavior," Sam concedes, his knee bouncing up and down, making my hand slap against it as it rises and falls. "But he's not the one that ran over Oshri's mom. Mom's the one who did it all on her own. Aba was just protecting his wife."

"Interesting logic." Joshua shakes his head, like this is all hard for him to comprehend—and I'm glad. Maybe now he'll see why we did what we did. Maybe he'll even keep this quiet for his brother. So we don't have to kill him.

"There's no way," Joshua finally says. "I don't believe that Mom killed Aba, and honestly, Sam, I don't understand how you've been harboring so much hatred for Mom all these years. Aba didn't accept you, not as you are. Mom's the one who didn't bat an eye when you came out. Mom's the one who saw you through every bout of rehab, who actually loved you!"

"Please," Sam spits. "Please don't tell me you believe all that bullshit that Mom's indoctrinated us with. I didn't come out—I was forced out! Mom's the one who showed Aba my journal, don't forget! You make her out like a saint, but she's the one who betrayed me—not him! Aba isn't the evil person you all make him out to be. Eventually, I know he would have come around and accepted me as I am! He didn't have a chance to, though. If he hadn't died—if Mom hadn't murdered him—everything would have been different."

Joshua shakes his head but doesn't say anything for a long time. When he finally speaks, he says, looking at me, "Bailey told me our brother had a new love interest. He was in Sam's contacts as O with a heart next to it. Sam said— What was it he told Bailey? That O-with-a-heart made him *happy*. O for Oshri." He exhales with a whoosh. "Aba told me once, he was happy going out on a game drive with me. And he told me the Hebrew words for happy. Osher, which is the root word of Oshri I'm guessing . . . and Asher . . . they both mean happy. I can't believe it. So you planned this? Both of you? For a long time, huh? It's so convoluted. So . . . *evil*."

"Oh, please—evil," I say, the word acrid in my throat. "Give me a break! Good and evil—it's so binary, Joshua. You haven't experienced tragedy like I have, so obviously you'd lean back on your high horse. But bad people aren't any different than good people like you. We're just good people who've been pushed so far that we can't help but do a bad thing."

Joshua eyes me with naked spite. "Well, if that's what you need to tell yourself, then. Oh!" Joshua turns to his brother. "I just realized—Gwen saw you at Markus's cabin."

I rub Sam's back so he knows not to confirm. But Joshua is on a roll, doesn't wait for either of us to interject before steamrolling forward. "So you took Markus's rifle, Sam? And what—put it in their suite for Asher to use? Is that how it happened? Sam would have his alibi—he was with Bailey, chatting away—and Asher would murder Mom?"

I nod slowly. And if I didn't know it before, I know it now for sure—we can't let Joshua live. I still can't believe he figured out the Oshri equals Asher thing. I thought I was being so clever. But Joshua knows everything. Way, way too much. We could never trust him to keep quiet. I know it intuitively—he wouldn't. He's too principled for that, no matter that I believe he does love his brother.

"But how did you get her back to the bonfire pit so late at night, Asher? What did you say to— Oh shit." Joshua stares at us, wide-eyed. "Her locket. That's it, isn't it?"

Sam shifts uncomfortably beside me.

"You gave Mom that massage! Rubbing her shoulders, pandering to her after your big fight. And you hugged Asher too. Is that when he gave you the key to their suite, Sam? So you could slip the rifle inside, after you'd stolen it? Or did you steal the key from the front desk? So the fight was staged—the whole thing was—"

"Mom and I are oil and water in the best of scenarios. It wasn't staged as much as maybe . . . exaggerated," Sam says.

"Right." Joshua gazes at his brother now with unconcealed spite. "*Exaggerated*, to facilitate her murder." Joshua's face crumples, like this is all too much to bear.

"Sam wasn't supposed to be so reactive," I hear myself grumble. Sam turns to me with a scowl. But my jaw stays set. It's true; he almost ruined it with his ridiculous tirade. He was supposed to apologize to his mother, bond with her, then take her locket. Not call more attention to himself, no matter how good his alibi was meant to be. But I've long known that Sam has many positive qualities—and control over his emotions isn't one of them. I shouldn't have been so handsy with Odelia in front of Sam. That was my mistake.

"The locket— She needed to lose it there," Sam says, "because we knew she'd be tipsy, maybe drunk. That was Asher's job, keep Mom drinking. So she wouldn't notice if the locket was there or not." Sam stares off with a stony set to his jaw, not looking at his brother, but also not looking at me.

"You pointed it out then," Joshua says flatly, eyes shifting to me. "Later, back in your suite. You told her it was missing, she must've lost it, and so of course she went back to the bonfire pit to look. She wouldn't wait until morning."

"Yes," I admit, surprised that he's figured it all out, even though we were so careful, so cunning.

I'm rather angry, to be honest, that he's unraveled the whole thing. I thought there was no way anyone would. *Ordeal by Innocence*, after all—my favorite, underrated Christie. In it, a man is convicted of murder, but he claims an iron-tight alibi: he was in a car with a stranger, nowhere near the scene of the murder. The stranger doesn't materialize as the alibi, though, and the man dies in prison. But after his death, the stranger comes forward and confirms the validity of the man's alibi. So the investigation reopens—and later it's discovered that the man convicted was in fact in on the murder plot, but he was conspiring with a second offender, the one who actually committed the murder.

It was perfect. The perfect crime. And unlike the Christie novel, Sam's alibi wasn't meant to be compromised. If Bailey hadn't disappeared after that elephant, Sam's alibi would have been set. And no one was supposed to suspect me; I had no motive. I think about telling Joshua the whole thing, so he, too, can admire the perfection our scheme should have achieved.

Goddamn him! Goddamn Joshua!

I gather myself, though. I need to get my emotions in check. Not fall into a rabbit hole from which I might not get out. Joshua's smart, granted, but he's at our mercy now. I need to focus ahead, not get sucked into a futile reexamining of our plans, and where we went wrong.

"I'm still confused, though," I finally say, "about where the locket's gone."

That damn locket—Delia was so obsessed. Always twisting it, snapping it open when she didn't think I was looking, to make sure that stupid key was inside. My father told me about the key—it was to Delia's parents' shed, over half a century ago. The girls used to meet there, a place to find comfort and security.

Security. Ha.

I know why Delia wore that locket until her death. The guilt was suffocating her alive. She was supposed to protect my mother, and instead she murdered her.

"Happened to it—yes." But something about how Joshua says it, not meeting my eyes, gives me an idea.

I stand and go over to Joshua and reach into his pants pocket. "It was you," I say, when sure enough, I rub against the familiar chain links, then the locket, my fingers brushing against the grooves, The Triple Threats etched in gold. But as I pull out the locket, my hand scrapes against something else, and I unveil that too.

A knife. Identical to ours.

Now there are two.

"You came prepared." I nod at Joshua, extending my genuine admiration.

"Not enough," he says, looking only at Sam now. His eyes pleading.

I place Joshua's knife on the coffee table and twirl the locket around in my fingers, then pop it open. I'm expecting to see the key, but instead there's something entirely else inside.

"What do we have here?" I ask, slipping a flash drive out. "Of course, this is how you knew—this is how—"

"It has all the notes, the ones you've been sending her. And a letter from my mother to Gwen, admitting everything!"

"Shit, Osh." Sam bends forward, massaging his scalp in his hands. "We're so fucked."

I don't respond, digesting everything. This is bad, indeed.

"But your mother didn't know it was me," I say. "You're the one who put it together. Who figured it out . . ."

"I told Davina!" Joshua says. "I told her if I'm not back immediately to call the police!" But I can tell instantly that he's lying.

I smile. "You didn't. It's the middle of the night. No one wakes the mother of a baby. Especially when you knew she wouldn't be in any danger staying behind. Because you knew you were coming *toward* the danger."

Joshua's face sags in. He knows I'm right, that he can't say anything back to dispute it. "I made copies of everything, it's all on my laptop," he says, but that, too, I can tell, is posturing. He didn't. This is the evidence, made its way to me by the grace of a very benevolent God. After I killed her, I sifted in Delia's things for the notes, so that I could destroy them. But I found nothing, and now I understand. She must have binned them and taken screenshots and put everything on this flash drive. She was smart. Of course.

I place the flash drive back inside the locket and put it on the table, next to the knife I confiscated from Joshua.

Okay. Okay. Think, Oshri.

Joshua must die. That's the incontrovertible conclusion I've come to.

And I'm going to have to massage things now, so Sam sees this can only end one way.

# CHAPTER THIRTY-FIVE

# JOSHUA

I fumble with the lamp cord binding my wrists behind my back, struggling to break free but without my captors noticing. My captors—fuck. This is so unreal. I try to catch my brother's eye, try to make him see this is lunacy. That he won't get away with it. That he has to let me go.

Sam helped kill our mother. I still can't comprehend it. And he's with Asher. Like, in *love* with Asher. Of course I knew Asher was bisexual. But him and Sam? No, I couldn't have fathomed this level of deception. How did none of us notice that Sam's barbs toward Asher were all a well-polished act?

"You should get an Academy Award," I say, trying to make Sam look at me.

"Huh?" But he doesn't make eye contact.

"All your angst and anger, like you hated Asher. A total act."

"Oh." Now he has the courtesy to meet my gaze. "I know. I'm sorry."

"You're sorry? You're sorry is all you can say?"

He shrugs. "I'm not sorry for what we did. She deserved it. She deserved it and then some, Joshua. You know she did. But . . . I'm sorry for *this*."

"Yes, well, you can let me go. Let me go, Sam. Whatever he's trying to make you do, you don't need to."

"He's not making me do anything! This has all been my choice." But Sam's face reads otherwise—like a wounded puppy. Unsure.

"Really," I counter, "because it seems like Asher is pulling all the strings.

Just like you always accused Mom of doing. You're not in control, Sam. Stop deluding yourself. You've just traded one puppet master for another."

"Shut up, shut the fuck up!" Asher shouts, his face reddening. "Don't listen to him, Sam. He's just trying to manipulate you." Asher checks his watch. "We're going to have to—" He flicks his head toward me. "Deal with your brother before sunrise, before the police arrive. You do know that, don't you, baby? You know we're going to have to. He knows far too much. We can't let him go."

My whole being prickles with alertness, scrambling for my next move. Asher gets up to draw the last of the blinds, then spins Mom's locket in his hands. How stupid of me. I'm livid at myself, that I brought it over here and practically handed him all the evidence—that I didn't leave it behind to be leverage. That I am the worst liar known to man.

I strain my hands against the cord as Asher and Sam whisper to each other on the bed, my brain working overtime. I start to puzzle something out. "You took the rifle. You . . . how did you know Mom would give Markus the day off?"

"I asked her to." Asher runs his fingers over the locket, then jangles it. The flash drive makes a click noise against the side.

"Why? I mean, under what pretense?"

"Because I didn't want Markus there on the day of our wedding. And I don't owe you an explanation." Asher eyes Sam almost delicately, and I have no idea what's going on.

"You knew?" Sam gasps.

"I . . . baby, let's talk about this later." Asher rubs Sam's shoulder, but Sam just stares like a statue at the black candelabras on the fireplace mantel.

I don't understand what's happening, but I have a surge of hope that I can exploit it.

"I don't get it," I say. "So you two are in love? So you were never in love with my mother, Asher? I have to admit, I hated the idea of your marriage, but I didn't suspect anything awry. You put on quite the act. That you loved her."

"I *did* love her!" Asher explodes.

"Oh, please." I spit the words, feeling like a fuse has been lit and the fire's unfurling up my spine. "Please, you can say a lot of things, but that? That's gross."

My eyes flicker at my brother, but Sam's face is blank, unreadable.

"I'm not lying. I did." Asher leans back, crosses his arms over his bare chest. "After all, what is hate if not calcified obsession? I was obsessed with Odelia—I can totally admit that. She's been the central woman in my life ever since she murdered my mother. So is it a stretch that I loved her too? I mean—hate. Love. A good fuck. And she was a *very* good fuck. It all runs on the same fumes. You have to care on some level. And you can't say I didn't care about your mother."

"You despised her," I say incredulously.

"I did. But I loved her, too, I guess." Asher looks pensive, lost in his memories. "She was gorgeous, powerful. Funny. The sex was epic, in fact. We even fucked right before I killed her. One last hurrah. I almost cried, I have to admit. It was so poetic."

"One last fuck?" Sam says, but not angrily, almost meekly, like a little boy. "You slept with my mother last night? You told me you would only sleep with her once or twice to convince her. That you didn't have any feelings for her—"

"I don't! I didn't," Asher says, going over to wrap his arms around my brother. "Not like I love you. It was— Sam, don't let your brother play you like this! Focus on what you know is true. I love *you*. Only you."

I stare at Asher, speechless. He's a sociopath. And then I think of Ruby, and a cry gurgles up my throat. Ruby. I have to make it out of this hell for her. But I think, too, of the little boy who watched his mother murdered in front of his eyes. Who *knew* what happened—knew there was a cover-up— but no one believed him. Mom created this monster, sitting in front of me. Both Mom and Aba did, I guess.

Still, it has to stop somewhere. I look at Sam, try to plead with him with my eyes. How can my brother listen to Asher say all that insanity, that he *enjoyed* sex with our mother before he killed her, and quietly withstand it? How can Sam *not* know it's every sort of fucked-up? Sam's a ballbuster, not a pushover. But right now, he looks like a shadow of himself. Lifeless. Like one of Ruby's stuffed animals.

"You did it for the money," I say, putting two plus two together. "Not just to support your boyfriend, Sam. Not just because you hate her. But because you want Mom's money, despite everything you said to the contrary. And what about killing me?" I force my voice to lower, not to squeak and show my sheer terror. "Because that's where this is going, too, isn't it? How do you explain away killing me?"

"That's where this is going. Yes." Asher looks at Sam for reassurance, but Sam doesn't chime in. "As for how we'll explain it away, well, the evidence is all here. No one's going to figure out what you did."

"Okay, but how do you plan on being together, then? Sam might have an alibi—he was with Bailey at the time Mom was murdered—but how will anyone buy that this wasn't a joint effort, once you come out with your relationship?"

"Oh." Asher looks preoccupied, likely plotting my death, and not too concerned with what I'm saying. "We're patient, Joshua. After all, we've been planning this for quite some time. We won't say we're together right away. Obviously not."

"Okay, but once you do, even if it's years from now on, people will suspect you. They'll look back, wondering if your origin story was earlier than you're saying."

"Not if there is a clear murderer. Not if we plant seeds suggesting it was someone else who killed Odelia."

"Okay," I say. "But who?"

Asher doesn't look stymied like I hope. "Gwen," he says simply. "There's plenty of circumstantial evidence. How jealous she was of Odelia, how threatened she was by our marriage. How anxious she's been acting. In a year, when Sam and I declare our love, it won't seem odd. We bonded in the wake of all this tragedy. That's what people will think. Everyone will buy that Gwen killed her best friend, then killed herself. Poetic justice, isn't it?"

I feel my breath suck in. I gape at him, not believing someone could be this calculating. This evil. "What did you do to Gwen?" I breathe.

"Fed her to the crocodiles." Asher stands and places one hand on top of the other with his fingers extended and then closes them with a sudden smack to mimic the jaw of a crocodile closing. "Like I'm going to do to you now too."

# CHAPTER THIRTY-SIX

# ASHER

'Ve made mistakes tonight, that's for sure. I've been too eager, too proud. I shouldn't have told Sam I slept with Odelia last night. Or admitted to Joshua what I did to Gwen. And been quite so blatant about my intentions going forward. But it'll all be fixed once Joshua's dead. He's the last obstacle before Sam and I can close this horrible chapter and start our lives together.

I need to right this ship now. Finish things for good.

"You killed Gwen? You . . ." Joshua's voice dribbles off as he stares at Sam. "You— You let him kill Gwen?"

"I didn't know he was going to." Sam flickers uncertain eyes at me. "I only found out after he did it."

"I had to," I say, as much for Joshua's benefit as for Sam's. "She saw—"

"She saw what?" Joshua spews. "What could she see that would possibly make you— So you fed her to the crocodiles? That's really what you did? She's basically our aunt, Sam. She's—"

"She saw my birthmark," I explain.

I scrape the hair up at the nape of my neck and show it to him. The birthmark doesn't have a particular shape—not like the ones that look like a star or the Empire State Building. It's just a dark red blobby thing. But apparently Gwen remembered it from when I was a child. Odelia didn't pay attention to those things—I was nothing to her when I was young. Disposable. Inconsequential. Plus, she was usually drunk. But Gwen must have noticed it, and since I cut my hair shorter recently, she spotted it. Maybe if Odelia hadn't died, Gwen wouldn't have put it together. She would have thought it was another boy, with another birthmark. But with Odelia gone, Gwen knew. I was careful; I never scraped my hair off my shoulders into a bun like I would have preferred. But Gwen spotted the birthmark as she was digging in the earth for the locket, when we all ran out in the storm to bring her back. She didn't confront me right away, in front of everyone. Maybe she wanted to think it through, make sure she wasn't inventing things out of thin air. Thank goodness for that.

"She recognized you," Joshua said. "And I think she put it together, too, your initials on the wreaths at the rehearsal dinner. OTB and ATB. After she saw the birthmark, the pieces fit."

I pause. "Oh. So . . . maybe she did. To be honest, it was raining hard, and there wasn't a lot of time for small talk."

"And you just threw her into the river? Alive?" Joshua's eyes widen, judging me.

"First of all, let's not pretend Gwen's Little Miss Innocent here. She might not have murdered my mother, not like Odelia, but she participated in the cover-up. But you're right—she isn't as culpable as your mother. I gave your mother a death fitting to what she'd done."

Joshua winces. "How did you even know how to shoot a rifle?"

"I practiced," I admit. "At the shooting range. Used a fake ID, so don't think there's a trail. I grew up shooting some, with my father. But a rifle is different. You have to know how to handle it." I'm almost proud, though I don't say so. I knew if I didn't hit Odelia on the first shot, I would just go at it again. The bonfire space is the perfect place to stage a murder—isolated. Far from the lodge. No one around for miles, except for the animals, who are perfectly silent witnesses.

"I said, *This is for Rachel Taubman Balsam.* Then she turned, and I shot her." I aimed for her stomach, so there'd be time before she died, time for me to say what I wanted to, but I got her heart instead. Bull's-eye. I don't say that, though—Joshua doesn't need to know. He's still her son. Even if his mother deserved the death she got.

"Did she die right away?" he asks in a voice achingly sad. I shake it off, though. I have to shake it off. I have to keep a clear head. Sometimes there are casualties, but I was justified in everything I've done. I deserve this next chapter—a life free of Odelia, a life not revolving its every day, every moment, around her.

"She died instantly," I say, to spare him. She didn't. What actually happened is what I'd hoped. I went to her and stood over her, I told her who I was. Oshri Balsam. Said that because of the rifle, I had to shoot her at far range. I wasn't trying to be a coward, hide it. On the contrary. She was conscious when I told her. Before Odelia's eyes shut for good, I could see she understood the whole thing.

I linger inside the memory of killing her, and telling her it was me who sent the notes, me who planned all this, but instead of triumph, I feel hollow again. And I realize I'm even angrier than ever at Odelia. How can that be, when she's finally gone? But I am indeed angry still. I'm angry that she left me. Even if I was the one responsible for it. She was a force—she was a joy—she catalyzed so much rage in me. And the rage is still here! But the joy's been whittled down.

Well, it's situational, I tell myself. We've had to deal with the fallout, so it's to be expected. When Sam and I are back in Miami Beach, even if we can't be out with our love right away, everything will revert to baseline. We'll start to make real plans for the rest of our lives. We have everything at our fingertips now. Money, love, youth, Circ. And a world rid of Odelia Babel!

"And Gwen? What did you do to her exactly? How did you . . ." Joshua stops, erupts into a fit of coughs. Sam unscrews a water bottle and goes over to him, puts it to his brother's lips. Joshua tips his head back and drinks.

"I didn't plan to kill Gwen. But once she knew it was me, I had to."

"How did you—"

I bob my head toward the bronze lamp base on the ground, the cord around Joshua's ankles. The bulb and lampshade are still separate, resting on the coffee table. The lamp's twin has its cord currently coiled around Joshua's wrists.

"I knocked her on the head with that. Knocked her out. Same as you. We were by the bonfire pit, and it was raining outside. Lucky—I knew no one would be able to track footprints. I dragged her over the electric fence grates and down toward the river. I loaded her pockets with rocks, so she'd sink faster, and—"

"You sunk her in the river? You— But she was still alive!"

"She was unconscious. And I'm sure it was fast. Between the crocs—and hippos . . ."

It's not a pretty death. I know that. I didn't intend it that way—Gwen might have been weak, and lacking morals, but she was generally harmless as a gnat. Only suddenly she wasn't harmless anymore. She was threatening to bring everything down. She *knew*. And she'd participated in the cover-up of my mother's death. So she wasn't blameless, not at all! There was no other way to kill her and cover up my tracks. I had to act fast.

Joshua is looking down at his lap now, avoiding my gaze. Sam chugs the rest of the water bottle and then tosses it with a thud to the ground. He lies back on the bed and stares at the planked wooden ceiling. I lean back and rub his arm.

"I had to do it. I had to, babe. You know that."

But no one speaks, just the sound of the fan, cycling round and round and round. I scoot forward on the bed and check my watch. 5:15. Sunrise is coming at us like a freight train. I'm going to have to act fast—convince Sam his brother needs to go, and that we'll need to dispose of Joshua's body before the lodge wakes. Before the police arrive.

Or somehow kill Joshua and claim self-defense? What to do, what to do?

From the corner of my eyes, I can see Joshua struggling with the cord around his wrists, trying to get out of the bind when he thinks I'm not looking.

But I'm looking. I haven't come this far—this long—for it all to fall apart now.

"This isn't going to work, this is so fucked!" Sam's writhing on the bed now, clutching his head in his hands.

"It's going to be fine." I try to sound soothing. "I promise, it's all going to be fine."

"It's not going to be fine!" Joshua says. "He wants to kill me. You can't let him kill me, Sammy. No matter what you've done—what you've agreed with him to do—you wouldn't murder me. We're brothers! I know that still means something to you!"

Sam stares at me with his wide blue eyes, not the self-assured Sam I first met, when he saddled up beside me at the bar at a company event right after I'd begun working there. The sparks between us smoldered, total fireworks.

Love—or lust—at first sight. Sam's always been confident, decisive. Knowing exactly what he wants and deserves. Only now he seems lost, unmoored.

"We can't kill Joshua," he whispers to me.

"We have to," I tell him. "And we have to do it now." I reach for the knife.

Sam jerks up to a sit. "I can't believe you slept with my mother last night."

"Sam, you really need to focus," I tell him, trying to quell my own fears that this is all spiraling beyond my ability to control it.

"I don't get it," Joshua says, still working at his bind, trying to prevent his shoulders from bobbing up and giving him away. It's almost comical, the exertion. I tied his hands tight. He's not breaking free.

"I don't get one thing—well, more than one thing, but—you went to fashion school. A master's in material futures. Your résumé is ridiculous—Balmain, for god's sakes. Did you hate our mother so much that you orchestrated your entire career around getting into her company?"

"No," I tell him, curling my fingers back around my knife. This, even more than most of his accusations, enrages me. "No! I've always been creative, drawing sketches and obsessed with fabrics and shapes and precise tailoring. And I guess after my mom died, I channeled my feelings into my designs. Instead of lashing out, or punching something, I can make a perfect garment. The sewing machine is my boxing ring—I don't know, that's how it's always been. And when I was a kid, I used to watch my mom get dressed up. I'd sit on the floor of her closet and tell her yes or no to her outfits."

I close my eyes, the memory wafting over me, pain coiling up my spine. "She loved clothes—she had beautiful ones, was into fashion—but she trusted my judgment. She used to say, *My Oshie has the best taste.* And I could see it—how when she put out the right outfit, it gave her confidence. That's why I love what I do. I'm not only giving people clothing—I'm giving them that feeling of walking out into the world confident, to give it your best shot. That's priceless. *That's* changing the world. I've always thought if everyone just dressed well, in beautiful outfits, we'd have a happier world. I've always, *always* wanted to be a designer."

I don't know what I expect of Joshua when I finish—maybe grudging reverence—but instead he laughs. "Right. Creating a happier world. Sure."

Anger surges, overtaking the sadness my mother's memory always provokes. "I am! And making fashion more sustainable too."

"Oh, please. You might be passionate about design, but you can't tell me the mycology thing wasn't all an act. A calculated way to get into Circ. Wasn't that your game plan? I mean, how long have you even been planning this?"

"I didn't go into sustainable design because of Circ! Not exactly. But so what if I didn't think about the fact that your mother owned a fashion conglomerate and how it might dovetail with my own plans? So fucking what? Sometimes you put a plant in your house against a wall, and it has to grow away from the wall, but it's still a thriving plant. So it grows in a little different direction than it might have done organically—so what? We're all indoor plants in some way. And I'm an acclaimed designer. Other design houses—far more prestigious than Circ—wanted me. So you flatter your mother, Joshua. You flatter her, to put her at the epicenter of my whole life." But as I say it, it feels rather false. Haven't I done what Joshua just accused me of? Even subconsciously? Orchestrated my life around the woman who destroyed it?

"And besides, my interest in mycelium for textiles—that's genuine," I say, trying to get back onto solid ground. "I believe in sustainability far more than even your mother did. She wanted a company floating all the buzzwords. But it was total greenwashing. You know that, and I know it too. Circ is far better off with her gone. Now it can finally get off its fast-fashion profit train and veer into something that actually takes care of our earth."

Joshua is quiet, and I know why: He can't object. He knows, just as I do, that his mother's lack of integrity bled into everything. Into her company too.

"So you changed your name . . ."

"Yes." I shrug. "A long time ago. Before college. I needed a fresh start, and it's not like my father cared or even noticed—he was always drunk, anyhow. I knew I couldn't stay Oshri Balsam—not if I wanted to give Odelia her due one day. My father once told me that he and my mother were deciding between naming me Oshri or Asher. They both mean happiness. They both always told me how happy I made them." I stop, shove down the memories. "So I decided to become Asher. Though Sam calls me O or sometimes Osh—I like that. It's nice that I've been able to bring him inside my real world." I shoot a smile at my love, but Sam merely stares dazedly back. "And I changed Taubman to Theodore, Balsam to Bach. Not so difficult."

"Mm-hmm, then you got into Circ and what—your plan was to take down the company from the inside? Or seducing my brother and our mother was always your endgame?"

I take a deep breath, the knife slippery in my clammy hands. I don't need to answer Joshua on this. I don't need to prove anything to him. Sam's the only one I care about—and Sam's been in on it from the beginning. Well, almost the beginning. And he knows I didn't deliberately seduce him. He knows my love for him is the realest thing there is.

"I thought I'd take down her company. That was my plan. I didn't know how, but I figured I'd improvise once I was in. And I knew I was a shoo-in as a hire. My pedigree was ace, plus I was Jewish! A Jewish high-fashion designer who wanted to slum it in fast fashion. She could blast my pedigree at Balmain in all the campaigns, and it worked to Circ's advantage—you know that as well as anyone. People started associating Circ on the level of the big-name designers. But two things changed once I started working there—"

"You met my brother," Joshua says flatly.

"Yes." With my other hand—the one not holding the knife—I smooth Sam's forehead up through his hair. "We met, and we fell fast."

"You confided in each other, you mean, about your mutual enemy."

I meet Sam's eyes, and he holds my eye contact. But then he breaks first.

"Yes," I concede. I remember it now, how Sam complained about his mother ad nauseam—about how she withheld money that was rightfully his, about how she murdered his father and covered it up. How finally I felt comfortable enough to join him on the Bash Odelia train, to admit my true intentions, what she'd done to my mother. And how relieved I was—so relieved—when Sam didn't shun me, didn't balk at my joining Circ with nefarious intentions. How we gripped each other tight, and I told Sam, *We can do something about your mother*, and he was quiet. Didn't disagree.

"Yes," I say. "But what I didn't expect was the . . . chemistry."

"With Sam?" Joshua asks.

"Well, yes, of course," I say carefully, "but also with your mother. We got along."

"You got along? You hated her! You were trying to bring her down."

"Somehow I could put that aside, compartmentalize. She's— Odelia was smart! Quick. She got things, she made fast decisions. She had keen business instincts. Good fashion sense. Honestly, she was old, but hot. You can't fake chemistry. And we had chemistry."

I'm talking so fast, feeling so passionate, that I realize I've gone overboard again. No matter how in love Sam and I are—no matter how committed we are to spending the rest of our lives together—no paramour wants to hear you were attracted to his mother.

"So you decided to propose?"

"I thought she would go for it, and that it would work to my advantage." I spring up from the bed, start to pace the room. I'm getting antsy answering the questions Joshua's peppering me with, but I also know I need more time, that Sam isn't fully on board with our having to get rid of his brother, so I've got to figure out how to placate him, convince him it's a necessary evil.

"The proposal was spontaneous. I could see Odelia was head over heels. She was all in, your mother, and I needed to be, too, so she didn't get suspicious."

I don't say that Bora Bora was a blast. That the sex was incredible. Sam certainly doesn't need to hear all that.

"Plus, I knew that she'd want to celebrate the marriage with you kids. She'd been talking about bringing me to Leopard Sands. She'd told me all about it, how special this place is. And I started to get an idea. I saw how Sam and I could get rid of your mother. How we could work together— no one would ever suspect it. Sam would have an ironclad alibi—"

"You didn't anticipate Bailey going off to save an elephant, though."

"No." I laugh dryly. "That's true. There've been crimps in this plan—"

"Joshua is one big crimp. Too big," Sam says, sounding more alert and upset. He stands from the bed and whispers in my ear, "We can't kill my brother, Osh. We have to figure out something else."

"We don't have a choice, babe. He knows everything."

"I don't care. I can't do this anymore. I could rationalize that God would forgive me for Mom, because of everything she's done. And Gwen—weak, pathetic Gwen, who was complicit in your mother's death. But Joshua is blameless. He has a daughter, O! Ruby needs a father. I lost mine, and I won't do that to her."

"Okay. We'll figure out another way." I stare at my love and try to give him a reassuring smile as I calculate what I'm going to have to do.

# CHAPTER THIRTY-SEVEN

# JOSHUA

Sam doesn't want to kill me—it's the first surge of hope I've had in this whole insane thing.

I watch my brother and Asher bicker quietly, and I work harder against the bind, trying to free my hands, but am unable to. I imagine a disappointed Aba in my head: *Be strong, Joshua. Be strong like your brother!*

But I'm not. I slump down. I can't break free.

"The police are going to be here soon!" I decide to say. "Right at sunrise." Actually they're not—Officer Monala said they wouldn't be able to depart until after sunrise, and that it might be closer to eight, even nine. But Asher doesn't know that. "And besides, my DNA is all over this place."

"All of you kids' DNA is all over this place," Asher says, sounding exasperated. "All of you, coming in to see Mrs. Moneybags. I haven't had the housekeepers in since Odelia died. So it's not a problem if your DNA is around. Sam, do you get it? I know you don't want to do this, but we have to. It's the only way this whole thing is going to work now."

"Seriously, you're deluded," I say loudly, trying to insert myself into my brother's vacillation. "You think you're going to march me out and throw me in the river and no one will know? It's going to be light out soon—people will see."

"That's why we have to do it now," Asher hisses to my brother, the two of them facing each other, like in a standoff. "So we can get him out, dispose of him, and get back to clean . . ."

*Dispose* of me.

He's so clinical—so assured—that I shiver.

I can feel Asher's tiring of me, that I'm pressing my luck. But if I'm going to die, I have to know. "You're not sleeping with my wife, then, are you?"

Instantly I know I'm wrong. That it is—and always has been—a ridiculous accusation.

"Sleeping with Davina? God no." Asher looks appalled. "You mean because she came here last night?" I didn't even know she had, but I don't say so. He laughs. "No. She was just checking I'm okay. After my fiancée died. Nice wife you have there, Joshua. I mean, she's attractive, I'll give you that. But no—it's all friendly. Sam is the only Babel I want. Trust me, sleeping with two people in this family was quite enough. I'm not jonesing to add a third. And I'm loyal. It's Sam I love. It's you." He turns to my brother, clasps his hands. "I would never cheat on you, babe."

As Asher makes googly eyes at my brother, I sag forward with some modicum of relief. I can't believe I ever doubted my wife. I realize now I've been fixed on things that aren't even real while the actual machinations loomed large and completely escaped my notice.

I watch my brother and Asher talk, voices tight, but I'm unable to rouse any more arguments for them to consider to spare me. To spare my life. My life rests in my brother's hands—a proposition not so reassuring since this is my brother who conspired to kill our mother. For not the first time since I came to, tied to this chair, a realization assails me, that I might never see my wife and daughter again.

I choke with a cry, as I mourn everything I might miss: Ruby at her first recital, on her first date, and in her graduation cap, reciting her speech as class valedictorian. And then I simultaneously realize that those are my projections—the things I imagine Ruby will do or that I want for her—but the truly worst part is that I won't see her turn into her own person, doing and saying things I can't possibly conceive of.

I think about all the times Dav and I joke about Ruby's future career and her little burgeoning personality. But babies are like lumps of clay, I realize now. And as parents, we try to mold them into who we want. And who we want is necessarily based on our own traumas and fears. How we think a person will need to be to survive in this world. My father believed I had to be strong, to be good at sports, and that knowing the Jewish halacha would lead to a good life. And maybe I can't fault him for who he pushed me to be. Because I don't know the particular cuts and wounds that led him to the beliefs that being strong and religious would help me in this uncertain, scary world.

I think about Asher—spending his whole life avenging his mother's death instead of so many other ways he could have directed that energy. I don't want Ruby to spend her life mistakenly believing she needs to fix mine. And even more than that, it occurs to me that my game with Davina is a bit toxic, where we speculate about Ruby's future, or call her our little extravert. Maybe I've wanted her to be an extravert because I never was, and those outwardly social attributes make fitting in easier. Or maybe I'll want her to get married and have children, because those things have brought me joy and I worry that if she doesn't do them she'll miss out on the joy train. But perhaps Ruby's joy will lie elsewhere, in places I can't imagine because they aren't my journeys to walk. And maybe Ruby isn't meant to fit in. Maybe she'll be shy, or funny, or serious, or irreverent, and all those things are more than okay. Not just okay, but perfect. My little girl is her own lump of clay. She gets to mold herself, and my only job as her parent is to make her feel safe and secure as she does it and to love every curve and bend. And if I get out of this alive, if I get to hold my baby girl again, that's what I'm going to do. Sit on the sidelines and be her biggest cheerleader and hug her when things go wrong and when they go right and just love her big. Love her so big for whoever she is and whoever she wants to be.

If I get out of this alive, I vow it right now, that's what I'll do.

I'm weeping quietly when I hear Asher say, "You'll have access to your trust. You'll be the trustee."

"With Bailey, though," Sam says.

"Your sister will be a figurehead, c'mon. You know she's not a control freak like him." Asher nods his head toward me, but his eyes don't leave my brother's. "This is the way, Sam. This is how you take the power back. How you have access to *your* money. You can fund Say Cheese—you can fund all the apps your heart desires. We'll be on the top of the world—we can live anywhere—go anywhere—nothing holding us back, no more . . . things we have to take care of."

I watch Asher try to rouse my brother to agree to kill me, and fear knots through my chest, because I know my brother is rousable. I can see what they have in common, what drew them together. Passion, fervency. They both seem to like yes-men, and to be that for each other.

"I want all that," Sam says, and I watch tears drip down his face. "I want all that with you."

"We're gonna have it, baby!" Asher places his hands on my brother's shoulders. Sam's taller than him, by almost a full head, so Asher gazes up at him. In a weird way, it's what I always wanted for my brother. For him to find a safe landing place, a person to whom he could devote all his wild, passionate energy. But not like this, of course. I thought after all the drugs and rehab, it couldn't get worse. But it has.

"We *can't* have it." Sam gasps and crouches to the ground, arms flopping over his knees. "It's starting to get light out. The police are coming, and Joshua knows, and everything's fallen apart . . ."

Asher kneels down and puts his hands on Sam's shoulders. "We'll say it's self-defense."

"Self-defense? That's— No one's gonna believe—"

"Yes!" Asher strikes his fist into the air, like Hitler at one of his speeches. "That's it—that's how this will work. We'll say Joshua came here, thinking I did it. Come to some crazy conclusion without any basis—thinking I killed his mother and then Gwen. He'd lost his mind. He came with a knife— Look, babe." Their eyes swivel to the coffee table a foot away, where my knife rests on a coffee table book about conservation. "I had to defend myself. This is rural South Africa—they're not, like, big on the complicated murder investigations. Have you seen the police? They've barely been around—"

"It was the storm, though; that's not why—"

"No." Asher gives his head a vigorous shake. "Honestly, people are murdered every second here probably. And I'd bet most of the cases go cold. They're not going to look too deep into it, especially given that Joshua did come over here with his knife. Cut-and-dried!"

He smacks his hands together again in a way that chills my bones. I'm shivering, literally shaking in the chair, at this plan. Because, fuck. It's not ridiculous. A rural police force has few resources. They might very well get away with it.

Sam can't go along with it, though. He won't. Right? But he did kill our mother, if not by his hands, with his plans. Long, long plans. I can't pretend to myself he's not capable of it.

"You'll get back," Asher is saying now, "before Bailey wakes up. Anyway, she'll be out cold, on the Ambien—"

"You slipped Bailey an Ambien?" I squeak, hating how weak and scared I sound. "Is that why she's acting so anxious and out of character? What, so you could come over here and *fuck* Asher?" I feel all my anger rush forward, all my fear.

"Sam didn't give Bailey an Ambien," Asher says. "Your wife did."

"Dav?" I go cold, processing that.

"Yes," Asher says, triumphant to tell me something about my wife I didn't even know. "She thought Bailey needed to sleep through the night, and when she came to check on me, she told me that she had. So I told Sam. Bailey's a light sleeper, as you know, but if she was out cold, we knew Sam could come over tonight without her being the wiser."

"I can't believe you'd think I would drug Bailey!" Sam says to me, blue eyes flashing, like I've offended his high moral virtue. "I would never! Not for anything."

Asher presses his hand against Sam's head, to swivel it back to facing him. "Focus, babe. You understand why it has to go this way, right? I'll take care of Joshua. I'll do it. You don't have to. I'll make it quick. He won't suffer."

I blanch, feeling like I'm going to vomit, wondering what that means. I gag a couple times, but nothing comes out. Does Asher know just where to cut me in my neck—yes, he probably does. I think about screaming—think for the millionth time about it—but the suites are significantly set apart, and there's the empty one beside us. No one will hear. My only salvation is that the sun's rising now—the drapes are drawn, but morning light is filtering in.

I struggle more with my wrists, wincing as I rub up against the bind. I know I've already drawn blood, that I'm digging the cord into my open wounds, but I have to keep going, have to give it my all.

Sam's sobbing now, saying nothing coherent, and Asher says, "I have to do it now. It's already morning. You need to be strong. Let me finish the job." I watch him grab hold of the knife, the one he threatened me with earlier, the identical version of the one I brought over.

I should have had mine out and ready when I got here. I should have been stronger. Braver. Stabbed first, asked later.

I take a deep breath and begin to scream.

"Shut up! I'm going to make you shut up!" Asher steps toward me, knife out, as I'm screaming and sobbing. I can make out the knife's jagged edges, the sunlight glinting on the metal.

But suddenly Sam lets out a primal growl and lunges toward Asher. The two roll around on the ground as I keep on screaming. Sam's bigger and stronger, but Asher's scrappy and strong, too, and manages to disentangle himself. He rights his grip on the knife and rushes toward me. But then I see Sam grab hold of the other knife—the one I brought over—and leap through the air.

Asher's almost at me—knife aimed toward my neck—and I watch in horror, frozen in place, as he nears. His jaw is set, focused, until he gasps, and his face wrenches. He cries out and falls to my feet, face forward, giving me full view of the knife lodged in his back.

As Asher bleeds out on the floor, my brother and I stare at each other without saying a word.

# CHAPTER THIRTY-EIGHT

# JOSHUA

It all happens so fast—like a flip-book I'm streaming through, my thumb on the fore edge, making the pages whiz by, missing frames, skipping chunks.

Bursting out of the suite and screaming into the pink shreds of morning. Davina rushing out—pale blue pajama top and matching shorts.

The staff converging too. Jabulani and Grace. Then Markus, with his rifle, though that's not needed anymore.

Sam stumbling out, too, crowding me, trying to talk to me, explain, like I need more explanations, as Davina crushes me to her chest.

I wrap my arms around my wife. I tell her everything, frantically, and she gapes at me and rubs my back like she always does, saying things I don't absorb but with a lulling tone I do.

The chopper touching down. Officer Monala. I'm so glad to see her I nearly kneel at her feet. Officer Botha, too, still wiggling up his pants over his potbelly and acting all self-important, like he's the one who cracked this whole case.

Handcuffs, onto Sam's wrist. Bailey is poof, here—where did she come from? Where has she been?

Right. Dead asleep. Ambien.

Bailey's sobbing, pleading, banging her fists on the ground—*It can't be Sam. No, don't take him. He didn't do it!*

I hold my sister in my arms and tell her, "He did do it. I'm sorry. But he saved me in the end."

Then officers emerge from Mom and Asher's suite, carrying a body bag.

I answer questions—in the lodge, over tea that I don't drink, pastries foisted upon me that I can't stomach. It's all too much. Mom. Gwen. Sam. I rub my wrists, still raw from where Asher tied them. One of the places is still bleeding. As Officer Monala starts to ask me where the flash drive is, I lick the spot that's bleeding. It's so savage that she stops, and I do, too, my tongue midlick.

What we've all been driven to won't be soon undone.

I tell her the flash drive is in the locket. That the password to Mom's letter is TheThreeTs.

Bailey is with Sam, doesn't leave his side, though she'll have to go soon. An officer is guarding him, but I know he's not going to flee. He's broken, my brother—a shell of himself. I suppose this is what's always been lying beneath the bluster. The scared little boy. Maybe as his older brother I should have protected him. Done more.

The thought—what's going to become of my brother—nearly undoes me. I should hate him, maybe, but I don't. Fact is, I never have.

———————

THE HEAT IS RELENTLESS as we walk out of the lodge with the officers, the sun brazen, as if yesterday's storm was a mirage. The river is crowded with buffalo and zebra, some of the zebras romping in deep, while others drink at the verdant banks. I try not to think about Gwen in there, about what it was like for her in those final moments. The police aren't going to dredge it; they've said that unfortunately there won't be any trace of Gwen left.

The officers guide a handcuffed Sam toward the chopper. He's subdued now, eyes cast down.

"We have more questions, of course," Officer Monala tells me, "but that can wait. You need a hot shower. And some rest. Don't leave the country for now."

"I can barely imagine leaving my room," I say weakly.

She nods. "And Violett—you'll tell her we want to talk to her too. I understand from your wife that she's taking care of your daughter this morning. What a blessing, *ja*? That your daughter was shielded from all this."

"Yes." I try to smile. "Truly."

"You know that—I'm not sure if I should say—no, you know what?" She pats my shoulder. "You have enough on your plate. More than enough."

"What?" My heartbeat quickens. Is she talking about Ruby? "Is it . . . something with my daughter?"

"No, why ever would you think that? Oh, because we were talking about her? No, it's about, well—Violett, actually. Just that we've been looking into things from headquarters, and we got ahold of your mother's bank statements. I do understand that you are now in control of your mother's assets, and I wondered, did you know that your mother transferred money to Violett recently? Two days ago, in fact."

"Transferred money?" We've made it to the tarmac now, and something that looks like Bambi—a bushbuck, maybe—scampers in the reeds, not far off. "What do you mean, Mom transferred Violett money? Mom owns this place, so, like, as salary?"

"Not as salary, no. That's paid out of the company account. This was from your mother's personal bank account. Nearly two million rand is what she sent. The equivalent of about one hundred thousand dollars."

"To Violett?" I shake my head; it's not computing.

"*Ja*. Does your mother have a personal relationship with her?"

"No! I mean—not that I know of—no. She's an employee. She's worked here—"

"Over twenty years. Yes." Officer Monala shrugs. "It's probably nothing. Maybe a bonus, for all her years of hard work. It clearly doesn't have anything to do with your mother's murder. Or Gwen's."

"Right." I roll it around in my head, snagging on something, maybe something meaningful. But it's of no use. My head is alphabet soup. I'm not going to make heads or tails of any of it now.

Bailey's clutching onto Sam's arm, looking absolutely desolate. Davina's hand is in mine, gripping it tight.

I whisper, "It's okay, Dav," and detangle my fingers. I go to my brother.

Sam's eyes crowd with tears, and it occurs to me that I've only seen my brother cry once. At Aba's funeral.

"I'm so sorry," Sam says. "I'm so sorry, Joshua."

I nod slowly. "I know."

Sam's lips curl, and he lets out a sound like a wounded animal in the bush. It sends me immediately back to when I was young, maybe five, and went out on a game drive with just Aba and the guide, whoever worked here before Markus, the image of that guy now nebulous. But I remember we came across a little deer on the ground. It had been attacked by a leopard and had maggots in its head. It was in agony, dying a slow painful death, and the guide said we needed to put it out of its misery. He got out his long *sjambok* knife and slashed the deer's neck. Aba called it a mercy killing—the whole thing is seared in my memory.

"Do you think I'm a lost cause?" Sam asks, and I'm surprised at the question. Surprised at Sam needing me to tell him that he's not. I always wanted a little brother who looks up to me like that, but that's never been our relationship. Only now, I wonder if there is so much more buried in my brother beneath his bluster and false bravado.

"I don't think you're a lost cause," I finally say, and I'm amazed to realize I mean it. I put my arms around my brother and hug him tight as he quivers, his hands bound in front of him so he can't hug me back.

"Thank you for saving my life," I say, as we break apart.

He nods and chews on his lip. Then Officer Botha says, "We have to go, son." Bailey stops abruptly and stares at the officer, perplexed.

But then her protests resume as the officer leads Sam toward the chopper. Bailey runs after them, her wails of distress nearly drowning out the vigorous sound of the propellers starting up.

Davina links her arm into mine as we watch Sam board the chopper, then disappear inside. The chopper starts down the landing strip and eventually takes off.

"I'm so sorry, Joshua," Dav whispers, but I don't reply, just watch the chopper as it drifts through the cloudless sky.

"Let's go get our daughter," I finally say, turning toward her. "The only thing I want right now is to see Ruby."

"Yes. Let's."

We make our way toward Violett's cabin on the exterior of the lodge. "What a blessing Violett could take her somewhere out of all the action," Davina says.

"I didn't see Violett anywhere," I say, practically bouncing on the balls of my feet now to hold Ruby in my arms. "Does she even know what's happened?"

"Of course!" Dav says. "Of course she would. That's why they weren't in the lodge. Violett was shielding Ruby from everything. The staff must have told her."

"Yeah. They've probably been sitting on her porch, playing." I don't say that Violett's likely giving Ruby biltong, like she did for me when I was a child. Dav's particular about Ruby's food, so she might not appreciate that, but I'm not so precious about those things. I used to sit on Violett's porch with her, drawing pictures of animals. It's a fond memory, and it's nice that Violett's kindness transcends generations, that she's taking a liking to my daughter now too.

But when we get to Violett's little hut, they're not on the porch. Dav knocks on the door, and after a while, when no one answers, we head back to the lodge, perplexed. Markus is there, and we tell him we can't find Violett. That she's with Ruby, and it doesn't seem like the two of them are at her cabin. So we check her office—but nothing. And then Markus gets a look on his face I can't quite place, but it's something that startles me, that gets my adrenaline circulating again. He takes off running toward the parking lot out front, by the guard's booth.

"What's going on?" Dav asks, her voice carrying a first trace of panic.

"Maybe they're at the bonfire pit," I say, but I can't imagine why they would be. "Don't worry, Dav. They can't have gone far." I glance back over my shoulder, as if Ruby's going to pop out and say a grand, giggly *Surprise*.

"Does Markus think they're hanging out in the parking lot?" she asks. "I don't get it."

But when Markus bursts back, he's running, winded. "Her car's gone."

"What— I don't understand?" I say.

"It means she's gone," Markus says. "I think . . . I think Violett took your daughter."

# CHAPTER THIRTY-NINE

# VIOLETT

I'm motoring along the sandy road, past the golf club where hippos some-times sprawl on the lawn, when I hear a police siren.

"*Fok!*" I veer over onto the shoulder, and so does the police car. "It's okay, Ruby," I trill out. "Just a little hiccup. We'll be on our way again in no time."

I turn down the volume on the rugby game. The Boks have a ten-point lead over the sluggish Wallabies and are about to clinch things, a distraction from my busy brain. I glance back to see Ruby strapped into her Doona car seat—incredible, how her stroller turns into one. Still, I've been driving slowly, being exceedingly careful. And thankfully Ruby's preoccupied now, too, chewing on the biltong I brought along. It's the mild kind; babies love them when they teethe. Ruby smiles at me with her glittering face, calming my nerves a bit now that the rugby's off.

They can't have noticed we're gone and reported a kidnapping this fast—can they? I touch my pistol at my side.

After what happened to me, I'm never without it.

The officer is at my window now, rapping hard. I roll it down as a *bakkie* whizzes by.

"Yes?" I try to sound disgruntled. Well, I suppose I don't have to try.

"You were going very fast, madam. Far above the speed limit."

I wasn't. Even though I'm in a rush, of course, having kidnapped Ruby,

I am being mindful of my speed. Precious cargo in the back. "I'm sure I was going the speed limit, or even below."

"Well, you also ran the *robot* back there."

"Ran the *robot*? You're mistaken. It was yellow."

"It was red. And you didn't pull over. Didn't you hear me all this way? You cannot ignore a siren, madam."

"Oh." Did I not hear the siren? I've been so preoccupied in my head that perhaps I didn't.

Ruby suddenly bleats, and the officer peers back. "Oh! Your baby."

"Yes." I remind myself—he's not going to question she's mine. And Joshua and Davina are probably still sleeping, enjoying their lie-in, thinking I'm feeding Ruby and showing her the animals at the river.

Ruby peals another giggle, and the officer smiles, doesn't seem like he suspects me of kidnapping.

"I'll have to give you a ticket," he says, but he doesn't take out his pad. I know why that is—he wants a bribe. Prefers that, over issuing a ticket from which he attains nothing.

"What can I do so that you let me go without a ticket?" It's certainly to my benefit, too—I don't want any trace of this drive on an official record. I drum my red fingernails against the side of the car in an alluring manner and give him a winning smile.

A minute later, I am five hundred rand poorer and driving along again with Ruby gurgling happily in back.

# CHAPTER FORTY

# BAILEY

The windows are all rolled down, so we aren't in a sealed box of our thoughts. But still, even with the wind gusting in my face, the sun dappling down, Dav's cries are cutting from the back seat. We pass a slew of hand-painted signs that advertise all manner of goods and services, from witch doctor to chickens, tire repairs to wooden giraffes. I stare out the window, my brain taking me on a Tilt-A-Whirl tour—Sam, Mom, Gwen, Ruby. It feels like my heart's new steady state is beating berserk.

Markus speeds his pickup truck along the dusty road toward Graskop, the town Violett is apparently from. He pronounces it *chrahs-kop*. Instead of *grass-kop*, my American inclination.

"How long until we get to the grass place?" Dav asks again.

"Just now," Markus says, like his prior answers too. Which I know could mean anything from ten minutes to ten hours in South Africa time.

"How come the cops couldn't drive into the lodge but we can drive to Graskop?" I ask.

"The rains destroy soil roads. Make them very muddy," Markus says. "So you can't get through for days. But sand roads are different. The rain evaporates. The roads up into Graskop are sand."

"And you're sure the chopper can't land there? They could get there before us! I don't understand," Joshua says.

"There's no landing pad," Markus says. "You need a runway—and Graskop is set into the mountain. It's all cliffs and jagged bluffs."

"And you really think Ruby will be there?" Joshua asks. "But why . . . I still don't understand. Why would Violett take our daughter—"

"*Kidnap*," Davina interrupts. "She's kidnapped her! Don't soften what she's done. She's kidnapped my baby!"

"Why would Violett kidnap our daughter and take her to her house? I mean, she'd know the police would be onto her in a moment."

Markus shakes his head. "Do you have any other ideas?"

"Not a one," Joshua admits.

Quiet now, just Davina weeping and the wind and my dovetailing thoughts. I grab my backpack from the floor and rummage inside for my Nalgene. As I do, some of my things spill onto the seat—a stray carabiner. My malaria pills. A key chain with a picture of my adorable mutt, Sunny. In all the hubbub, I haven't even texted Junie to see how he's doing. My heart races even quicker; I'm getting accustomed to this feeling, that it's going to actually burst out of my chest.

"What's that?" Markus asks sharply.

"What's what?"

"That." He reaches over and holds up my malaria pills. He swivels it around to read the label. "Oh my days, Bailey. Have you been taking these?"

"It's just malaria pills," I say in surprise.

"Who prescribed them to you?"

"I don't know—some doctor at a clinic in Florida."

"Some doctor at a clinic? You mean, your mother's doctor? Bailey, these pills have been involved in lawsuits. It's rare to have an extreme reaction to them, but they've made people psychotic, even led some to commit suicide."

I stare at him, perplexed. "Seriously?"

"Your mother's doctor prescribed them?" he asks again, looking astounded. "I mean, they are still prescribed around the world, but I'd understood the backlash was pretty big in the United States. I didn't think they were being prescribed as much there."

"No. Well, actually . . . Mom was on me to make an appointment, but I forgot."

I didn't actually forget. It whooshes back now, all the anger boiling in me, as over breakfast one morning a few weeks back, Mom ticked off her checklist of to-dos. Things for the company, and that I needed to make a haircut before safari—my hair was looking scraggly. And malaria pills. She'd made me an appointment with her doctor.

Rage had churned inside me that, on a rare occasion, I allowed to explode. I told her I'd cut my own hair if I pleased and make an appointment for malaria pills when I decided to! That she didn't control me.

And she just said, *Okay, then*. With this curt air, as if she knew she did in fact control me, and that she was going to find some way to hold even this minor infraction against me.

By the time I realized I needed malaria pills, it was too late to get an appointment at my doctor's office, so I went to a random travel clinic.

What a time to make a stand, Bailey.

"Could this be the reason for—" Joshua says from the back seat. "Some of Bailey's behavior lately?"

"*Ja.*" Markus nods grimly. "I thought it was out of character—Bailey going after the elephant—"

"And about to leap into the river to save Gwen? With the crocodiles?" Joshua says. "That isn't Bails. She's thoughtful. Not the skydiving type. So I didn't understand—"

"This . . . oh my god." I feel a torrent of relief. That I'm not insane. Or being drugged. The crazy thing I've thought, ever since I learned my brother was in on a plot to kill Mom, wondering if he'd slipped me pills. Not the Ambien Dav gave me, but if Sam was maybe actually drugging me, to facilitate his plans. . . .

"I've felt so anxious," I finally say, still feeling the stabbing anxieties in my chest. "So not myself . . . like I'm going crazy . . ."

"You're having a bad reaction to the pills. No wonder you've been completely hectic. *Ag,* man, we're just lucky it wasn't worse, that you didn't—" Markus breaks off, his face stormy, and it takes me a moment to place the feeling I get, something almost daughterly and fatherly, or at least like he cares about me a lot. I experience a swell of guilt, of anger, too, that I push down. "We need to get you to the hospital."

"What . . . something could still happen to me?"

"They can treat this. Now that we know. Don't take any more pills, though."

"Of course not. I won't." I stare numbly at the orange bottle.

"But we won't go right to the hospital," Dav says. "Sorry, Bails, but can we go after we find Ruby? Please, we just need—"

"After we find Ruby, of course," I agree. Anyway, I'm not itching to check into a hospital in South Africa for however long and have them do—what exactly? Some sort of detox? I still want to go see Sam. Parse through a million competing thoughts.

"Why did she take her?" Joshua asks for what feels like the millionth time. "I don't understand."

"Markus," I say quietly, when Dav and Joshua are speculating again in the back, and Dav is moaning that her breasts are becoming engorged, without Ruby to feed. "Is Violett . . . is she—"

"Let's just get there," Markus interrupts me tightly. "Let's get to Graskop and find Ruby." He indicates Joshua and Davina in the back seat. "We don't want to make this harder on them now, right? I promise I'll tell you. I'll tell you everything I know. But not now. Do you trust me?"

"I do," I finally say.

---

IT'S MISTING OUTSIDE AS we arrive at Graskop, a spectacular place filled with waterfalls and dramatic mountain cliffs overlooking a green, fertile expanse. As we approached, Markus pointed out local attractions, and all of them pushed our buttons.

God's Window—a stunning sweep out into a forested ravine. "Where the fuck is God right now?" (Davina)

Bourke's Luck Potholes—rock formations with circular holes owing to the swirling water that's worn them down over millions of years. "Where is our luck on this trip?" (Joshua)

Mac Mac Falls—twin falls plunging into a gorge below. "*Twins.*" (Me)

Now we've inadvertently taken in enough beauty to give our eyeballs a good plunge, and we pour out of the truck into the steamy day before a house that can only generously be called a house. It's at the end of a rambling road, perched precariously on a cliff, and it looks like it might have seen its best days—if it ever had best days—one hundred years prior. The shingles are peeling, the red brick dingy, the roof patchy in parts. There's a stoop, with a few plastic chairs scattered haphazardly, one upturned.

"This is Violett's home?" I'm having trouble reconciling it with the polished, beautiful woman who manages Leopard Sands.

"Her grandmother's," Markus says, as we follow Joshua and Dav to the door. "But, yes, Violett lives with her. Has always lived with her."

Dav's taken off in a sprint, already banging on the door.

"The house is . . ." I think of a nice way to put it. "Kind of . . . sad?"

"Well, they haven't had it easy. Never enough money. Violett's grandmother's had heart issues her whole life. She couldn't work, and Violett's mother died when Violett was a teenager."

"Oh."

Of course I think about my own mother.

"Her mother died here, actually." He points toward the cliff. "She tumbled over the edge when she was drinking."

"Oh." I clap my hand over my mouth. "That's horrible."

"*Ja.* Violett took over her mother's job as waitress at Leopard Sands. Worked her way up. But it's a lot on young shoulders. She had to support her grandmother, her aunt and uncle, too . . . no-goods, them. She hasn't had it easy. Not one bit."

"Do you think she'll hurt Ruby?" I whisper.

He shakes his head. He doesn't say, *I've already answered this a million times in the truck.*

"I know she won't. I promise you, Bailey. Your niece will be fine. We'll get to the bottom of this. Violett doesn't have a cruel bone in her body even though life has been cruel to her. She's a good one. Tough shell, crusty sometimes, but a good heart. She has a very good heart."

"How do you know Ruby will be okay? How do you know . . ." My voice cracks. "How do you know I'll ever see my niece again?"

Markus opens his mouth, then closes it. "I just do." He checks his phone, scrolls. Then begins typing, his tongue sticking out in concentration. I'm surprised to realize I do the exact same thing.

"Are you talking to the police?"

"*Ja,* they're on their way."

We join Joshua and Dav on the stoop. It's quiet, eerily so, none of us saying the obvious. It's the middle of the day, and not a flicker of life. It doesn't look like Violett and Ruby are here.

No one's answered the door, and now Joshua's gone to one of the windows covered in steel bars and peers in. "I don't see anyone," he calls.

"What the fuck?" Dav bangs on the door some more. "Open up, Violett! Open the fuck up!"

I start to go right, to check the back of the house, when out of the corner of my eye I spot a boy, probably around ten, kicking a ball down the street. I approach him, and as I do, he waves. Then he sends the ball straight toward me.

"Whoa!" It's unexpected, and I fumble for it, but eventually manage to stop it. When I look down, I notice it's not a soccer ball, but a dingy, punctured volleyball. I kick it back. But the ball only rolls halfway toward him.

"You have to kick it harder," he says. "Violett kicks it harder than you."

"Violett? You know her?"

"*Ja natuurlik*," he says.

"What does that mean?"

"*Ja*," he says again. "Yes."

"Do you know where she is? She isn't answering the door and she's taken—" I was about to say my niece, but that's a bit dark to rope a little boy into. "She has something of ours."

"Oh." He sends the ball back to me. This time it flies high, and I manage to jab my foot beneath it, before it even touches the ground, and send it flying back.

The boy nods his approval at me. "Better. Violett's at the hospital, won't she be?"

"The hospital?" Now Dav and Joshua have come over. "What hospital?" Dav asks, looking frantic, like she wants to grab this boy and shake all the information he has out of him.

"*Ja*, Mapulaneng."

I look at Markus to decipher that and he says, "*Ag*. The hospital by Hazyview. You're sure? That's where she is?"

"I'm not sure," the boy says. "But her ouma is there—"

"Her ouma?" Dav asks.

"Violett's grandmother," Markus says. "Her grandmother is sick."

"Okay," Joshua says. "What are we waiting for? Let's go. I'll call Officer Monala in the car. And let's pray that they're there."

We all start toward the truck.

"You look like her."

I swivel back. The boy isn't looking at us as he continues to weave his ball around on the road.

"What?" Davina asks sharply.

The boy kicks the ball toward Violett's house, then emits a squeal of glee when it makes it toward the porch, which is apparently his goalpost.

"What?" I ask.

The boy says, "Him." He points.

I follow the line of his finger point to Joshua.

"Wha— What?" Joshua shakes his head. He glances behind him, then uncertainly back. "Are you talking to me?"

"Yeah, I don't know." The boy shrugs. "Just saying. You look like Violett. Are you her brother or something?"

# CHAPTER FORTY-ONE

# VIOLETT

I push through the waiting room, clutching a screaming Ruby to my chest. "Shhh, it's okay, *shongololo*. Almost there."

The room is overflowing, people waiting in the halls—as always, not enough staff to get through the hordes of would-be patients. Once I sat here with Ouma, waiting, while she wheezed, barely able to breathe, in the throes of pneumonia, while the man beside us clutched his hand to his scalp, bleeding. I asked him if it was serious, if he needed to be seen urgently, maybe I could convince a nurse, and he shrugged, and said, *Nah*, and then kept on waiting all day. Later, when they finally took him in, they discovered there was a bullet lodged in the back of his head. That's why he was bleeding! But he didn't even know it. South Africa for you.

Down the hall, turn right, then another right. Ruby's wailing harder— she doesn't like it here, and I understand that, baby girl. The antiseptic smell, the fluorescent lights. It's all horrible, but still far better than you'd get on the rest of the continent.

I stop at the end of the hall and pull out my phone. I scroll to Joshua's contact, which I only have because of the Leopard Sands information forms. I stab out a text, my fingers trembling as I type. *Ruby is safe. My grandmother is sick, and I had to come see her, and I didn't want to wake you and Davina up. I figured this was the easiest solution. I'm so sorry! She's completely safe, and I'm bringing her right back to you. Not a hair harmed on her beautiful head.*

I blink back tears, shove my phone in my pocketbook, and turn the doorknob.

It's a tiny room, but Ouma has been blessed with the window partition—a view onto the parking lot, but all around it, trees. I fought for this placement. She was originally in a different room, with a nurse I didn't like, but I can be fierce when I need to be. When I enter, I see my tannie sleeping on the chair. I don't wake her—she is mostly useless, my tannie. Gambles and drinks, like my mother used to do. But my tannie does have one redeeming quality: she loves Ouma.

"Ouma." I'm already crying as I approach the bed, the frail shape beneath the threadbare blue blanket. She used to be so big, Ouma. Three different stomach rolls, each one a new landscape to curl into, each one a gentle hug to bury my tears inside.

She stirs, and then a smile spreads across her peeling lips. Her smile falters, though, as her eyes fasten on the bundle in my arms.

"*Is dit Ruby?*"

"*Ja.*" Tears collect in my eyes as I bend the baby down, for my grandmother to soak in a full view. She doesn't know—it doesn't matter—how much I've sacrificed to bring Ruby here now. But for the sheer awe and pleasure on my dying grandmother's face, I would do it all again a million times over.

I switch to English, so Ruby can understand. Because babies are people, and they know. I do believe that.

"Ruby, meet your oumagroot." I tremble as I lower Ruby to my grandmother. Ruby has stopped crying now, stopped whimpering, and is fixing her big brown eyes on Ouma in wonder. Staring almost rapturously at Ouma's hollowed, wrinkled, beautiful face.

"Ouma, meet your great-great-granddaughter."

———

SUDDENLY, THERE WAS A baby.

Isn't that how every story begins? The good ones, at least. Though this was not a good one, and not a bad one, either. It had both aspects, twisted together, as many stories do.

The bad part? Well, maybe I should start with the good part. Because there was only one.

Joshua.

Well, before he was Joshua, he was Frederich. It means "peaceful ruler," and I felt in giving him that name I was infusing him with a hallowed intention.

But now we get to the bad parts. I gave birth to Frederich when I had just turned fifteen. It took me a long time to understand I was pregnant, and when I did, it was the worst, most unfathomable thing that could happen to a person. Because I knew where this baby came from.

And so did my mother.

Her boyfriend.

He lived with us—all of us together—but before my tannie moved in, it was just us and Ouma, with enough bedrooms for me to have my own. I didn't like my mother's boyfriend, the way he looked at me, kind of leering. One day it was the two of us alone in the house, and I don't need to describe it, do I? What he did to me? I told my mother right after—and she didn't believe me.

I was too ashamed to tell Ouma. Until I became pregnant. Then I did tell her, but it was too late.

Ouma banished my mother from the home, and her boyfriend too. I didn't have to lie awake at night anymore, with my dresser pushed in front of my door, in case he tried anything again. But I was left with the spoils. The baby.

I worried I wouldn't love him. That I wouldn't be capable of it.

I was wrong.

Frederich arrived, and he was perfect. But I struggled—of course I did. I hadn't asked for a baby, and not in this way. I was a mere child myself. I felt shame and love and hate, all at the same time. Sometimes I stared at Frederich's rolls and his gurgle and smile and surged with motherly love. Sometimes I gave him to Ouma and went to work for a few days and tried to forget he existed at all. My mother had gotten me a job at Leopard Sands as a housekeeper. She was a waitress, had worked her way up—surprising, because she gambled and was angry—but she was magnetic. She could work a guest; they loved her. Charismatic and flirtatious. Beautiful too.

Can you tell how much I hate her? Can you tell where this story is going?

———

PERHAPS I AM GLOSSING over things, but the story is too painful to dig for details and excavate them one by one. That's meant for a person who has the time, money, and inclination for therapy, who wants to line up her traumas on a shelf and pore over them, rinse, repeat.

My traumas? I prefer them buried deep—locked with a key.

How did Frederich, my son, become Joshua Babel, son of Aryeh and Odelia?

Well, because my mother sold him to them.

———

ONE DAY, I CAME home from work, and he was gone. Simple as that. When I understood what had happened, what my mother had done, for money—money she eventually frittered away—it was too late. Frederich was gone.

"You didn't even want to be a mother," she said, as if she'd done me some great favor. "He will live a far better life than you could provide."

Aryeh and Odelia Babel were wealthy people who had spent a couple years in Jozi and now visited their lodge, Leopard Sands, whenever they pleased. I don't know what my mother told them, how selling my baby was brokered. Did they ask her to find them a baby? Did she mention she had one for sale? Did she say Frederich was a product of rape? Did she tell them I sang him lullabies at night, that I spent hours stroking his soft skin in the moonlight? Or did she tell them I didn't want him? Is that what all three of them wanted anyhow to believe?

It doesn't really matter, because Aryeh and Odelia absconded soon after with my baby. I understand they had a passport procured quickly. A few thousand rand, and all that would be smoothed over. Legal, stamped. Easy. They went back to Florida and didn't return to Leopard Sands for over five years.

Could I have gone after them? Could I have told the authorities, pressed charges, against my mother and the Babels? Claimed international kidnapping? Worked the diplomatic channels, like you see on movies?

Pah. If I went to the authorities, then the job I had—employed by the Babels themselves—was all but guaranteed to go kaput. And I probably wouldn't get Frederich back in any event. I would have to prove that I, an unmarried teenager, was his mother. That he wasn't theirs. Up against their millions or billions in legal muscle to fight me. Connections. Bribes. Corruption in the government, in the police, the people I'd have to turn to for protection and redemption.

Was it horrific?

Yes.

You may wonder—however did I cope with it?

Well, I killed my mother.

———

OR, I DIDN'T KILL her, but I didn't save her. Semantics, maybe.

After it happened, after I discovered what she'd done, we fought in the yard, by the cliff. It was night. My mother had stumbled home. Her boyfriend—not the one who'd violated me, but a new one, two boyfriends down the line by now—had kicked her out. She was flush with cash, some gambled away, but some left, and she wanted to buy me something. A watch? A necklace? What did I want? She didn't say it, but it was meant to be compensation.

I railed at her, devastated. Distraught. I can't put into words how I felt—it's too tremendous, even now, to describe the feelings that ticked in me like a bomb.

And then that bomb detonated.

My mother called Frederich a bastard. She accused me of not even wanting him—of shunning him even. Maybe I had. I curdled with shame. But she took no responsibility—not for bringing that man into my life, or for selling my baby. She was drunk, arms flailing, and I kept screaming at her, lunging forward, forcing her to retreat backward, closer and closer to the edge of the cliff.

The gorge below was hundreds of feet down, the entire way punishing rock. We had talked about putting in a guardrail, but you needed money for that.

You see where this is going? It had rained recently. The ground was still wet. My mother slipped and cried out, and maybe I could have reached for her. Pulled her back.

But I didn't.

---

OUMA RUNS A ROUGH finger against Ruby's bicep. "She is beautiful."

"Beautiful," I agree. "Perfect."

"And a Jew!" Ouma smiles. "A Jew! Jesus was a Jew. This little one comes from the land of Jesus!"

"She comes from me, Ouma."

"Her mother is a Jew, *is sy nie*? That is what you told me."

"Yes. That is true. Davina is Jewish."

"Jewish, just like Jesus. They let you take her? They let you bring her to me?"

"No," I admit, my sadness stopping up my throat. "No. But I needed you to meet her before . . ."

"Before I go." Ouma gasps, then her head falls back on her pillow and she doesn't say anything more, just stares at Ruby with a look I can't decipher. Grief and happiness, and acceptance, maybe. Ouma's here, I realize, but she's someplace else, too, and I know that her molecules are migrating to that other place more and more. Still, I feel something peaceful inside, that no matter what happens now, to me or to her, Ruby is bound to us too. No longer a photograph or a theory. No longer a thing to observe from afar with longing and regret. But skin to skin to skin. Stamped and engraved. Loved.

I want to collect all the moments. I want to hold them tight and press pause.

After some time, I hear commotion at the door. I hold Ruby tighter and soak in her intoxicating smell and kiss her head. Bury my face in her thick, lustrous hair.

Like her father's. Like mine.

"I'm sorry, I'm sorry, I'm sorry," I'm already saying, barely able to see through the wall of my tears, as Joshua and Davina storm into the room, and Davina pulls her daughter from my arms.

# CHAPTER FORTY-TWO

# BAILEY

*Two Weeks Later*

Nice not going out on a game drive with a checklist," Markus says, setting up his little stove to make our coffees. He chuckles. "Sometimes it's like all that are out there are springboks, and I need to do some good customer satisfaction massaging."

I don't reply, just stare at the sun beginning to break over the trees, its oranges and reds rippling across the low, pale sky.

"Or did you want to keep going?" He indicates his rifle. "We could take a walk. Could—"

"No, I don't want to walk. Seeing One Horn was a treat enough." One Horn is the oldest rhino in these parts, a black rhino, exceedingly rare these days. Endangered. We watched him grip leaves with his hook lip, and yes, it was very nice.

"*Ag, ja,*" Markus says, misunderstanding. "Maybe we need some time to pass . . . since our *adventure* before we—"

"No, I'm . . . I don't know. Maybe. Maybe that's it."

"Look." Markus points at the bird soaring above the termite mound. "That's a plum-colored starling, in his breeding plumage."

I stare up at it but can't muster an excited response.

"You okay, Bails?"

Markus hands me my *moer koffie.*

"Thank you. Yes, I'm fine." I sip on the sweet coffee, then I swirl a rusk inside.

"You sure? Maybe they shouldn't have let you out of the hospital yet?"

"I'm sure. My inflammatory markers were all back to normal."

"Okay, then what's up, Bails?"

The way he says it—so familiar—makes my chest spasm.

"I'm not Bails!" I say, my reaction unexpected even to myself.

"How's that?"

"It's like . . . you think just because I'm your daughter . . . just because you saved me from the bush that night, you can call me that! I'm only Bails to the people I'm closest to. Sam and Joshua call me Bails. Mom and Gwen did too. But you—you don't—"

"I don't get that right." Markus looks somberly away. "It's okay. That's fair."

"*Is* it fair, though? Is it? Is anything about anything that's happened *fair*?"

Markus removes his cap and rakes a weary hand through his blond hair smattered with grays. "Maybe it's the pills still in your system," he finally says. "Because I know this has been a terrible few weeks—but this isn't you—this doesn't seem like—"

"This is me!" I say, white-hot rage shooting all over. "Maybe this is me! This is me, when I'm not thinking about another person's feelings over my own!"

For a while, we tramp on in silence, with Markus looking side to side, checking the trees for leopards and the ground for resting lions. Checking the thick, rich grass on the outskirts of a watering hole for zebras or wilde-beest. But for now, nothing—no animals visible, just the tension fomenting between us and an occasional bird hoot or a distant *kwe-kwe-kwe*, and the scents of wild sage and tannin—peaceful, nice, but suddenly not mine. For my entire life, the bush was my escape. Coming here was my break from regular life, from my parents and Circ. But for the last two weeks I was in the hospital, mostly alone, though Joshua, Dav, and Ruby visited, and Markus too. I had a lot of time to think. And I thought about so much.

"You don't have to shield my feelings," Markus says. "I'm sorry—I know what a horrible time this has been for you. And what a shock it must have been to find out I'm your father. I guess I thought . . ." He gives me a crooked smile. "We've always been buds, me and you. So I thought—"

"You thought I'd slot you into the daddy role," I say weakly.

"No, not like that." Markus grimaces.

"It's okay. It's not just you. It's, like, in a week, all three of us Babel kids lost a parent and also gained a new one. We should be grateful, huh?

"No. C'mon. I know it's more complicated than that."

I shrug. "Well, it *is* more complicated. More nuanced. The situations with you and Violett are different." Joshua's filled me in by now, after the whole ordeal. "Violett was a child, for one. You weren't a child." I feel a bit badly twisting the knife, but facts are facts. "And Joshua was stolen from her. Sam and I weren't stolen from you. You let us go. You gave us away."

"It was more complicated than that," Markus says softly, twisting his fingers into his bracelet. It's part gold chain, part brown leather, and there's a little charm of a lion. He's worn it forever, but I have no idea what it represents, why it's meaningful to him. I don't know so many things about him.

"Part of me wishes I could easily acclimate to you being my birth father," I admit. "But if I'm honest—"

"Please. Please do be honest. You can always tell me the truth, Bailey."

"Okay." I think about what my hospital nurse, Themba, to whom I ended up spilling my life story, said. She was quiet as I rambled on, and then when I'd finished, she told me she'd studied psychology, too, in addition to nursing. And that my parents sounded like textbook narcissists, which can cause their children to be constantly walking on eggshells. Codependent. People pleasers. And overachieving.

I tell Markus about it, about my revelations, and he listens quietly.

"That makes sense. They were big personalities," he finally says, when I've finished. "I'm so sorry, Bail—Bailey. I know I only knew you from afar. From our little interactions when you came here. I didn't know your whole life."

"But you saw them!" Tears smother my cheeks, and it feels impossible to stop them. "I mean, Mom wasn't awful, but Aba was. And you must have known—you saw how he acted down here, like he ruled the world, mean to his staff, to Mom, to us. Well, really to my brothers. Me he just ignored. Acted like I didn't exist."

*You let me be raised by that man*, I want to scream, but I guess he knows that's what I'm feeling, if he reads between the lines.

"It was a different time, Bailey," Markus finally says. "You know what the legal presumption is for a woman pregnant by her husband? That the child is his. Your father believed you and Sam were his—of course he did. What was I going to do? Fight them in court? Fight your father? With what money? Your mother would have said it wasn't true, and I would have been out of a job and without you guys, anyway. In the end, I guess . . . I guess I thought I was giving you the better life."

"I don't know," I finally say, processing that, that things are more complex than I imagined them to be. "Maybe you gave me the life that was easier for you. You never wanted children. You told me that once, when I asked you why you didn't have them."

Markus's shoulders sag. "Maybe I said that because it's always felt painful, having you and losing you, in an endless loop. You'd pop over here to Leopard Sands—you and Sam—and then your parents would take you back to Florida for months or years at a time. But you're right—maybe I still should have fought for you kids. I regret it now . . . that I didn't. But I'll tell you one thing, Bailey. I've always cared about you. About you and Sam. Joshua too. I've always—whenever I knew you kids were coming here, I felt on pins and needles, waiting. I do love you. Even if the way I've shown it has been imperfect."

His words settle something in me. It doesn't make everything okay, but maybe that's a ridiculous expectation, anyway, for everything to even be okay. I do feel some sort of peace, though, hearing Markus's explanation. And maybe even more, having said how I feel. I'm determined to do that more often now.

"I decided I'm going to apply to veterinarian school when I get back to Florida," I tell him.

"Really?" A slow smile spreads across Markus's face. "That's fantastic."

"Yeah. I haven't been happy at Circ—pretty much ever. And I realized—I mean, I don't want to blame it all on Mom, because I get that I'm an adult. I have to take responsibility for my own choices. But I've basically been living this life she's wanted me to live. The biggest stand I ever made was to go to a shady doctor and get those malaria pills. Figures." I laugh ruefully. "I know I'm making a difference at Circ, sort of, but chief conservation officer, I don't know—it's like a made-up title Mom gave me to make me feel useful. I was a figurehead. She was the one in charge."

"Well, your mom isn't at the helm anymore," Markus says. "So you could still—"

"Nah." I shake my head. "I'll make a bigger difference being a vet. And I'll be happier."

I suddenly feel light, buoyant almost, imagining getting to do this thing I've always wanted to do with no one telling me I should be doing something else.

"That's wonderful," Markus finally says. "I've always thought you were like me—that you need the animals. The quiet."

"I do."

"You could . . ." He pauses.

"What?"

"You could always come train here, with me."

"Like . . . to be a guide?"

Now his smile widens, and I feel that familiar sinking in my chest, a preliminary knowing I'm going to either let down a parent or let down myself. Usually myself.

"I'd love it. I'd love to have you here. Show you the ropes. I've always thought you'd be amazing at it."

"Oh." An image pops into my mind, of little Bailey. Running her ant hospital, digging for worms, begging to go to the park so I could play with other people's dogs. And I find myself making a silent promise to the girl, that it's her I'm going to do right by from now on.

"That's an amazing offer. But no. No, thank you. I want to go back and move out of my mom's and get my own place. And give vet school a try. I'm happy in Palm Beach, I think. Joshua's there, and Dav, and Ruby. And if it doesn't feel right after all, then I need to decide what is. On my own."

*With no one I'm beholden to*, I think.

I push down the lump in my throat and think about visiting Sam in jail, about what he said as we sat across from each other. How praying has been getting him through everything, though he still won't acknowledge—or face—Markus being our birth father. Not now, at least; denial is a powerful coping mechanism. But Sam did say that he does want to face up to me and Joshua, to repent to the two of us, especially, and to repent to God.

Sam said that he realized the voice he was listening to—the voice saying to conspire with Asher to kill Mom, the voice hating Mom, blaming her for so many things—wasn't actually God. Because God's voice is infinitely loving and forgiving; that's what his rabbi said. So Sam is talking to the real God now, listening, trying to do better. And I asked him how he does that, how he hears the real God, and he said it's a little voice in his head speaking to him that feels true and good. And that he's still learning to tell the difference between the dueling voices. I had a light bulb moment when he said it, because I have that little, true voice, too, and all my life I've been mostly disregarding it. Telling it to stop, go away—because I felt I couldn't follow it. I had to do what Mom and Aba wanted. And now I just want to go home and listen to that little, true voice and do what it says. Without other people's voices and opinions crowding it out.

I even emailed Mrs. Thatch, my old beloved teacher. She's in her nineties now, I realized. I was so afraid that she'd maybe have died. And I'd have missed all this time—missed this chance to connect and tell her how much she meant to me when I was a kid, how I'm so sorry that after Aba died, I closed the door on the religious world, and also on her. But she's alive and well. I'm going to go see her when I get back to Florida. I can hardly wait.

"Sorry," I eventually tell Markus. "As much as I love it out here, this doesn't feel like where I'm supposed to be now. I need to go home."

"You don't have to apologize," Markus says softly. "I'm proud of you. I think your mother would be too."

I laugh then. "She wouldn't be. Trust me. She'd be pissed I'm leaving Circ. I interned for a vet hospital in high school, and she and Aba were totally against it. They only agreed because I also interned at Circ. They were determined to show me how much more money and power I'd have working in the family business."

"Eh, I don't know. I think the evolved part of your mother—maybe she wouldn't be happy with your decision. But I do think she'd eventually respect it." For a while it's quiet between us, and then Markus says, "Anyway, what do you think? Shall we start back?"

I breathe out. "Yeah."

He slides into the front seat and starts the motor, but before we head off, I say, "Markus?"

He turns. "Yeah?"

"Will you—" I think how to say it. "Will you watch out for Sam after I leave? I'll be back, for his trial, and to see him. But I can't stay here now. And Sam . . . what he did was horrible—but he's a good person deep down. Our parents messed him—all of us, really—up. And he's going to need—"

"Bailey," Markus interrupts. "You don't have to ask me. I would have done it anyway. I'll look out for Sam. Of course I will. I care about him just as much— Well, I care about both of you. Always have. Always will."

"Thank you."

"Sure, kiddo." Markus presses on the gas and we lurch forward through a thicket of banana palms. Then he glances over at me, uncertain. "Is that okay? I mean, if kiddo is too, I don't know, fatherlike for you, I can—"

"It's fine." And I find that I'm smiling a little as we head back toward the lodge.

# CHAPTER FORTY-THREE

# VIOLETT

There's a knock on the door, I've been expecting it. I patter over and open my little cabin to my son.

He's so beautiful—his goodness shining from his every pore—that it's all I can do not to maul him, to run my hands over his arms and shoulders and marvel at his everything. I never got to do that, not really, and I suppose I'm still a bit starved.

But he just raises a hand in a sheepish wave and says, "I came to say a last goodbye."

"Oh."

I force myself to breathe, to calm, but tears are already swimming in my eyes. I know this. He's leaving now, and Davina and Ruby too. I already said goodbye to them last night, Even if Davina still hasn't forgiven me for taking Ruby, even if she avoided looking me in the eye and held Ruby tight as I leaned down to kiss my granddaughter goodbye, I think she sort of sees—mother to mother—why I did. She didn't press charges, at least. That was a huge kindness.

"I'm sorry." Joshua frowns. "I didn't mean to—"

"No." I wipe my eyes. "It's just Ouma . . . and now you're going . . . and Ruby . . . and we've only now . . ."

I don't know what to call it. Reunited? Is that what this has been? So much has happened. Nothing has truly sunk in and integrated. I know

Joshua needs time, to settle, to process his mother . . . Gwen . . . Sam . . . Asher . . . me.

To figure out what he wants from me going forward, if anything at all.

I manage a smile. "Do you have a few minutes to sit?" I indicate the chairs looking out on the river. "I have oat crunchies."

"*Your* oat crunchies?" he asks, and my heart leaps that he remembers. I made them for him when he came over sometimes, as a child. Really, I won him over with them.

"Yes."

"Okay." He checks his watch. "I only have a few minutes, though."

I hurry inside to grab the crunchies on a plate, then rush back outside and place them on the little table. I ease down into the seat.

"I'm so sorry, Joshua. I really— I hope you can understand how desperate I felt. I—"

"You don't have to explain it again," Joshua says, staring off at the river. "We've been through it, and frankly, Davina is still pretty traumatized. Well, to be honest, we both are . . ."

He grimaces, and my heart clenches, because I know he's not only referring to what I did. I still can't believe how close Joshua came with Sam . . . and Asher. I knew something was up with that smarmy Asher. I just knew it. I should have protected my son. I've made so many mistakes.

"You could have done it differently," Joshua says, "you could have told me—"

"How could I tell you? *Joshua, I'm your mother, and I want you to meet my grandmother before she dies.* It would have been putting so much on you."

"And taking my daughter didn't?" he asks quietly. "What did you think was going to happen?"

I redden. "I thought I would explain it as an emergency," I explain again. "Ouma needed me—I didn't want to wake you and Davina—"

"Come on, Violett. You knew it was going to be bigger than that ridiculous explanation."

"Maybe." I sigh. "I wasn't thinking straight. I was so emotional. You and Ruby were here, but you weren't mine. Not mine to have, at least. I always felt that way about you, but with Ruby here, it was all doubled. She looks so like you as a baby, when you were still mine. I guess I went a little crazy."

Joshua bites into his crunchie. "I don't really understand," he says quietly, and my heart hitches. "After Mom died . . . why you didn't want me to meet Ouma too?"

"Of course I wanted you to meet Ouma! And her to meet you. Of course I did, Joshua." I try to push down the emotion that swells up. "I've always wanted that, so very much. But after your mother died, it was too . . . fraught. I didn't think it would be fair to you, to spring this information on you when you were grieving."

"But it was fair to—take my daughter?" he asks evenly. I look down, aware he nearly said *kidnapped*, but avoided it to spare my feelings.

"No, of course it wasn't," I say quietly. "I lost my mind. I can see that now. But Ruby was never in any harm. I took good care of her. I even brought her milk along that Davina had pumped, and a bottle, all in that little portable cooler."

"Well, truth is, you weren't the only one who went crazy this week. And Ruby was okay." He shoots me a smile I probably don't deserve. "She smiles whenever you're around. Seems like she's taken to you."

"I've really taken to her too." I swallow, trying to stave off the enormity of that feeling. "Thank you for coming to Ouma's funeral."

Joshua nods. "I wish I would have gotten to know her. That I'd have had more time, to—"

"I know. But you got to meet her. And she got to meet you and Ruby. That means . . . that means a lot to me. And it meant a lot to her too."

"To me too."

We're quiet until I spot a boomslang snake slithering up the side of the stoop, not far before it makes it to our feet. In a flash, I'm up. I grab my shotgun leaning against the side of the cabin and shoot at the boomslang. It slithers fast away into the bush.

Joshua gasps.

"Salt pellet," I tell him, sitting back down, exhaling slowly. "It's not to kill, it's just to get him gone. You have to protect yourself, as a woman in South Africa, but especially in the bush."

"That's true," Joshua finally says. "I never thought of that. You're not afraid?"

"No. Animals don't scare me. Only humans do."

Joshua is quiet for some time, until he says, "Violett, I have to ask you something."

"Anything."

"You asked my mother for money—you blackmailed her, didn't you? Said you would expose the fact that she more or less stole me?"

I shiver but don't speak. Fear overtakes me, that this is the end. My son has managed to forgive me for everything I've done. Kidnapping his daughter. Knowing all this time I was his mother—and keeping it from him. And now he knows about the blackmail. Isn't it too much?

There is a wall, I know, beyond which a person can no longer forgive.

"Yes," I admit at last.

"But why? You . . . you needed money? Or you just hated her that much?"

"Both, Joshua." I'm shaking. "Look, I needed the money for experimental treatments for Ouma. I thought we could still save her when I asked your mother for money! I really, truly did. But also, yes, maybe I got some satisfaction from it too. She stole my baby, Joshua. Even if she didn't know—even if she thought my mother had gotten my permission. Even if she didn't know all the circumstances, she *bought* a baby and left the country quickly. She barely even looked at me whenever she came back. She knew—she knew you were mine! That I was fifteen when you were born. And she knew she had all the power, that I needed this job. I hated her. I did. Maybe some of it was unfair. Because I hated my own mother, and the . . . man who— And I hated *your* birth father, and your adoptive father too. The Leopard, oh my word. And in the end, your mother was the only one left. The only one remaining to put all that hate on."

I'm panting as I finish, and I try to push the words back down my throat. This isn't fair to him. My son was a helpless pawn in all this. And I do believe that Odelia loved him. For all her flaws—and she had many—I do believe she tried to give him the best life she could.

"I don't really know how to be a mother," I finally tell Joshua. "I'm sorry. I'm really sorry. I'll try to be better. If you . . ."

*If you allow me to be in your life*, I almost say, but then I don't. I didn't tell him what happened to my own mother, except saying that she died when I was a teenager. Even if it might make me feel better to admit it, to say it aloud, to somehow hope he will pardon me, say it was justified, I know better.

There are some things in life you just have to live with knowing you did.

Joshua nods, then says something unexpected. "I wanted to tell you—I'm thinking about moving some of Circ's production back to the local villages here. The artisans, using natural weaving techniques and materials."

"Oh, really?" I rub my eyes, try to return to this moment from where I've gone, onto that cliff in the dark with my mother. "That's . . . wonderful."

"Yes. You remember, my father used to employ local artisans, before Mom stepped in after he died and changed our supply chain. Tried to make Circ more fast fashion. But I've been thinking a lot about how I'm going to change things as CEO. And I want to stop the greenwashing, put true emphasis on conservation and really being a company that's good for our planet. Supporting local weavers, like my father originally conceived. Even if our profit margins suffer."

"That's . . . that's beautiful, Joshua." I want to say I'm proud of him, but that feels a step too far. "And it's nice to imagine you'll be back here more often—to set up the production in the villages, I mean."

I clear my throat. I don't want him to feel pressure to visit me.

"Well, I'm sure I will be. Though I'm thinking I'll appoint a dedicated role, perhaps someone living here locally, to manage things. And maybe I'll even open a South African office at some point, in Johannesburg. Let's see."

"Oh," I say, pushing down my disappointment. "Yes. Sounds smart."

Joshua checks his watch. "I'm going to have to go now, Violett."

I heave out a breath. Everything in me feels tight.

"Of course." I try to make my voice light. "I wish you all the best in the world, Joshua. I'm so sorry again for everything."

"I know." Joshua stands, and I stand too.

"Do you want me to package up the crunchies? For the plane?"

"No, that's okay."

"Okay." I try not to sound disappointed. Devastated. I try to reclaim my smile that's faded.

"No, it's just— There's plenty of food on the plane and, anyway, I was thinking maybe you could make us some crunchies in person. That is . . . if you're up for it?"

"Oh?" I shake my head, not understanding.

"I was thinking you could come to Florida, I mean. To visit us sometime. If you want?"

"I . . . I—"

"It's not to say everything's been forgotten— I think that will take Davina some time still. And me, too, if I'm being honest."

I nod, not trusting myself to speak.

"But you haven't had it easy, not at all, Violett. And I've always felt you are a good person. I still feel that way. And it's not . . . it's not to say we won't be back to Leopard Sands. We will. For Sam's trial, especially. And I love it here, despite what's happened. But Ruby's so young, and we . . ." Joshua's smile turns sheepish. "We want more children. Sooner than later. And I think Circ is going to require a lot of my energy now too. Shifting things there. So it might be hard for me to travel often, to get back here soon, and I thought . . . I thought you might want to come—"

"I *do* want," I say, feeling my shoulders quake. "I would really love that. More than you can possibly know. I know I have to prove myself, to you and Davina, and I will, Joshua. I'll do anything. I'll do anything to be a part of your life, and Davina's and Ruby's, as much as you want me to." I think about adding, How soon can I come? But I don't want to seem too eager. I want to let him lead things. I don't want to throw myself and my love at him all at once.

"Good." Joshua smiles and steps toward me with a question in his eyes. Like, is it okay if we hug?

I nod, scarcely able to believe I will soon hold my son in my arms. It's never been appropriate for us to hug, so we haven't, plain as that.

*Die poppe gaan dans* pops into my head. It's a saying we have in Afrikaans that I've felt kinship with all my life. Literally, it means "the dolls will dance," which indicates there will be trouble. Something bad will happen. It's the mantra I've been living by my whole life.

But suddenly, something good is happening.

My whole body buzzes as my son wraps his arms around me. I try not to press into him, not to crush him to me the way I want to, to give him space. To give him time. And to believe this isn't the end. Crazily enough, this may be some kind of new beginning that I never dared to dream I'd get.

## CHAPTER FORTY-FOUR

# JOSHUA

I head back to our suite to get Dav and Ruby right as the jet roars in and swoops toward the trees.

"They're here," I tell my wife, walking into the neat suite that looks nothing like the disaster we've unleashed on it these past few weeks. Jabulani's already taken the bags toward the landing strip. "Ready?"

"Yes." Dav fiddles with the zip on the diaper bag. "Hard to believe we're finally going home."

"I know."

My wife's been such a trooper—staying here while we dealt with everything. Until Bailey got out of the hospital. And until Ouma's funeral was over. Not pressing charges against Violett.

Ruby looks up at me and peals with a laugh, and I marvel at it, that she's back here with us, that she's ours.

"You okay?" Dav comes toward me, cuddles against my chest, and I stroke her pink hair.

"Yes."

She tips her head up, eyes blinking question marks.

"Really. I'm really okay."

I kiss her head, still ashamed I ever doubted her loyalty.

How wrong I was—about so many things.

"Let's go get Bails and get out of here?"

"Yeah." Dav tickles Ruby's chin. "We're going home, Ruby-Rube. God, I can't wait to go home. I never want to leave home again. Bury me in our bed."

"What?" I ask in mock shock. "You mean, you don't want the bigger life anymore?"

"What do you mean?"

"The bigger life—you told me that recently." I try to say it casually, but the old hurt travels through me, even though so much has happened since. "Remember? After meeting that yoga couple who move around all the time, you told me you felt like you wanted a bigger life? The humanitarian aid worker and her flexible husband?"

"Oh." Dav shrugs. "Was he flexible? I don't even think I could place him if I saw him in a lineup. And anyway—haven't you learned not to listen to what I say?"

"Um . . . no. Not sure if you've noticed, but I always listen to what you say."

"Well, I probably said it in some hormonal fever dream. Sometimes I just say shit! I didn't actually mean it. I love our life, Joshua. I want our life. I don't want anything more or bigger." She folds herself back into my chest and grips on tighter.

"Oh. Okay, then. If that's settled." I smile down into her hair.

"It is." She smiles back up at me.

When we untangle, I sling my dad-pack over my shoulder, making sure I have spare diapers in there, too, then usher my girls out of the suite.

"You go ahead," I tell Dav. "I'll get Bailey and meet you at the jet."

I walk the length between our suite and Bailey's slowly, taking in the last moments of the bush, of this place I've now discovered runs rightly in my bones. I laugh to myself, remembering Violett shooting a salt pellet at the snake.

"Bails?" I knock.

Soon my sister emerges with her wild hair and faded backpack.

"Ready, Freddy?" I ask, surprised to hear the rote phrase come out of my mouth. Aba used to say it in rare moments of good humor.

"Yep. Ready," she says, instead of answering *ready, Freddy* back.

"You okay?"

"I mean." She shrugs.

"Leaving Sam?"

"Yeah."

"I know."

We walk in quiet for a bit until I say, "I got a text from Officer Monala this morning."

"Oh?"

"They're gathering evidence against Officer Botha. Apparently, they'll have enough to arrest him soon. It's clear he's been tipping off the poachers, making sure the patrols avoid the areas they're in. Officer Monala said that if you hadn't recognized his voice as the head of the poaching ring on the speakerphone, they never would have figured it out. And Junior too—he gave Masasana's location to the poachers. You were right, Bails, about all of it. You should be really proud of yourself. Officer Monala said that because of you, the rhinos and elephants here are all so much safer."

"Oh, wow." Bailey looks at me in surprise. "That's—"

"Amazing is what it is. You've always loved animals. It still astounds me, what you did to save Masasana."

"That was the crazy-making malaria drug's doing." Bailey tries to laugh.

"Maybe. But you acted on your impulse out of love. That's why you did it. You had the best of intentions."

"Yeah. I guess. I really hope I'll get into vet school now."

"You will. Of course you will." I'm happy for my sister, so happy she's on this path now. Small blessings, or even big ones, with Mom gone. No longer ruling the roost.

The jet is in the distance now, and I can see Dav and Ruby boarding the stairs. Bailey walks ahead toward them, but I stop.

"Bails?"

"Yeah." She looks back.

I step forward, slip beside her, my heart racing. I could *not* say this. I know I could keep it forever, never speak it aloud. Or I could wait, until some time soon, after we've all started healing, the words slip out of me. But I also know that boarding this plane means entering a new era, for all of us. And I want to leave this conversation here. I don't want to carry it forward.

"Pineapple, Bails?" I say.

Bailey's face instantly pales. "Wha— What?"

"Sam said Mom killed Aba. That's what he said to me, in Asher's suite, when . . ." I swallow hard. "He said there was pineapple in Aba's system. That

that's what the autopsy showed, but Mom covered it up, to protect herself. Because she'd killed Aba. Intentionally."

Bailey is silent, just staring at me with her fiery blue eyes. Eyes that I've always thought belied her personality, so soft and acquiescent.

But maybe not. Maybe I haven't seen all my sister's angles. We're all more than one thing, aren't we, after all?

"It was you," I whisper. "Aba used to ask you to make his afternoon coffee. You must have slipped in some pineapple juice and . . . Mom knew, didn't she? She covered it up."

Bailey lets out a noise that is half cry, half grunt. A noise that sounds like an animal in pain.

"Sam never suspected you," I say quietly. "He was sure it was Mom's doing."

I can see tears glistening in my sister's eyes. And I know that I'm right.

"Yes. Oh my—how did you—yes." Bailey shudders and grunts, doesn't look at me as she speaks. "Yes. I bought a little cup of pineapple at the cafeteria at the animal hospital. I knew we weren't supposed to have pineapple at home, and I wasn't intending to kill Aba—not at all—but still, I brought it home. He'd just sent Sam into conversion therapy, and I was so angry. So, so angry, Joshua. Everything had built up. Now Sam has a revisionist memory. He's demonized Mom and made Aba a saint. But Aba was horrible to him! Aba fucked him up. Aba made him think his desires—and Sam *himself*—were despicable. And Aba was awful to you too. You could never live up to his standards, Joshua, never be what he wanted—that time he called you a sissy. How he always yelled at Mom, berating her. How he always froze me out."

I nod, as our childhood floods back at me and my nervous system tenses up.

Bailey wipes the back of her palm against her eyes. "Aba asked me to bring him his coffee that day and I don't know what came over me— I poured a little of the pineapple juice from my fruit cup inside, then added his Baileys. But I didn't want him to die!"

Now Bailey chokes with sobs. "I just thought—I don't know what I thought—I'd hurt him. I'd hurt him like he'd hurt me. Like he'd hurt all of us! But I wasn't trying to kill Aba! I don't know— Yes, I knew he was allergic, but I'd never seen him affected by it. He said he got hives as a kid. We even went to Hawaii and he was fine! He worried about cross-contamination, sure, but I thought he'd get hives or something again, and be really mad. I thought that he'd suffer a little, like he'd caused to all of us! And I stayed close, Joshua—in case he cried out and I needed to get his EpiPen, but he didn't. And I was mad, actually. I thought it figured that the one time I rebelled even slightly it totally failed. But then I heard Mom scream. And I ran over to his study . . ." Bailey gasps.

We're quiet for some time, remembering. How Mom called an ambulance, and they sped him to the hospital. They did what they could, but the heart attack was severe, and he never regained consciousness. Aba died three days later.

"Mom knew," I finally say.

"I had to tell her. We had to get rid of the coffee cup. In case—" Bailey looks desolately out toward the river. "You know, he named you guys biblical names."

"What?"

"Aba always said that Joshua was Moses's successor. He led the Jews into the Promised Land. And that Sam—Sam comes from the phrase *heard from God*. And Aba would tell the story—"

"About how Hannah asked God for a child and her prayer was answered."

Bailey stares up at me with shining eyes. "Yes, Aba's prayers were answered. He prayed for another child, and Sam and I came. Doesn't matter that Aba was shooting blanks—he got his wish, thanks to Markus. There came Sam, who Aba wanted. And good old Bailey, who he didn't. You know why he named me Bailey, don't you?"

"No." Now that I think of it I don't, even though Aba did tell me frequently the meanings of mine and Sam's names.

"Because Aba liked Baileys in his coffee sometimes. *Sometimes*. That's what he told me, when I asked. *That's* the meaning he attached to me." Bailey gives me a pained smile, and I can see it all—the fact that even with her antagonistic feelings, she loved our father. Of course she did. And maybe all the times she spouts about how awful Aba was is her own way of ameliorating her guilt. I'm struck by so much emotion now, at the horrible way our father died, at what Bailey's been living with, at how Sam believed it went down and what he did because of that mistaken belief. More than anything, at what we've all lost.

"See, I'm no better than Sam! All this time, everyone thinks I'm Perfect Bailey, Obedient Bailey—but I'm not. And the worst part is, I've hated myself ever since I did it. I took a life, Joshua! I violated the Ten Commandments. And so the Torah says I deserve to die myself."

I look at my sister, oozing pain she's hidden for so long, and I find myself unable to summon words.

"It's in Exodus, Joshua. *He who strikes a man so he dies shall surely be put to death.* You know—" Bailey looks off. "Mrs. Thatch told me once how the thing she's most proud of in her life is that she didn't lose her humanity in Auschwitz. Because she saw the worst of humanity—and that was an invitation to sink right down too. Some people did. But Mrs. Thatch said she gave her little food to her sisters, because they needed it more." Bailey wipes at her eyes. "And what did I do? I wasn't in Auschwitz, Joshua. I was in a gorgeous mansion with Mom and Aba. And I totally lost my humanity."

"It was cruel how he ignored you." I put a hand on my sister's back, feeling her tremble. "He acted like you were barely important. Barely even there."

"Oh." Bailey makes a squeaky, throaty sound, and I know I've nailed it, finally, the deepest thing.

"You didn't mean to kill him."

"I don't know anymore." Bailey wipes her eyes. "What if deep down I did?"

"That's why you stopped being religious," I finally say quietly. "I always thought you loved it. Even though it was Aba's thing too."

"I couldn't face them! I couldn't face Mrs. Thatch. Not after what I'd done. Mom knew, you know. We never spoke of it, though. Not even once."

"No. She wouldn't." But I wonder about things now—if the reason Bailey followed every single thing Mom ever wanted for my sister is because of the invisible string that connected them after Aba's death.

"It's crazy—none of us is actually a Babel by birth," Bailey says softly. "Isn't it . . . wild?"

"It is," I say. "It really is."

"I've been thinking about it, Joshua. In the hospital, I couldn't stop thinking about it. How the Torah places infinite value on each human life. God places a spark of himself in each human, and I played God. I decided to play God! However awful Aba was, he was a human being. And humans are just a different kind of animal, Joshua!" My sister looks at me with pained eyes, and I know what she's saying. How Bailey loves every animal—even the lions who take down a buffalo or rip apart a leopard. Bailey can find a place in her heart for each one of them, but not for Aba, not in the moment she put the pineapple juice in his coffee. And maybe not, ever since what she did, for herself.

"I'm glad you know. I'm glad you finally know." Bailey bites down on her lip. "Are you . . . are you going to tell anyone?"

"No, Bails. I'll follow Mom's last request. Time to *let the dead stay dead*."

# ACKNOWLEDGMENTS

My third thriller—it's hard to believe! Writing these books brings me inordinate joy, and this book in particular feels like a full circle moment. (Full *Circ*-le, if you will.) When I quit my job as a lawyer nine years ago to travel the world and try for my dream career of writing novels, my first international destination was South Africa. There is something undeniably magical and even spiritual about an African safari. I've been meditating twice a day for over a decade, and being in the presence of these glorious animals in their natural habitat, I felt the same time-suspending transcendence of meditation. South Africa is a special place, and I bookmarked it for a future book locale. I didn't know then that mysteries would become my writing addiction—or that a safari would make a perfectly eerie locked-room thriller locale.

My biggest thanks to my agent, Rachel Ekstrom Courage. This was the year we finally got to hug, twice! Thank you for being the most fantastic publishing partner and friend. You are caring and wise and advocate so brilliantly for me and my books. I appreciate you beyond measure. And my sincerest thanks to Heather Baror-Shapiro and Tara Timinsky for championing my books internationally and for film and TV.

A huge thank-you to my wonderful editor, Lara Jones. I feel like the luckiest author to get to work with you. Your genius edits make my books so much better, and chatting and brainstorming with you on a regular basis adds such joy to my days. I've said it before but it's just so true: every time I get an email from you, I smile! I am also so fortunate to work with the most spectacular team at Atria/Emily Bestler Books. Thank you from the bottom of my heart to Emily Bestler, Libby McGuire, Dana Trocker, Megan Rudloff,

Aleaha Renee, Dayna Johnson, Hydia Scott-Riley, Karlyn Hixson, Morgan Pager, Claire Sullivan, James Iacobelli, Paige Lytle, Shelby Pumphrey, Jason Chappell, Nicole Bond, Abby Velasco, and everyone on the sales, audio, and education/library teams. From the most fabulous publicity and marketing campaigns to covers beyond my wildest dreams, and so much more, I can't imagine a more dedicated, kind, and talented team.

This book required a substantial amount of research, and I am immeasurably grateful to the many people who took the time to speak with and educate me. Any errors I've made are mine alone. First and foremost, thank you to the incredibly kind, generous, and brilliant Peter Allison. I first came across Peter because I read his dazzling, hilarious, bestselling books about his experiences as a safari guide: *How to Walk a Puma*; *Don't Look Behind You!*; and *Whatever You Do, Don't Run*. If you haven't read them, you *should* definitely run to get yourself copies. They are truly some of the best books I've ever read, and were hands-down the most fun research material to pore over. I reached out to Peter, asking if he'd be open to a phone call, and to my great excitement, he agreed. I wouldn't have been able to write a murder mystery on safari without Peter's invaluable thoughts and wisdom. Thank you, Peter, from the bottom of my heart. A huge thank-you also to Sean Rubinstein, another amazing safari guide in Africa, who helped me iron out plot kinks— I am so grateful!

Enormous thanks as well to the bevy of generous South Africans who met and shared insights with me. To Kim Feldman, Jodi Notelovitz, Leah Goldberg, Tracy Nestadt Josef, Tashima Gordon, and Daniella Scherr, this book deeply benefited from your wisdom and stories. A big thank-you to Rabbi Michele Faudem, who has been a mentor and friend to me since she was the rabbi at my middle school and generously spoke with me, sharing Jewish experiences, teachings, and customs. Thank you to my cousin Jesse Adler who spoke with me about sustainable fashion and her fascinating research that I used loosely as inspiration for Asher's career. And a huge thanks to Robin De Lano, my tarot reader/psychic/coach extraordinaire, without whom I would not have been able to craft the tarot portions of this book. Thank you for providing me with excellent tarot insights and spreads for this book—in accordance with the crazy parameters I set out—and for being such a light in my life.

Thank you to the authors who blurb my books. To Lisa Barr, Alex

Finlay, Katy Hays, Hank Phillippi Ryan, and Finley Turner, I am enormously grateful for your support on my last book. Thank you to Nicole Hackett, my wonderful critique partner and friend, whose next brilliant novel will be out soon; I count my lucky stars that I get to share this journey with you. Thank you to my friends Jill Salama Handman and Allison Hill for promoting and circulating my books far and wide; you both touch me so much, and I deeply value our friendships. Thank you to my wonderful author friends, especially the ladies of Artists Against Antisemitism whose light lifted me up many times this past year. In particular, thanks to Lisa Barr for your support, love, and check-ins; I adore you and your stunning books and cherish our special connection. And thank you to the bookstagram community who posts about my books, the podcasters who host me for meaningful conversations, and the book clubs who gather to read my books. And to the booksellers and librarians who spread the word. I love meeting and chatting with all of you and am bowled over by your love and support. And a big heartfelt thanks to you, my wonderful readers. It is because of you I get to do this thing that I deeply love!

A particular special thanks honoring Mrs. Riva Thatch, ז"ל. Mrs. Thatch was my Hebrew teacher in fifth grade and had a big, beautiful influence on my life. She survived the Holocaust and was a strong, inspiring woman. The Mrs. Thatch of this book is named in homage to my wonderful teacher; she was in fact a survivor of Auschwitz, though I changed all other personal details about her life.

Thank you from the bottom of my heart to the very best family and friends. To Mom, Dad, Bubs, Suz, Nadav, Jas, and Arica—I would pick each of you a million times over to be my family. Thank you for supporting and cheering me on in such a massive way, every step of the way. Suz, you in particular play such an instrumental part in the creation of my books. Not sure how I got so lucky that my sister is also an all-star editor, to the point that my writer friends ask if they can borrow her. (No, she is the busiest person I know, and only freelance edits my stuff, ha!) You are so on point and precise in your critiques, my books benefit invaluably from your input. Thank you for being in the trenches with me for each one of them; I couldn't—and would never want to—do any of this without you. And to the most huggable and lovable nephews and nieces, Liad, Reagan, Griffin, Noa, Archer, and Ari, you are such lights in my life, and I love being your Auntie Jac. And to the rest of my family and friends—you know who you are, and you are the very, very best. I'm hugging you through these pages, always.

I'd like to express a final, perhaps unconventional, thanks: to myself. I don't think we always take the time to appreciate ourselves, and so in this full circle moment, I'd like to do so. I'm very proud of myself for where I stand today. Doing this writing thing I've dreamt about doing since my earliest memory. Writing and publishing a book is a vulnerable endeavor. Or as Brené Brown so wisely calls it—being in the arena. I wouldn't want to be anywhere else.